Death Dance

Death Dance

TWENTY-FIVE

STORIES BY

Angus Wilson

THE VIKING PRESS

NEW YORK

Viking Compass Edition

Issued in 1970 by The Viking Press, Inc.
625 Madison Avenue, New York, N.Y. 10022

SBN 670–26112–2 (hardbound)
SBN 670–00284–4 (paperbound)

Library of Congress catalog card number: 69–15654

Printed in U.S.A.

"Realpolitik" and "What Do Hippos Eat?" orig-
inally appeared in *The Listener*; "Crazy Crowd,"
"Mother's Sense of Fun," and "Totentanz" in
Horizon (London); and "More Friend than
Lodger" and "Once a Lady" in *The New Yorker*.

Gratefully to John and Ann Dizikes

Contents

FROM *A Bit Off the Map*

FROM
The Wrong Set

The Wrong Set

⁂

Just before the club closed, Mrs. Lippiatt asked very specially for a medley of old numbers. Mr. Pontresoli himself came over and told Terry. "It's for your bundle of charms," he said, "so don't blame me." Vi wanted to refuse when Terry asked her—she had a filthy headache and anyway she was sick of being kept late. "Tell the old cow to go and . . ." she was saying, when Terry put a finger on her lips. "Do it for me, dear," he said. "Remember, without her I don't eat." Poor kid! thought Vi, having to do it with an old trout like that, old enough to be his grandmother—still she stank of money, he was on to a good thing if he could keep it. So she put on a special sweet smile and waved at Mrs. Lippiatt. "Here's wishing you all you wish yourself, dear," she called. Then she smiled at Mr. Pontresoli, just to show him how hard she worked for his lousy club—might as well kill two birds with one stone. "Let it go, Terry," she called, and the two pianos jazzed out the old duet routine—"Souvenirs," "Paper Doll," "Some of These Days," "Blue Again," everything nice and corny.

It was while they were playing "The Sheik of Araby" that she noticed Mrs. Lippiatt's face—all lit up with memories. Christ! she must be old if she goes back to that, thought Vi, and then she said to herself, "Poor old bitch, she must have been pretty

Written in 1946; published in 1949; scene laid in the Labour Government years immediately after the Second World War.

once, but, there you are, that's life, makes you hard." At least she'd got a nice bit of stuff in Terry, best-looking boy in the place; not that she didn't prefer something a bit nearer her own age herself, and she gazed proudly over at Trevor, with his wavy grey hair and soldier's moustache, talking to Mr. Pontresoli. Funny how class told. Old Pontresoli could have bought Trevor up any day, but there he was, respectful as anything, listening to what Trevor had to say. She could hear Trevor's voice above the music. "My dear old Ponto, you'll never change that sort of thing in this country till you clear out the Yids." If Mr. Pontresoli knew what Trevor really thought of him! "Filthy wop," he'd said, but he'd agreed to be nice because of Vi's piano act, and until he got a job they needed all the money she could earn.

After closing time she had a drink with Terry and Mrs. Lippiatt. Mrs. Lippiatt said what was the good of having money, there was nothing to spend it on. Vi thought to herself what she would like was to have some money to spend, but aloud she said in her smart voice, "Yes, isn't it awful? With this government you have to be grateful for the air you breathe. Look at the things we can't have —food, clothes, foreign travel."

"Ah, yes, foreign travel," said Mrs. Lippiatt, though she knew damned well Vi had never been abroad. "It's bad enough for you and me, Mrs. Cawston, but think of this poor boy," and she put her fat, beringed hand on Terry's knee, "*he's* never been out of England. Never mind, darling, you shall have your trip to Nice the day we get a proper government back."

Mr. Pontresoli and Trevor joined them. Trevor was the real public-school boy with his monocle and calling Mrs. Lippiatt "my dear lady." Vi could see that Terry was worried—he was frightened that Trevor was muscling in; but that was just Trevor's natural way with women—he had perfect manners. Later in the evening he asked Vi who the hell the old trout was.

"The Major's got a good one about Attlee," said Mr. Pontresoli in his thick, adenoidal Italian cockney, his series of blue-stubbled chins wobbling as he spoke.

"It's impossible to be as funny about this government as they are themselves," said Trevor. He had *such* a quiet sense of humour. "They're a regular Fred Karno show." But they all begged to hear the story, so he gave it to them. "An empty taxi drove up to No. 10," he said, "and Mr. Attlee got out." Beautifully told it was, with his monocle taken out of the eye and polished just at the right moment.

"Well, Sir Stafford gives me the creeps," said Terry. No one thought that very funny except Mrs. Lippiatt, and she roared.

"Are you ready, young woman?" Trevor said to Vi with mock severity. "Because I'm not waiting all night."

As she was coming out of the ladies', Vi met Mona and her girl friend. She stopped and talked to them for a minute although she knew Trevor would disapprove. It was true, of course, that that sort of thing was on the increase and Trevor said it was the ruin of England, but then he said that about so many things—Jews and foreigners, the Labour Government and the Ballet. Anyhow Mona's crowd had been very kind to her in the old days when she was down to her last sausage, and when they'd found she wasn't their sort there'd never been so much as a word to upset her.

"For Christ's sake, kiddie," said Trevor, "I wish you wouldn't talk to those lizzies."

On the stairs they met young Mr. Solomons. Vi *had* to talk to him, whatever Trevor said. First of all he was important at the club, and then his smile always got her—nice and warm, some-how like a cat purring, but that was what she felt about a lot of Jews. "She's stood me up, Vi," he said, his eyes round with pretended dismay, "left me in the lurch. Ah! I ought to have stuck to nice girls like you." Vi couldn't help laughing, but Trevor was wild with anger. He stood quite still for a moment in Denman Street under the electric sign which read Passion Fruit Club. "If I catch that lousy Yid hanging around you again, girlie," he said, "I'll knock his ruddy block off."

All the way in the tube to Earls Court he was in a rage. Vi wanted to tell him that she was going to visit her nephew Norman tomorrow, but she feared his reception of the news. Trevor had talked big about helping Norman, when she told him the boy had won a scholarship at London University and was coming to live with them. But somehow her sister Ivy had got word that she wasn't really married to Trevor and they'd sent the boy elsewhere. She and Trevor had taken him out to dinner once in the West End—a funny boy with tousled black hair and thick spectacles who never said a word, though he'd eaten a hearty enough meal and laughed fit to split at the Palladium. Trevor said he wasn't all there and the less they saw of him the better, but Vi thought of him as her only relative in London and after all Ivy *was* her sister, even if she was so narrow.

"I'm going to see Norman tomorrow," Vi said timidly as they crossed the Earls Court Road.

"Good God!" cried Trevor. "What on earth for, girlie?"

"I've written once or twice to that Hampstead address and had no reply."

"Well, let the little swine stew in his own juice if he hasn't the decency to answer," said Trevor.

"Blood's blood after all," countered Vi, and so they argued until they were back in their bed-sitting-room. Vi put on a kimono and feathered mules, washed off her make-up, and covered her face in cream until it shone with highlights. Then she sat plucking her eyebrows. Trevor put his trousers to press under the mattress, gave himself a whisky in the toothglass, refilled it with Milton and water, and put in his dentures. Then he sat, in his pants, suspenders, and socks, squeezing blackheads from his nose in front of a mirror.

All this time they kept on rowing. At last Vi cried out, "All right, all right, Trevor Cawston, but I'm *still* going."

"Okay," said Trevor. "How's about a little loving?"

So then they broke into the old routine.

When the time came to visit Norman, Vi was in quite a quandary about what to wear. She didn't want the people he lived with to put her down as tarty—there'd probably been quite enough of that sort of talk already; on the other hand she wasn't going to look a frump for anyone. She compromised with her black suit,

white lace jabot, and gold pocket seal, with coral nail varnish instead of scarlet.

The house when she got there wasn't in Hampstead at all but in
Kilburn. Respectable, she decided, but a bit poor-looking.

"Norman's out at the demo," said Mrs. Thursby, "but he
should be back any time now. You'll come in and have a cup of
tea, won't you?"

Vi said she thought she would. She hadn't quite understood
where her nephew was, but if he was coming back soon she might
as well wait. The parlour into which she was ushered brought her
home in Leicester back to her—all that plush, and the tassels and
the china with crests on it, got her down properly now. One
thing they wouldn't have had at home though, and that was all
those books, cases full of them, and stacks of newspapers and magazines piled on the floor, and then there was a typewriter—probably a studious home, she decided. She did wish the little dowdy,
bright-eyed woman with the bobbed hair would sit down instead
of hopping about like a bird.

But Mrs. Thursby had heard something about Vi, and she was
at once nervous and hostile; she stood making little plucking gestures at her necklace and her sleeve ends and shooting staccato
inquiries at Vi in a chirping voice that had an undertone of sarcasm.

"Mrs. . . . Mrs. Cawston, is it?"

"That's right," said Vi.

"Oh, yes. I wasn't quite sure. It's so difficult to know sometimes
these days, isn't it? With . . ." and Mrs. Thursby's voice trailed
away.

Vi felt she was being got at. But Mrs. Thursby went on talking.

"Oh, the man *will* be sorry you came when he was out." By
calling Norman "the man" she seemed to be claiming a greater
relationship to him than that of a mere aunt. "He's talked of you"
—and she paused, then added drily—"a certain amount. I won't
say a great deal, but then he's not a great talker."

"Where did you say he was?" asked Vi.

"At Trafalgar Square," said Mr. Thursby. "They're rallying there to hear Pollitt or one of those people. My two went, they're both C.P., and Norman's gone with them. Though I'm glad to say he's had the good sense not to join up completely. He's just a fellow traveller, as they call them."

Vi was too bemused to say much, but she managed to ask for what purpose they were rallying.

"To make trouble for the government they put into power," said Mrs. Thursby drily. "It makes me very angry sometimes. It's taken us forty years to get a real Labour Government, and then just because they don't move fast enough for these young people, it's criticism, criticism, all the time. But, there it is, I've always said the same, there's no fool like a young fool," and she closed her tight little mouth with relish. "They'll come round in time. Hilda, that's my girl, was just the same about the Chapel, but now it seems they've agreed to the worship of God. Very kind of them, I'm sure. I expect you feel the same as I do, Mrs. Cawston."

Vi wasn't quite sure exactly what Mrs. Thursby did feel, but she *was* sure that she didn't agree, so she said defiantly, "I'm Conservative."

"Lena," said Mrs. Thursby in a dry, abrupt voice to a tall, middle-aged woman who was bringing in the tea-tray, "we've got a Tory in the house. The first for many a day."

"Oh, no!" said Lena, and everything about her was charming and *gemütlich*, from her foreign accent to her smile of welcome. "I am so pleased to meet you, but it is terrible that you are a Tory."

"Miss Untermayer teaches the man German," said Mrs. Thursby. "Mrs. Cawston is Norman's aunt."

"Oh!" cried Miss Untermayer; her gaunt features lit up with almost girlish pleasure. "Then I congratulate you. You have a very clever nephew."

Vi said she was sure she was pleased to hear that, but she didn't quite like the sound of these rallies.

"Oh, that!" said Miss Untermayer. "He will grow out of that.

All this processions and violence, it is for children. But Norman is a very spiritual boy. I am sure that he is a true pacifist."

"I'm sure I hope not," said Vi, who was getting really angry. "I've never had anything to do with conchies."

"Then you've missed contact with a very fine body of men," said Mrs. Thursby. "Mr. Thursby was an objector."

"I'm sorry, I'm sure," said Vi. "Major Cawston was right through the war."

"The important thing is that he came out the other side," remarked Mrs. Thursby drily.

"There are so many kinds of bravery, so many kinds of courage. I think we must respect them all." Miss Untermayer's years as a refugee had made her an adept at glossing over divisions of opinion. All the same she gave a sigh of relief when Norman's voice was heard in the hall; at least the responsibility would not be on *her* any more.

"Hilda and Jack have gone on to a meeting," he shouted. "I'd have gone too but I've got to get on with this essay."

"Your aunt's come to see you," shouted back Mrs. Thursby.

Norman came into the room sideways like a crab, he was overcome with confusion at the sight of Vi, and he stood running his hands through his hair and blinking behind his spectacles.

"You were such a long time answering my letters that I thought I'd better come down and see what sort of mischief you'd got into," said Vi, "and I have," she added bitterly. "Demonstrations indeed. I'd like to know what your mother would say, Norman Hackett."

Norman's face was scarlet as he looked up, but he answered firmly, "I don't think Mum would disapprove, not if she understood. And even if she did, it couldn't make any difference."

"Not make any difference what your mother said! I'm ashamed of you, Norman, mixing up with a lot of Reds and Jews."

"That's enough of that," cried Mrs. Thursby. "We'll not have any talk against Jews in this house. No, not even from Rahab herself."

Vi's face flushed purple underneath her make-up. "You ought

to be ashamed," she cried, "an old woman like you, to let a boy
of Norman's age mix up with all this trash."

"You've no right to say that . . ." began Norman, but Mrs.
Thursby interrupted him. "Oh, let the woman say her say, Norman. I've had a windful of Tory talk before now and it hasn't
killed me. If Father and I have taught the man to stand up for his
own class, we're proud of it. And now, Mrs. Cawston, if you've
nothing more to say to Norman, I think you'd better go."

Vi arrived at the Unicorn sharp at opening time that evening.
She'd got over most of her indignation—after all, Ivy didn't think
much about *her*, and if the boy wanted to go to pot, good riddance. She had a couple of gins and lime as she waited for
Trevor.

Mr. Pontresoli came across the saloon bar. "Hullo, Vi," he said
in this thick voice. "Have you heard the news about Solomons?
Dreadful, isn't it?"

It really gave Vi quite a shock to hear that they'd charged
young Mr. Solomons—something to do with clothing coupons.
She had felt quite guilty towards him after speaking out like that
against the Jews, and now to hear of this, it made you wonder
what sort of a government we *had* got. As Mr. Pontresoli said,
"It's getting to be the end of liberty, you mark my words."

"Trevor'll have something to say about this, Mr. Pontresoli,"
Vi said, and then she remembered what Trevor said about the
Jews—it was all too difficult, one could never tell.

Mr. Pontresoli offered her another gin, so she said yes. "I'll tell
you what," said Mr. Pontresoli, "it's going to make a difference
to me financially. Solomons was one of my best backers at the
club. It may mean cutting down a bit. We shan't be needing two
pianos."

What with the gin—will you have another? said Mr. Pontresoli,
and, yes, said Vi—and the tiring day she'd had, Vi felt quite cast
down as she thought of Terry out of a job. A nice boy like that.
But then he'd got Mrs. Lippiatt.

"Poor Terry, Mr. Pontresoli," she said, her eyes filling with tears. "We *shall* miss him at the club. Here's wishing him more Mrs. Lippiatts," and she drained her glass. "This one's on me, Mr. Pontresoli," she said, and Mr. Pontresoli agreed.

"We couldn't afford to let Terry go," said Mr. Pontresoli, "that's certain. Mrs. Lippiatt says he draws all the women, and she ought to know, she spends so much money."

Vi worked all this out and it seemed to come round to her. This made her angry. "Why, that's nonsense, Mr. Pontresoli," she said, and she smiled broad-mindedly. "Surely you know Terry's a pansy."

Mr. Pontresoli's fat, cheerful face only winked. "That gets 'em all ways," he said and walked out of the saloon bar.

Vi felt quite desperate. She couldn't think where Trevor had got to. "Have you seen my husband, Major Cawston, Gertie?" she asked the barmaid. No one could say I haven't got dignity when I want it, she thought. Gertie hadn't seen Trevor, but Mona's girl friend said she had, twenty minutes ago at the George *and* stinking. No job and Trevor stinking. It all made Vi feel very low. Life was hell anyhow, and with all those Reds, she'd go after Trevor and fetch Norman back. She was about to get down from the high stool when she noticed that Mona's girl friend's eyes were red. "What's the matter, dear?" she asked.

"Mona's gone off with that Bretonne bitch," said the girl.

"Oh, dear," said Vi solemnly. "That's very bad." So they both had another drink to help them on.

Vi was in battling mood. "Go out and fetch Mona back," she cried. "You won't get anywhere sitting still."

"You do talk silly sometimes," said the girl. "What can I do against a Bretonne, they're so passionate."

The sadness of it all overcame Vi; it was all so true and so sad and so true—all those Bretonnes and Reds and passionates, and Trevor going off to demos, no, Norman going off to demos, and Mr. Solomons in the hands of the government, and her nephew in the hands of the Reds. Yes, that was the chief thing.

"I must let my sister know that her son's in trouble," she said. "How can I tell her?"

"Ring her up," suggested Mona's friend, but Vi told her Ivy had no phone.

"Send a telegram, dear, that's what I should do," said Gertie. "You can use the phone at the back of the bar. Just dial TEL."

It took Vi some time to get through to Telegrams—the telephone at the Unicorn seemed to be such a difficult one. I mustn't let Ivy know that I'm in this condition, she thought; she was always the grand lady with Ivy, so holding herself erect and drawling slightly, she said, "I want to send a telegram to my sister, please. The name is Hackett—44 Guybourne Road, Leicester. Terribly worried." It sounded very Mayfair, and she repeated it. "Terribly worried. Norman in the Wrong Set. Vi."

"I feel much better now, Gertie," she said as she stumbled back to the bar. "I've done my duty."

Saturnalia

—————————————————————

❯❯❯❮❮❮

"I really can't understand it," said Ruby Mann to her friend Enid. "I thought things would have been humming long ago. Hi there," she shouted to the two medicos from Barts, "a little action from the gang, please."

"It isn't a bit like the Mendel Court to be so slow. It's more like that morgue the Ventnor," Enid answered. Scrawny-necked and anæmic, since childhood she had been drifting from one private hotel to another. She knew.

There was no doubt that the first hour of the staff dance had proved very sticky; servants and guests just wouldn't mix. Chef had started the evening in the customary way by leading out Mrs. Hyde-Green, and the Commander had shown the young chaps the way to do it in a foxtrot with Miss Tarrant, the receptionist. But these conventional exchanges had somehow only created greater inhibitions. A class barrier of ice seemed to be forming; and though a few of the more determinedly matey both of masters and men ventured from time to time into this frozen no-man's-land, they were soon driven back by the cold blasts of deadened conversation. A thousand comparisons were made between this year's streamers and last year's fairylights; every measurement possible and impossible was conjectured for the length of the lounge; it would have verged on irony to have deplored even

—————————————————————

Written in 1947; first published in 1949; scene laid on New Year's Eve, 1931.

once more the absence through illness of the headwaitress, who had been such a sport the year before. By nine o'clock the rift was almost complete.

The manageress, Stella Hennessy, looked so pretty in her dove-grey tulle; with her soft brown hair and her round surprised eyes, she fluttered about like some moth with a genius for pathos—"a little bit of a thing," as Bruce Talfourd-Rich remarked—no one would have believed that she had a son at a public school. If *she* couldn't make things go nobody could. She had such grit and determination—never having sewn even a button on and then buckling to like this when the crash came. She was so exactly the right sort of person for the Mendel Court Hotel, thoroughly up-to-date and broad-minded—one old colonel even went so far as to say that she was "O. T. Mustard," but then one heard afterwards that she'd been forced to put the poor old thing in his place. For there was no doubt that the Mendel Court was different from most other hotels in South Kensington—it was brighter, more easy-going, less fusty, less stuffy. They hadn't so many old tabbies and crocks with one foot in the grave. There was a poker set as well as a bridge set. Over half the residents were divorced or separated. Lots of them did interesting jobs, like being mannequins or film extras, or even helping friends to run night clubs, only showing how splendidly the right class of people could turn to when they had to. If they failed to pay their bills it was not from any ashamed indigence but because they thought they could get away with it.

It was something like a blow to prestige, then, when the dance seemed to hang fire. The lack of gaiety even disturbed Claire Talfourd-Rich, whose position as "injured wife" was so generally respected in the hotel that she could usually glide like Cassandra through any celebration. She looked strikingly injured tonight, her marble-white skin and deep-set dark eyes funereal against the heavy white silk, ankle-length gown with its gold-wire belt. Bruce too was giving her every provocation with Stella Hennessy—though to her trained eye it was clear that Stella's babyish nagging would soon kill that *affaire*—not that she any longer really noticed his infidelities, her mind was too intent upon the cultivation of a Knightsbridge exterior with a Kensington purse, but a certain dull ache of self-pity at the back of her consciousness made her hold to the marriage with sullen tenacity. To cry woe as you moved among the motley was one thing, to form part of a group of hired mutes quite another, and Claire soon found herself declaiming against the failure of the evening to "get going."

"It's too shame-making," she said in her deep contralto—she had managed to get that new book *Vile Bodies* from the library and was making full use of the Mayfair slang before it was too widely known in S.W.7.

"It'll be better soon when all the old tabbies go to bed," said Enid, and sure enough a moment later Mrs. Hyde-Green made preparations to depart.

"I can't bear to tear myself away from the fun," she said, and it was clear that she really meant it. "But early to bed, you know. I'm sure *I* could do with a lot more wealth," she added with a sigh. Soon she had collected a party of the more staid around her to take a last cup of tea in her sitting-room, for she was an old-established resident and had three rooms with a lot of her own furniture. Miss Tarrant, the receptionist, was kindly included in the party, so that on the staff side too there was a sense of relief. Only old Mrs. Mann declared that she would stay to watch her daughter dance.

Mrs. Hyde-Green's departure saved the situation. Liquor flowed freely, and by ten-fifteen, as Enid pointed out, nearly everyone was a wee bit squiffy. Stella's eyes were round with innocence as she called out to Claire in her baby drawl, "What shall I do with this man of yours? He keeps saying the most impossible things. The trouble is, Mrs. Talfourd-Rich, that he's been too well taught." Only drink could have allowed her to let the bitch so far out of the bag.

"Pipe down, kiddie, pipe down," said Bruce, but Stella only giggled. "We're making rather an exhibition of ourselves, aren't we?" she said with delight.

The pretty waitress Gloria had gone very gay. "Take it away," she cried to the band. Her shoulder strap was slipping and a bit

of hair kept flopping in her eyes. It was difficult to snap your
fingers when your head was going round. She and young Tom
the porter were dancing real *palais de danse* and "Send me, darling, send me," she cried.

Bruce felt only too ready to oblige; he had no desire to stay
with Stella all the evening if she was going to be difficult—these
bitches were all the same after a bit. Soon he was dancing with
Gloria, his shoulders moving exaggeratedly, for he prided himself on fitting in with all classes.

"Send me," Gloria kept calling out.

In the hinterland of old Sir Charles' mind some classroom memory earlier even than the glories of his colonial governorship was
stirred. Waving a bridge roll unsteadily, his swivel eye fixed on
the ceiling, "The lady's repeated demands to be sent," he cried,
"remind me of the Hecuba. You know the lines," he said to Mrs.
Mann.

"It's funny," she replied. "Ruby's the only one here with a
bandeau tonight." No one was by to tell her that it would have
been curious in 1925 but was far from strange in 1931. "Queen
Hecuba, you know, in her distress asks to be taken away," Sir
Charles continued, "and then you get that wonderful accumula-
tion of words in which the Greeks excelled. *Labete, pherete, pem-
pet, aeirete mou*," he cried excitedly.

"The old boy's three parts cut," said Bruce, and he pressed
Gloria closer to him.

"We all think he's cuckoo." She giggled.

"You know you're a very lucky girl to be dancing with a handsome man like me," Bruce continued—it was one of his favourite
lines.

"Says who?" Gloria cried.

"Lovely maidens have cast themselves from high towers for my
sake," he went on.

Of course it was all silly talk, but you couldn't help liking him,
he was good-looking too, with his little moustache, even if he was
a bit old and baggy under the eyes.

Bertha, the crazy Welsh kitchenmaid with the bandy legs, was dancing with page in a very marked manner. "I don't know what you young fellows are at," said Sir Charles to Grierson, the youngest student from Barts, "letting a boy of that age monopolize the women." Grierson protested that he was only two years older than page, but Sir Charles soon had him dancing with Bertha. "You're nice," she said, and years of yearning spent in institutions sounded in her voice. "Press closer," she added, and she rubbed her thighs against his. Sir Charles had no idea that page was an expert swimmer, and he examined his life-saving medal with keen interest. He himself was a daily Serpentine man. "The main thing is to keep practising your crawl," he said paternally.

Tom the porter's Irish glance had soon detected Stella's discomfiture. She was hot stuff all right, he thought, and then to be the friend of the manageress might be very useful. "You look beautiful tonoite, Mrs. Hennessy, if you'll pardon the familiarity," he said. "That grey stuff—chiffon d'ye call it?—looks like the lovely sea mists." But Stella had fought too hard to maintain her class position to have it obscured by poetic words. In any case, with her, sexual flirtation was far too closely bound up with social ambition. "You've had more liquor than is good for you," her carefully lipsticked cupid's bow snapped at him, and her baby eyes were as hard as boot buttons. "Ye little God a'mighty bitch," he muttered.

" 'Ten cents a dance, that's what they pay me, gosh! how they weigh me down,' " the band played and Gloria sang with the tune. She was almost lying in Bruce's arms as he carried her through the slow foxtrot. Wouldn't it be wonderful, she thought, to be a dance hostess and to make your living dancing with hundreds of men every night. " 'Though I've a chorus of elderly beaux, stockings are porous with holes in the toes,' " she sang on, " 'I'm here till closing time, dance and be merry, it's only a dime.' " "By God, that's a true song," said Bruce, choking slightly as he thought of the tragedy of it. "Poor kids, what a god-awful life dancing with any swine that likes to pay." Suddenly Gloria saw it like that too and she began to cry. "Bruce," she said, "Bruce," and she buried her head in his shoulder. "There, there, baby," he replied soothingly.

Bertha's red curls danced in the air as she bobbed up and down holding young Grierson tightly to her, and her teeth showed forth black as ebony as she smiled at him. Cinderella had found her Prince Charming, the orphan girl's dream had come true. "What are you looking all round the room like that for, my sunshine boy?" she asked. "You don't want anything to do with that trollopy lot. Keep your eyes on me." From the horror of his fixed gaze she might have been the Medusa.

Page too was staring in alarm at Sir Charles as the old man's hand banged against his chest. "You'll have to broaden those shoulders, my lad," the old man was saying. "You wait. They'll get you into uniform yet and teach you discipline. A bit of the barrack square, that's what you need."

Old Mrs. Mann kept smiling to herself. "I really think your mother's the tiniest bit *geschwimpt*," said Enid to Ruby—she had picked up the phrase on a Rhineland holiday. "Are you all right, Mother?" asked Ruby, but the old lady had turned to Claire Talfourd-Rich, who was standing by her chair. "Isn't it a funny thing," she said, "Ruby's the only one here with a bandeau tonight."

Tom the porter stared across at Claire. There was no doubt she was beautiful enough, with her dark eyes and her sleek black hair. She was a proud bitch all right, a different class altogether from that manageress. It would be something worth talking about to make her, and she'd be worth making too. "Would ye do me the honour of giving me a dance, madam?" he said, his Irish blue eyes all a-dancing, just the straightforward, sensible boy that he was. "That's very nice of you, Tom," drawled Claire. "I should love to."

"Did anyone ever tell you that you were a very fine dancer?" Claire asked as half an hour later they were still waltzing together. "I think it's that beautiful look of yours in your lovely white dress that's brought out the lilt in me," Tom said, and he looked so

straight at her that she felt that she couldn't be offended with the
boy. You're in, Tom my boy, he thought, you're in.

Gradually, as drink broke down the barriers of self-consciousness, the classes began to merge. The servility of the staff began to give way to the contempt that they fell for the pretentious
raffishness of their superiors. To the residents the easy moral
tone of the staff was more surprising, for how were they to know
that conditions of work in the hotel could attract only the scum
of that great tide of labour which the depression had rolled into
London. But like called to like. The Colonel's lady and Judy
O'Grady were both *lumpen* under their skins.

Over the heads of the dancers, as they formed a circle to welcome 1932, floated the balloons—red, blue, green, silver, sausage-
shaped, moon-shaped. Claire pressed Tom's hand tightly and
her booming contralto sounded above the other voices in "Auld
Lang Syne." Bertha's New Year resolution was a thick whisper
in the ear of young Grierson. Enid, who was nearby, started in
surprise for she thought she heard an awful word that ought not
to be spoken. Mrs. Mann's resolution too was mumbled, but she
wanted, it seemed, more bandeaux worn in 1932, while Ruby resolved never to go to another dance.

Sir Charles held a balloon in his hand. "I trust there will be
greater comradeship in the coming year," he said pompously.
"Following the example of Achilles . . ." But before he could
finish his sentence the balloon burst in his face to the sound of
page's delighted giggles. Bruce, sitting alone—for Gloria had
gone for a moment to you-know-where to adjust her shoulder
straps—was overcome by melancholy and resolved to have no
more to do with women. Tom caught at an old music-hall memory. "Oi resolve to hang on to that beautiful rainbow wherever I
see't this year," he said and remarked with relief that the meaningless sentiment seemed what Claire had expected of him. She
leaned back with her eyes half shut and, blowing smoke rings, she
produced the same smartly cynical resolution that she had used
for the five preceding years. "I resolve," she drawled, "to do good
wherever I see a chance," and added with the same perennial

laugh, "to myself," but somehow the flat little cynicism seemed
to have more meaning to her than ever before. There really did
appear to be something besides clothes that might interest her
as she looked deep into Tom's eyes. The hard, babyish tones of
Stella Hennessy interrupted their reverie. "I had no idea you
were a Socialist, Mrs. Talfourd-Rich," she said, her eyes great
circles of surprised blue. "You seem *quite* resolved to break down
class barriers. I shall have to make my New Year resolutions
about labour problems too," she added curtly, and she gave Tom
a threateningly contemptuous glance.

But Stella Hennessy was to have more serious difficulties with
the staff before the dance was over. A quarter of an hour later she
passed the little waiting-room in the annex, on the way to her office. Through the half-open door she could see by the faint light
of the window that there were two figures on the couch—
Bruce lay half across Gloria, whose dress had fallen from the shoulders to reveal full breasts which he was fondling. Stella drew
back to pass unobserved. Gloria began to giggle drunkenly. "I
s'pose this is what you do to old Mother Hennessy," she said. Bruce
belched slightly. "Christ," he said, "that old cow! Why, I'd rather
squeeze milk out of a coconut." Stella felt quite sick; for a moment she almost doubted whether the drudgery of her life was
worth while even to keep Paul at Malvern.

" 'If it's a crime, then I'm guilty, guilty of loving you,' " sang
Tom in his low, crooning Irish tenor. "You're disgustingly handsome, you know," said Claire. After all, there was nothing socially wrong about Lady Chatterley or Potiphar's wife, so why
not? "I'm dazzled to look at you, you're so beautiful," Tom replied. It was all so like a film that he felt quite carried away by his
own words. "Ye've no roight to waste all that beauty," he went
on. Breaking through the layers of social snobbery and imitated
sophistication, dissipating even the thick clouds of self-pity
which had covered her emotions for so many years, physical desire began to awake again in Claire. She thought of how often
she had said that she dressed only to please herself; it's a bloody
lie, she realized, I'd rather far dress to please men. "Will ye let

me come to ye tonight?" said Tom hoarsely, then he remembered
with dismay that she shared a double room with Bruce. "Oi'll
show ye where ye can foind me, where we can be happy together." Through tears of pleasure Claire smiled at him. "Perhaps," she said. "Perhaps."

Across the ballroom Sir Charles was throwing streamers at
page. " 'Fear wist not to evade, as Love wist to pursue,' " he intoned, but for once Francis Thompson was wrong, for when Sir
Charles looked again page had disappeared through the green
baize door to the service wing.

"You're not dancing, Ruby," said old Mrs. Mann, "and your
bandeau's slipped, darling." "Blast the bandeau," cried Ruby
and, tearing it from her head, she threw it into the old lady's lap.
"I haven't danced the whole bloody evening," she cried and, in
tears, she ran from the room. "I thought Ruby was a little overwrought," said her friend Enid.

From the little service room near the dining-hall there emerged
a triumphant Bertha leading a dejected Grierson. Her face was lit
with happiness; life had given her all she asked. But young Grierson looked very white, and as he approached the main staircase
he was violently sick. "Steady the Buffs," called his fellow student from Barts. "Pardon me, chaps, while I see old Jerry to bed."

"It would be stupid to talk to you about the kindness of the
management, wouldn't it?" said Stella Hennessy, and her little
rosebud mouth rounded as she spoke, making her look like a baby
possessed by a malevolent devil. "Your class has never understood
the meaning of gratitude. After this evening's disgusting exhibition you won't, of course, get the week's notice that you people
are always talking about. I could send you away now, at once,
but we will say tomorrow morning early. Do you hear me," she
said, suddenly raising her voice, for Gloria was staring so strangely,
"or are you too drunk?" Indeed, the girl might have represented
Drunkenness in a morality play as she sat opposite the office desk
to which she had been summoned; the pink satin dress was half
torn from her shoulders, pink artificial flowers and locks of brown
hair fell alike across her face, her lipstick had smudged onto her

cheeks, her tongue continually passed over her dry lips. Yet even
in this condition she looked so young that Stella's face was suddenly distorted with rage and jealousy. "You filthy creature!"
And hysteria seized her. "Get out, get out!" she screamed. Gloria rose with drunken dignity. "You silly old cow," she said, refinement giving way to full cockney. "You won't send me away,
you won't, not on your ruddy life. I know too much about you,
my treasure, old Mother Have-me-if-you-like Hennessy."

Bruce moved away from the frosted glass door of the office. It
wasn't pleasant to hear women recriminating like that. He could
not help resenting their apparent forgetfulness of himself in their
hatred of each other. No place for men, he thought as he moved
slowly back to the dance floor.

Claire was standing by a pot of hydrangeas; the return of
physical desire had animated her features as he had not seen them
since the early years of their marriage. He walked over to her.
"Hullo, Pookie," he said. "Care for a dance?" The use of her pet
name after so many years came strangely to Claire. She knew
quite well that his sudden interest was only an interval in the
usual routine of their lives; she knew that there was no reciprocal
feeling in herself, that she would regret the loss of her new hunger for Tom, but habit was very strong and it shut down upon
her emotions; she could not resist an opportunity to strengthen the
frayed marital tie. "Of course, darling," she said, stumping out
her cigarette.

When Tom came back with the whisky she had requested he
saw them dancing together—so that drunken fool had pushed
his way in. "Now ye haven't forgot the dance ye promised me,
Mrs. Talfourd," he said, and he winked very slightly over Bruce's
head.

Claire never achieved such a successfully strangulated Knightsbridge tone as when she answered. "Oh, Tom, how awful," she
said. "I'd quite forgotten. I haven't told you, darling," she said to
Bruce, "how sweet Tom has been in looking after me all the evening. But now this wretched husband of mine has deigned to turn

up, I suppose I shall have to reward him by keeping an eye on him."

"Thanks for looking after my old trouble and strife," said Bruce as they moved away. "I'll do the same for you someday, old man, come you're married."

"Christ! the bitch," murmured Tom, "and I thought I was in."

There were only a few more dances before the band packed up, but everyone agreed that the Talfourd-Riches were the finest couple on the floor; indeed, the evening would have been nothing without them. "Well, after all," drawled Claire, "if one can't put oneself out for the servants for *one* evening. It isn't very much to ask. Only *one* evening in the whole year."

Sir Charles looked so miserable as, with a red paper crown on his head and a wooden rattle in his hand, he prepared to go to his room. "Alas, yes, dear lady," he said. "The Saturnalia is at an end."

Realpolitik

➤➤➤◄◄◄

John Hobday sat on the edge of his desk and swung his left leg with characteristic boyishness. He waited for the staff to get settled in their seats and then spoke with careful informality.

"I know how frightfully busy you are. As a matter of fact I am myself," he said with the half-humorous urchin smile that he used for such jokes. Only his secretary, Veronica, gave the helpful laugh he expected. It was not going to be an easy meeting, he decided. "So I'm not going to waste your time with a lot of talk," he went on. "I just thought . . ." He paused and beat with his pencil against the desk while Mrs. Scrutton moved her chair fussily out of the sunlight. "Ready?" he asked with an over-elaborate smile. "Right. Then we'll start again. As I was saying, we're all very busy, but all the same I thought it was time we had a little meeting. I've been here a week now and although I've had some very helpful chats with each of you in turn, we've never had a chance to get together and outline our plans." None of the three who formed his audience made any response. Veronica, who remembered him taking over new departments at the Ministry during the war, thought, He hasn't got the right tone, he doesn't realize that he's coming up against deeper loyalties with these people, loyalties to scholarship and ideas. She almost felt like letting him fend for himself, but old habits were too strong.

"I'm sure it's what everybody's been wanting," she said in her

Written in 1947; first published in 1949; scene contemporary.

deep voice. She had gauged rightly; his moment of uncertainty
had gone, her faithful bark had guided him at the crucial moment.
Mrs. Scrutton tried to discomfort him. She rustled the papers
on her lap and whispered audibly to Major Sarson, "Our plans.
His plans for us would be more honest." But it was too late; she
had missed her chance. John merely frowned at the interruption,
and it was Mrs. Scrutton who was left with burning cheeks, hiding her embarrassment by lighting a fresh cigarette.

"As you know," John went on—and Veronica could tell by the
loud, trumpeting, rhetorical note of his voice that he was once
more the confident salesman lost in the dream world of the grandi-
ose schemes he was putting before them—"I've got some very
big ideas for the gallery. I'm not an expert in any way, as you
people are, but I think that's possibly why Sir Harold's executors
chose me for the job. They felt the gallery had already got its full
weight of scholars and experts; what it needed was a man with
administrative experience, whose training had led him to take an
over-all view of things, to think, shall I say, widely rather than
deeply. That's why they got me in. But I'm going to be absolutely frank with you"—tossing a lock of brown wavy hair
from his forehead, he stared at his audience with a wide-eyed appeal—"I need *your* help; without my staff I can get nowhere."

Major Sarson winced slightly. All this theatricality and the loud
pitch of John's voice got on his nerves; besides, he could feel a
draught round his legs. It's like some damned Methodist preacher
fellow, he thought.

"You've been grand in this first week," John went on, "absolutely grand. I don't mind telling you now that when I arrived
I was dead scared. You'd all been here for years, you knew the
collections backwards, you had your own ways of running the
place, and above all you'd had the inestimable advantage of knowing Sir Harold, of hearing exactly what was in his mind when he
bought this picture or that object, of knowing what his ideals were
in giving the public the benefit of his taste and experience. I felt
sure you were bound to resent me as an outsider, and I knew I'd
have done the same in your place."

The faces in front of him were quite unresponsive. He isn't going to get anywhere with sentimental appeals, thought Veronica; these people are idealists, there's nothing more hard-boiled. The damned fools, thought John, they have the chance of turning this tin-pot, cranky provincial gallery into a national institution and they won't play ball. Well, if they can't see which way their own chances lie, they're not getting in the way of mine. They'll have to come to heel or go. His voice became a little sharper, a shade less ingenuous and friendly.

"You've all told me your views in our various little chats. Sometimes we've agreed, sometimes we haven't. You've inclined to the feeling that all is for the best in the best of all possible worlds; I've felt that some changes were needed, that the scope of the work here wanted broadening, that the organization wanted, let's face it, bringing up-to-date a bit, and in all this the board has agreed with me."

Tony Parnell's baby face had grown steadily more pouting and scowling as John had been speaking. To think of this mountebank in charge of the gallery, a professional careerist, who understood nothing of Sir Harold's ideas and aims, who had even laughed when he'd spoken to him of the metaphysical aspects of technique in painting. He had banked so much on becoming curator. Sir Harold had spoken so often of him as "my torchbearer, the youngest member of our staff," and now these awful businessmen who had got control of the estate had put this creature in. Major Sarson and Mrs. Scrutton were too old to fight these changes; he had promised before the meeting that *he* would make the challenge. Now was his opportunity. Red in the face, he opened his mouth, but in his nervousness his voice emerged a high falsetto.

John smiled across at Veronica.

"The board haven't had much opportunity of agreeing with us since they haven't heard our views," Tony squeaked.

"My dear Parnell," said John, and his tone was purposely patronizing and offensive. The old ones he regarded without rancour as dead wood to be cleared away, but Tony he disliked personally for his assumptions of scholarly disinterestedness and moral superiority. "Don't let that worry you. As soon as you've got your ideas clear, come along and push them at the board as much as you like. I shouldn't use too much of your favourite art jargon if I were you; the board are anxious to help but they're only ordinary businessmen and they might not understand. If you follow my advice you'll come down to earth a bit, but of course that's entirely your affair."

Mrs. Scrutton fingered the buttons on her checked tweed coat nervously. "There's no need to bully Mr. Parnell," she said.

"Oh, come," said John jocosely, "if Parnell's going to have the ladies on his side I shall have to surrender." To his delight he saw that Tony was frowning with annoyance.

"Do let me deal with this in my own way," Parnell said to Mrs. Scrutton, whose lip began to tremble.

So that severe grey bobbed hair and man's collar and tie could dissolve early into tears, thought John, so much the better.

"Mrs. Scrutton was only trying to help you, Parnell," said Major Sarson. "Don't let us forget our manners, please."

John yawned slightly. "When the little civil war's over," he said, "I'd just like to outline our main functions. As I see them they're these: Relations with the Public, that's you, Parnell; Display, Mrs. Scrutton; Research, Major Sarson. Miss Clay"—he indicated Veronica—"is maid of all work. And I, well, I'm the Aunt Sally, ready to stop the bricks and pass on the bouquets."

Major Sarson looked at his watch impatiently. "I quite agree with you, Major," said John, "the sooner we get finished, the better. No true gentlemen continue to hold meetings after opening time." The old man's face twitched violently; no one before had referred overtly to his notorious weakness.

"I'd like to take the public first," said John. "You've done a first-rate job, Parnell—within its limits. But you haven't gone far enough. You've got real enthusiasm and that's half the battle—but only half. You give the public first-rate value in lectures and catalogues when they get here, but you don't try to get them to come. I know what you're going to say: 'They'll come if they're interested.' But aren't you being a bit hard on the poor, tired, pushed-around public of today? They've got to be told about the place. You've got to compete with the cinema, the football team, *and* the fireside radio. In short, you've got to advertise, and you can't do that unless you have figures." Here John paused and picked up a file of papers.

"You have all the figures there," said Tony sulkily.

"I know," said John, "but don't you think they're just a bit too general? 'So many people visited the gallery on August 5th, so many on November 3rd.' But what sort of people? Whom are we catering for? Were they Chinese, shopgirls, farmers, or just plain deaf-mutes? To tell us anything, these figures want breaking down into groups—so many foreigners, so many over-forties, so many under-twenties. That's the way to build up a picture. Now supposing you run over these figures in the way that I suggest and we'll talk again."

Tony was about to protest that this task was impossible, but John held up his hand. "No, no, time's very short and there's one more point I want to raise before we pass on to Display." Mrs. Scrutton drew her coat tightly round her. "It's about the lecture-room. Sir Louis Crippen was saying something at the last board meeting about its not being free for his archæological society when he needed it. Do you know anything about that?"

Tony Parnell hesitated. "Well, actually," he said, "Mrs. Scrutton makes all the lecture-hall arrangements."

"But isn't it the P.R.O.'s pigeon?" asked John.

"Yes," said Tony, "but . . . well . . . Mrs. Scrutton . . ."

"I see," said John coldly. "Perhaps you'd enlighten me then, Mrs. Scrutton."

The grey bob shook as she answered, an involuntary shake that was to prove the prelude to age's palsy. "Sir Louis asked for Tuesday, and Tuesdays are always booked by Miss Copley," she said.

"Miss Copley?"

Mrs. Scrutton guessed that he knew the answer and her reply attempted a rebuke. "Miss Copley is an old and true friend to the gallery," she said. "She's been giving her lectures to schools on Tuesdays for many years."

"No doubt," said John, "but I still think Sir Louis should have preference."

"I don't agree at all," said Major Sarson. "It would be most unfair."

"Yes, why should Sir Louis receive special treatment?" asked Mrs. Scrutton.

"Well, frankly," replied John, "because although Miss Copley may be a very old friend, Sir Louis is a very influential one, and the gallery needs influential friends."

Before Mrs. Scrutton there floated Sir Harold's features, like Erasmus she had thought him, the last of the humanists. Major Sarson too remembered his old friend's handshake and his firm clear voice. "Sarson," he had said, "this money came to me through false standards, false distinctions. There shall be no distinctions in its use but those of scholarship." The eyes of both these old people filled with tears.

John turned to Veronica. "You've nothing to do, Miss Clay," he said. "In future you will take on the lecture-hall arrangements. Anything important you'll refer to me." Mrs. Scrutton made a gesture of protest. "No, no," said John. "I'm not going to let you wear yourself out on these minor details, you're far too valuable to the gallery. Besides, you've got more than a full-time job with Display if it's properly carried out."

Tony Parnell half rose from his chair. "I thought the lecture-hall arrangements came under Public Relations?"

"So did I," said John, "until you disillusioned me.

"Next we come to Display. I suppose no side of our work has been more revolutionized in recent years. The Philadelphia report, you know, and the Canadian Association series," he went on, smiling at Mrs. Scrutton. She suddenly felt very tired; she had seen these documents but had never been able to bring herself to read them. "But there's no need for me to mention these things to you," John continued. "Your arrangement of the miniature collection"—and he sighed in wonder—"well, I'm going to pay you a great compliment there. Your arrangement of the miniatures not only makes one want to look at them, it makes it impossible for one not to look at them. I'm sure, Mrs. Scrutton, you'll agree with my wish that some other sides of the collection had the same advantages as the miniatures—the jewellery, for instance, and the armour. But that's not your fault. There's just too much for one person, that's all there is to it. The same applies to the research. I'm not going to embarrass Major Sarson by talking about his position as a scholar"—he waved his hand towards the old man who went red round the ears—"suffice it to say what we all know, that the gallery is honoured by the presence of the world's greatest authority on the Dutch school, and a great scholar of painting generally. Though I doubt, by the way, whether the Major's exactly fond of the moderns. I sometimes wish that the gallery possessed only paintings—I'm sure Major Sarson does. Unfortunately that isn't the case. I fully sympathized with him when he spoke to me as he did of 'those wretched pots and pans' "—here John laughed patronizingly—"but I doubt if a ceramics man would. Frankly," he said, turning to Major Sarson, "I consider it disgraceful that a scholar of your calibre should be taken off your real work in this way. Now how, you may ask, do I propose to remedy the situation? Well, the answer is that I propose to treble the staff. From next month new staff will begin to arrive—some students from the universities, some more experienced men from other galleries and museums."

There was silence for a minute, then Mrs. Scrutton spoke. "Does the board know of this?"

"Yes," said John, "they fully approve the scheme."

"Do they realize the expense involved?" asked Tony, the practical man.

"The board are businessmen," said John. "They know that outlay must precede returns." He looked round at their faces. "Well, I think that's all," he said. "I know you will give the new members of the staff the same co-operation you have given me, whether it is a question of instructing and training them, or in some cases of working under them." His tone was openly sarcastic.

"Do I understand that people will be put over us?" asked Mrs. Scrutton.

"In cases where experts are brought in, it may be necessary to make revisions in seniority," said John.

"You realize, of course, that in such an eventuality we should resign," said Major Sarson.

"That would be a great loss to the gallery, but we could not, of course, control your decisions," replied John and, opening the door, he bowed them out.

"Golly," said Veronica, "you do tell some lies, don't you? Or have the board ratified your staff changes?"

"How many more times must I tell you, Veronica, that truth is relative," said John.

Veronica looked down for a minute. "I'll make you some coffee," she said.

"Yes," said John. "Victory always makes me thirsty. I cannot help being satisfied when I think of the well-merited unpleasant few weeks those three are going to have. The punishment of incompetence is always satisfactory."

"Mmm," said Veronica doubtfully.

"What's that mean? You've not fallen for this sentimental stuff about Sir Harold, have you?"

"Good Lord, no," said Veronica. "It's not those misfits I'm worrying about, it's you."

"Me?" said John. "Why?"

"You're getting too fond of bullying," said Veronica. "It interferes with your charm, and charm's essential for your success." She went out to make the coffee.

What Veronica said was very true, thought John, and he made a note to be more detached in his attitude. All the same these criticisms were bad for his self-esteem. For all her loyalty Veronica knew him too well, got too near home. Charm was important to success, but self-esteem was more so. His imagination began to envisage further staff changes, perhaps a graduate secretary would really be more suitable now.

Union Reunion

➤➤❯❮❮❮

They could hardly keep their gaze on the low, one-storeyed house as they came up the long, straight drive, so did the sunlight reflected from the glaring white walls hurt and crack their eyeballs. Down the staring white façade ran the creepers in streams of blood —splashes of purple and crimson bougainvillea pouring into vermilion pools of cannas in the flower beds below, the whole massed red merging into the tiny scarlet drops of Barbton daisies and salvia that bordered the garden in trim ranks. The eyes of the visitors sought relief to the left of the verandah where the house came to an abrupt end, revealing the boundless panorama of the Umgeni valley beyond. The brown and green stretches of the plain lay so flat and seemed so near in the shimmering air that Laura felt as though she could have stretched out her hand to stroke the smooth levels far, far out into the white heat mists of the horizon, could have dabbled her fingers in the tiny streamer-like band of the great river as it curved and wound across the middle distance, and, imitating Gulliver, could have removed with a simple gesture the clusters of corrugated iron huts with which coolie poverty had marred the landscape. Here it lay—the background of her girlhood to which she had returned after twenty years and over so many thousands of miles.

For a moment she paused and stared into the distance. Nothing

Written in 1946; first published in 1949; scene laid in 1925.

seemed to have changed since her childhood, and now it was as
though its sleeping beauty had been awakened by the kiss of her
sudden return. Thoughts and feelings which had lain dormant
since she had left South Africa as a girl of twenty came pouring into her mind. Fragments of the scene had been with her, of
course, throughout the years, distortedly as the background of
her dreams or like flotsam attracted to the surface for a moment
by some chance smell or sound in a London street, but always
evasive, sinking back into the subconscious before she could see
clearly. Now at last there was no puzzle; the blur of intervening
years was gone and she saw it once more with the eyes of her
youth.

But it was not with the Umgeni valley that she had to deal, it
was with the family group drawn up to meet her. She could not
indulge in the slow, soothing nostalgia of unchanged nature, must
face the disturbing conflict of changed humanity. The harsh visual discord of the façade of the house seemed repeated upon the
verandah with the men in their bright duck suits standing uneasily at the back and the women in their violently coloured linen
and silk dresses seated in deck chairs in the foreground.

How enormous her sisters-in-law had grown, Laura reflected,
but then it was easy to understand in this hot climate where they
ate so much and moved so little; it was the price one had to pay
for plentiful food and cheap motorcars. Certainly the new short
dresses with their low waists and shapeless bodices were not an
advantage to stout women and made them look so many brightly
painted barrels. She had been so angry at detecting superiority in
Harry's manner towards her family on their arrival, but with all
his faults she had married a man who appreciated smartness, and
really there was no other word for her sisters-in-law but blowsy.
Flo, in particular, who had been such a fine dark-haired girl, almost Spanish-looking, people had said, seemed to have cheapened
herself dreadfully. Harry had said she looked as though she kept
a knocking shop, and although, of course, it was a most unfair
remark, one couldn't help laughing. Laura tried for a moment to
visualize Flo at one of her bridge parties in Kensington or Worth-

ing—what *would* Lady Amplefield have said? The badly hennaed hair, the overrouged cheeks, and the magenta frock with its
spray of gold flowers—could it be? yes, it actually was made of
velvet, and in this heat—but it was wrong to make fun of Flo like
that, for in spite of all that mischief-makers might say, the doctor
had told her that Flo had been very kind to her little David at the
end. It was terrible to think of her son dying out here so far away
from her and she tried never to dwell on it, but she must always
be thankful to Flo for what she had done.

That must be Flo's girl Ursula, she decided, who was winding
up the gramophone. How everyone seemed to like that "What'll
I Do?" But then waltz tunes were always pretty. She wondered
whether her nieces had as many boys as she had had at their age.
Of course it would all be different now, but though she had grown
to accept the more formal standards demanded of young people
in "the old country," she remembered with pleasure the free and
easy life she had led as a girl, and that was in 1900, so what would
it be like in this post-war world of 1924? Of course such ways
wouldn't do in England, she quite saw that; but it had been a
happy childhood.

Here was Minnie coming to meet them. So she still took the
lead in the family, and Flo and Edie probably still resented it; well,
more fools they for putting up with it. Minnie, at least, had kept
some trace of her looks, with her corn-coloured hair and baby-
blue eyes; her skin too was still as delicate as ever, but she'd let her
figure go. What a lot of one's life was wasted in unnecessary jealousies, Laura thought as she watched her youngest sister-in-
law approaching. She could remember so well the countless picnics and dances that had been spoiled for her through envy of
Minnie's tiny hands and feet, and now such features were not even
particularly admired, and on poor Minnie's mountainous body
they looked positively grotesque. She watched the enormous figure in powder-blue muslin teetering towards them on high-heeled
white shoes, the pink-and-white angel's face, with its pouts and
dimples and halo of golden hair, smiling and grimacing above the
swaying balloonlike body, and she was filled with the first revul-

sion she had felt that day. If only it had not been Minnie with whom she had to make first contact. She could not overcome her distrust and dislike of her youngest sister-in-law. Her other sisters-in-law kissed her and squeezed her arm and gave her confidences and she did not shrink back, but with Minnie it always seemed so false. Of course they had all felt that Minnie had tricked Bert into the marriage and Bert had been her favourite brother, but then it was all so long ago now and Bert was dead. She really must try to forget these things—being away so long had kept them fresh in her mind. Queen Anne's dead, she said to herself with a grimace, but she knew that she would never really forgive Flo and Edie if they had forgotten that Minnie was an intruder into the family. The clipped, pettish voice and the childish lisp had not disappeared anyway, she reflected as her sister-in-law's greeting became audible. Surely Harry would not be fascinated with Minnie's baby talk now that it came out of an elephant, as he had been in 1913 when Bert had brought his slim, attractive bride to London for their honeymoon.

Minnie at any rate was determined that her smart English brother-in-law should remember their earlier flirtation. "But you're not changed at all, Harry," she said, "not one tiny bit. Is he still as wicked as ever, Laura? But you needn't tell me, I can see he is. Well, you mustn't think you're going to play any of your tricks with the Durban girls of today. They're up to everything, they're not little schoolgirls like I was when I listened to all your stories. But still it was rather nice not knowing any better," she added, looking at Laura to see the effect of her words. "You've no right to have such an attractive husband, Laura, and if you have you should keep him under control. Laura hasn't changed either," she continued less confidently, "but then we knew she'd be the same dear old Laura as ever," and she pressed her sister-in-law's arm. The family seized upon the formula eagerly.

Although Stanley and the other sisters-in-law had already seen Laura and Harry at the docks, this was the first family celebration of their visit. They had been awaiting this moment with nerv-

ous expectancy; there seemed to be so little in common except
memories, and yet it was not as if they could move immediately
into the world of the past. After all they were not old people
like Aunt Liz, for whom past and present were irrevocably confused in a haze of sweet satisfaction. The contemplation of the
past years still gave an immediate answer to them, the sum of what
lay behind still added up to the mood of today, the business deal
of tomorrow, the trip to the Cape next month. Unconsciously they
had hoped that all difficulties would vanish in the mists of sentiment. It would give Aunt Liz such pleasure to hold a family re-
union at her home, one was not eighty-eight every day. And then
there was dear old Laura—she had had so many knocks, losing little David like that and, if all the stories were true, leading a dog's
life with old Harry, having to put up with other women and his
gambling and extravagance—she deserved a break if anyone
did, always so proud and never letting on about her troubles,
it would do her good to feel the family were gathered round her.
So Stanley, the only living brother, reasoned, and the women fell
in with the plan, partly from sentiment and partly from curiosity,
but chiefly as an exercise of their matriarchal power. It was they
who had declared war, and now they would arrange a truce. If the
meeting provided nothing else, it would be an opportunity for
acquiring ammunition for the future—first-hand observation and
scandal to replenish the decreasing stock of hearsay.

The actual meeting, however, had not gone smoothly; there
were too many suspicions and jealousies to allow conversation to
flow freely, so that they had awaited Laura's arrival to set the
wheels in motion. Yet as soon as they had seen her coming up the
drive they had realized that she too was a stranger, and something
worse than a stranger, an alien. Whatever their dissensions and
hatreds, and these still remained, they were South Africans not
only by birth but by life and habit, a feeling of unity was sensed
among them. Though Edie frowned and turned aside when Flo
whispered to her, "She's still very much the duchess," Flo had
hit upon the general sentiment. Let Laura and Harry think them
colonials—under the weight of that judgment they were at once

proud and ill-at-ease. Their childhood in common with Laura was overshadowed by their memories of her as they had seen her in London on their trips "home." Time was needed before the community of the past, the ties of kinship, could be revived, and Minnie had provided the magic phrase to cover those first uneasy minutes when a heightened awareness of what they were today seemed to banish all hope of recapturing the sense of what they once had been. "The same dear old Laura as ever"—the words bridged the gap between past and present. For the first few moments they all kept repeating it, and the fact that they none of them believed it seemed of no importance.

Rapidly the uneasiness and friction vanished as the drinks were handed round by the *umfaan* in his white cotton vest and shorts with their red edgings. The conflicting emotions of strangeness and of too great intimacy dissolved into the badinage and trivialities of the conventional middle-class party.

The men stood in a group at the back of the verandah, helping themselves liberally to whiskies and sodas. Stanley, with his pink, smooth, podgy face, his white trousers stretched like a drum over his swollen belly and fleshy rump, the two top fly buttons undone where the waistband would not meet, acted the genial host. Edie's two boys sprawled in deck chairs, bronzed, with a hidden and nervous virility, but with so great an external passivity that they appeared a neutral breed beside the aggressive self-certainty of Harry's English raffishness as he chaffed his brother-in-law, patronized his nephews, and laid down the law in consciousness of a superior sophistication. They were soon engaged in a series of arguments about sports and politics, amid loud, boisterous laughter at jokes which came near to insults, their voices rising now and again in dogmatic assertions which trembled on the edge of loss of temper.

"My dear old pot-bellied, fat-headed friend," Harry was saying in answer to a poker story of Stanley's, "if you care to raise the game on a busted flush, you bloody well deserve to lose. You should give up poker, old boy, and take to tiddlywinks. Tiddlywinks would be your uncle's strong suit," he added, turning to one of the boys. A moment later and they were involved in an argument upon a point of fact, each asserting the superiority of his memory with a clamour that would have done credit to the Greens and Blues.

"No, no, Harry, you've got it wrong," Stanley asserted. "Maclaren never made a century during the whole of that tour. You're thinking of that famous innings of Lord Hawke's."

"Well, since both Archie Maclaren and Martin Hawke are extremely old pals of mine I suppose I might be allowed to know something about it."

"You mustn't scare us with big names," said Stanley. "We're only poor colonials, you know, Harry," and he winked at his nephews.

But Harry knew when to take a joke against himself; in a moment he was expansive Britannia putting out a hand to pat the prize pupil on the head. "Good God, Stanley, I don't know what we'd have done without you in '16, colonials or not," he said, his shoulders squared and his eyes staring straight ahead. "You put up a damned fine fight at Delville Wood. Don't think you aren't appreciated at home. Why, they tell me the South Africans have put on the best show of the whole lot at Wembley. They're keeping it on next year, so you'll all have to come back with us, if they can find room for old Stanley in Piccadilly with all the traffic," he added, laughing.

It was the Union's turn to be handsome now. "I'm afraid our racing's going to be small beer to you, Harry," said Stanley, "but you must let me make you a member while you're here. I've bought one or two horses myself lately and I'd like to have your opinion on them."

"Glad to give it, old boy. As a matter of fact I was talking to a pal of mine connected with the Manton stables just before we left and he asked me to keep my eyes skinned while I was over here. Said he'd heard you'd got one or two promising two-year-olds."

It was a proud moment and they all felt happy as they thought of praise from such a quarter. Emboldened by the conversation, Edie's younger boy ventured a question.

"What do you think of our Natal boys' rugger, Uncle Harry?" he inquired.

But Harry felt he had conceded enough. "Too busy studying the form of the Thirsty Tiddlers," he replied.

"Perhaps you don't know much about South African rugger," said the boy angrily. "I think . . ."

"Don't, laddie, don't," interrupted his uncle. "It can be a very painful process if you haven't the requisite grey matter."

They were soon united again as the conversation turned to politics, for there was no Nationalist nonsense about Natal, everyone believed in Smuts and the S.A.P., everyone stood by the old country; yet what was the meaning of all this Labour and strikes, were the people at home turning Bolshie?

"Don't you worry about that," Harry answered them. "It's just a crowd of agitators, like this Indian Saklatavala. He's a nasty piece of work . . ."

"That's our trouble," said Stanley, "the Indians. We ought never to have allowed them to stay when their indentures were up. It was all due to master bloody Gandhi. We pretty near tarred and feathered him, you know, Harry, and we'd have slung him in the bay as sure as life if old Sir Joseph hadn't stopped us. More's the pity. The trouble is it makes the native boys so difficult to handle. *They* have to be indoors at curfew and the coolies don't. You can't blame the Kaffirs for not liking it, but it's making them cheeky. You can't get a decent houseboy now, what with the missions and one thing and another."

"I'm sorry Stanley should choose to speak against the mission boys," said Edie, her little bloodless lips compressed together in her sharp, yellowed, and lined face.

"Take no notice of anything Stanley says; he just likes to hear himself talk. I know, I'm married to him," Flo drawled in her slow South African whine.

But the common topic of the natives had broken down the barrier between the two sexes, overshadowing the fascinations of sport and gambling for the men, of clothes and operations for the women. Only Laura and Harry remained unaffected, attempting to maintain the former flow of chatter. But Harry's jokes and Laura's oblique movements towards that other field of feminine interest, domestic service, were not proof against the intensity of emotions that welled up in the others. Pride and courage were high as they thought of all that had been achieved by the whites; yet for a moment the anxieties and fears that were buried so deep shot through them with cruel sharpness as they thought of their small numbers and the thread by which their security hung. It was but a faint glimmer of their historical position that came to them, but, faint as it was, it was enough to outshine the selfishness of their everyday materialism. They sensed the brutal nature of their power, yet realized that if it was for a moment relaxed the answer would be swift and yet more brutal. The thought of the violence and the force upon which their lives rested excited them all, helping the gin and the whisky to thaw the gentility and pretension which ordinarily froze them, allowing the common crudity of their minds and feelings to flow and mingle. To the women, in particular, this sense of danger, of brutal, even sexual violence was most strongly appealing and the nature of their answer to it least ashamed.

"I wonder you don't worry about your sister," said Flo to Edie. "I hear she's over fifty miles from the nearest white station, and I suppose her husband has to be away an awful lot."

"My sister's in God's hands and her own," said Edie grimly. "She doesn't fear for herself, that's why she's so respected. Norman says the natives are more afraid of her than they are of him."

"Well, I should be terrified if my man wasn't there," drawled Flo. "You hear of such dreadful cases in Zululand these days. It's always these educated boys of course. An old schoolfriend wrote me that she sleeps with a revolver under the pillow."

"That's because people have spoiled the natives," said Minnie. "We had over fifty boys on our farm in the old days and my father never had any trouble with them. If he had a boy who seemed cheeky he gave him a taste of the sjambok. My brother does just the same now and *he* never has any trouble."

Even Aunt Liz's scattered memory was disturbed into some

sort of equilibrium by the excitement of the topic. "The sjambok isn't always enough," she croaked. "I shall never forget that
boy we had called Whiskers, he was a real skellum. Your cousin
was only a girl at the time, a skinny little thing. She was forever
complaining of faces looking in at her window, so your uncle and
I waited outside all one night. Not that I was much size to deal
with a man, but my blood was up and I'd have given him something to remember me by. It wasn't until early morning that he
came creeping through the bushes by the back verandah. He
must have seen us, I think, for he suddenly bolted, but your uncle didn't hesitate, he shot him through the foot. Oh, there's no
doubt God watched over us in those days."

"And He does now, Auntie," said Edie piously.

The others, who had put off their Nonconformity with their
childhood, became embarrassed by the religious turn of the talk.
Nevertheless they were proud as they looked at Aunt Liz, so frail
and bent and shrivelled; what fine brave people they had been,
those old pioneers! Really one felt ashamed to be so impatient with
the old girl, even if she did forget who one was, and whine and
complain so; they wouldn't see her like again, it was a dying
breed. Laura too felt drawn back to the community of her family as she remembered the early days when Aunt Liz and Mother
had come out from England; they had been windbound for six
weeks—or was it six days? anyway, for a very long time—and
eventually they had landed from the boat in baskets, fancy that,
in baskets. There was no doubt that she came from a tough pio-
neering stock who could hold their heads high. She looked proudly
across at Harry as she turned to Aunt Liz.

"You certainly had hard times, Auntie," she said, smiling at
the old lady, who had so far failed to recognize her. "Why, I remember so well when the Zulus were coming south, though I
was only five. Father was all ready to shoot us children if they
should get as near as Maritzburg. Those were terrible days."

If the Kaffirs attacked The Maples, thought Minnie, I should
have no man to defend me. Flo has Stanley, and Laura has Harry,
and Edie has her boys. I have no man. No woman was made to

be petted and cared for more than me and yet I have no one. My hair is a lovely corn colour and my figure is beautiful; Mother always saw to it that I held myself well. I have to smile at the way they run round me. Even these raw colonial boys see that I am a grand lady. It might be an English general or a foreign count. "How can so small a hand be so lovely?" I trace figures in the sand with the tip of my cream lace parasol, but I do not look up. I am playing with him as Woman must. "Why is she so mysterious, so enigmatic?" He has snatched a kiss, and I am in my white muslin ball dress 'midst the scent of the geraniums, just a crazy girl after her first dance. No, perhaps more interesting than that, a woman of the world, lovely, with her white satin nightdress clinging loosely about her limbs. "You should not have come to my room. You may kiss my hand and then you must go." Nothing nasty, no horrid contact, just a long flirtation, Woman's eternal spell cast over Man. I used to have such beautiful attachments, such wonderful *affaires*, only men always spoiled it, wanting to rush into bed, treating one so brutally, never content to worship at arm's length. And now there is not even that, no one even wanting my body now as Bert did, and Harry too, for all that Laura looks so proud. Now I am fat and shapeless and Harry hasn't noticed me, but I have not altered, I am still there smiling with my round blue eyes, kitten's eyes you used to call them, Harry. I should like to talk to him in our old baby language, to say, "Oo's naughty, Hawy; Minnie won't love 'oo if 'oo's so cruel." They would all laugh at me. I shall scream and scream until he takes notice of me, he can't just let me scream. Dr. Gladstone did. I lay on the bed in my pink crêpe de Chine and kicked and screamed. He said I disgusted him, that I looked like a pink jellyfish. Why am I unhappy? It ought to be so lovely for me, I was born for beauty and happiness. I can't bear it, I can't bear it. I won't face it. Come along, Minnie, you're exaggerating; it's true you're not a girl any longer, but you're a woman of experience. Harry has made no sign yet because of Laura, but he will. "You're grown up, Minnie, you're not my Baby any longer, but you're something much more, something that a mere man can only stand before in humble silence." How kind and thoughtful Edie is, for all her narrow religion; she has put me next to Harry at dinner, it is now he will whisper to me under cover of the conversation.

The long dining table was so richly decked that hardly a trace of the white tablecloth could be seen beneath the array of polished silver, the napkins folded like rosebuds, and the scarlet and cream poinsettias twining their way among the cutlery. The old lady, though nominally hostess, had soon lost any real understanding of what was taking place. Stanley, however, had felt that a woman's hand was needed for so festive an occasion, so Flo had indulged to the full her taste for colour and decoration. The young people sat at a side table which was embellished with china models of Bonzo and Felix the cat. Stanley himself had seen to the menu and had ordered a massacre in the poultry yard that would have challenged Herod—a goose, a turkey, two ducks, and two fowls had all shed their blood that Laura might feel welcome and Aunt Liz's eighty-eighth birthday not pass unhonoured.

Edie presided over the vegetables, doling great heaps indiscriminately upon each plate—pumpkin, boiled rice, sweet potato, English potato, mealie cobs and peas, and over all a thick brown gravy. If there were any protests she would put them aside with one of her dry little Chapel jokes. "Nonsense, the Inner Man must be fed," she would say, or "You can't help your neighbour on an empty stomach." Laura at first felt a little shy at such profusion, remembering the toast Melba and vol-au-vent of Lady Amplefield's luncheons in Hans Crescent, but the effect of three dry martinis and her childhood memories soon brought back the appetite of her youth. Aunt Liz ate greedily from her wheel chair, picking the wishbones in her fingers, and then dozed off before the second course.

Everyone was anxious to know what Harry thought of the South African hock, and was relieved when he passed it as capital, though perhaps a shade sweet. Wait, they cried, till he tasted the Van Der Hum after the meal, then he would see what the Union could do. Apple pies, peach and apricot tarts, bright pink stewed guavas, bowls of pulpy salad made from pawpaw and gran-

adilla followed, all covered with cream. Not until the fruit was on
the table, however, did the clash of colour reach its highest note.
In one bowl were the litchis with strange coral-like skins, and
next to them the round granadillas, their wine-coloured shells
cracked and dented like broken pingpong balls. In a third bowl
were heaped the tawny mangoes flecked with black and smelling
of the sugar refineries. In the centre of the table stood a cluster of
pineapples, their tawny squares contrasting with the dozens of
oranges of all sizes that surrounded them, from the tiny nartjies
through tangerines and green mandarins to the great navel oranges with their umbilical tops. For the discriminating palate there
was savoury salad of avocado pear with its oily texture and its
taste of dressed crab. But few palates were so discriminating as
this, and the avocado pear was eaten up in the mechanical round
in which everything else was consumed, a deliberate locustlike
advance that finally left the table a battlefield of picked bones, broken shells, dry skins, and seeds.

The physical effects of such consumption of food and drink
became increasingly marked as the meal progressed. Stanley's
veins seemed to stand out in his temples, his neck seemed to swell,
and his brow to be bathed in sweat. Flo's high make-up became
confused with an artificial and purple flush. Edie's face was dif-
fused with a greasiness that seemed somehow to derive more from
an inner piety than from the fatty liquids that clung to her faint
black moustache. Laura's corsets were giving her trouble, while
Minnie's flirtatious footplay with Harry was somewhat marred by
an occasional hiccough. Indeed, the belching and breaking of
wind that soon began to visit the adults like a Mosaic plague was
the occasion of much giggling and laughter at the side table.
Aunt Liz awoke from her doze for one minute to a violent bout
of flatulence.

"Did you hear that?" sniggered Edie's young son, and his elder
brother whispered loudly, "I think it was an old tin lizzie back-
firing."

It was not long before Stanley was caught up in the tide of
coarseness that flowed from the juvenile table. With his bon-

homie and his almost simple outlook he was always a favourite
with the children. "Keep the seat warm for me," he called to his
nephew as the latter departed for "where you can't go for me."

"Oh, Pop," shouted his daughter, "don't you go to the loo, or
you'll get stuck again," and they all went into peals of laughter
at the famous family joke.

"I don't think even a crane could move you this time, darling," said his wife, "you've got so broad in the beam."

By a coincidence Harry's voice was heard in man-of-the-
world explanation to Minnie. "My dear girl, it's as broad as it's
long." Even Edie had to join in the laugh, and Stanley said with
mock annoyance, "You leave my behind out of your powwows."

"Oh, for God's sake," said Harry, "keep your filthy mind to
yourself," and Minnie smiled sophisticated agreement, but they
were in the minority. The heat of the room and the working of
the digestive juices had completed the dissipation of self-consciousness begun by drink and family sentiment. Childhood was
being recaptured in all its crudity.

A moment later Harry, anxious to accommodate himself to the
company, attempted a hackneyed smoking-room story, but this
was too great a sophistication, and indeed, in its allusion to sex,
almost shocked Edie back into prudish gentility. Laura it was
who saved the situation; taking up a chocolate, she smiled at her
sister-in-law. "You'd better look at your bottom, Edie; mine's got
paper stuck to it." Dear old Laura, she was one of the best really,
and "What price the duchess?" whispered Flo.

Stanley picked up his glass and in a mock bow to his sister—
"Here's to you, Laura, your face my bottom." "You wretch,"—
his sister laughed—"I'd put you over my knee if I had half a
chance."

After this sally of Stanley's, Edie's "Bottoms up" said with a
giggle sounded a little feeble, but, still, coming from Aunt
Edie! . . .

" 'Chase me, Charlie, chase me, Charlie, I've lost the leg of my
drawers,' " sang Flo softly. This was more like it, no silly airs and
fancies, just like that funny picture in the album at home, "A

rare old rickety rackety crew." There was nothing like a joke
to make you feel young again and no one like Stanley to provide
the joke, a real comical kid, think how he dressed up in the old
girl's petticoats that night and kept them all in fits, pretending to
get spoony. There he was now, though, winking and giggling at
her, he'd probably want it before they got home. That was the
trouble with him when he got tight, always wanting it. Why
can't they have a good time without that? But it wasn't only the
men who were the cause, whatever women said. The women
were half to blame by fussing about it so. Look at Minnie, never
so happy as when she was leading them on and then going all my
lady and refusing them what they wanted, silly cow. It wasn't as
if there was anything to it, though she liked a bit of fun herself
occasionally, and if men wanted it bad then it was nice to give
it to them, like those poor kids they sent out as Tommies in the
war. But when it was all over the best you got was to feel sleepy;
now a good party like this and having what you wanted, that
was the way to live your life. That was one blessing in being
married to Stanley, he knew how to make money and he knew
how to spend it, not frittering it away with a lot of splash, but
having the comforts you wanted and putting by for *anno Domini*.
All the show Laura and Harry put on, and Minnie too—un-
crowned Queen of Durban that English piano player had called
her, and how she lapped it up—well, Stanley could buy them up
any day, that was one satisfaction, and heaven knows what would
happen when they got old, come cap in hand to her probably,
and of course she'd fork out, for when all's said and done blood's
blood, but rather them than her. Comfort in old age and the girls
well provided for, that was what Stanley and she had secured. It
wouldn't stop you dying though, like young David with those
oxygen tubes, and his pinched blue face. Poor old Laura, she must
have felt it, losing the only child like that. Probably wanted to ask
her all sorts of questions, any mother would, but say what they
liked they couldn't blame her. After all she'd been very good to
the boy, never asked to have him parked on her, wouldn't have
done if Grandpa hadn't died suddenly like that. No one else would

take him on, not even Edie for all her religion, and you couldn't
ship him back in wartime, what with the *Lusitania* and the rest.
He was a nice enough kid though a bit dreamy, but she couldn't
do with sick people, and when he was dying, well, that put the lid
on it, too damned scaring. Of course she'd seen he had the best
that money could buy and the girls were in and out of his room all
the time, but the kid had noticed her absence, asked for his Auntie
Flo. She'd tried to stay with him at the end, but it had frightened
her too much—time enough when one had to go oneself. She'd
shocked herself as she sat there wishing him dead to get it over,
and in the end she'd run out of the room. God knows, Laura
would feel bitter if she knew, but Dr. Gladstone understood how
she had felt, he would tell Laura that everything possible had
been done. So long as those bitches didn't gossip too much, everything would be all right; what the eye didn't see was a very true
motto. All the same she hoped to God there weren't many like
herself, neglecting you when you were dying and wishing it
over. God, it frightened you to think about it, everything out of
your hands and nothing to be done about it. Still that wasn't the
way to enjoy oneself. Thank God, the kids had started a bit of
music, that would liven things up. That elder boy of Edie's was
stuck on Ursula, that would upset Edie, thought her children
weren't good enough, bad moral influence. She wouldn't trust the
girls alone with either of those boys, deep and dirty, she knew
the Sunday-school type. " 'And how in the hell can the old folks
tell that it ain't gonna rain no mo?' "

So sang Flo, but Edie and her boys preferred "how in the heck,"
and Laura, who was sitting near to Edie, just left a blank. Stanley
was the first to go to the old Joanna, and when Edie's boys produced their ukuleles everything was set for a really nice sing-
song. A few jolly choruses were always a help in breaking the ice.
"Felix kept on walking" made everyone laugh, especially when
Edie's younger boy walked up and down copying the cartoon.
Stanley was, as usual, slow to sense a change of mood. "With his
tail behind him"—he laughed, winking at Edie. "Well, I don't
know where else he'd keep it." But Edie was already regretting

the slight looseness of their earlier talk. "Don't be more of a fool than God made you, Stanley," she snapped.

Matters were not improved when Flo's girl, Ursula, persuaded Edie's elder boy to play for her. Ursula was certainly "fast" and she could only be described as making "goo-goo eyes" as she sang to her cousin, " 'If you kiss a ukulele lady, will you promise ever to be true,' " and again, " 'Where the tricky wicky-wackies woo, if you like a ukulele lady, ukulele lady like-a you.' " Laura became worried at Edie's obvious restiveness. "Do sing us something, Minnie," she cried. "All these modern things sound alike to me." She was to regret her impulsiveness, as a moment later Harry moved up to the piano to play "The Temple Bells" for his sister-in-law. Soon Minnie's deep contralto filled the room, hooting somewhat with the emotion of the words "I am weary unto Death, O my rose of jasmine breath, and the month of marriages is drawing nigh." Even Ursula was forced to breathe, "Oh, that was lovely, Aunt Minnie. Sing some more, please." So Minnie gave them "Where My Caravan Has Rested" and "In the Heart of a Rose." Harry followed with his cockney imitation of Albert Chevalier in "My Old Dutch," and though most of the family did not follow his words, Laura's heart was glad at the compliment. Finally Stanley got out his banjo and accompanied himself with a soft strumming in "Oh, Dem Golden Slippers" and "White Wings They Never Grow Weary." His low, light voice and the deep sentiment which he lent to every word soon welded the party together in a mood of sleepy sadness.

Father used to sing these old songs so beautifully, thought Edie; how fine he used to look with his broad shoulders and his thick beard. God grant that my boys may grow up as their grandfather, always paying their way, asking nothing of any man, afraid to look no sinner in the face and call him to repentance, but always sweet and loving to their kith and kin as Father was. He had never been narrow like the Baptists, would sing these old songs so sweetly, though there never could be anything but sacred on Sundays. She had relaxed that rule with the boys, but sometimes she wondered if these changes were wise. Of course she did not want to be a spoilsport, liked them to have their motorbikes and their sports rifles, swimming and surfing too, even dancing. There was no harm in girls and boys playing games together, indeed there was a lot about the modern girl that she admired, more open and free, she liked the short skirts and the bobbed hair, but covering up the faces God had given them with paint and powder—that was different. Pray God she did not allow her love for these boys to close her eyes to their weaknesses. Swearing or drunkenness, how often she had told them that there was nothing truly manly about these things. But they were good boys, they were her boys and Grandfather's boys, never smoked and only a glass of wine on a party occasion like this. All the same she wished in a way she had not brought them here, there could be no good in hearing the silly, boastful weakness of her brothers-in-law, and as for her sisters-in-law, they were bad, frivolous women: it wasn't the atmosphere she would have chosen for the boys. If it hadn't been that she had wanted to please Aunt Liz . . . It was a thousand pities that Ursula was there— stupid little minx, she would like to put her across her knee. So different from the girls that she hoped the boys would bring home one day, not yet of course, for the elder was only just twenty-one, but someday. A girl they had met out swimming or at the Chapel picnic on the island. "Welcome to our home, my dear," she would say to this daughter-in-law of hers, and afterwards as they sat sewing together on the porch, for such a girl would love to help Mother with the sewing and the linen, she would look straight at her and tell her, "I give you a husband, my dear, free from blemish, from evil thought or deed." They would come together spotless, and spotless they would grow beneath a loving mother's eye. Yes, decidedly she would speak to that Ursula before any harm was done.

Edie had been sitting musing so long that there was general astonishment when her voice was suddenly raised above the general conversation. "Now, my girl," she said to Ursula, "you leave

those boys alone. There's plenty of young fools to make sheep's
eyes at you down in the town, but good boys are scarce and I
won't have you meddling with mine."

Ursula stared at her aunt for a moment, scarlet in the face, then
rushed from the room, holding her handkerchief to her eyes.
Edie's elder boy moved unhappily from one foot to the other,
while the younger one sniggered at his brother's discomfiture.

"Ursula has no need to run after anyone, I can assure you," said
Flo. "My God, I hope she can do better than cut some namby-
pamby from his mother's apron strings."

"Go on, go on," said Edie in her driest tones, "get it off your
chest, woman. You'll feel better for it. But it won't alter the fact
that my boys are not going to get mixed up with shameless girls
like Ursula."

"Ursula's a decent, straightforward girl, not a damned, creeping little toad, like your son. I heard about him making filthy suggestions to the youngest Palmer girl and using the dirty bits in
the Bible to do it."

"You're a very silly, angry woman," said Edie, "who's saying
things she doesn't understand. You had better put your own house
in order before you go listening to wicked lies, neglecting the dying . . ."

"What do you mean by that, may I ask?" queried Flo.

"Oh, don't be so silly, Flo," said Minnie. "You know very well
what Edie means, we all do, except perhaps Laura, and if she
doesn't it's high time she did."

The mellowing effects of the feast had worn off, leaving an irritation in every mind that was quick to flare up in anger. Already Stanley was telling Edie's sons that they should be
ashamed to let their mother boss them about in public like that,
to which his nephews retorted that such a remark was rich when
everyone knew Aunt Flo wore the trousers.

Only Laura, bewildered by the undercurrents that were rising
to the surface, had remained aloof. She could not, however, wholly
disregard Minnie's remark. "What ought I to know?" she asked
coldly.

"Why, that Flo neglected little David when he died, that she never went near the little fellow in his last illness," said Minnie, speaking rapidly.

"It's a lie!" shouted Flo dramatically. "I swear it's a lie, Laura."

"The doctor has said that Flo did everything she could," said Laura, but she did not take Flo's outstretched hand.

"Well, of course, if you prefer to believe what strangers tell you," said Minnie.

"I choose to believe what the doctor told me, and in any case I think you've interfered in my affairs enough for today."

"Interfered in your affairs, what *do* you mean, Laura? Harry, I appeal to you, what *is* all this about?"

"I think you've appealed to Harry enough too for one day," said Laura with unconscious wit.

"Poor old Harry," said Minnie, laying her hand on his arm. "So this is the sort of life she leads you."

"Look here, Laura, you know . . ." began Harry, but if Minnie was relying on male support for her victory she was ignoring Laura's marital ascendancy.

"Now, Harry, that will do," she said. "*We* don't want to quarrel," and her husband was silenced.

The sense of unity was finally shattered, like Humpty Dumpty, beyond repair. Nothing remained but to pack into the family Fords and Humbers, Wolseleys and Oldsmobiles, and depart in mutual silence. Only Laura was left alone for a moment with Aunt Liz. "Thank you for a lovely party, Aunt Liz," she said.

The old lady came to consciousness from her gorged sleep, and by a strange chance recognized Laura for the first time that day.

"So you came to see us after all, Laura. They said you would, but I wasn't sure. People get so selfish being abroad, wrapped up in themselves. Well, you've aged a lot, but I don't suppose you're too old to learn from your family. The family doesn't meet often enough," she mumbled, sinking into her dozy state again. "It does you all good, makes you think of something besides self for a bit."

A Story of Historical Interest

➤➤❯❮❮❮

It was clear, thought Lois, that no real provision was made in these ambulances for relatives—of the deceased, she was about to say but recovered herself in time—of the sick, of course. My legs are quite stiff, she thought, and my bottom will never be the same again after sitting for so long on this little bench. How selfish! How dreadfully selfish to think of oneself when Daddy was lying there dying, or at any rate possibly dying, for no one, not even the doctor, seemed to know whether he would recover from the effects of this stroke. His face looked so strange, almost blue-grey, and at intervals he was sick into the little white bowl which she or Harold held up to him—not really sick, she thought, remembering with horror those bouts of vomiting she had undergone as a child after parties—this wasn't like that at all, just a thin watery fluid with globules of green phlegm floating in it. His hand, too, constantly brushed feebly at his face or picked at his lips as though he were removing an imaginary cobweb. He was more comfortable now though, since they had had the nurse to wash him.

Perhaps the most awful moment of the three awful days, since she had been summoned back to the hotel from the office, had been the realization of her own clumsiness and of the pain she was causing him when she had tried to wash him on that first after-

Written in 1946; first published in 1949; scene laid in 1939 some months before the outbreak of war.

noon. The thick hairs had got coated together and stuck to the body with sweat and urine, and she had pulled at them in her efforts to sponge him. His eyes had gleamed red and small with hatred as he had cursed her for it. "God damn you, you bloody bitch," he had said again and again, for he was impatient of any pain and behind it all, though she tried hard not to believe it, terrified of dying, angry like a trapped animal. She had gone on relentlessly, however, hoping that at such times it was necessary to be cruel to be kind. It had angered her too, for she longed to show him her tenderness, to envelop him in a deep, almost maternal love, but by her blundering roughness she had failed. She had hated him for underlining her clumsiness; if he had not been cowardly and inconsiderate she would never have guessed at her failure.

How different the nurse had been! She could still see those "frank" Irish eyes with their sly, sexy twinkle, could hear that soft brogue jollying him on, while the plump hands moved him about like a baby, turning him over, powdering him, making him easy. "It's a wicked boy ye've been, I can see, and will be again. Ye've not finished with the poor girls yet with those great eyes of yours," and her father's chuckle, sensual still though feeble. "What do you know about me and the girls, Nurse? I'd like to know." She had seen herself suddenly as Mummy, awkward, unattractive, without gaiety; and the nurse as a symbol of those other women who had made up the pattern of his life. It seemed so unfair that the drab, clumsy part of her which came from her mother should have made its appearance at that moment, putting her at a disadvantage, alienating him from her as he was fading out of life. Ever since Mummy's death she had suppressed that side of herself, had deliberately cultivated gaiety, had flirted with him to hold him at home as she felt Mummy should have done—and she had succeeded so that he had said she was "the nicest kid he'd ever run around with," called her "Daddy's little pal." She could hear her own voice now as she spoke to the nurse, prim and tense like an affronted governess: "Mr. Gorringe has never been very fond of women's chatter, Nurse, so I expect you'll find him rather impatient. It's only a question really of keeping him comfortable. I'd have taken it on myself but we don't know how long the illness will last and I can't stay away from work indefinitely." "Not fond of women now, Oi'm surprised to hear't with his little twinklin' eyes. But it's merciful you got a nurse in when you did, the poor thing's been pulled about cruelly." She had almost struck the bitch. Nevertheless she had been just: Daddy needed a nurse and so the nurse should stay. No, it was only that dreadful letter which had made it imperative to dismiss her.

When nurse appeared dressed for the street Lois felt a greater antipathy even than before. Really, she thought, she's no better than a little shopgirl, an "amateur pro." She had seen such little creatures, with their black hair, badly put on lipstick, and insolent eyes, hanging on the arms of soldiers in the Edgware Road. The sort of horrible women whose full animal natures only appeared when they were drunk, singing and shouting obscenities on the tops of buses. What an unsuitable person to be Daddy's nurse, and she thought of those brown leather wallets of his, smelling of lavender water and packed with letters from the women of his past, clever, beautiful women—actresses, wives of friends, models, all the distinguished bric-à-brac of Edwardian wild oats. How degrading that at such a time he should be making moribund passes—I didn't mean those words, she thought with shame, they just slipped into my mind—flirting with a cheap Irish wanton. "A nice reliable girl," Dr. Filby had said; he must be insane. And then into her mind came other incidents—Daddy leaving her with an excuse at Leicester Square to speak, as she well know, to a hard-faced, peroxide prostitute; Mummy finding that cretinous Welsh housemaid in bed with him; that nursemaid who appeared on the stairs with her hair down, laughing and shouting curses at Mummy . . . My God, she thought, perhaps it isn't so unsuitable after all. I'm allowing myself to dramatize the situation, she decided; after all I'm very overtired. The girl's private life is no concern of ours; she's a good competent nurse and she makes Daddy comfortable, that's all that matters.

"Won't you have a cup of tea before you go, Nurse?" she asked.

"Well, now, that's kind of you. I'll not say no." Really the girl had a most pleasant smile.

They sat uneasily in Lois's room while the kettle boiled on the gas-ring.

"Yours must be a tiring life, Nurse," said Lois at last, in dead tones. "But then I expect you wouldn't have taken up nursing unless you had felt a great call to it. I mean it always seems to me to be a vocation rather than a profession." What a flat Kensington platitude, she thought, and, oh, my God, the girl's probably a Catholic and she'll think it blasphemous to say "vocation."

"It is grand work indeed to feel that you can help the poor things in their trouble," Nurse replied.

I am a fool, thought Lois, always seeing depths in people where they don't exist. "We shall all have need of you," she said, "if war comes. That is if any of us are left alive after the first hour."

"Do you think it'll come to war then?" said the nurse, and her voice took on a sudden excited note, accentuating the brogue. "God in heaven, I pray not. But they do say they have the coffins ready for us, in their thousands, and made of cardboard too, such terrible massacres they're expecting. Mind you, if it came it would be a righteous war, they've been doing the devil's work there in those concentration camps. But there's worse than that they've done, dividing father against son, destroying homes."

Really, thought Lois, I thought I was covering an awkward silence and I've let loose the Abbey Theatre. Aloud she said, "I can see you feel very strongly about it, Nurse. I wish I could feel as certain as you, but the papers are so lying, one doesn't know what to believe."

"Oh, if my brother could hear you say that, it's what I'm always telling him. He's turned a Red," she said in a hushed whisper, "and they'll no more receive him at home. He fought in Spain with that dreadful International Brigade. It was fighting against God, I told him, but he only laughs. He's forever speaking of the dreadful things the Fascists did at Barcelona and such places. 'It's the truth I'm telling you,' he says, but how can one believe him? Oh, why can't they leave us alone?" And to Lois's ear she seemed almost to be wailing, Don't we have our own private thoughts that are aching in us?

She was silent for a few minutes, and Lois suspected that she was embarrassed at her outburst; then, putting down her empty cup, she handed Lois a blue envelope. "I must be going," she said. "Will you give this to Dr. Filby, please? It's a note of the patient's temperature. You'll be sure to give it to him?" she added.

"Of course," said Lois. How hysterical she seems for a nurse, she thought, and then felt unjust—after all she too was probably overtired.

After the nurse had left, Lois returned to sit in her father's room. She felt overwrought after the alarm of yesterday and the first sleepless night of sitting by the sickbed. Nothing has changed, she thought as she lay back in the armchair—the rows and rows of brown, highly polished shoes each with its shoetree; the ivory and silver brushes and combs with the Gothic monograms; the silver-framed photograph of her parents taken on their honeymoon, and a later one of Mummy in a chiffon blouse with a cameo brooch—all these were objects of familiar vision. And she could guess at so many others—the neatly pressed grey-checked suits on their hangers; the stovepipe trousers of the old Edwardian narrowness, some even with shoestraps; the two grey bowlers which he was so proud to display in these degenerate, sloppy days; the photographs of Duke Rodney, his champion bulldog—everything smelling of his beloved lavender water. That familiar scent filled the room, closing all round her in her drowsiness, but behind it there was another scent, sharp, acrid, disgusting. Suddenly she was roused from the sleep that was enveloping her—for a moment she had been forgetting the awful thing that had happened, but that scent had recalled it—the sharp stench of vomit, the faint, sickly odour of fæces. That was why the room was so unbearably hot, why, although sunlight was pouring in through the

windows, the gasfire was burning at full height. The stroke that
had robbed Daddy of the power to move his legs had left him
perpetually numbed, so that he who had so loved fresh air seemed
always to be complaining that the room was cold.

Stroke was a well-chosen name, she decided, for it had descended upon them so suddenly, out of the void, shattering their
happiness. She had suffered moments of apprehension that such a
blow would fall ever since Daddy had passed his seventieth
birthday, but he was so active and gay, and people lived to such
an age nowadays, that she had always put the thought from her
mind. She was too busy understanding him, letting him do what
he wanted and preventing Harold from hearing of it. That was
what had aged him, she felt no doubt of it, feeling dependent on
Harold for his money. *She* never allowed him to feel that the little
bit he got from her was anything but his own. But Harold was always grumbling at the way the money was spent, just like Mummy
had done. *She* understood Daddy better than that, he was like a
naughty child; of course he'd always been spoiled, but he was so
sweet when he had his own way. He wanted the good things of
life, needed the excitement of gambling. Harold was such a horribly *good* man, he never wanted to do anything he shouldn't. It
was true he would pay Daddy's debts, but always with such a
long face and sometimes even with a lecture. It hurt Daddy's pride
so, and she couldn't bear to see him humiliated at his age, so that
she was always interceding for him, pretending the money was
needed for the household, getting at Harold when Daisy was not
there.

It was Daisy really who was so unkind, she who was not even
one of the family, except by marriage. They were always suggesting that Daddy should live with them at Tunbridge Wells; but he
would have hated it, away from the West End, his poker and his
racing, treated like an old dependent. She and Daddy had fought
them and had won. "You don't want to be rid of your old daddy,
do you, Lois?" he had asked after one of Daisy's visits, and she
had knelt on the floor by his side, rubbing her cheek against his

poor, worried face, running her fingers through his hair. "Silly," she had said, "I must have my old daddy to bully or what should I do when I was cross?"

But now that this awful thing had happened, how were they to meet it? She could not afford to leave her job, and who would look after him in a hotel? No one would say whether the paralysis was permanent. They would take him away from her, put him with the incurables. No! Oh, God! No, rather let him die than that, she said half aloud, and for a moment she fancied that the drawn face on the pillow had smiled at her. Perhaps he would recover, perhaps it was only a temporary thing, a warning for the future. Oh, God! let him recover, and we will take such care not to offend again, she murmured. If only he could move about even a little they could carry on as before. The main thing was to know what was happening. That nurse knew, she had probably written it all in the letter—"Mr. Gorringe has only three days to live." They had no right to ignore her so; it was bad enough to treat poor Daddy like an animal to be ordered about at will, just because he could not move, but *she* could not be treated so, she was still able to protect him. She picked up the blue envelope and tore it open. Nothing was written on the notepaper but temperature recordings and the times at which medicine had been given. She flung the paper down in disgust, and then on the reverse she saw what seemed to be a private letter. "What's eating you, honey?" she read. "It's over four weeks and more that I've never seen you, and none of my letters getting an answer. Darling, you know I'm mad about you. I can't sleep for thinking of it. When shall I see you again? You know where you can find me and I think you know I can make it worth while to you. For God's sake, give me a break, Fil. Kath."

Private thoughts that are aching in us, thought Lois. My God, how disgusting!

The ambulance lurched slightly as it avoided a careless cyclist. Mr. Gorringe's shoulders seemed to heave as he retched again, the green globules slipping down his beard in snail tracks. Lois wiped his chin with a hand towel. She could hear him murmuring

faintly, "I'm very ill, God help me, I'm very ill," and his eyes
stared with fright as his body shook at a sudden hiccough. Harold
held up the basin. "Poor old chap," he whispered to Lois. "He's
so very helpless." Lois pretended not to hear; it was just what
Mrs. Cooper had said at that awful interview in the hotel office—
the interview that had finally sent Daddy from her. After the
first moments of fury, she could have disregarded that disgusting,
cheap letter, have treated the nurse and Dr. Filby as though she
had never read it, or at the worst doctor and the nurse could
have been changed, but Mrs. Cooper's statement had been so final,
so irrevocable.

There were residents at the St. Mary Abbot's Hotel who said
that Mrs. Cooper's office was the most spacious room in the house,
and on this warm July afternoon their belief would have seemed
amply justified. It was more of a sitting-room than an office, with
its rich lacquer suite from Maples, the noticeably antique grandfather clock, and the Edwardian curio table containing silver
spoons and ostrich eggs. On this particular afternoon the room was
a riot of blue—delphiniums, lupins, love-in-a-mist, and anchusa, all
brought from Mrs. Cooper's country home near Midhurst—for
Mrs. Cooper loved blue, it was "her colour"; with her baby-blue
eyes and her carefully waved white hair, she felt sure that "blue
suited her," as her turquoise earrings and butterfly-wing brooch
could attest.

Lois always felt at a disadvantage with Mrs. Cooper; the hard
eyes, the drawling voice, with its occasional glottal stop betraying an East End origin, seemed to assert success and comfortable
security, to underline her own genteel penury. She hated to think
that this vulgar woman knew so exactly Daddy's financial vagar-
ies, had even refused him little loans to meet gambling debts.
This afternoon's summons to the office had completely unnerved
her, cutting through her private grief, overwhelming even the horror of that disgusting letter. It was so unlucky that Mrs. Cooper
should happen to be there, for in these last years a rising bank
balance had taken her on cruises to Norway and to Greece, on

trips to Monte and Bordighera and Biarritz, leaving more malleable manageresses as vicereines, but 1939 had brought an uncertainty that daunted even her.

"Sit yourself down, Miss Gorringe," said Mrs. Cooper. "I don't think you've met my nephew," and she waved her hand towards an overdressed young man with a Ronald Colman moustache.

"Pleased to meet you," said the nephew.

"Now, Tony, you great lump," said Mrs. Cooper, "stir yourself and get Miss Gorringe a cigarette."

"No, thank you," said Lois, and she thought, Pray God that he goes soon. Why should I have to hear their conversation when Daddy's so ill? She will try to separate us and I am determined to fight her, but if I have to talk about other matters I shall lose my resolution. She has done it on purpose to break my nerve.

"I've just been telling this boy that if things go on like this he'll have to be measured for a uniform," said Mrs. Cooper. "We'll have you in khaki yet, Tony," she added with a laugh.

"If things come to a head I shall join the Air Force," said the young man.

"You'll go where they send you, my lad," said his aunt. "Hitler means war, you mark my words."

"I can't believe he can be so crazy," said Lois.

"Can't you?" replied Mrs. Cooper. "I can. Well, Tony, give my love to Mother. See you next month, Hitler willing."

At last he has gone, thought Lois. Now I must be firm. Attack is the best defence. "I'm so glad you asked to see me, Mrs. Cooper," she said. "I was intending to come down anyway. There are one or two things my father will be wanting now that he is ill."

"Yes?" said Mrs. Cooper, without appearing to hear. Then she said rather distinctly, "You'll miss him, won't you, Miss Gorringe? But Tunbridge Wells isn't far—you'll be able to run down whenever you want to. Has your brother made arrangements yet?"

"My brother couldn't possibly accommodate my father," said Lois firmly.

"Couldn't he? What a pity! Well, I expect he'll find a nearby nursing home."

"Daddy wouldn't like that at all. He values his independence so much. Besides," Lois added ingratiatingly, "he's so fond of the hotel."

"And we're so fond of him," said Mrs. Cooper. "He's the nicest guest I've got. You tell him that from me, it'll cheer the old dear up. Don't worry, my dear, they often rally from these strokes, but he'll be an invalid, of course. He couldn't possibly get the attention he needs in a hotel. Poor old chap, he's so very helpless."

"But we've got a nurse," said Lois.

"Now, my dear Miss Gorringe, do you imagine I'd ever keep any maids if all the guests had nurses in attendance? You know as well as I do how badly that class get on with each other. Why! there's been trouble already. No, you make other arrangements; shall we say not later than a week from today?" And Mrs. Cooper turned to her account book.

"Aren't you rather presuming?" began Lois.

Mrs. Cooper laid down her fountain pen and her smiling blue eyes were quite unflinching. "No, my dear, I'm not," she said sweetly. "The situation's quite impossible. You're tired out or you'd see the point at once. You take my advice and ring your brother up now. Doctors can be very callous sometimes; they see so many of these cases, of course. It would be a pity if he insisted on sending your father to the hospital—it's so difficult to get them out once they're there." And she returned to her accounts.

The movement of the ambulance had become faster but yet more smooth. Lois guessed that they had reached the open country. Mr. Gorringe was seized with a new bout of hiccoughs, great shaking, bursts of wind that seemed to rack his whole frame. His cheeks were flecked with green, and dull white patches appeared on his cheekbones, which reminded Lois of his appearance in a fit of rage. It was quite possible, she thought, that he *was* in a rage; he kept murmuring, but the words were too faint to be understood. She helped Harold to prop his body forward with the pillows, while the attendant wiped his forehead. His face was suffused with sweat after the exertions caused by the hiccoughs, and Lois noticed that the sweat smelled rank, almost as though the body was putrefying. At last the bout came to an end, and he lay back, exhausted and snoring.

Harold looked apprehensive. "I don't like that stertorous breathing at all," he whispered, but soon the patient was sleeping more quietly. "I don't want to say anything against Dr. Filby, but I shall be glad when Dr. Grimmett sees the old man. Filby's diagnosis seems so vague, in fact his whole handling of the case wants a bit of explaining. Oh, don't think I'm complaining," he continued as he saw a shadow cross his sister's face. "You've done your best in a very nasty jam, but I think it was just as well the old man was moved when he was." The awful thing is, thought Lois, that I can't defend myself. Dr. Filby's whole behaviour was most unsatisfactory, he never really came to the point, but what could I have done? If Harold knew of that letter from the nurse he'd make an awful row. She noticed that the bedclothes had slipped away from the patient's feet, and, as she tucked them in, she saw again the strange brown scabs on her father's legs. The whole of that perplexing, unsatisfactory interview with the doctor came back to her.

They sat in the corner of the lounge in great deep armchairs, so that Lois was forced to perch on the edge in order to hear what he said. She felt all the time as though she were slipping off the seat. It's absurd that he should look so like a stage doctor, she thought, with his well-cut morning coat and striped trousers, with that bronzed, handsome face and strong jaw, and, crowning all, the iron-grey wavy hair of the matinee idol. As the interview progressed she found herself wondering at moments whether he was not, in fact, an actor and no real doctor at all, so exactly right was the form of his speech and yet so tenuous and vague was the information it contained. "Impostor deceives Kensington girl," she thought, but that was absurd. She really must listen more carefully to what he was saying, and she tried to set her face as she did when Harold talked to her about the workings of the Special Jury System or Daddy about Rugby Union Rules.

"Of course it's rather difficult to be specific when one doesn't come into the case until this late stage," he said.

Oh, dear! thought Lois, he's offended. Aloud she said, "He's not consulted anyone else, Dr. Filby," but judging by its result the apology did more harm than good.

"I imagine not," said Dr. Filby coldly. "The legs are entirely paralyzed, of course, but that is not necessarily a permanent condition."

"You mean you think he may recover?" said Lois.

"He might well improve," said Dr. Filby. "He's not young, of course. Poor old chap, he keeps his sense of humour, doesn't he? We can all do with that in these days."

Lois laughed obediently. "And if he doesn't get better, will he linger on like this for long?" she asked.

"I should think he must have had a little stroke before this. Can you remember anything of the kind?" said Dr. Filby. "Of course, these attacks are often so slight that they pass off without much notice."

Lois thought for a moment. "He had a bad giddy spell at the club some six months ago," she said.

"Very likely," said the doctor. "I understand movement has been difficult at times."

"He shuffles more than he used to," Lois replied, "and sometimes his legs seem to run away with him. But then he's over seventy and up to now he's been so active and cheerful." He isn't listening to what I'm saying, she thought, he doesn't even seem to be listening to himself, he's quite abstracted, it's really hopeless to talk to him. I shall make one more serious effort to get some information. "Do you think he's dying, Dr. Filby?" she asked. "If so, don't be afraid to tell me."

"He's in a bad condition," said the doctor. "I'll send a nurse around, a nice reliable girl; you'll like her. No meat or eggs, I think. Otherwise let him rest; he'll sleep a lot."

"I know names and that sort of thing aren't important," said Lois, "but I should like to be able to give my brother some exact statement. He's a bit fussy, you know," she added apologetically. Dr. Filby laughed. "No meat or eggs," he repeated. "The kidneys are affected. There's definite albumen in the water. I suppose your father was a bit wild when he was younger. You'll excuse my asking, but do you know of any V.D. story?"

"I've never heard of anything," said Lois.

"I'm just a bit puzzled by those marks on his legs," said the doctor. "There's a possibility of a tertiary syphilis, but don't worry about it; even if it is so, it can only be of historical interest."

"Are there any medicines I should get, Dr. Filby?" Lois asked.

"These hotels must be very comfortable," said the doctor, "but a bit gloomy at times," and he shivered. "Nurse'll look after any medicines. In a few days' time we can see how he is and then if necessary I'll get him admitted to hospital."

"Do you mean to give him treatment then?" Lois asked.

"Hardly that," said Dr. Filby. "But he may live on for a long time yet, you know, and he'll need hospital attention."

At last he's given a straight answer, thought Lois. How dare he suggest putting Daddy in a hospital ward like that, among the incurables probably? How dare he? How dare he? "Oh, my brother and I couldn't permit that," she said. "My father would eat his heart out with misery in a public ward."

"I'll write a note for the matron and get them to put a screen round the bed."

I *must* stop this, thought Lois, or I shall hit him. How dare he talk to me like this just because we're not rich? He treats us as though we were working-class people. "If it's necessary for my father to be moved," she said, "he will, of course, go to my brother's place, but I shall have to feel very convinced that the move is necessary."

Once more Dr. Filby reverted to the indirect answer. "I'll look in tomorrow morning," he said, "about eleven. We're going through difficult times," he added, "but I think Chamberlain's do-

ing his best. I'd like to see what some of these critics would do if
they were in his shoes."

Lois felt that she too had a right to be abstracted now, so she
merely replied, "Yes."

"Well," said Dr. Filby, "good-bye. Don't worry. And don't sit
too much in this lounge, it's like a funeral parlour."

Mr. Gorringe was sleeping peacefully at last, though now and
again he would wake at some jar in the movement of the ambulance and give vent to a mumbled obscenity. "I hope the old man
doesn't start cursing Miss Wheeler," said Harold. "We're almost
there now."

"I don't think I should worry," said Lois, "they're probably
used to that sort of thing at the nursing home."

"Oh! she's a good old sort," said Harold. "I don't suppose she'll
bat an eyelid, but still she *is* doing us a kind turn really, and then
she's got all the children to consider."

"All the children? I don't understand, Harold."

His voice in explanation was worried and apologetic. "Look,
old dear, I haven't had the time to tell you about this end, but
we've had a dickens of a time finding anywhere that will take the
old man. The nursing homes are simply nests of robbers, they want
ten or twelve guineas a week, and even then one doesn't hear
anything too good about them. Anyhow, I won't beat about the
bush with *you*. Business is at such a standstill with all these crises,
people just won't take a risk; I simply feel I can't afford to lay out
a sum like that as things are now. After all, it may be for a long
time. The old man'll probably get much better, he may hang on
for a couple of years, but he'll need proper attention. Miss
Wheeler's just the person for him, Daisy thinks no end of her.
She's a trained nurse of course," he said proudly. "She'll look
after him like a child. But it *is* rather a favour, because, you see,
normally she only takes babies and things—children that aren't
wanted, you know, poor little blighters. Awfully nice kids, I saw

some of them the other day. I should say she made them very happy," he added.

"How gratifying to hear," said Lois savagely.

"Of course she wouldn't do this for everyone," continued Harold, "but Daisy's won her heart as usual. They've worked together on some Conservative Committee."

Thank heaven Harold never recognizes sarcasm, thought Lois. I won't lose my temper, I won't, I won't, for Daddy's sake. It may be some time before I can move him and I don't want any unpleasantness. I'll never forgive them, never. Darling Daddy, they shan't treat you like this and go unpunished. Aloud she merely said, "We'll have to see how it works, won't we, Harold?"

Her brother was buoyant again at once. "I'm sure it's just the thing. Daisy's up to her eyes at the minute, trying to jog the local party into action, but you can rest assured, Lois, she'll see that everything's up to standard. By the way," he went on somewhat timorously, "you won't see her at Miss Wheeler's. She's got a very important committee meeting on, and there didn't seem much point in her coming down anyway. I mean the less there are to get in Miss Wheeler's way the better," he ended lamely.

It suddenly struck Lois that he thought she would mind Daisy's absence more than the muddle about the nursing home. How fantastic! "That's all right, Harold," she said. "I understand," and then she began to laugh wildly, hysterically.

Harold put a hand on her arm. "I say, old girl, steady on," he said. "You're just about all in, you know, the sooner we get you to bed the better."

If only she *could* escape to bed, thought Lois as she cut a piece of her anchovy egg into smaller and smaller squares at supper that night; if only she could escape from this endless monologue of Daisy's. They really were the two most selfish, thoughtless people she had ever known—if anything, Harold was worse than Daisy. He knew what a strain she had been through that day; she had already been at breaking point when they arrived at Miss Wheeler's but had steeled herself to meet the ordeal of her father's reception. Daddy had been so terribly ill after the slight jolting when he was carried upstairs; at one point fluid seemed to be pouring from every part of his body at once. She had to admit that Miss Wheeler and Dr. Grimmett had been very kind and, what was more important, efficient. But it had been pitiful to see his poor body when they had washed him, and he had cried with the pain—great, heavy sobs. She had never heard him cry before, and she had almost broken down. Despite Miss Wheeler's kindness, the whole house seemed so unsuitable, with sounds of babies' yelling and a smell of nappies on the landing. She had sworn an oath that she would rescue him, but meanwhile things were better than she had dared to hope.

It was well after nine o'clock before they got back to the house, and Daisy had still not returned. She had wanted to go to bed, but Harold had said that Daisy would be so disappointed, had assured her it would only be a question of a few minutes. It was ten o'clock before Daisy came in and they sat down to what she was told was a "scratch meal." Now it was almost eleven, and all that time Daisy had been talking and eating continuously—sausage rolls, sardine sandwiches, savoury eggs, rock cakes, anything within reach. Lois had felt too tired to hear most of what her sister-in-law said, so that she had been watching this voracious consumption as though she had been lucky enough to arrive at the Mappin Terrace at 4 p.m. And really it was exactly like some animal, for Daisy opened her mouth very wide, talking all the time that she was eating, and swallowing enormous mouthfuls, yes, and spitting wet globules of food all over the table, added Lois spitefully.

There seemed to be so much of Daisy—enormous bosom, rows of teeth, wisps of hair that knew no control, huge arms, and a voluminous black-and-white foulard dress with angel sleeves, the ends of which dipped into every dish as she reached across the table. She must have a digestion like an ox to eat all this heavy food so quickly. I know I shall never sleep after what I've eaten, Lois thought.

"Rubbish, Harold!" her sister-in-law was saying. "The trouble with the City of London is that they haven't got any guts.

They're simply putting their own financial interests before the country's good. Anything more shortsighted than their so-called realism I cannot imagine. A ten-per-cent dividend may be very nice, but it's not much help if we're going to sit by and sink to the position of a second-rate power."

"I think you're inclined to misjudge the government a bit, you know, old dear," said her husband. "There's a point beyond which we shall never concede. But modern war's a nasty business, it's not like the old days of shining armour. You can't go to war over every tin-pot European country created at Versailles by a lot of men who didn't know geography. I think we can rest assured Chamberlain's keeping an eye open, and if they go too far with us we shall say no."

"And meanwhile we're letting that man take every key point in Europe. Really, Harold, as if I didn't have enough of it all the evening. I'm as loyal a Conservative as anyone, but I hope I shall never put party before country."

"I suppose you'd rather have the Labour Party."

"With peace ballots and unilateral disarmament, no, thank you. No, we're the only party who can save the Empire, and that's exactly why we've got to pull our socks up. There's too much attachment to individuals, that's the trouble. Some of the old guard have done wonderfully well, but they aren't big enough for the situation and if they can't adapt themselves they must go, that's all. Thank God, Mrs. Faulkner tells me her brother in the War Office says the service chiefs have started kicking up a row at last, about time too. Have you heard anything of that, Lois?" she asked.

"I haven't heard about any of it," said Lois. "You see, I've been nursing Daddy."

Daisy was taken aback for a moment, then she got up from her seat and put her hand on Lois's shoulder. "Poor old Lois," she said. "Too bad, my dear. Never mind, we'll be taking the burden on now."

Lois moved away from her. "I have been proud to do it."

Daisy decided to ignore this remark. "Motion before the house: bed," she said. "Carried unanimously."

When they visited Mr. Gorringe the next morning he showed a remarkable improvement; he was sitting up in bed in a little camel-hair jacket, his white hair neatly brushed, even his eyes quite bright. Daisy too, although she had put off her morning engagements, was bright and cheerful, while Miss Wheeler seemed to Lois to be odiously eupeptic. Everyone seems awfully pleased, thought Lois, except me. Miss Wheeler took her aside to tell her that the change for the better in her father's condition was miraculous. "I really thought last night that he was going to pop off the hooks," she said, "but he's wonderfully rested, dear old gentleman. Dr. Grimmett says we'll have him out and about in a wheel chair in next to no time if he goes on like this."

Lois could not help wishing that she too could feel "wonderfully rested" as she thought bitterly of the battles she had fought all night in defence of her father, the tears she had wept in anger at the day's events.

"Miss Wheeler and I are famous friends," said Mr. Gorringe. "We've made a bargain—she cuts my beard and I give her the winner of the 2:30."

Miss Wheeler laughed appreciatively and winked across at Daisy. It was just as Harold had promised, she treated Daddy like a child, but somehow Lois had to admit that he did not seem to mind.

"I hear you've made great friends with a little kiddy here," said Daisy.

"It's wonderful," explained Miss Wheeler, "the baby took to him at once. She calls him Foonoo." A moment later she came back with the baby in her arms. "Foonoo," she said, pointing at Mr. Gorringe. "Foonoo" and "Foonoo" said the baby. Mr. Gorringe laughed delightedly.

"Well, Father," said Daisy, substituting the Schools Programme for the Children's Hour, "what do you think of the mess the country's in?"

"We've got to tell Hitler and Musso where they get off," said Mr. Gorringe. "Good for you, Father," said Daisy, "that's what I told the local party yesterday," and "Good for you," said Mr. Gorringe.

A little later Lois managed to get close to her father while Miss Wheeler and Daisy were busy talking. "Are you sure you're all right, Daddy darling?" she said. "You don't have to stay if you don't like it. I'll get you away."

Mr. Gorringe looked puzzled. "Don't you worry your head, girlie," he said, "the old woman's a very decent sort. You ought to be cutting back to town, you don't want to upset them at the office."

Lois bent down and kissed her father. "As if the office counted beside you, darling," she said.

But Mr. Gorringe only answered rather impatiently, "I'll be all right, girlie." Then he looked up at the baby in Miss Wheeler's arms. "That kid's a second Dempsey," he said. "Look at those wicked uppercuts with the right."

Suddenly Lois's voice sounded in the room shrill and shaking. "I shall go now," she said. "I'll get the next train. Yes, really I must. Don't bother, I can find my way to the station. I shall be at Marjorie Boothby's for the next few days—you can find it in the phone book if you want me. Good-bye, darling," and she kissed her father's brow. "I'll come and see you again soon."

Lois was doing her hair and Marjorie was in the bath when the telephone rang. They were dining in Soho with the Travises, but they had promised to look in at Mavis Wayne's party before dinner. "See who it is, darling," called Marjorie. When Lois lifted the receiver she recognized Daisy's voice.

"It's me speaking, Daisy," she said. "Oh, Lois dear, I rang to tell you Father's not so well. He's had a relapse. It's definite uremia, Dr. Grimmett says. He's not conscious, in a coma, you know. Harold and I thought we should tell you; the doctor says he may go at any time. He's not suffering any pain though, Lois. I know you'll be glad to hear that. Shall we expect you down?"

"No," said Lois. "It's really only of historical interest," and she realized suddenly that she was repeating Dr. Filby's words.

"What did you say, dear? I couldn't hear." Daisy sounded puzzled.

"I said there doesn't seem to be much point in my coming down if he's in a coma," said Lois. "You'll let me know if he asks for me, of course."

"Of course," repeated Daisy and she still sounded puzzled.

"Well, good-bye," said Lois and she put down the receiver. "Are you nearly ready, Marjorie?" she called. "Will there be hundreds of interesting new people? I'm rather in the mood to meet hundreds of interesting new people."

Crazy Crowd

❧❧❦❦

Jennie leaned forward and touched him on the knee. "What are you thinking about, darling?" she asked.

"I was thinking about Tuesday," Peter said.

"It was nice, wasn't it?" said Jennie, and for a moment the memory of being in bed with him filled her so completely that she lay back with her eyes closed and her lips slightly apart.

This greatly excited Peter, and he felt the presence of the old gentleman in the opposite corner of the carriage as an intolerable intrusion. A moment later she was staring at him, her large dark eyes with their long lashes dwelling on him with that sincere, courageous look that made him worship her so completely.

"All the same, Peter, I wish you didn't have to say Tuesday in that special voice."

"What should I have said?" he asked nervously.

"I should have thought you could have said, 'I was thinking how nice it was when we were in bed together,' or something like that."

Peter laughed. "I see what you mean," he said.

"I wonder if you do."

"I think so. You prefer to call a spade a spade."

Written in 1947; first published in *Horizon* in 1948; scene immediately after Second World War, when alcoholic drinks and many foods were still in short supply and many people objected to using small dollar purchasing power to acquire Hollywood movies.

"No, I don't," said Jennie. "Spades have nothing to do with it." She lit a cigarette with an abrupt, angry gesture. "There's nothing shocking about it. No unpleasant facts to be faced. It's just that I don't like covering over something rather good and pleasant with all that stickiness, that hesitating and making it sacred with a special kind of hushed voice. I think that kind of thing clogs up the works."

"Yes," said Peter, "perhaps it does. But isn't it just a convention? Does it mean any more?"

"I think so," said Jennie. "I think it does." She put on her amber-rimmed glasses and took out her Hugo's Italian Course.

Peter felt completely sick; he must make it all right with her now or there would be one of those angry silences that he could not bear. "I do understand what you mean," he said. "I just didn't get it for a moment, that was all."

Jennie wrinkled up her nose at him and pressed his hand softly. "Never mind, silly," she said and smiled, but she went back to her Italian grammar.

Peter longed to say something more, to make sure that everything was all right, but he remembered what Jennie had said to him about wasting time trying to undo things that were done. As he looked at her peering so solemnly at the book in front of her and making notes on a piece of paper from time to time, he felt once more how privileged he was to have won her love. She was so clearsighted, so firm in her judgments, so tenacious in her application. Here she was learning Italian, and learning it competently, not just playing at it, and all because she intended a visit to Italy some time next year. They had almost quarrelled about it some weeks ago when she had refused to go to Studio One to see the Raimu film because she had her next lesson to prepare. "Aren't you being rather goody-goody about all this?" he had said, but she had shown him immediately how false was his perspective. "No, darling, it's not a question of being good, it's just a matter of thinking ahead a little, being sensible even if it means being a bore sometimes. If I went to Italy without having read something of their literature and without being able to speak adequately I

should feel such a fraud." "You mean because you would be having something on easy terms that others could appreciate more."
"No, no," she had cried, "Damn all that about others, that's just
sentimentality. No, I'm thinking of myself, of my own integrity.
Peter, surely you can see that one must have some clear picture
of one's life in front of one. You can't just grab at pleasure like a
greedy schoolboy, Raimu this evening because I want it, no Italian because I don't. The whole thing would be such an impossible
mess." Then she had leaned over the back of his chair and stroked
his hair. "Listen to me," she had said, "talking to you like this—
you who have done so much with your life even at twenty-
seven, fighting that dismal Baptist background, winning scholarships, getting a First, being an officer in His Majesty's Navy, and
now being an Assistant Principal at the Ministry and a jolly good
A.P. too. That's really the trouble, you've read everything, you
know all the languages, I don't. Be patient with me, darling, be
patient with my ignorance." She had paused for a moment, frowning, then she had added, "Not that I think you should ever stop
learning. The trouble is, you know, that you've got swallowed
up by the Ministry. Town planning is a wonderful thing but it
isn't enough for someone like you, you need something creative
in your leisure time too."

Of course he realized that she was right, he had fallen into the
habit of thinking that he could rest on his laurels. There had been
so much activity in the past few years, constant examinations,
adapting himself to new situations, new strata of society, first
Cambridge, then the Navy, and now the Ministry and life in London, he had begun to think that he could rest for a bit and just
have fun, provided he did his job properly. But Jennie had seen
through that. It wasn't as if she could not have fun too when she
wanted it, and in a far more abandoned, less inhibited way than
he could ever manage, but she had a sense of balance, had not
been thrown out of gear by the war. And so he had promised to
resume his university research work on The Pléiade.

Peter opened the new book on Du Bellay and read a few
pages, but somehow with Jennie sitting opposite he could not

concentrate and he began to stare out of the window. Already
the train was moving through the flats of Cambridgeshire: an
even yellow surface of grass after the summer's heat, cut by the
crisscross of streams with their thick rushes and pollarded willows;
only occasionally did the eye find a focal point—the hard black
and white of some Frisians pasturing, the rusty symmetry of a
Georgian mansion, the golden billowing of a copse in the September wind, and—marks of creeping urbanization—the wire fences
and outhouses of the small holdings with their shining white geese
and goats. It seemed strange to think that Jennie's home, which
she had painted in such warm, happy, even, if the word had not
been debased, cosy colours, should lie among such plain, almost
deadening landscape. But as Peter gazed longer he began to feel
that there was a dependability, an honest good sense, about these
levels that was much what he admired so in her, and perhaps as
she had built that brilliant, gay, attractive nature upon plain and
good foundation, so the Cockshotts had created their home, alive,
bright, happy-go-lucky, "crazy," Jennie had often described it,
upon this sensible land.

He tried to picture her family from the many things she had
said about them. His own home background was so different
that he found it difficult to follow her warm, impulsive description of her childhood. Respect for parents he understood, and
acceptance of the recognized forms and ceremonies or else rebellion from them, but he had been far too busy winning scholarships and passing examinations to attempt the intimate undertones, the almost emotional companionship of which Jennie
spoke, nor would his parents, with their austere conceptions of
filial obedience, tempered only by their ambitions for his future,
have understood or encouraged such overtures. He felt greatly
drawn to the easy familiarity that she had described, yet much
afraid that her family would not like him.

It was clear that the only course was to maintain a friendly
silence and trust to Jennie to interpret as she had done so often in
London. Her affection for her father was deep, and he imagined
it was reciprocated. Indeed, the wealthy barrister who had re-

tired from the law so early sounded a most attractive gentle creature, with his love of the country, his local antiquarianism, and
his great artistic integrity, which had caused him to publish so little, to polish and polish as he aimed at perfection. A survival, of
course, but a lovable and amusing person; Peter's only fear was
that he would fail to grasp the many leisured-class hypotheses by
which Mr. Cockshott obviously lived, but there again Jennie had
explained so much.

Her stepmother, Nan, remained more vague. Some children,
certainly, would have resented the intrusion of an American
woman into their home, but Jennie and her brother had apparently completely accepted Nan, though there were clearly
things in her that Jennie felt difficult to assimilate, for she often
said laughingly that her stepmother had on such and such an occasion been "rather pathetically Yankee." Thinking of the gar-
rulous, overearnest American academical women he had known,
Peter had thought this an unpleasant condemnation; but his acquaintance was very limited, and Jennie had explained that South-
eners were quite different—"awfully English really, only with
an extra chic for which any English girl would sell her all." Peter
thought that perhaps Nan might be a little alarming but obviously
very worth while.

Then there was Jennie's brother Hamish, who had been her
companion in all those strange, happy, fantasy games of her childhood. She had explained carefully that he was not an intellectual
but that he was very learned in country lore and had read all sorts
of out-of-the-way books on subjects that interested him. Jennie
admired him because he had hammered out ideas for himself in so
many different spheres—had his own philosophy of life and his
own views on art and politics. Some of these views sounded
strangely crazy to Peter, and perhaps a bit cocksure, but still he
was only twenty-two, and, as Jennie had pointed out, views didn't
matter when one was young, what really counted was thinking
for oneself. It would be necessary to go very easy with a fellow
like that, Peter reflected, thinking of his own obstinate defence of

heterodox ideas at that age: it had been mostly due to shyness he remembered.

And last there was Flopsy, who was some sort of cousin, though he could never unravel the exact relationship. She was certainly somebody outside his former experience, not that he was unused to the presence of elderly unmarried female relations in the homes of family friends, but their activities were always confined to household matters, women's gossip, or good works. This Flopsy was a much more positive character, for not only did she run the household—and with such a happy-go-lucky family she must be kept very busy—but she appeared also to be the confidante of all their troubles. The extent to which even someone so self-reliant as Jennie depended upon her advice was amazing, but she was obviously a rare sort of person. He felt that he already knew and liked her from the many stories he had heard of her downright tongue, her great common sense, and her sudden frivolities; he only hoped that he would not fall too much below her idea of the ideal suitor, but at least he felt that so shrewd and honest a woman would see through his awkwardness to his deep love for Jennie. Anyhow, he decided, if anything went wrong it would only be his own fault, for it was really a privilege to be meeting such unusual people who were yet so simple and warm-hearted; above all it was a great privilege to be meeting Jennie's family.

As she stepped from the carriage onto the little country platform Jennie looked back for a moment at her lover. "Frightened, darling?" she asked. And as Peter nodded assent, "There's no earthly need," she said. "I'm pretty certain you'll approve of them and I know they'll love you. Anyhow, anyone who fails to make the grade will have to reckon with me. So you've been warned," she ended with mock severity.

A sudden gust of wind blew from behind her as she stood on the platform, causing her to hold tightly to the little red straw hat perched precariously on her head, blowing the thick, dark wavy hair in strands on which the sun played, moulding her cherry-and-white-flowered dress to her slender figure, underlining the beauty of her long, well-shaped legs. It gave a moment's sharp desire to Peter that made him fear the discomfort of the weekend, doubt his ability to keep their mutual bond that parental feelings were to be respected, lovemaking forsworn.

But desire could not endure, already they had been claimed by Nan. "Honey," she cried in her soft Southern drawl, throwing her arms round Jennie's neck. "Honey, it's good to see you. I know it's only a week, but it's seemed like an age."

"Darling Nan," cried Jennie, and her embrace was almost that of a little girl as she kicked her feet up behind her. "Darling Nan, this is Peter. Peter, this is Nan."

The sunburnt, florid face, with its upturned freckled nose, turned to Peter, the blue eyes gazed steadily at him, then Nan broke into a broad, good-natured smile, the wide, loose mouth parting to reveal even white teeth. She gave Peter's hand a hearty shake. "My, this is a good moment," she said. "A very good moment." Then she turned again to Jennie and, holding her at arm's length, "You look awfully pale, dear," she said. "I hate to think of you up there in those dreadful smoky streets, and it's been so lovely here. We have the most beautiful autumns here, Peter."

"They're the same as autumns anywhere else, darling," said Jennie.

"That they're not," said Nan. "Everything's kind of special round here. You just wait till you see our trees, Peter, great splendid red and gold creatures. I better warn you I shan't like you at all if you don't fall in love with our countryside. But I know you will, you're no townsman, not with those powerful shoulders. I like your Peter," she said to Jennie.

"There you are, darling, she likes you."

"Well, for heaven's sake, look at that," cried Nan. "Hamish hasn't moved out of the car," and she pointed at a tall, dark-haired young man whose legs seemed to fill the back of the grey car towards which they were advancing.

It gave Peter a shock to see Jennie's eyes staring from a man's face. He felt the moment had come to be positive. "Hullo, Hamish," he said with what he hoped was a friendly smile, but the young man ignored him.

"That's a revolting dress," he said to Jennie in a mumble that came from behind his pipe.

"Not so revolting as a green tie with a blue shirt," said his sister. "Really, darling, you need me here to take your colour sense in hand."

"Parkinson's wife been took again, and it's a mercy she come through, what with being her eighth and born with a hump like a camel," said Hamish.

"Never," said Jennie, "and her such a good woman. What be they callin' the littl'un?"

"They don't give 'er no name," said Hamish, "for fear she be bewitched."

" 'Appen it'll be so," said Jennie.

"For heaven's sake, you two," said Nan. "What will Peter think of you? Aren't they the craziest pair? Look at poor Peter standing there wondering what sort of place he's come to."

Peter endeavoured to explain that he understood them to be imitating rustics, but Nan would not allow him to comprehend. "My dear, there's no need to hide it from me. I know exactly what you're thinking: 'What ever made me come down to this crazy place among these crazy people?' And so they are—the crazy Cockshotts. My dear," she called to Jennie in the back of the car, "it's going to be the most terrible picnic, I've just not thought a thing about what to eat or what to drink, so heaven knows what you'll find, children."

"Never mind, darling," called Jennie, "the Lord will provide."

"He'd better," said Nan, "or I'll never go to that awful old church again."

To Peter, sitting in front with her, it seemed that Nan never ceased speaking for the whole nine miles of their drive to the house. He could not help feeling that in her garrulity she was much like other American women, but he felt sure that he was missing some quality through his own obtuseness. He found it easy enough to answer her innumerable questions, for a murmur of assent was all she required; her sudden changes, however, from talk about the village and rationing or praise of the countryside to a more intimate note confused him greatly. "I do hope you're going to like us," she said, fixing him with her honest blue eyes, to the great detriment of her driving, "because I know we're going to like you very, very much."

As a background to Nan's slow drawl he could hear a constant conversation, in varying degrees of rustic accent, coming from the back of the car, sometimes giving place to giggles from Jennie and great guffaws from Hamish, sometimes to horseplay in which wrestling and hair pulling were followed by shrieks of laughter. Only twice did the two conversations merge. "Jennie," called Nan once, "you never told me Peter was a beautiful young man. He's beautiful."

"Nan, Nan, don't say it. You'll make him conceited," said Jennie.

"I can't help it," said Nan. "If I see anything beautiful, whether it's trees or flowers or a lovely physique, I just have to say so."

"He's certainly better than Jennie's last young man," said Hamish, "the one with spavins and a cauliflower ear. Peter's ears appear to be of the normal size."

"We pride ourselves on our ears in my family," said Peter, trying to join in the fun, but Hamish was intent on his own act.

"Then there was the young dental mechanic, a charming fellow, indeed brilliant as dental mechanics go, but unfortunately he smelled. You don't smell, do you?" he called to Peter.

"Don't be rude, Hamish," said Jennie, and Nan chimed in with, "Now, Hamish, you're just being horrible and coarse."

"Ah, I forgot," said Hamish, "the susceptibilities of the great bourgeoisie; no reference must ever be made to the effects of the humours of the human body upon the olfactory nerves. Peter, I apologize."

Luckily Peter was not called upon to reply, for Nan directed his attention to a Queen Anne house. "My, what a shame!" she said. "The Piggotts are from home. I know you'd just adore the

Piggots. They're the most wonderful old English family. They've lived in that lovely old house for generations, but to meet them they're the simplest folk imaginable. Why, old Sir Charles looks just like a dear old farmer!" And she continued to discourse happily on the necessary interdependence of good breeding and simplicity, occasionally adding remarks to the effect that having roots deep in the countryside was what really mattered. Suddenly she paused and, shouting over her shoulder to Jennie, she called, "My dear, the most awful thing! I quite forgot to tell you we've all got to go to the Bogus-Smiths' to tea."

"Oh, Nan, no!" cried Jennie, "not the Bogus-S's."

"We always call them the Bogus-Smiths," said Nan by way of explanation. "They're a terribly vulgar family that comes from heaven knows where. They've got the most lovely old place, a darling old eighteenth-century dower house, but they've just ruined it. They've made it all olde-worlde, of course they just haven't got any taste. Don't you agree, Peter, that vulgarity is the most dreadful of the Deadly Sins?" Peter murmured assent. "I knew you would," said Nan. "I wish you could see Mrs. Bogus-Smith gardening in all her rings. I just hate to see hands in a garden when they don't really belong to the soil. The awful thing is, Jennie," she added, "that everything grows there. I suppose," she ended with a sigh, "people just have green fingers or they haven't."

"The Bogus-S's have *money*," said Hamish, "and a sense of the power of money, that's what I like about them. If the people who really belong to the land are effete and weak and humane, then let those who have money and are prepared to use it ruthlessly take over. I can respect the Bogus-Smiths' vulgarity, it's strong. When I'm with them it's gloves off. Mr. Bogus-S sweats his workmen and Mrs. Bogus-S her servants, but they've got what they want. I like going there, it's a clash of wills, my power against theirs."

"Hamish is crazy on Power," said Nan, explaining again. "Very well, darling, you shall go and Peter and Jennie can stay at home. The Brashers will be there."

"Oh, hell," said Hamish, and Jennie, roaring with laughter, began to chant—

> *"In their own eyes the Brashers*
> *Are all of them dashers.*
> *The boys are all mashers*
> *And the girls are all smashers"*—

a chorus in which Hamish joined with a deafening roar, and even Nan hummed the tune. "The Brashers shall serve my will and that of the Bogus-Smiths," said Hamish. "They shall be our helots."

"Thus spake Zarathustra," said Jennie with mock gravity. Hamish began to pull her hat off, and had they not turned into the drive at that moment there would have been another wrestling bout.

They approached a long, grey early-Victorian house with a verandah and a row of elegant French windows with olive-green shutters. "Now isn't it just the ugliest house you've ever seen?" asked Nan. Peter thought it had great charm and said so. "Well, yes," said Nan, "the children love it and I suppose it is quaint. But think if it was one of those lovely old red-brick Queen Anne farmhouses."

A bent old man in a straw hat was tending a chrysanthemum bed. Jennie began to shout excitedly through the window. "Mr. Porpentine, darling Mr. Porpentine," she cried.

"What a curious name," said Peter, whose mind had indeed begun to wander under the impact of Nan's chatter.

"Oh, Peter, darling, really," said Jennie. "It isn't his real name, it's because he's so prickly—you know, 'the fretful porpentine.' Only of course he isn't really prickly, he's an old darling."

Further explanations were cut short by their arrival at the front porch. Nan led the way into a long, high-ceilinged room, into which the sunlight was streaming through the long windows. "This is the sitting-room," said Nan. "It's in the most terrible mess. But at least it *is* human, it's lived in." And lived in it clearly was—to an unfamiliar visitor like Peter the room appeared like a

chart of some crowded group of islands: deep armchairs and
sofas in a faded flowered cretonne stood but a few feet from each
other, and where the bewildered navigator might hope to pass between them there was always some table or stool to bar his way.
Movement was made the more dangerous because some breakable
object was balanced precariously on every available flat surface.
There were used plates and unused plates, half-finished dishes of
sandwiches, half-empty cups of coffee, ashtrays standing days
deep in cigarette ends; even the family photographs on the mantelpiece seemed to be pushing half-finished glasses of beer over
the edge. It was impossible to sit down, for the chairs and sofas
were filled with books, sewing, workboxes, unfolded newspapers,
and in one case a tabby cat and two pairs of pliers. When at last
some spaces were cleared the chair springs groaned and creaked
beneath the weight of their sitters. Peter sank into a chair the
springs of which were broken, hitting the calves of his legs against
an unsuspected wooden edge. It was clear that the chairs and sofas
were each the favourite of some member of the family, had indeed
been overlong lived in.

"My dears," said Nan, "I'm ashamed," and she waved her hand
towards a plate of unfinished veal-and-ham pie that was placed on
the "poof." "Suicide Sal's away and we've been picnicking."

"Oh, I'm so disappointed," cried Jennie. "I had so wanted Peter
to see Suicide Sal."

"My dear, she's had another accident."

" 'Tis Jim Tomlin 'ave got 'er into trouble this time," said Hamish. "They do say she be minded to throw 'erself in pond."

"Oh! Hamish, don't be so dreadful," said Nan, and she began
to repeat the story of her servant problems that Peter had heard in
the car.

Suddenly the door opened and a little birdlike elderly woman
in a neat grey skirt and coat seemed almost to hop into the room.
She had a face of faded prettiness with kitten eyes, but at this moment her lips were compressed, her forehead wrinkled, and she
was pushing back a wisp of grey hair with a worried gesture. "Oh,
Nan, there you are at last," she said. "I just can't get that lemon

meringue pie of yours right. The oven won't come down and I'm sure the wretched thing will burn."

"Flopsy," cried Jennie, and "How's my canary bird?" said Flopsy as they embraced.

"Flopsy, this is Peter."

"How do you do?" said Flopsy. "You're taller than I expected and thinner. That young man of yours needs feeding, Jennie. Well, Peter or no Peter, he won't get any dinner tonight if we don't look after that pie. Come on, Nan."

"Happy, darling?" asked Jennie. Peter was too exhausted to do more than smile, but alone with her he felt he could do so sincerely. "Good," she said; then, "Where can Daddy be?" she asked and began to call, "Dads, Dads, where are you?"

Mr. Cockshott was a much smaller man than Peter had expected. Despite his bald head fringed with grey and his grey toothbrush moustache he had a boyish, almost Puckish expression which made him seem younger than his fifty-seven years. He wore an old, shapeless tweed suit with bulging pockets and a neat grey foulard bow-tie. "Jennie, darling, you're looking very pretty," he said, kissing her on the forehead as she sat on the sofa and running his hand over her hair.

"Dads," said Jennie, "darling Dads. This is Peter."

"So you're the brave man who's had the temerity to take on this little wretch," said Mr. Cockshott.

"It doesn't require much courage," said Peter, "the reward is so great."

"Good, good," said Mr. Cockshott absently. "How are things at the Ministry—humming, I suppose?" It was the first question about himself that anyone had asked Peter, and he was about to answer when Mr. Cockshott went on. "Of course they are. I never yet heard of a government office where things were *not* humming. Though what they're humming about is rather a different question, eh? Well, you'll find things very quiet down here. Not but what there's not been a deal of trouble about Abbot Gladwin's yearly returns. These mortmain tenures are liable to cause a rumpus, you know," he said, turning to Jennie. "It's not like a simple scutage where the return is a plain *per capitem*. Between you and me, the abbot's had a lot of trouble with his *own* tenants. I'm by no means sure that Dame Alice hasn't suppressed a pig or two, and as for Richard the Smith, frankly the man's a liar."

"Darling, don't mystify Peter. He's talking about his old twelfth century, Peter. Have you had a reply from the Record Office yet, darling?"

"Yes," said Mr. Cockshott, "most unsatisfactory. Of course it was a turbulent century, Barrett," he said to Peter, "and the turbulence was not without repercussions even in our remote part of the world. For instance, I've been able to relate the impact of Richard Cœur de Lion's ransom directly to . . ." But there he was interrupted by the return of Nan.

"For heaven's sake, Gordon," she said, "just look at you. You dreadful, disreputable creature. I appeal to you, Peter, doesn't he look just like the wrong end of a salvage campaign? I just can't imagine what that starchy Mrs. Brasher will say if she sees you."

"If Mrs. Brasher does see me, and considering her myopic tendencies I consider that very unlikely, she will undoubtedly, as the current phrase goes, fall for me."

"May be, dear, may be," said Nan, "but nevertheless your trousers are going to get a patch in them. Flopsy," she called, "Flopsy, bring a needle and help sew up Gordon's pants."

"Poor Dads!" said Jennie. "Aren't you shockingly bullied? Cross my heart, spit on my finger," she added, "I'll never treat my man like this virago," and she pressed Nan's elbow tenderly.

Peter smiled uneasily and uncrossed his legs. But Mr. Cockshott was purring as a buzz of feminine interest surrounded him. "I'll tell you a secret, Barrett," he said. "Women are like touchy collie dogs, they need humouring."

Peter was about to reply, in what he felt to be a suitable man-to-man vein, when he was startled by finding a large bodkin thrust into his left hand. "Hold that," said Flopsy, "and don't sit gaping." The kindness that lay behind her gruff voice was almost unbearable. "You'll have to learn to be useful if you want to earn your bread and butter in this house. No drones here."

"Oh, for crying out loud," said Nan. "Flopsy, you're scaring the poor boy into fits."

"Peter's not frightened, are you, darling?" said Jennie. "Why, it didn't take him any time to see how much Flopsy's bark meant."

Peter laughed and tried to smile at Flopsy. "I shan't eat you up, young man," she said.

But Mr. Cockshott was growing restive; his face took on an expression of caricatured thoughtfulness and he bit on his pipe. "Of course, I might appear with no trousers at all," he said. "Æsthetically I should be perfectly justified, for I still have a very fine leg. Hygienically—well, the weather is very warm and trousers are an undesirable encumbrance. Socially I make my own laws. I have only one hesitation, and that is in the moral sphere. I have no doubt at all that the sight of my splendid limbs would cause Mrs. Brasher to become discontented with her own spouse's spindly shanks; and while I have the greatest contempt for that horsetoothed, henpecked gentleman, I have also the highest respect for the institution of marriage. No, I must remain a martyr to the cause of public morality."

A chorus of laughter greeted this sally, and Nan declared he was impossible, while Jennie dared him to carry out his threats. "Oh, do, Dads, do," she cried. "I'd so adore to see Mrs. Brasher's face. Go on, I dare you," but Dads just shook his head. "Flopsy shall make me a kilt in the long winter evenings," he declared.

"I'll make you a bag to put your head in if you don't stand still while I'm patching you," said Flopsy, laughing.

"Heathenish woman, how right they were to give you that outlandish name."

"It's not an outlandish name," said Jennie. "Flopsy's a lovely name. It comes from the Flopsy bunnies in *Peter Rabbit*."

"It does not," said Hamish, entering the room. "It is taken from the immortal English surrealist Edward Lear and his Mopsikon-Flopsikon bear."

After what seemed to Peter an age the family were ready to depart. He would not have dared to confess to Jennie his relief as he heard the car disappear down the drive.

Despite all Nan's apologies that the evening meal was just a picnic, Peter decided that they lived very well; with the combined produce of the garden, neighbouring farms, and American relations, it was clear that austerity had not seriously touched them. Sweet corn and tunny fish was followed by roast chicken, and the meal ended with open apple tart and lemon meringue pie. Everybody ate very heartily, while deploring the hard times in which they lived. To Mr. Cockshott no regime could be called civilized that compelled a discriminating palate to take beer rather than wine with dinner. Hamish was unable to see what else could result from a sentimental system designed to level down. Flopsy suspected that to get decent food it would soon be necessary to descend the mines, where she had no doubt that caviar and foie gras were being consumed hourly. Nan adored the farmhouse simplicity of it all and had always wanted to live on such wholesome fare, but she deplored the disappearance of the old English hospitality which scarcity compelled. Jennie, with one eye on Peter, remained silent, but in face of such unaccustomed plenty Peter was in no critical mood. Indeed, as he sat in an armchair with a cup of Nan's excellent American coffee and a glass of Cointreau unearthed by Mr. Cockshott from his treasure house, he did not even feel alarmed that he had been left alone with Hamish.

For a time there was silence as Hamish looked at the evening paper gloomily, then quite suddenly he said, "Well, we've reached the final point of fantasy. Vitiate the minds or what pass for the minds of the people with education, teach them to read and write, feed their imaginations with sexual and criminal fantasies known as films, and then starve them in order to pay for these delightful erotic celluloids. *Circenses* without *panem* it seems."

"Yes," said Peter, "it's pretty bad. I don't suppose anyone would be the worse for the disappearance of a lot of the films we get from America. But you tend to forget perhaps the routine nature of so many jobs today; people need recreation and some emotional outlet."

"I don't accept industrialization as an excuse for anything," said Hamish. "We made the machines, we can get rid of them.

People seem to forget that our wills are still free. As to recreation, that died out with village life. I don't know quite what you mean by emotional outlet; judging by most films, I take it you refer to sexual intercourse—there I'm old-fashioned enough to believe that marriage for the purposes of procreation is still quite an intelligent answer. But if you mean the need for something not purely material, some exercise of the sense of awe, you people killed that when you killed church-going."

Peter laughed and denied that he was responsible for the decline in church congregations.

"*Do* you go to church?" said Hamish.

"No," said Peter. "I suppose I incline to agnosticism in religion."

"You incline to agnosticism," said Hamish scornfully, "which means, I suppose, that you prefer to believe the latest miracle performed by some B.Sc. London to the authority of two thousand years."

"I don't think the divergence of science and religion is quite the issue nowadays," said Peter as calmly as he could manage. "After all, so many modern physicists are by no means hostile to religious belief."

"Very kind of them I'm sure," said Hamish. "In any case I was not talking about what the B.B.C. calls 'belief in God,' that is not a thing for discussion really. I was talking of church-going. The greatest dereliction of duty in an irresponsible age is the failure of the educated and propertied classes to set an example by attending their parish churches."

"You would hardly advocate attendance at church by non-believers."

"My dear fellow," said Hamish, "all this talk about belief or non-belief is rather crude. A Roman gentleman might privately be a Stoic or an Epicurean but that didn't prevent him from performing his duty to his country by sacrificing to the gods. We have privileges and we must act accordingly by setting an example to our inferiors."

"I think," said Peter angrily, "that that view is crazy as well as un-Christian."

"Yes," said Hamish, "so does the *Sunday Express*. *I* think that the only dignified approach to the modern world *is* to be classed as crazy."

Further acrimony was prevented by the appearance of Mr. Cockshott with some papers, and Hamish retired.

"Where has Jennie gone?" asked Peter rather restively.

"In these unhallowed times," said Mr. Cockshott, "even the fairest of women have to partake in the household duties—in short, the women of the house are assisting cook with the washing up."

"But can't I help?" asked Peter.

"Good heavens, my dear boy. No. Let us retain some of the privileges of our sex. Jennie tells me you have a taste for literature, so I've brought you a few occasional writings of mine for a little light bedside reading."

Peter took the offprints with a sincere interest. "I should very much like to read them," he said.

"Thank you," said Mr. Cockshott, "thank you. I project a longer work—a history of North Cambridgeshire which will be at once, I hope, a scholarly account of the changing institutions and a work of literary value and entertainment describing the social scene with its quaint everyday characters and customs. Unfortunately my position as a J.P. and a local landlord, though only of course on a small scale, leaves me less time for writing than I should like. In any case I am not one who is content with information without style. That's why I'm afraid I quarrel with our good neighbours the Cambridge Fellows. I find most of their painstaking researches quite unreadable, but then I'm neither a pedagogue nor a pedant. On the other hand, though I believe that imagination must infuse the pages of history if they are to live, I could not write what is known as the popular historical biography. I have too much sense of accuracy and too little interest in the seamy side of the past to do that, nor have I the requisite standard of vulgarity in my writing. In fact, I am rather a fish out of water, a fact that is always brought home to me when I attend the meetings of historical or antiquarian societies."

It seemed to Peter that Mr. Cockshott talked for hours about the various quarrels he had engaged in with eminent historians and authors; he began to feel more and more drowsy, and the desire to be with Jennie, to touch and feel her, became stronger and stronger. At last the door was opened and Nan appeared. "Oh, Gordon," she said, "look at poor Peter, he's so tired and white. You want to go to bed, don't you?"

"I am rather tired after the journey," said Peter, but he hastened to add, "It's all been awfully interesting and I'm very much looking forward to reading these articles."

As he walked along the corridor to his room he passed an open door of another bedroom. Inside two figures were locked in each other's arms. He went quickly and, he hoped, silently past. He told himself that he had always known how tremendously fond Jennie was of her brother, but all the same the droop of her body and the force of Hamish's embrace troubled him much that night.

Peter sat in a deck chair after breakfast the next morning attempting to read Mr. Cockshott's account of the Black Death in Little Fromling, but he could not attend to the essay. He felt tired and irritable, for he had slept very poorly. He found himself wondering where Jennie had gone; she had slipped away after breakfast to make the beds, promising to join him in a few minutes, and now nearly an hour had passed. He decided to go and look for her. He found Mr. Cockshott in the morning-room, writing letters. "Do you know where Jennie is?" he asked.

"Ah, where indeed?" said Mr. Cockshott. "That's what I'm always asking when she's here at the weekends. I never seem to see anything of her. We're all a bit jealous over Jennie. But her independence is part of her charm. She will be free, she won't be monopolized."

"I had no intention of monopolizing her. I just wanted to talk to her, that's all."

"My dear boy, I quite understand your feelings and it's very naughty of her to have left her guest like this. But we're rather a crazy family, lacking in the conventions, or rather perhaps I should say we make our own."

Peter decided to seek her elsewhere. He went upstairs to his bedroom; there he found Flopsy making the bed. "You can't come up to your room now," said Flopsy. "The chambermaid's at work."

"I was looking for Jennie."

"Well, you mustn't look like an angry dog, you'll never hold Jennie that way. You like her a lot, don't you?"

"I'm very fond of Jennie," said Peter, "very fond indeed."

"Good heavens, I should hope so and more! Any man in his senses would be head over heels about Jennie. But there," she added, "I'm partial." But she obviously did not think so.

"If it's any satisfaction to you," said Peter savagely, "I'm in love with Jennie and that's why I want to see her."

"Good for you," said Flopsy. "But don't bite my head off. We Cockshotts are a crazy crowd, you know, you can't drive us. Well, now be off. I must make this bed."

Peter wandered out into the garden, where he found Nan, in an old waterproof and a battered felt hat, making a bonfire. "Have you seen Jennie?" he asked.

"Oh, Peter," she said, "has she left you on your own? No! That's too bad. But there you are, that's the Cockshotts all over, they're completely crazy."

"Don't you find it rather a strain?" asked Peter.

"Maybe at first I did a little, but they're so natural and simple I love that way of living." For a moment she looked away from him. "They do ask rather a lot from people," she said, and her voice sounded for the first time sincere. A moment later her blue eyes were looking at him with that frank, open stare which he was beginning to mistrust. "It's not that really, it's just that they ask a lot of life. You see, they're big people, and big people are often kind of strange to understand." She laid her hand on Peter's arm. "Go see if she's in the tree house," she said. "It's a kind of funny old place she and Hamish made when they were kids and they still love it. It's down at the end of the garden by the little wood."

Jennie and Hamish were sitting on a wooden platform up in an elm tree when Peter found them. They were practising tying knots in a piece of rope. Peter's anger must have shown itself, for Jennie called out, "Welcome, darling, welcome to the tree house. You ought to make three salaams before you're allowed in, but we'll let you off this time, won't we, Hamish?"

"Certainly," said Hamish, who also appeared anxious to placate Peter.

"I thought you went to church on Sunday mornings," said Peter.

"Everything must give way to the hospitality due to friends," said Hamish with a charming smile.

"There was no need to have stayed away for me."

"Now, Peter," said Jennie, "that's rude after Hamish has been so nice."

"We ought to saw some logs," said Hamish. "Would you like to give a hand?"

"Oh, yes, do let's" said Jennie. "You and Peter can take the double saw, and I'll do the small branches."

Peter did not find it very easy to keep up to Hamish's pace; he got very hot and out of breath, the sawdust kept flying in his face, and the teeth of the saw stuck suddenly in the knots of wood so that they were both violently jolted.

"I say," said Hamish, "I don't think you're very good at this. Perhaps we'd better stop."

"No," said Jennie, who was angry at Peter's inefficiency, "certainly not. It does Peter good to do things he's not good at."

Peter immediately let go of his end of the saw so that it swung sharply round, almost cutting off Hamish's arm. "Bloody hell," said Hamish, but Peter took no notice; he strode rapidly away down the path through the little copse.

Jennie ran after him. "Good heavens, Peter," she called, "whatever is the matter? Don't be such an idiot. Just because I said it was good for you to go on sawing, and so it would have been."

"It's a great deal more than that," said Peter tensely, "as you'd see if you weren't blind with love of your family."

"Darling, what has upset you? Surely you aren't annoyed with Hamish. Why, he's only a child."

"I'm well aware of that," said Peter, "a vain, spoiled child to be petted and fussed one minute and bullied and ordered about the next. And your father's just as bad. Well, I don't want a lot of women petting and bullying me, not Nan, nor your beloved Flopsy, no, nor even you."

"Peter, you're crazy."

"Good God, I'm only trying to live up to your family! I've had it ever since I arrived—'The Crazy Cockshotts,' and bloody proud of it. I've had it from you and your father, from Flopsy and from Nan—wretched woman, she ought to know all about it—and I've had it from your Fascist brother. You're all a damned sight too crazy for me to live up to."

Jennie was getting quite out of breath, trying to keep up with Peter's increasing pace. Suddenly she flung herself down in the thick bracken at the side of the path. "Stop! Peter, stop!" she called.

Peter stood still over her, and she stretched out her hand to him, pulling him down on top of her. Her mouth pressed tightly to his, and her hands stroked his hair, his arms, his back, soothing and caressing him. Gradually his anger died from him and the tension relaxed as in his turn he held her to him.

A Visit in Bad Taste

--->>><<<---

"He looks very much older," said Margaret. "It's aged him dreadfully and made him servile."

"I should imagine that prison does tend to kill one's independence," said her husband drily.

"Oh, yes, that's all very well, Malcolm, you can afford to be rational, to explain away, to account for. But he's my brother and no amount of reasons can make it any better to have him sitting there fingering his tie when he talks, loosening his collar with his finger, deferring every opinion to you, calling old Colonel Gordon 'sir,' jumping up with every move I make. It's like a rather pathetic minor public-school boy of nineteen applying for a job, and he's sixty, Malcolm, remember that—sixty."

"I think, you know," said Malcolm Tarrant as he replaced his glass of port on the little table by his side, "that public school has always meant a lot more to Arthur than we can quite understand. The only time that I visited him in Tamcaster I was struck by the importance that they all attached to it. As a bank manager there, and a worthy citizen of the town, it was in some kind of way a passport to power, not just the place you'd been at school at. And now, I imagine, it's assumed an importance out of all perspective, a kind of lifebuoy to a drowning sailor. We're inclined to imagine prison as peopled with public-school boys, each with a toothbrush

_____

Written in 1947; published in 1949; scene contemporary.

94

moustache and an assumed military rank, 'ex-public-school boy jailed,' but they only make so much of it because it's so unusual. God knows what sort of awful snobbery the presence of a 'public-school man' arouses among the old lags, or the warders too for that matter—people speak so often of the horrors of war but they never mention the most awful of them—the mind of the non-commissioned officer. Depend upon it, whatever snobbery there was, Arthur got full benefit from it."

Margaret's deep black eyes showed no sign of her distress; only her long upper lip stiffened and the tapir's nose that would have done credit to an Edward Lear drawing showed more white. The firelight shone upon her rich silver brocade evening dress as she rustled and shimmered across the room to a place a log on the great open fire. She put the tiny liqueur glass of light emerald —how Malcolm always laughed at her feminine taste for crême de menthe!—upon the mantelpiece between the Chelsea group of Silenus and a country girl and the plain grey bowl filled with coppery and red-gold chrysanthemums.

"If you mean that Arthur is vulgar," she cried, "always has been, yes, yes. At least, not always"—and her thin lips, so faintly rouged, relaxed into tenderness—"not when we were children. But increasingly so. My dear, how could I think otherwise, married to that terrible little woman—'How do you keep the servants from thieving, Margaret?' 'Give that class an inch and they'll take an ell'—dreadful, vulgar little Fascist-minded creature."

"Dear Margaret," said Malcolm, and he smiled the special smile of admiring condescension that he kept for his wife's political opinions. "Remember that in Myra's eyes you were a terrible Red."

"It isn't a question of politics, Malcolm," said his wife, and she frowned—to her husband she was once again the serious-minded, simple student he had found so irresistible at Cambridge nearly forty years before. "It's a question of taste. No, it was a terrible marriage and a terrible life. It was the one excuse I could make for him at the time. To have lived for so many years against such a background was excuse enough for any crime, yes, even that one. I felt it all through the trial as I sat and watched Myra being the injured wife, with that ghastly family round her."

"That's where we differ," said Malcolm, and for a moment his handsome, high-cheekboned face with its Roman nose showed all his Covenanting ancestry. "I could never excuse his actions. I tried to rid myself of prejudice against them, to see him as a sick man rather than as a criminal"—it was not for nothing, one felt, that the progressive weeklies were so neatly piled on the table beside him—"but when he refused psychiatric treatment the whole thing became impossible."

Margaret smiled at her husband maternally as she speared a crystallized orange from its wooden box with the little two-pronged fork. "It must be wonderful to have everything all cut and dried like you, darling," she said, "only people don't fit into pigeonholes according to the demands of reason. Arthur would never go to a psychoanalyst, you old goose; in the first place he thinks it isn't respectable, and then deep down, of course, he would be frightened of it, he would think it was witchcraft."

"No doubt you're right. No doubt Arthur does still live in the Middle Ages." He moved his cigar dexterously so that the long grey ash fell into the ashtray rather than onto his suit; he narrowed his eyes. "I still find his actions disgusting, inexcusable."

"Offences against children," said Margaret, and she spoke the phrase in inverted commas, contemptuously. "I suppose there is no woman whose blood does not get heated when she reads that in the newspaper. But somehow it all seemed so different when I saw it at the trial. Arthur seemed so shrunken and small, so curiously remote for the principal actor, as though he'd done it all inadvertently. He probably had too," she added fiercely, striking the arm of her chair with her hand, "in order to forget that dreadful, bright woman—that awful, chromium-plated, cocktail-cabinet, old-oak-lounge home. And then those ghastly people—the parents—there are some kinds of working-class people I just cannot take—servile and defiant, obstinate and shifty. I believe every word Arthur said when he told of their menaces, their sudden visits, their demands for money. Oh, they'd had their pound of flesh all right," she said bitterly, "in unhappiness and fear. Even the children, Malcolm, it sounds so moving in the abstract, poor little creatures not comprehending, their whole lives distorted by a single incident. When Rupert and Jane were little, I used to think that if anyone harmed them I would put his eyes out with hot irons. But these children weren't like that—that cretinous boy with the sudden look of cunning in his eyes and that awful, painted, oversexed girl."

"It's a pity you ever went to the trial," said Malcolm, but Margaret could not agree. "I had to suffer it all," she cried, "it was the only way. But that Dostoevskian mood is over. I don't want any more of it, I want it to be finished." She fitted a cigarette into one of the little cardboard holders that stood in a glass jar on her work table, then suddenly she turned on her husband fiercely. "Why has he come here? Why? Why?" she cried.

"I imagine because he's lonely," said Malcolm.

"Of course he is. What can be expected? But he'll be just as lonely here. We aren't his sort of people, Malcolm. Oh, not just because of what's happened, we never have been. This isn't his kind of house." She thought with pleasure of all they had built up there—the taste, the tolerance, the ease of living, the lack of dogmatism. Her eyes lighted on the Chelsea and the Meissen figures, the John drawings, the Spanish metalwork, the little pale-yellow spinet—eclectic but good. Her ears heard once more Ralph Tarrant telling them of his ideas for Hamlet, Mrs. Doyle speaking of her life with the great man, Professor Crewe describing his theory of obsolete ideas, Dr. Modjka his terrible meeting with Hitler. Arthur had no place there.

"You want me to ask him to go," said Malcolm slowly.

Margaret bent over the fire, crouching on a stool in the hearth, holding out her hands to the warmth. "Yes," she said in a low voice, "I do."

"Before he's found his feet?" Malcolm was puzzled. "He knows, I think, that he must move eventually, but for the moment . . ."

"The moment!" broke in Margaret savagely. "If he stays now

he stays forever, I'm as certain of that as that I stand. Don't ask me *how* I know, but I do."

"Ah, well, it won't be a very pleasant talk," said her husband, "but perhaps it will be for the best."

Only the frou-frou of Margaret's skirt broke the silence as she moved about the room, rearranging the sprigs of winter jasmine, drawing the heavy striped-satin curtains across to cover a crack of light. Suddenly she sat down again on the stool and began to unwrap some sewing from a little silk bundle.

"I think the last chapter of Walter's book very pretentious," she said in a voice harder and clearer than normal. "He's at his worst when he's doing the great panjandrum."

"Poor Walter," said Malcolm. "You can't go on playing Peter Pan *and* speak with the voice of authority . . ."

They had not long been talking when Arthur came in. His suit looked overpressed, his tie was too "club," his hair had too much brilliantine for a man of his age. All his actions were carried out overconsciously, with military precision; as he sat down he jerked up his trousers to preserve the crease; he removed a white handkerchief from his shirt cuff, wiped his little toothbrush moustache, and cleared his throat. "Sorry to have been so long," he said. "Nature's call, you know."

Malcolm smiled wryly and Margaret winced. "You don't take sugar, do you, Arthur?" she said as she handed him his coffee.

"Will you have a glass of port, old man?" asked Malcolm, adapting his phraseology to his brother-in-law.

"Oh, thanks very much," said Arthur in quick, nervous tones, fingering his collar. Then, feeling that such diffidence was unsuitable, he added, "Port, eh? Very fruity, very tasty."

There was a long pause, then Margaret and Malcolm spoke at once.

"I've just been saying that Walter Howard's new book . . ." she began.

"Did you have an opportunity to look at the trees we've planted?" said Malcolm. Then, as Margaret, blushing, turned her head away, he continued, "We ought really to have more trees down, if this fuel shortage is going to materialize. I'll get on to Bowers about it."

"Oh, not this week, darling," said Margaret. "Mrs. Bowers is away with her mother, who's ill, and young Peter's got flu. Poor Bowers is terribly overworked."

"Next week then," said Malcolm. "I must say, I've never known such a set for illness."

"Give them an inch and they'll take an ell," said Arthur.

The reiteration of her sister-in-law's phrase enraged Margaret. "What nonsense you do talk, Arthur," she cried. "I should have thought the last few months would have taught you some sense." She blushed scarlet as she realized what she had said, then more gently she added, "You don't know the Bowerses. Why, Mrs. Bowers is the best friend I have round here."

Arthur felt the old order was on its mettle; he was not prepared to be placated. "I'm afraid my respect for your precious British workmen has not been increased where I come from," he said defiantly.

"I doubt if you saw the British workman at his best in prison," said Malcolm carefully, and as his brother-in-law was about to continue the argument, he added, "No, Arthur, let's leave it at that—Margaret and I have our own ideas on these things and we're too old to change them now."

Arthur's defiance vanished. He fingered the knot of his tie and mumbled something about "respecting them for it." There was a silence for some minutes, then Malcolm said abruptly, "Where do you plan to go from here?"

Arthur was understood to say that he hadn't thought about it.

"I think you should," said Malcolm. "Why don't you go abroad?"

"The colonies?" questioned Arthur with a little laugh.

"I know it's conventional, but why not? You can always count on me if you need any money."

Arthur did not speak for a moment; then, "You *want* me to go from here?" he asked.

Margaret was determined to fight her own battle, so, "Yes, Arthur," she replied. "You must. It won't do here, we don't fit in together."

"I doubt if *I* fit in anywhere." Arthur's voice was bitter.

Malcolm would have dispelled the mood with a "Nonsense, old man," but Margaret again took up the task. "No, Malcolm, perhaps he's right." Suddenly her voice became far away, with a dramatic note. "When Malcolm was at the Ministry in London during the raids and Rupert was flying over Germany, I had to realize that they might both be killed and then, of course, *I* wouldn't have fitted in. I took my precautions. I always carried something that would finish me off quickly if I needed it. Remember, Arthur, if anything should happen I shall always understand and respect you."

Malcolm looked away, embarrassed. These moments of self-dramatization of Margaret's made him feel that he had married beneath him.

Arthur sat, thinking—the colonies or suicide, neither seemed to be what he was needing. "Well," he said finally, "I'm very tired. I'll be toddling off to bed, I think. A real long night'll do me good."

Margaret got up and stroked his hair.

"Ee," he said, "it's a moocky do, lass, as nurse used to say."

This direct appeal to sentiment repelled her. "You'll find whisky and a syphon in your room," she said formally.

"Yes, have a good nightcap," said Malcolm to the erect over-military back of his brother-in-law.

"Thank God that's over," he sighed a few minutes later. "Poor old Arthur. I expect he'll find happiness sometime, somewhere."

"No, Malcolm," said Margaret fiercely, "it's been an unpleasant business, but if it's not to turn sour on us we've got to face it. Arthur will *never* be happy, he's rotten, dead. But we aren't, and if we're going to live, we can't afford to let his rottenness infect us."

Malcolm stared at his wife with admiration—to face reality, that was obviously the way to meet these things, not to try to escape. He thought for a few minutes of what she had said—of Arthur's rottenness, socially and personally, and of all that they stood for, individually alive, socially progressive. But for all the realism of her view, it somehow did not satisfy him. He remained vaguely uneasy the whole evening.

Raspberry Jam

-»)«-

"How are your funny friends at Potter's Farm, Johnnie?" asked his aunt from London.

"Very well, thank you, Aunt Eva," said the little boy in the window in a high, prim voice. He had been drawing faces on his bare knee and now put down the indelible pencil. The moment that he had been dreading all day had arrived. Now they would probe and probe with their silly questions, and the whole story of that dreadful tea party with his old friends would come tumbling out. There would be scenes and abuse and the old ladies would be made to suffer further. This he could not bear, for although he never wanted to see them again and had come, in brooding over the afternoon's events, almost to hate them, to bring them further misery, to be the means of their disgrace, would be worse than any of the horrible things that had already happened. Apart from his fear of what might follow, he did not intend to pursue the conversation himself, for he disliked his aunt's bright, patronizing tone. He knew that she felt ill-at-ease with children and would soon lapse into that embarrassing "leg-pulling" manner which some grownups used. For himself he did not mind this, but if she made silly jokes about the old ladies at Potter's Farm he would get angry and then Mummy would say all that about his having to learn to take a joke and about his being highly strung and where could he have got it from, not from her.

Written in 1946; first published in 1949; scene contemporary.

But he need not have feared. For though the grownups continued to speak of the old ladies as "Johnnie's friends," the topic
soon became a general one. Many of the things the others said
made the little boy bite his lip, but he was able to go on drawing
on his knee with the feigned abstraction of a child among adults.

"My dear," said Johnnie's mother to her sister, "you really
must meet them. They're the *most* wonderful pair of freaks. They
live in a great barn of a farmhouse. The inside's like a museum, full
of old junk mixed up with some really lovely things all moulder-
ing to pieces. The family's been there for hundreds of years and
they're madly proud of it. They won't let anyone do a single thing
for them, although they're both well over sixty, and of course the
result is that the place is in the most *frightful* mess. It's really
rather ghastly and one oughtn't to laugh, but if you could *see*
them, my dear. The elder one, Marian, wears a long tweed skirt
almost to the ankles—she had a terrible hunting accident or something—and a school blazer. The younger one's said to have been
a beauty, but she's really rather sinister now, inches thick in
enamel and rouge and dressed in all colours of the rainbow, with
dyed red hair which is constantly falling down. Of course Johnnie's made tremendous friends with them, and I must say they've
been immensely kind to him, but what Harry will say when he
comes back from Germany I can't think. As it *is*, he's always complaining that the child is too much with women and has no friends
of his own age."

"I don't honestly think you need worry about that, Grace,"
said her brother Jim, assuming the attitude of the sole male in the
company, for of the masculinity of old Mr. Codrington, their
guest, he instinctively made little. "Harry ought to be very
pleased with the way old Miss Marian's encouraged Johnnie's
cricket and riding; it's pretty uphill work too. Johnnie's not exactly a Don Bradman or a Gordon Richards, are you, old man?
I like the old girl, personally. She's got a bee in her bonnet
about the Bolsheviks, but she's stood up to those damned council
people about the drainage like a good 'un; she does no end for
the village people as well and says very little about it."

"I don't like the sound of 'doing good to the village' very much," said Eva. "It usually means patronage and disappointed old maids meddling in other people's affairs. It's only in villages like this that people can go on serving out sermons with gifts of soup."

"Curiously enough, Eva old dear," Jim said, for he believed in being rude to his progressive sister, "in this particular case you happen to be wrong. Miss Swindale is extremely broad-minded. You remember, Grace," he said, addressing his other sister, "what she said about giving money to old Cooper when the rector protested it would only go on drink—'You have a perfect right to consign us all to hell, Rector, but you must allow us the choice of how we get there.' Serve him damn well right for interfering too."

"Well, Jim darling," said Grace, "I must say she could hardly have the nerve to object to drink—the poor old thing has the most dreadful bouts herself. Sometimes when I can't get gin from the grocer's it makes me absolutely livid to think of all that secret drinking, and they say it only makes her more and more gloomy. All the same, I suppose *I* should drink if I had a sister like Dolly. It must be horrifying when one's family-proud like she is to have such a skeleton in the cupboard. I'm sure there's going to be the most awful trouble in the village about Dolly before she's finished. You've heard the squalid story about young Tony Calkett, haven't you? My dear, he went round there to fix the lights and apparently Dolly invited him up to her bedroom to have a cherry brandy, of all things, and made the *most* unfortunate proposals. Of course I know she's been very lonely, and it's all a ghastly tragedy really, but Mrs. Calkett's a terribly silly little woman and a very jealous mother and she won't see it that way at all. The awful thing is that both the Miss Swindales give me the creeps rather. I have a dreadful feeling when I'm with them that I don't know who's the keeper and who's the lunatic. In fact, Eva my dear, they're both really rather horrors and I suppose I ought never to let Johnnie go near them."

"I think you have no cause for alarm, Mrs. Allingham," put

in old Mr. Codrington in a purring voice. He had been waiting
for some time to take the floor, and now that he had got it he did
not intend to relinquish it. Had it not been for the small range
of village society he would not have been a visitor at Mrs. Allingham's, for, as he frequently remarked, if there was one thing he
deplored more than her vulgarity it was her loquacity. "No
one delights in scandal more than I do, but it is always a little distorted, a trifle *exagéré*—indeed, where would be its charm if it
were not so! No doubt Miss Marian has her solaces, but she remains a noble-hearted woman. No doubt Miss Dolly is often a
trifle naughty"—he dwelt on this world caressingly—"but she
really only uses the privilege of one who has been that rare thing,
a beautiful woman. As for Tony Calkett, it is really time that that
young man ceased to be so unnecessarily virginal. If my calcula-
tions are correct, and I have every reason to think they are, he
must be twenty-two, an age at which modesty should have been
put behind one long since. No, dear Mrs. Allingham, you should
rejoice that Johnnie has been given the friendship of two women
who can still, in this vulgar age, be honoured with a name that,
for all that it has been cheapened and degraded, one is still proud
to bestow—the name of a lady."

Mr. Codrington threw his head back and stared round the
room as though defying anyone to deny him his own right to
this name. "Miss Marian will encourage him in the manlier virtues, Miss Dolly in the arts. Her own water colours, though perhaps lacking in strength, are not to be despised. She has a fine
sense of colour, though I could wish that she was a little less bold
with it in her costume. Nevertheless, with that red-gold hair,
there is something splendid about her appearance, something especially wistful to an old man like myself. Those peacock-blue
linen gowns take me back through Conder's fans and Whistler's
rooms to Rossetti's Mona Vanna. Unfortunately, as she gets older,
the linen is not overclean. We are given a Mona Vanna with the
collected dust of age, but surely," he added with a little cackle,
"it is dirt that lends patina to a picture. It is interesting that you
should say you are uncertain which of the two sisters is a trifle

peculiar, because, in point of fact, both have been away, as they used to phrase it in the servants' hall of my youth. Strange," he mused, "that one's knowledge of the servants' hall should always belong to the period of one's infancy, be, as it were, eternally outmoded. I have no conception of how they may speak of an asylum in the servants' hall of today. No doubt Johnnie could tell us. But, of course, I forget that social progress has removed the servants' hall from the ken of all but the most privileged children. I wonder now whether that is a loss or a blessing in disguise."

"A blessing without any doubt at all," said Aunt Eva, irrepressible in the cause of Advance. "Think of all the appalling inhibitions we acquired from servants' chatter. I had an old nurse who was always talking about ghosts and dead bodies and curses on the family in a way that must have set up terrible phobias in me. I still have those ugly, morbid nightmares about spiders," she said, turning to Grace.

"I refuse," said Mr. Codrington in a voice of great contempt, for he was greatly displeased at the interruption, "to believe that any dream of yours could be ugly; morbid, perhaps, but with a sense of drama and artistry that would befit the dreamer. I confess that if I have inhibitions, and I trust I have many, I cling to them. I should not wish to give way unreservedly to what is so unattractively called the libido; it suggests a state of affairs in which beach pyjamas are worn and jitterbugging is compulsory. No, let us retain the fantasies, the imaginative games of childhood, even at the expense of a little fear, for they are the true magnificence of the springtime of life."

"Darling Mr. Codrington," cried Grace, "I do pray and hope you're right. It's exactly what I keep on telling myself about Johnnie, but I really don't know. Johnnie, darling, run upstairs and fetch Mummy's bag." But his mother need not have been so solicitous about Johnnie's overhearing what she had to say, for the child had already left the room. "There you are, Eva," she said. "He's the strangest child. He slips away without so much as a word. I must say he's very good at amusing himself, but I very much wonder if all the funny games he plays aren't very bad for him. He's certainly been very peculiar lately, strange silences and sudden tears, and, my dear, the awful nightmares he has! About a fortnight ago, after he'd been at tea with the Misses Swindale, I don't know whether it was something he'd eaten there, but he made the most awful sobbing noise in the night. Sometimes I think it's just temper, like Harry. The other day at tea I only offered him some jam, my best home-made raspberry too, and he just screamed at me."

"You should take him to a child psychologist," said her sister.

"Well, darling, I expect you're right. It's so difficult to know whether they're frauds, everyone recommends somebody different. I'm sure Harry would disapprove too, and then think of the expense. You know how desperately poor we are, although I think I manage as well as anyone could . . ."

At this point Mr. Codrington took a deep breath and sat back, for on the merits of her household management Grace Allingham was at her most boring and could by no possible stratagem be restrained.

Upstairs, in the room which had been known as the nursery until his eleventh birthday but was now called his bedroom, Johnnie was playing with his farm animals. The ritual involved in the game was very complicated and had a long history. It was on his ninth birthday that he had been given the farm set by his father. "Something a bit less babyish than those woolly animals of yours," he had said, and Johnnie had accepted them, since they made in fact no difference whatever to the games he played; games by which, could Major Allingham have guessed at them, he would have been distinctly puzzled. The little ducks, pigs, and cows of lead no more remained themselves in Johnnie's games than had the pink woollen sheep and green cloth horses of his early childhood. Johnnie's world was a strange compound of the adult world in which he had always lived and a book world composed from Grimm, the Arabian Nights, Alice's adventures, natural history books, and more recently the novels of Dickens and Jane Austen. His imagination was taken by anything odd—strange faces, strange names, strange animals, strange voices, and catch phrases—all these appeared in his games. The black pig and the white duck were keeping a hotel; the black pig was called that funny name of Granny's friend, Mrs. Gudgeon-Rogers. She was always holding her skirt tight round the knees and warming her bottom over the fire, like Mrs. Coates, and whenever anyone in the hotel asked for anything she would reply, "Darling, I can't stop now, I've simply got to fly," like Aunt Sophie, and then she would fly out of the window. The duck was an echidna or spiny anteater who wore a picture hat and a fish train, like in the picture of Aunt Eleanor, and used to weep a lot because, like Granny when she described her games of bridge, she was "vulnerable," and she would yawn at the hotel guests and say, "Lord, I am tired," like Lydia Bennet. The two collie dogs had "been asked to leave," like in the story of Mummy's friend Gertie who "got tight" at the Hunt Ball; they were going to be divorced and were consequently wearing "co-respondent shoes." The lady collie, who was called Minnie Mongelheim, kept on saying, "That chap's got a proud stomach. Let him eat chaff," like Mr. F.'s aunt in *Little Dorrit*. The sheep, who always played the part of a bore, kept on and on, talking like Daddy about "leg cuts and fine shots to cover"; sometimes when the rest of the animal guests got too bored the sheep would change into Grandfather Graham and tell a funny story about a Scotsman so that they were bored in a different way. Finally the cat, who was a grand vizier and worked by magic, would say, "All the ways round here belong to me," like the Red Queen, and he would have all the guests torn in pieces and flayed alive until Johnnie felt so sorry for them that the game would come to an end. Mummy was already saying that he was getting too old for the farm animals: one always seemed to be getting too old for something.

In fact, the animals were no longer necessary to Johnnie's games, for most of the time now he liked to read, and when he wanted to play games he could do so in his head without the aid of any toys, but he hated the idea of throwing things away because they were no longer needed. Mummy and Daddy were always throwing things away and never thinking of their feelings. When he had been much younger Mummy had given him an old petticoat to put in the dustbin, but Johnnie had taken it to his room and hugged it and cried over it, because it was no longer wanted. Daddy had been very upset. Daddy was always being upset at what Johnnie did. Only the last time that he was home there had been an awful row, because Johnnie had tried to make up like old Mrs. Langdon and could not wash the blue paint off his eyes. Daddy had beaten him and looked very hurt all day and said to Mummy that he'd "rather see him dead than grow up a sissy." No, it was better not to do imitations oneself, but to leave it to the animals.

This afternoon, however, Johnnie was not attending seriously to his game; he was sitting and thinking of what the grownups had been saying, and of how he would never see his friends, the old ladies, again, and of how he never, never wanted to. This irrevocable separation lay like a black cloud over his mind, a constant darkness which was lit up momentarily by forks of hysterical horror as he remembered the nature of their last meeting.

The loss of this friendship was a very serious one to the little boy. It had met so completely the needs and loneliness which are always great in a child isolated from other children and surrounded by unimaginative adults. In a totally unself-conscious way, half crazy as they were and half crazy even though the child sensed them to be, the Misses Swindale possessed just those qualities of which Johnnie felt most in need. To begin with, they were odd and fantastic and highly coloured, and, more important still, they believed that such peculiarities were nothing to be ashamed of, indeed were often a matter for pride. "How delightfully odd," Miss Dolly would say in her drawling voice when Johnnie told her how the duck-billed platypus had chosen spangled tights when Queen Alexandra had ordered her to be shot from a cannon at Brighton Pavilion. "What a delightfully extravagant creature that duck-billed platypus is, *caro Gabriele*,"

for Miss Dolly had brought back a touch of Italian here and there
from her years in Florence, while in Johnnie she fancied a likeness to the angel Gabriel. In describing her own dresses too,
which she would do for hours on end, extravagance was her chief
commendation: "As for that gold-and-sliver brocade ball dress,"
she would say, and her voice would sink to an awed whisper, "it
was richly fantastic."

To Miss Marian, with her more brusque, masculine nature,
Johnnie's imaginative powers were a matter of far greater wonder than to her sister and she treated them with even greater respect. In her bluff, simple way, like some old-fashioned religious
army officer or overgrown but solemn schoolboy, she too admired the eccentric and unusual. "What a lark!" she would say
when Johnnie told her how the Crown Prince had slipped in some
polar bears dressed in pink ballet skirts to sing "Ta-ra-ra-boom-
deay" in the middle of a boring school concert which his royal
duties had forced him to attend. "What a nice chap he must be
to know." In talking of her late father, the general, whose memory she worshipped and of whom she had a never-ending flow of
anecdotes, she would give an instance of his warm-hearted but distinctly eccentric behaviour and say in her gruff voice, "Wasn't it
rum? That's the bit I like best."

But in neither of the sisters was there the least trace of that
self-conscious whimsicality which Johnnie had met and hated
in so many grownups. They were the first people he had met who
liked what he liked and as he liked it.

Their love of lost causes and their defence of the broken, the
worn-out, and the forgotten met a deep demand in his nature,
which had grown almost sickly sentimental in the dead, practical
world of his home. He loved the disorder of the old eighteenth-
century farmhouse, the collection of miscellaneous objects of all
kinds that littered the rooms, and thoroughly sympathized with
the sisters' magpie propensity to collect dress ends, feathers,
string, old whistles, and broken cups. He grew excited with them
in their fights to prevent drunken old men being taken to work-
houses and cancerous old women to hospitals, though he sensed

something crazy in their constant fear of intruders, Bolsheviks, and prying doctors. He would often try to change the conversation when Miss Marian became excited about spies in the village, or told him of how torches had been flashing all night in the garden and of how the vicar was slandering her father's memory in a whispering campaign. He felt deeply embarrassed when Miss Dolly insisted on looking into all the cupboards and behind the curtains to see, as she said, "if there were any eyes or ears where they were not wanted. For, *caro Gabriele*, those who hate beauty are many and strong, those who love it are few."

It was, above all, their kindness and their deep affection which held the love-starved child. His friendship with Miss Dolly had been almost instantaneous. She soon entered into his fantasies with complete intimacy, and he was spellbound by her stories of the gaiety and beauty of Mediterranean life. They would play dressing-up games together and enacted all his favourite historical scenes. She helped him with his French too, and taught him Italian words with lovely sounds; she praised his painting and helped him to make costume designs for some of his "characters." With Miss Marian, at first, there had been much greater difficulty. She was an intensely shy woman and took refuge behind a rather forbidding bluntness of manner. Her old-fashioned military airs and general "manly" tone, copied from her father, with which she approached small boys, reminded Johnnie too closely of his own father. "Head up, me lad," she would say, "shoulders straight." Once he had come very near to hating her, when after an exhibition of his absent-mindedness she had said, "Take care, Johnnie, head in the air. You'll be lost in the clouds, me lad, if you're not careful." But the moment after she had won his heart forever, when with a little chuckle she continued, "Jolly good thing if you are—you'll learn things up there that we shall never know." On her side, as soon as she saw that she had won his affection, she lost her shyness and proceeded impulsively to load him with kindnesses. She loved to cook his favourite dishes for him and give him his favourite fruit from their kitchen garden. Her admiration for his precocity and imagination was open-eyed and childlike.

Finally they had found a common love of Dickens and Jane Austen, which she had read with her father, and now they would sit for hours talking over the characters in their favourite books.

Johnnie's affection for them was intensely protective and increased daily as he heard and saw the contempt and dislike with which they were regarded by many persons in the village. The knowledge that "they had been away" was nothing new to him when Mr. Codrington had revealed it that afternoon. Once Miss Dolly had told him how a foolish doctor had advised her to go into a home, "for, you know, *caro*, ever since I returned to these grey skies my health has not been very good. People here think me strange; I cannot attune myself to the cold northern soul. But it was useless to keep me there. I need beauty and warmth of colour, and there it was so drab. The people too were unhappy, crazy creatures, and I missed my music so dreadfully." Miss Marian had spoken more violently of it on one of her "funny" days, when, from the depredations caused by the village boys to the orchard, she had passed on to the strange man she had found spying in her father's library and the need for a high wall round the house to prevent people peering through the telescopes from Mr. Hatton's house opposite. "They're frightened of us though, Johnnie," she had said. "I'm too honest for them and Dolly's too clever. They're always trying to separate us. Once they took me away against my will. They couldn't keep me— I wrote to all sorts of big pots, friends of Father's, you know, and they had to release me."

Johnnie realized too that when his mother had said that she never knew which was the keeper, she had spoken more truly than she understood. Each sister was constantly alarmed for the other and anxious to hide the other's defects from an un-understanding world. Once when Miss Dolly had been telling him a long story about a young waiter who had slipped a note into her hand the last time she had been in London, Miss Marian called Johnnie into the kitchen to look at some pies she had made. Later she had told him not to listen if Dolly said "soppy things" because, being so beautiful, she did not realize that she was no longer young. Another day, when Miss Marian had brought in the silver-framed photo of her father in full-dress uniform and had asked Johnnie to swear an oath to clear the general's memory in the village, Miss Dolly had begun to play a mazurka on the piano. Later she had warned Johnnie not to take too much notice when her sister got excited. "She lives a little too much in the past, Gabriele. She suffered very much when our father died. Poor Marian, it is a pity, perhaps, that she is so good, she has had too little of the pleasures of life. But we must love her very much, *caro*, very much."

Johnnie had sworn to himself to stand by them and to fight the wicked people who said they were old and useless and in the way. But now, since that dreadful tea party, he could not fight for them any longer, for he knew why they had been shut up and felt that it was justified. In a sense, too, he understood that it was to protect others that they had to be restrained, for the most awful memory of all that terrifying afternoon was the thought that he had shared with pleasure for a moment in their wicked game.

It was certainly most unfortunate that Johnnie should have been invited to tea on that Thursday, for the Misses Swindale had been drinking heavily on and off for the preceding week and were by that time in a state of mental and nervous excitement that rendered them far from normal. A number of events had combined to produce the greatest sense of isolation in these old women whose sanity, in any event, hung by a precarious thread. Miss Marian had been involved in an unpleasant scene with the vicar over the new hall for the Young People's Club. She was, as usual, providing the cash for the building and felt extremely happy and excited at being consulted about the decorations. Though she did not care for the vicar, she set out to see him, determined that she would accommodate herself to changing times. In any case, since she was the benefactress, it was, she felt, particularly necessary that she should take a back seat; to have imposed her wishes in any way would have been most ill bred. It was an unhappy

chance that caused the vicar to harp upon the need for new fabrics for the chairs and even to digress upon the ugliness of the
old upholstery, for these chairs had come from the late General
Swindale's library. Miss Marian was immediately reminded of her
belief that the vicar was attempting secretly to blacken her father's memory; nor was the impression corrected when he tact-
lessly suggested that the question of her father's taste was unimportant and irrelevant. She was more deeply wounded still to
find, in the next few days, that the village shared the vicar's view
that she was attempting to dictate to the boys' club by means of
her money. "After all," as Mrs. Grove at the post office said, "it's
not only the large sums that count, Miss Swindale, it's all the
boys' sixpences that they've saved up." "You've too much of your
father's ways in you, that's the trouble, Miss Swindale," said Mr.
Norton, who was famous for his bluntness, "and they won't
do nowadays."

She had returned from this unfortunate morning's shopping to
find Mrs. Calkett on the doorstep. Now the visit of Mrs. Calkett
was not altogether unexpected, for Miss Marian had guessed from
chance remarks of her sister's that something "unfortunate" had
happened with young Tony. When, however, the sharp-faced,
unpleasant little woman began to complain about Miss Dolly with
innuendoes and veiledly coarse suggestions, Miss Marian could
stand it no longer and drove her away harshly. "How dare you
speak about my sister in that disgusting way, you evil-minded little woman," she said. "You'd better be careful or you'll find yourself charged with libel." When the scene was over she felt very
tired. It was dreadful, of course, that anyone so mean and cheap
should speak thus of anyone so fine and beautiful as Dolly, but
it was also dreadful that Dolly should have made such a scene
possible.

Things were not improved, therefore, when Dolly returned
from Brighton at once elevated by a new conquest and depressed
by its subsequent results. It seemed that the new conductor on
the Southdown, "that charming, dark Italian-looking boy I was
telling you about, my dear," had returned her a most intimate

smile and pressed her hand when giving her change. Her own smiles must have been embarrassingly intimate, for a woman in the next seat had remarked loudly to her friend, "These painted old things—really, I wonder the men don't smack their faces." "I couldn't help smiling," remarked Miss Dolly, "she was so evidently *jalouse*, my dear. I'm glad to say the conductor did not hear, for no doubt he would have felt it necessary to come to my defence, he was so completely *épris*." But, for once, Miss Marian was too vexed to play ball; she turned on her sister and roundly condemned her conduct, ending up by accusing her of bringing misery to them both and shame to their father's memory. Poor Miss Dolly just stared in bewilderment, her baby-blue eyes round with fright, tears washing the mascara from her eyelashes in black streams down the wrinkled vermilion of her cheeks. Finally she ran crying up to her room.

That night both the sisters began to drink heavily. Miss Dolly lay like some monstrous broken doll, her red hair streaming over her shoulders, her corsets unloosed, and her fat body poking out of an old pink velvet ball dress—pink with red hair was always so audacious—through the most unexpected places in bulges of thick, blue-white flesh. She sipped at glass after glass of gin, sometimes staring into the distance with bewilderment that she should find herself in such a condition, sometimes leering pruriently at some pictures of Johnny Weismuller in swimsuits that she had cut out of *Film Weekly*. At last she began to weep to think that she had sunk to this. Miss Marian sat at her desk and drank more deliberately from a cut-glass decanter of brandy. She read solemnly through her father's letters, their old-fashioned, earnest, Victorian sentiments swimming ever more wildly before her eyes. But, at last, she too began to weep as she thought of how his memory would be quite gone when she passed away, and of how she had broken the promise that she had made to him on his deathbed to stick to her sister through thick and thin.

So they continued for two or three days with wild spasms of drinking and horrible, sober periods of remorse. They cooked themselves odd scraps in the kitchen, littered the house with unwashed dishes and cups, never speaking, always avoiding each other. They didn't change their clothes or wash, and indeed made little alteration in their appearance. Miss Dolly put fresh rouge on her cheeks periodically and some pink roses in her hair, which hung there wilting; she was twice sick over the pink velvet dress. Miss Marian put on an old scarlet hunting waistcoat of her father's, partly out of maudlin sentiment and partly because she was cold. Once she fell on the stairs and cut her forehead against the banisters; the red-and-white handkerchief which she tied round her head gave her the appearance of a tipsy pirate. On the fourth day the sisters were reconciled and sat in Miss Dolly's room. That night they slept, lying heavily against each other on Miss Dolly's bed, open-mouthed and snoring, Miss Marian's deep guttural rattle contrasting with Miss Dolly's high-pitched whistle. They awoke on Thursday morning, much sobered, to the realization that Johnnie was coming to tea that afternoon.

It was characteristic that neither spoke a word of the late debauch. Together they went out into the hot July sunshine to gather raspberries for Johnnie's tea. But the nets in the kitchen garden had been disarranged and the birds had got the fruit. The awful malignity of this chance event took some time to pierce through the fuddled brains of the two ladies as they stood there, grotesque and obscene in their staring pink and clashing red, with their heavy, pouchy faces and bloodshot eyes showing up in the hard, clear light of the sun. But when the realization did get home, it seemed to come as a confirmation of all the beliefs of persecution which had been growing throughout the drunken orgy. There is little doubt that they were both a good deal mad when they returned to the house.

Johnnie arrived punctually at four o'clock, for he was a small boy of exceptional politeness. Miss Marian opened the door to him, and he was surprised at her appearance, in her red bandana and her scarlet waistcoat, and especially by her voice, which, though friendly and gruff as usual, sounded thick and flat. Miss Dolly too looked more than usually odd, with one eye closed in a kind of perpetual wink and with her pink dress falling off her shoulders. She kept on laughing in a silly, high giggle.

The shock of discovering that the raspberries were gone had driven them back to the bottle, and they were both fairly drunk. They pressed upon the little boy, who was thirsty after his walk, two small glasses in succession, one of brandy, the other of gin, though in their sober mood the ladies would have died rather than have seen their little friend take strong liquor. The drink soon combined with the heat of the day and the smell of vomit that hung around the room to make Johnnie feel most strange. The walls of the room seemed to be closing in and the floor to be moving up and down like sea waves. The ladies' faces came up at him suddenly and then receded, now Miss Dolly's with great blobs of blue and scarlet and her eyes winking and leering, now Miss Marian's, a huge white mass with her moustache grown large and black.

He was only conscious by fits and starts of what they were doing or saying. Sometimes he would hear Miss Marian speaking in a flat, slow monotone. She seemed to be reading out her father's letters, snatches of which came to him clearly and then faded away. " 'There is so much to be done in our short sojourn on this earth, so much that may be done for good, so much for evil. Let us earnestly endeavour to keep the good steadfastly before us' "; then suddenly, " 'Major Campbell has told me of his decision to leave the regiment. I pray God hourly that he may have acted in full consideration of the Higher Will to which . . .' "; and once grotesquely, " 'Your Aunt Maud was here yesterday, she is a maddening woman and I consider it a just judgment upon the Liberal Party that she should espouse its cause.' " None of these phrases meant anything to the little boy, but he was dimly conscious that Miss Marian was growing excited, for he heard her say, "That was our father. As Shakespeare says, 'He was a man, take him for all in all,' Johnnie. We loved him, but there were those who sought to destroy him, for he was too big for them. But their day is nearly ended. Always remember that,

Johnnie." It was difficult to hear all that the elder sister said, for Miss Dolly kept on drawling and giggling in his ear about a black charmeuse evening gown she had worn, and a young donkey boy she had danced with in the fiesta at Asti. "*E come era bello, caro Gabriele, come era bello.* And afterwards . . . but I must spare the ears of one so young the details of the *arte dell' amore,*" she added with a giggle, and then with drunken dignity, "It would not be immodest, I think, to mention that his skin was like velvet. Only a few lire too, just imagine." All this too was largely meaningless to the boy, though he remembered it in later years.

For a while he must have slept, since he remembered that later he could see and hear more clearly though his head ached terribly. Miss Dolly was seated at the piano, playing a little jig and bobbing up and down like a mountainous pink blanc-mange, while Miss Marian, more than ever like a pirate, was dancing some sort of a hornpipe. Suddenly Miss Dolly stopped playing. "Shall we show him the prisoner?" she said solemnly.

"Head up, shoulders straight," said Miss Marian in a parody of her old manner. "You're going to be very honoured, me lad. Promise you'll never betray that honour. You shall see one of the enemy punished. Our father gave us close instructions. 'Do good to all,' he said, 'but if you catch one of the enemy, remember you are a soldier's daughters.' We shall obey that command."

Meanwhile Miss Dolly had returned from the kitchen, carrying a little bird which was pecking and clawing at the net in which it had been caught and shrilling incessantly—it was a little bullfinch. "You're a very beautiful little bird," Miss Dolly whispered, "with lovely soft pink feathers and pretty grey wings. But you're a very naughty little bird too, *tanto cattivo.* You came and took the fruit from us which we'd kept for our darling Gabriele." She began feverishly to pull the rose breast feathers from the bird, which piped more loudly and squirmed. Soon little trickles of red blood ran down among the feathers. "Scarlet and pink, a very daring combination," Miss Dolly cried.

Johnnie watched from his chair, his heart beating fast.

Suddenly Miss Marian stepped forward and, holding the bird's head, she thrust a pin into its eyes. "We don't like spies round here looking at what we are doing," she said in her flat, gruff voice. "When we find them we teach them a lesson so that they don't spy on us again." Then she took out a little pocket knife and cut into the bird's breast; its wings were beating more feebly now, and its claws only moved spasmodically, while its chirping was very faint. Little yellow and white strings of entrails began to peep out from where she had cut.

"Oh," cried Miss Dolly, "I like the lovely colours, I don't like these worms."

But Johnnie could bear it no longer. White and shaking, he jumped from his chair and, seizing the bird, he threw it on the floor and then he stamped on it violently until it was nothing but a sodden crimson mass.

"Oh, Gabriele, what have you done? You've spoiled all the soft, pretty colours. Why, it's nothing now, it just looks like a lump of raspberry jam. Why have you done it, Gabriele?" cried Miss Dolly.

But little Johnnie gave no answer. He had run from the room.

Mother's Sense of Fun

>>><<<

Donald had awoken at six to hear those sounds of bustle and activity that he knew so well—quick scurryings that sounded like mice in the wainscotting, and hushed, penetrating whispers to cook. There could be no doubt that his mother was up and about and that she intended to be particularly considerate to him after his journey. Overlong intimacy had invested each sound that she made with a particular significance, so that he soon recognized in the youthful jauntiness of her movements a pleasure in his return that went beyond her usual pride in being up so early. She was being especially thoughtful that he might have no cause for complaint, was laying up indulgence for herself, acquiring merit so that any independence he might claim would appear as ingratitude. No martyr could walk so bravely to her doom as she to the stake she had built for herself.

Why should these household noises have such an accusing ring? He knew there were no duties that could not be performed later in the day, yet it seemed impossible to believe that in carrying them out so quietly his mother was not having to skimp them or expend extra energy upon them—and all this sacrifice, of course, was for him.

I am not equal to the fight, he thought bitterly. "The contest between Mrs. Carrington and her son for the prize of the latter's

Written in 1946; first published in *Horizon* in 1947; scene contemporary.

independence was an unsatisfactory one to the spectators, for the
fight was very unequal. Mrs. Carrington, though a veteran in
the ring, showed her old undiminished energy, while her punch
seemed to have lost nothing of its force. Her speed and tactics
were completely superior to those of her opponent, who seemed
dazed and tired from the start. She sprang from one corner of the
ring to another, seeming to be everywhere at once and dealing
blows from the most unexpected angles. It was all so intensely unfair, he reflected; she had so many virtues, and it was exactly
those virtues which made life with her impossible. The crowd too
was so often on her side, so often succumbed to her charm, all
but his own few friends, those that she had not appropriated, and
they, of course, were "impossible" people. "What a wonderful pal
your mother must be," people would say to him, "so easygoing
and alive and such a terrific sense of fun." It was, of course, absolutely true. At times she moved and even looked like a young girl,
and she could then be a delightful companion, ready to go anywhere at any moment, and investing the most ordinary events
with a sense of adventure. Despite her continuous anxieties and
frets about household matters, she was ready to leave them aside
at a moment's notice if she could share for a minute in his life. "I'm
the mistress of the house," she would say, "not the house of me."
Since she rose at six and never retired before midnight she had,
as she claimed, plenty of time to get things done. It was the other
members of the household who suffered.

Looking back, Donald realized that he could not remember
leaving a theatre or an evening party without the sick apprehension that he would have to pass an hour or more before he was allowed to sink exhausted into bed. She always had a letter to write
on which he could advise, or something to finish off in the kitchen
if he wouldn't mind giving a hand, or, in default of other employ-
ment, she could bustle about making a last cup of tea, which she
would then bring to his bedside. "I really think this is my favourite moment of the day," she would say, sinking into the armchair,
"when we can both relax at last. What an extraordinary hat Olga
had on . . ." It was, of course, a nice Bohemian refusal to be

dominated by routine, but it meant that they were both always a little overtired, always a little on edge.

As if to emphasize the underlying tension of his life at home, Mrs. Carrington's voice came floating towards him from the room outside, its cheerful metallic timbre striking a chill in him even as he lay in bed. "Nonsense, Cook," she was saying. "You know very well you like standing in these queues. You take to them like a duck to water, they're just up your street." It was almost obscene, he decided, that one's mother should be so like a hospital nurse. It was difficult to decide which of her two voices more completely suggested the private ward. The sweet cooing which she used in moments of intimacy roused greater suspicion in him, for it called so openly for surrender. But his hostility was chiefly reserved for the high-pitched jollity of her everyday speech, which, apart from being more aurally revolting, revealed her insensitive and bullying nature. All day long it seemed to shrill about the house in a constant stream of self-satisfied humour and obtuse common sense. The words she employed, too, were surely specially designed to rob the English language of any pretensions to beauty it might possess. It was not exactly that she used outmoded slang like Miss Rutherford, who was always "unable to care less" about things or to "like them more," or even the earlier slang of Aunt Nora, with her "top holes" and "purple limits." He had often thought that to find his mother's phrases one would have to go to English translations of opera or the French and German prose books that he had used at school. It always "rained cats and dogs," that is, if the rain did not "look like holding off"; Alice Stockfield "was a bit down in the mouth" but then she "let things get on top of her"; Roger Grant was "certainly no Adonis" but she had "an awfully soft spot in her heart for him." At the end of a tiring day he would often wait for one of these familiar phrases in an agony of apprehension that he feared to betray, for he knew that criticism would be met by wounded silence or the slow, crushing steamroller of her banter, the terrible levelling force of her sense of humour. She and cook were having a "good old laugh" at that very moment. "Well, I suppose we must have looked rather silly,

ma'am," he could hear cook saying. "Of course we did," his
mother replied. "You standing there with flour all over your face
and me in that terrible old green dress and in front of us on the
floor—a pudding. Didn't you notice his face? I've no doubt at all
that when he got home to dinner that night at Surbiton or wherever inspectors of taxes live he told his wife that he'd seen a couple
of lunatics—and of course we *are* completely crazy in this household."

The same cosy, family jokes, he thought, the same satisfaction
with her own little world. The difficulty was that in attacking her
in this way one felt so grossly unfair. If she had been someone
else's mother one would have felt different. She had an eye for
the ridiculous that was all-penetrating, and, in a great degree, that
rarer quality, a sense of fun, so that he seldom went anywhere with
her without having, what she so delighted in, "a good laugh."
"That rare gift in a woman," Major Ashley had called it, "the
ability to laugh at herself." And it was quite true—on occasion she
would even mock the very jargon in her speech which he criti-
cized. "So I said to him in my bright, jolly way," she would say.
But the self-satisfaction with which she laughed at herself! thought
Donald bitterly. There was never any real self-criticism in her
humour. No, the criticism was reserved for everything else—the
ideas she could not understand, the beauty she could not see, the
feelings she could not appreciate. Heaven preserve me from the
laugh of a really good woman! he said aloud.

As if to mock his mood the laughter and conversation outside
his room grew louder. It was clear that the period of respite
granted to him was approaching its end. Soon she would fill the
room with that proud sense of possession of which her early morning embrace was almost a symbol. As he looked round the bedroom he realized how much he hated it. The careful, dead, good
taste of its furnishings bore the imprint of her withering hand.
Yet how much she delighted in emphasizing that it was *his* room
—"Donald's part of the world." She would be longing to emphasize his return to it, waiting for him to say how happy he was to
be back there—well, she would have to say it for him. Nothing

nauseated him more than this pretence that he enjoyed a separate establishment. It was a primary article of the household creed, which she reiterated every day, that "civilized people could not live on top of each other," "everyone must have his own little place where he could do what he liked." As long as he could remember she had fostered the belief in him that his room was his private domain, only, it would seem, to create stress by her constant invasion of it. The very fiction of independence itself had been used as a weapon against him, when as a boy he had resisted her claims —"Remember, Donald," she had declared, "I'm only a visitor here and visitors should be treated with some semblance of good manners."

At times he fancied the room as a battlefield littered with the skulls and skeletons of his past hopes. It brought before him a series of ever more dispiriting pictures: sickbeds surrounded by cloying and fussy affection; nursery teas when his every private fantasy and ambition had been taken out, laughed at, and put away with the nonsense knocked out of it; adolescent hours of study and dreams riddled through and through with nagging and banter and summons to petty errands—over twenty years now of nauseating futility. Over these years there had grown up between him and his mother a thickly woven web of companionship and antipathy, and beneath that an inner web of love and hatred. As time passed, the antipathy and hatred had grown paramount, as she gradually coiled round his life, breaking his moral fibre, softening and pulping so that at the last she could swallow him. " 'The Night-mare Life-in-Death was she,' " he quoted, "who thicks man's blood with cold.' "

The kiss with which his mother greeted him as she brought in the breakfast tray was brisk and businesslike; the sting lay in the gesture with which she followed it—the stroking and rumpling of his hair. The same routine had persisted since his thirteenth year; he could almost hear her say the words he had known so well in his schooldays: "We're a bit too old for kisses now, aren't we, darling? But we're still Mummy's boy." This morning he could see that she was hungry for some demonstration of the affection she had missed during his six months' absence; well, as far as he was concerned it should be a struggle *à l'outrance*.

"I hope you're quite rested, darling," said Mrs. Carrington, "because you'll have to nerve yourself for a heart-to-heart with cook. Only wild horses or a fond mother's love could have prevented her from waking you up hours ago."

Donald made no answer but lay back with his head on the pillow and his eyes closed; he was determined to show no sign of appreciation, determined to express no pleasure at being home once more. He watched his mother as she moved quietly but briskly about, settling his clothes and books with the business-like reverence of a modern Martha. A ray of sunshine from the window picked out her neat grey shingled head—she had always refused to succumb to the more fashionable bleached hair, for she felt that white gave such a hard line to the face—outlined the bright, birdlike features with their pastel colouring of powder and faint rouge upon the cheeks—lipstick was all right for young girls, she would say, but not for old women like her. She looked like a robin, he decided, that had come in for warmth from the Christmas-card snow scene outside as she hopped from object to object, folding her son's ties, rearranging the Christmas roses in the pewter mug on the mantelpiece; her bright, quizzical eyes and her jolly little smile, her well-cut grey woollen costume and her crimson silk blouse, all helped to enhance the picture. "Look," she seemed to say, "I'm really rather wonderful for fifty-eight, so cheerful, almost 'cheeky'; of course life hasn't been easy and it's taken a lot of pluck to keep going." And then, if you liked robins on Christmas cards, you would be filled with the requisite warmth towards her, would surrender to the appeal for protection and make a place for her by your fireside.

And if you did, he thought, you would be lost. No, it was on quite other things that you must concentrate if you were to save your soul alive. The brave, humorous little smile was there, but the underlip stuck out in a discontented babyish pout; the blue eyes shone brightly, but they shone with the hard light of egotism; above all, the lines that ran down from her cheeks were lines of self-pity. It was true that he had left the liner at Southampton yesterday with mixed feelings, but he had not guessed how soon the old misery would descend upon him. It had only taken one evening in her company to realize what "home" and "mother" meant to him; shades of the prison house had indeed begun to close round the growing boy, and the horror of it was, he reflected, that it was not even as if he was a growing boy, he was twenty-five, an old "lag." The six months' lecture tour in America had been his first escape since university days. When he was over there it had seemed as though he was free at last, but of course he had really only been a ticket-of-leave man. America, in any case, was a thing of the past—that she had made clear to him in their conversation of the night before. "Well," she had said with half-humorous patronage, "they seem to be very much like other foreigners. Perfectly easy to get on with, so long as you remember that you are dealing with children. They don't sound as sensible as the French, but at any rate they're not so pompous as the Germans. Quite frankly, I'm afraid the trouble with them is that they're all really rather common." It wasn't a period of his life she had shared in, and the sooner it was forgotten the better. She had not done with the subject, he noticed, as he tried not to hear the comments she made while tidying his clothes.

"I hope you like the Christmas roses. I had almost to sell the family diamonds to buy them, but there, I'm forgetting they're probably two a penny in New York. . . . You don't imagine you're going to *wear* this terrible American tie, do you, darling? Unless you intend to take me to a guest night at the Ancient Order of Buffaloes. Somehow I don't think we'd fit in very well. . . . Gracious! How old-fashioned they must be over there, all those naked girls on magazine covers! Why, it's just the sort of thing your Great-uncle Tom used to hide in the desk in the billiard room."

God! Why must she protract the agony like this? thought Donald. If she wanted to remove his self-reliance from him, let her wheel him into the operating theatre and get it over with; let him at least be spared this bright sickroom talk, these preliminary flashes of the surgeon's scalpel.

At last Mrs. Carrington herself grew impatient of skirmishing. "Your room hasn't changed much, darling, has it?" she asked in a voice yearning for affection.

"The room hasn't changed at all," he answered flatly, and as he said it he was sucked down by tiredness at the truth of the statement. Nothing had changed; all the illusions he had built up in his absence, all his beliefs in new powers of defence, faded before the persistence of her attack. He could see before him the outline of the coming week—the week of holiday before returning to the office on which he had counted so much as a preparation for a new life of independence. There would be successes for her when boring relatives came to the house, when they visited Aunt Nora at Richmond or when she showed off his tricks before friends she had made in his absence. There would be Pyrrhic victories for him when *his* friends came to the house and she gently but humorously put them out of their ease. There would be truces when he shopped with her at Harrods, lunched with her at her club, or accompanied her to the family solicitor. There would undoubtedly be at least one major conflict with loss of temper and tears and sulking; and, at last, he would return to work, broken in and trained to carry on life at home.

Some weeks later Donald lay back in bed, luxuriating in the pleasure of a sleep already closing in upon him at the early hour of half-past ten. How strangely exact his forecast of that week had been, save for one major event! Yes, he thought, one must still call it a major event, though perhaps in a few months, or even weeks, it would no longer be "major," for one must recognize the strange tricks of human memory and affection—not that he would have called himself cynical, only that time had taught him to be a realist. Yes, it had been a most typical week, almost a symbol of his whole relationship with his mother.

First there had been the meeting with Alec. How she must

have resented his imposing Alec upon her in that first week at home. How typical of his own subservience, he reflected bitterly, that he had told her of meeting his friend at all. There were certain of his friends of whom she had never approved and Alec Lovat was one of them. A clever Scottish secondary-school boy was not the sort of Cambridge friend she had imagined for him, and their common literary enthusiasms, in which she could not share, did not improve the situation. She had been so very eager to make this shy and angular youth feel at home, but his lack of response had not been encouraging; he persisted in remaining her son's friend and not hers. He recalled the little frown of displeasure with which she had heard of the meeting. "Alec!" she had said. "Well, that *is* jolly. I expect he's changed a lot. The army's probably knocked most of the corners off him. He could be so nice when he forgot for a moment that he'd worked his way up from the bottom. He was so very proud of his childish opinions and so very ashamed of his delightful Scots accent."

"The Scots accent's quite disappeared now," he had told her. "Gracious me," she had said, "then he must certainly be laughed back into it."

When the telephone rang that evening she had run to answer it. "But of course you must come," he had heard her say, and a moment later, "Och! but what ha'e ye done wi' your gude Scots tongue? I hope ye no ha'e left it in Eetaly."

She had chosen to invite a young French girl to meet Alec at dinner. She had a great liking for the dead conventionality and empty chic of French middle-class women, and this girl had been a superb specimen of her kind. The evening had not been a success. Poor Alec's shyness had vanished only for a moment, when he began to speak of his new-found enthusiasm for the early Wordsworth. "It's all nonsense," he had said excitedly, "to expect the Prelude without that first attempt at a new freshness. Some of it's absurd if you like . . ."

"Now you're very naughty, Alec," broke in Mrs. Carrington. "*I* know you're only pulling our legs, but gracious me, you'll have Mademoiselle Planquet thinking you mean it. Remember the dignity you have to uphold as the first real live Professor of English she's ever met." When Alec protested his sincerity, she laughed a little and then said abruptly, "Fiddlesticks; why, I suppose you'll be telling me next that 'The Idiot Boy' is the finest poem in the English language. I expect just the same nonsense goes on in France, Mademoiselle Planquet. As soon as we've got one stuffy old writer put safely away in the cupboard, these ridiculous children have to fish him out and dust him up again. They haven't got enough to do, that's the trouble."

The Samuels' cocktail party, of course, had been asking for trouble, but his mother had insisted on going. If she disliked Alec Lovat, she hated Rosa Samuel. The Samuels were richer and more sophisticated than she was. But above everything, she was jealous of Rosa. That innocent visit he had made to them in Essex in summer 1942 had been the root of the trouble.

"Rosa Samuel behaved very stupidly with Donald," she had told Aunt Nora.

Rosa, in her own words, "had gone all 1912." Her sleek, dark hair was piled up high on her head with some construction of scarlet fruit and feathers in it, and her scarlet velvet dress, which spread out in a train round her ankles, was cut up the side of its very tight skirt. Donald remembered that as she had come forward to greet them his heart had jumped with triumph—here at least he was on friendly soil, for Rosa had been his confidante and ally in all his battles. Almost immediately, however, he had felt sure that his mother would win. So, indeed, it had proved, for Rosa, in her mingled shyness and dislike, had foolishly set out to shock. She greeted them with a self-consciously amusing account of her return journey from Switzerland. It appeared that she had got into conversation with a young girl "with the face of the Little Flower, my dear," but it had soon become clear that the relations of the saintlike creature with her elderly uncle were not entirely conventional. "Apparently, duckie," Rosa had said in her deep yet strangulated voice, "he makes her stand in nothing but her stockings and thrashes her with a cowhide whip. But the incredible thing was that she told me all the horrifying details in an offhand, bored way, just as though she was describing a shopping expedition to the greengrocer's."

His mother had rocked with laughter. "Goodness gracious, Mrs. Samuel," she had said, "it takes a really moral person like yourself to imagine that the lives of people like that *are* anything but very boring."

"Old bitch," Rosa had said to him later in the evening. "I know she was as shocked as hell, but you can never catch her out." His mother had not waited for her hostess to pass out of earshot before she had said to him, "How it all reminds me of those Edwardian parties at Grandfather Carrington's down at Maidenhead. All this silly smoking-room smut, they want a good smack on the behind."

"I can't help liking Rosa Samuel," she had said as they made their way home afterwards. "She's so very stupid that it would really be impossible to *dis*like her. Someone ought to tell her about her clothes though, darling. Whatever *had* she got that ridiculous Christmas tree on her head for? And that scarlet dress! It was just like an early film of Pola Negri's. I kept on thinking she'd bring a secret message out of her bosom."

He had tried, he remembered, to turn the conversation to a young woman archæologist whom he had met at the party and liked; *her* clothes, at least, had been of the simplest variety. His mother, however, had been quite equal to this; indeed, there was nothing she liked better than to have things both ways. "I thought she was a very nice girl," she had said. "It seemed such a pity that she had to wear those lumpy clothes and sensible shoes. You have to have such a very good complexion, too, to go without make-up like that. Anyone could see she was an intelligent person without all that parade. Dear me! They'll be wearing placards next, with B.A. Oxon or whatever it is written on them."

A mood of compromise had descended upon him. Let me betray anything, let me sacrifice Rosa, let me forswear my belief in intellectual standards, he had thought, only let me be at peace with her, let us agree. He happened to have overheard a pretentious conversation about the theatre between three people at the party, and this he had told her, knowing that in so doing he was feeding her with ammunition for future attacks on his "clever" friends. "I sometimes wonder if they know themselves what they mean when they use this jargon," he had said. "They were discussing a play, Mother, and Olive Vernon said she didn't like it although she thought it was good theatre. 'Good theatre,' said her husband, 'I thought it was thundering bad theatre.' Then that stupid Stokes boy broke in, 'I really don't think it was theatre at all—I mean, you have to have some glitter if you're going to have theatre and it was so drab.' 'Oh, but that sort of drabness,' said Olive in her silliest voice, 'surely *is* just a kind of inverted glitter.' " His mother had been delighted with the story. "They really *are* a pack of ninnies," she had exclaimed.

How different she had been with Commander and Mrs. Stokes, who dined with them the following evening! The Stokeses, whom she had met during his absence, had proved to be a dull and somewhat self-satisfied couple, and it had been clear from the start that they were to be a kind of private joke between them. Whenever Mrs. Stokes had said something unusually snobbish, his mother had taken great delight in catching Donald's eye, while, at the end of a particularly long story of the Commander's about life aboard the *Nelson*, she had smiled sweetly and said, "Well, that's most interesting. I feel as though I'd been afloat for years, don't you, Donald?" After their guests had gone she had sat down and roared with laughter. "You really are wicked, Donald," she had cried, "making me laugh at the poor creatures like that. They'll never set the Thames on fire, but still they're better than those silly intellectuals we met at the Samuels'. Ah! Well, thank God for a sense of humour, without it the evening might have been very dull." How he had longed to say that even with it the evening had not been very interesting.

Politics, of course, had come under discussion when Uncle Ernest came to lunch. The open ruthlessness of his uncle's particular brand of City conservatism always outraged his social conscience, and they had soon been engaged in a heated argument. His mother had been so amusing at both their expenses. "You haven't given the Labour people a chance, Ernest," she had declared. "They've had no time to do anything yet. Remember that it's all quite new to them. Most of them have been mayors or town councillors or some other dreadful smug thing and they're bound to be a bit dazed now they've got to *do* something. Why, by this time next year they'll be as sound old Tories as even *you* could want."

The visit to Aunt Nora, of course, had brought the usual row with it. He flattered himself that he recognized the sense of duty and real kindness of heart that inspired these determined visits to that impoverished and irritating woman. It was true that Aunt Nora would have felt snubbed if they had not been to see her, but when he reflected that her silliness would lead his mother to say a hundred snubbing things before they had left Rose Cottage, it was not surprising that he had always found these expeditions depressing and pointless.

It had been without eagerness, then, that he walked through Richmond Park towards Aunt Nora's house. The day, he remembered so vividly, had been sunny and cold and he had stood for a moment to gaze at the twisted grey elm trunks and their tracery of black boughs outlined against the sky. "It would be nice," he had said, "to spend a day in the country before the holiday is over." "I dare say," his mother had replied, "but that's no excuse for being late for Nora. You know how she looks forward to this visit." Suddenly the futility of the whole week had impressed itself upon him. "Damn Nora and damn you," he had shouted. "I never do a bloody thing I want to." "Really, Donald, that's ridiculous. The whole week's been given up to amusing you. In any case we sometimes have to do our duty, even though we don't like it."

The calm common sense of her reply had been more than he could bear. It was too unfair that she should always have her cake and eat it in this way, he had felt. He had let out at her where he knew it would hurt most. "Oh, for God's sake, spare us your quotations from Samuel Smiles. I know all about your religion," he cried out, "but the whole thing's meaningless. I don't believe you have any real *faith*, just a lot of sentiment and cherished illusions you've kept from your childhood." His mother had begun to cry, for, as he well knew, in attacking her religion he had dealt her a serious blow. She had a number of ethical principles, and these she held firmly. She had also a certain private devotional life which centred in the prayerbook she had been given at her confirmation. He had looked into this book when he was younger and had found between its leaves some love letters from his father written during their engagement, that happy period of her life before the physical contact of marriage had come to awaken and shock her, when she lived in that state of emotional flirtation which she had tried to re-create with him. Of real religious beliefs concerning God and immortality she was quite uncertain, and far too afraid of her doubts to probe further. In speaking so violently, he had attacked the secret citadel of her life, and she had only been able to find refuge in tears.

In a sense it had been his only victory of the week, for after it she had been most anxious to make amends. She had realized that she must have annoyed him very deeply to provoke him to such an attack. "My poor darling," she had said, "you must certainly have your walk in the woods." They must go to his favourite Epping on the Friday, she had announced.

Friday had proved to be a wet and dismal day but nothing would deter her from making the expedition. "Nonsense! The walk will do you good," she had said in answer to his protestations. They had been marooned in the Forest during a violent rainstorm and had been drenched to the skin. On Saturday she had woken with a bad cold but had remained on her feet with a depressing and determined cheefulness. That night she had complained of sharp pains in the chest and on the next day she had developed pneumonia. Was it unnatural, he wondered, to have felt so little about it? No, surely, things had gone too far between them for him to have felt anything but an ashamed relief. The fight she had put up had roused his pity and admiration, though. She was a tough little woman and she had a strong will to live, but she was, after all, fifty-eight, and death had taken her all the same. She had been

conscious only once during the last two days of her life, and Donald had been at her beside. He had hardly been able to recognize
the little thin blue-grey face or the vague, alarmed kitten's eyes,
for she had known that she was dying and she had been very
frightened. He had wished so much to comfort her, but he had
only felt very, very tired. She had signed to him to bend down
beside her and had run her hand feebly over his hair. "My poor
boy," he had just been able to hear her murmur. "My poor boy
will be very lonely without Mother."

Yes, life had been very hectic after her death, Donald thought
as he stretched his limbs sensuously. His days were his own now
to do as he liked, though it was strange how difficult he found it
to decide what to do with them. That was to be expected with a
new-found freedom, it was bound to take a little time, the main
thing was that he was free. She had said that the walk in the Forest "would do him good," he thought sardonically. Poor Mother—
it was not really the sort of joke that she would have cared for. It
was with a smile on his lips that he slipped into sleep. . . .

He was at a reception, many hundreds of people were there
and he was talking animatedly. They were in a long, lofty room
with great, high windows and heavy curtains; it appeared to be in
some medieval castle. Gradually a storm blew up outside, the
winds howled and the heavy curtains flapped about in the huge
room, like enormous birds; it began to grow very dark. The other
people in the room huddled together in close little groups, but he
was left standing alone. Soon the people began to fade away and
it grew darker and darker. Somebody ought to be with him, he
could not be left alone like this, somebody was not there who
should have been there. He began to scream. He awoke with his
face buried in the pillow and he felt dreadfully lonely, so lonely
that he began to cry. He told himself that this sense of solitude
would pass with time, but in his heart he knew that this was not
true. He might be free in little things, but in essentials she had
tied him to her and now she had left him forever. She had had the
last word in the matter as usual. "My poor boy will be lonely,"
she had said. She was dead right.

Et Dona Ferentes

-->>)(((<--

"I'll have a cigarette too, Mother," said Monica to Mrs. Rackham. "It'll help to keep the midges off. That's why I always hate woods so. Oh, don't worry, Elizabeth," she added as she saw her own daughter's look of alarm. "That's why I *hate* woods, but there are hundreds and hundreds of more important reasons why I *love* them—especially pine woods. To begin with, there's the scent, and *you* can say what you like, Edwin"—she smiled up at her husband, who was frowning as he cut inexpertly at a block of wood with a pocket knife—"about its being a hackneyed smell. But, apart from the scent, there's the effect of light and shade. The only time that you can really see the sunlight out of doors is when it shines through dark trees like these. When you're in it, you're always too hot or too dazzled to notice anything. So you see, darling"—she turned again to her daughter—"I *do* love pine woods." For a moment she lay back, but the smoke from her cigarette got into her eyes and soon she was stubbing it out on the bed of pine needles beneath. "How I *do* hate cigarettes," she cried, "and how I *do* hate hating them. It puts one at such a social disadvantage. Oh, it's all right for you, Mother; everyone in your generation smoked, and *smoked* determinedly; and it's all right for Elizabeth, when she's eighteen—don't let's talk of it, there's only two years—nobody will even think of smoking, it'll be so dowdy; but with women in the forties like me there was always

Written in 1947; published in 1949; scene contemporary.

that awful choice—to smoke or not to smoke—and I chose not to, and there I am, of course, on occasions like parties and things with nothing to do with my hands. Now let's all lie back and relax for a quarter of an hour," she went on, and the nervous tension in her voice seemed even greater than before as she said it, "and then we can have a drink before lunch. Don't you think it was clever of me to remember to bring gin? People *always* forget it on picnics and yet it's so lovely to be able to have a drink without needing to be jolly. I hope nobody is going to be jolly, by the way. I forbid anyone to be jolly," she said with mock sternness and then, turning to her son, who was watching a squirrel in a nearby tree, "Richard, darling, take that knife away from your father before he does himself an injury."

"It wouldn't be a very serious injury, Mother, and then Elizabeth could show her prowess as a First-Aider or whatever they're called in the Guides," said Richard, but nevertheless he moved slowly towards his father. Before he could offer assistance, however, a tall, fair-haired youth had sprung forward.

"Allow me, please, Mr. Newman," he said, the stiffness of his foreign English relieved by the charm and intimacy of his smile. "I am very able to cut wood with these kind of knives."

"That's very kind of you, Sven," said Monica. "There you are, darlings, you see, Sven has manners. I'm surprised you weren't able to learn a few, Richard, when you were staying with him in Sweden. I'm afraid we lost all our manners here while we were busy fighting the war."

Two sharp points of red glowed suddenly on the Swedish boy's high cheekbones, and his already slanting eyes narrowed and blinked.

Edwin Newman glared angrily at his wife, his prominent Adam's apple jerking convulsively above his open-necked shirt. He placed a hand on Sven's shoulder. "You have given us so many useful lessons since you arrived, Sven, if you use the same charm to re-educate us in everyday courtesy, we shall be fortunate," he said.

"You are too kind to say these many good things to me, Mr. Newman," replied the boy. "I hope I shall not quite fail to deserve them."

"You two ought to be talking in Latin," said Richard. "You sound like Dr. Johnson, Dad, when he met famous foreign scholars. By the way, Grannie, have you been getting at Sven about his reading? I can't persuade him to read anything decent like De Quincey or Dickens or Coleridge. He seems to think for some reason or other that he's got to wade through *Rasselas* in order to 'appreciate literature,' as he calls it. I must say, I shouldn't have thought even you would have inflicted that torture upon anyone."

Mrs. Rackham's heavy, square-jawed face lost its look of grimness for a moment as she spoke to her beloved grandson. "I am delighted to hear of a blow being struck at this neo-romantic nonsense. Like Miss Deborah, I think that nothing but good can arise from reading the works of the great Lexicographer. Continue to read *Rasselas*," she said to Sven, "and you may yet know what the English language should really sound like. Take no notice of Richard's attempts to lure you into reading Dickens. He only wants you to fall under a railway train like a famous English retired officer, Captain Brown, whose unhealthy interest in Boz led him to that horrid end."

"That just shows how little you understand about it, Grannie. Captain Brown was reading Pickwick, and Pickwick's nothing to do with the real Dickens. Anyhow, it was Pickwick in weekly parts, which couldn't happen now."

"Isn't it time you two stopped all this Who's Who in Literature?" said Edwin. "In any case, if Sven's going to waste his time on novels, surely he might read modern authors like Huxley or even Lawrence."

"Dear Edwin," replied Mrs. Rackham, "even I know that Huxley or even Lawrence"—and she imitated her son-in-law's hesitant tones—"daring though they may be, are not *modern* authors."

"In any case I am reading *Rasselas* because it is demanded for the higher examination. I am not really so greatly interested to read books." Sven lay back and stretched his arms out to a spot where the sunlight had broken through. "I think I prefer more to follow outdoor games when the sun shines, like Elizabeth does," and he smiled lazily towards the clearing where Elizabeth was staking little wooden sticks around a clump of late bluebells.

Seen upside down, it's more like a cat's than a satyr's, thought Edwin.

Elizabeth only scowled. "This isn't an outdoor game," she said. "I'm just messing around. Come down to the stream with me, Mummy," she called.

"May I come too?" said Mrs. Rackham.

Elizabeth gave no answer, but Monica looked pleased and held out her hand to assist her mother from the ground. The family likeness showed clearly as they walked away—three generations—hand in hand.

"It's the most lovely stream, Mummy," said Elizabeth, squeezing Monica's arm. "I wish we had it all for our own."

"Yes," said Monica, "I would plant Japanese irises here—the dark purple kind with the spear-like leaves to contrast with the yellow flags. It's funny how profuse nature is with yellow—now if I had made the universe I should have had much more contrast of colour and more subtlety too with wild flowers. I wonder if fritillary would grow here, the place could do with something a bit more strange."

"But, Mummy, it would be awful to change it when it's so beautiful."

"I don't think so, darling," said Monica. "I don't know, of course, but I've always thought that was a false sort of romanticism. I don't believe you really become aware of the beauty of a scene until you see how it could be made more beautiful. What do you think, Mother?"

Mrs. Rackham smiled. "I think I just see the stream and the

meadows behind," she said, "and then I feel a great sense of peace and solitude."

"Oh, yes, that, of course," cried her daughter, "but there's something else too. You have to look at it properly, surely, to see the patterns of shape and colour, and that's when you see what's needed to complete them." She thought for a moment, then added, "Yes, I'm sure you have to do that, otherwise it's all a blur and you don't really see anything."

"Look, Mummy, those holes," cried Elizabeth. "I think there must be badgers. If you were here at night you would see them come down to drink."

"I should like that," said Monica, "when there was no moon —at dusk or dawn—with black water and those nightmare-deformed willow trees and then lumbering grey shapes coming down to drink. But not by moonlight, that would be too expected."

"We've been imagining the badgers drinking in the stream," said Elizabeth to her father when they returned.

"Is that one of Brock's nightly prowls?" asked Edwin.

"No, darling," replied Monica, "*not* Brock and *not* nightly prowls. Just badgers drinking. There were rabbits too, but they weren't wearing sky-blue shorts, they were just brown rabbits with white tails." Then, seeing her husband's hurt expression, she put her hand on his arm. "Never mind, darling," she said. "You like imagining in that whimsical way, I don't; but I think it's only because I don't know how to."

Edwin smiled. "How about that gin you were talking about?" he asked.

"It's in the shaker, darling, with some French. You do the shaking, you're so professional."

Indeed, with his boyish face and long black hair, dressed in a Saxe-blue Aertex shirt and navy-blue Daks, Edwin looked very much like some barman from a smart bar in Cannes or like some cabaret turn. He seemed almost to be guying the part as he waved the shaker to and fro, dancing up and down and singing grotesquely "Hold That Tiger."

"Idiot," cried Monica and, relenting further, she turned to Sven. "Do respectable fathers of families ever behave so absurdly in Sweden?"

"I do not imagine Mr. Newman a father of a family. I imagine him to have continual youth."

Monica turned away sharply. "At eighteen, of course, one can imagine so many ridiculous things," she said.

But Edwin ended his dance with a mock bow. "The spirit of youth is infectious," he declared.

Sven lay back and laughed with delight, showing his regular white teeth.

It was while they were eating their lunch that Edwin got onto his hobby horse. "There's supposed to be a Saxon camp across on that hill over there," he said, pointing to the east. "If my theory is right it may well be an example of a Saxon settlement existing alongside a British one."

He was so used to a completely silent audience that he was quite startled when Sven said, "Can that really be?"

"I believe so, but it's a view which is only gradually gaining ground," said Edwin, and he looked across at Sven, who sat clasping his legs, with his knees up to his chin, staring seriously before him. It's like talking to Pan, he thought, and he went on hurriedly, "Of course, the whole of this Thames Valley area is very important from the point of view of Saxon migrations. It's almost certain that a great part of the inhabitants of Wessex came from the east and crossed the river near here at Dorchester."

"But that is most interesting," said Sven.

"Do you really think so?" asked Elizabeth and then, turning away contemptuously, she added, "I don't believe you know anything about it."

"That is true," said the boy, "but your father makes the story so alive."

"If you're really interested we might go to the edge of the wood and see the hill from a closer vantage point," suggested Edwin.

Sven was on his feet immediately. "I should like that so much!" he exclaimed.

"Are you coming, Richard?" asked his father, but Richard was deep in a first reading of *The Possessed* and merely shook his head.

Mr. Newman bounded lightly across the tree trunks that lay in the path, his sandals thumping against his heels.

"Of course, when I say that Saxons and British dwelt side by side, I don't deny that there *were* cases of horrible violence," they could hear him saying, and Sven's answering voice replying, "But violence, I think, is often so beautiful."

"How happy Edwin seems," said Mrs. Rackham to her daughter. "That boy's quite right, he *has* got the spirit of 'continual youth' as he called it."

Monica made no answer. "I'm going down to the stream again," she said.

"I've never seen him look so young and gay," went on Mrs. Rackham.

"How funny," said her daughter as she walked away. "I was just thinking how absurd he looked, like a scoutmaster or something."

If I was one of those Virginia Woolf mothers, thought Mrs. Rackham, I should have been told what all this means long ago. It's much better as it is, however, she decided. Fond as I am of Monica, I wouldn't be able to help, whatever may be wrong. She has no power of resignation, no ability to seek refuge, she insists on fighting, on living even when life is unpleasant. Edwin too has that same total absorption in the affair of the moment. They want to wring every drop out of life. She smiled as she thought how they must despise her for living so much in books. A second-hand life they would probably call it. I prefer to have my people pre-digested, she decided, it's easier, yes, and wiser. Today's undercurrents, for instance, how wearying! . . . and life was so short. She turned to her book, then laughed out loud as it came to her how little even she profited from her reading. Let me remember Miss Woodhouse's folly in interfering in the affairs of others, she said, and began her twenty-third reading of *Emma*.

Monica took the lime-green coat she was carrying over her arm and placed it on a large white stone by the edge of the stream. Then she sat down and rippled her fingers through the water. Every now and again she dabbed her forehead or smoothed her eyelids with her wet fingers. The afternoon had become intensely hot; there seemed to be no breath of air anywhere. Overhead, mosquitoes and midges hummed so that she was forced to pluck some wild mint from the stream to attempt to drive them away. The mint grew so shallowly that the whole plant came away suddenly as she touched it, and mud from the roots splashed over her white dress. Everything seemed discordant to her—the yellow-green of her coat against the emerald grass, the crimson ribbons of the large straw hat which lay at her side against a clump of pink campion. Suddenly she saw a creature slithering up the trunk of an old tree, a creature brown-grey like the tree itself—it was a tree-creeper, but for a moment the little bird seemed to her like a rat. The rusty bullocks farther up the stream stamped and swished their tails as they tried to drive the horseflies from their dung-caked flanks. There were always creatures like that who lived upon dirt, who nosed it out and unearthed it, however deeply it was hidden, however long, yes, even though all trace of it seemed vanished for twenty years, she thought. A shallow, vain, egocentric creature like that, with those untrustworthy, mocking cat's eyes. Twenty years ago, when they were first married and Edwin had told her, she had been so anxious to help. There had been incidents, it was true, but they had been so unimportant and they had become closer through fighting them together. But now after twenty years she felt she could do nothing; her pride was too hurt. All this fortnight, since the holiday began, she had been telling herself it could not be true and yet she knew she was not mistaken, today especially she felt sure of it. What could have altered things to make it possible? she reflected. It was true that she had been a bit uncertain in her feelings herself this year, but Edwin had understood so well that it was change of life that was coming to her early. Change of life had such strange results, that must be it—she seized on the idea eagerly—it was all fancy. How horrible that anything purely physical could make one believe such things and how cruel to Edwin that she had indulged them. How cruelly she had behaved, even if it was true, and somehow she felt again that it was. She had withdrawn her sympathy at the very moment Edwin needed it most; it was easy enough to realize that with one's mind, she thought, but the emotional revulsion was so great after twenty years' forgetfulness that she might only overcome it when events had moved beyond her reach.

Whatever happens, she thought, I shall be so much to blame; and to Elizabeth, who came running towards her along the bank of the stream, she said aloud, "If anything should go wrong, darling, in our lives, always remember I am to blame. I hadn't the courage to do as I should."

The moment she had said it she could have bitten her tongue out. The child was already too inclined to histrionics in this new phase of schoolgirl religious enthusiasm through which she was passing. Monica's fears were quite justified. Elizabeth rose at once to the situation, though she had no idea of the meaning of her mother's words.

"Brave Mummy," she said, putting her hand on Monica's arm.

Monica spoke almost harshly. "No, darling, *not* brave Mummy. Self-dramatizing Mummy, if you like, Mummy who's got the heroine's part quite pat at rehearsals and in the wings, but who always fluffs her words when it comes to the night. Anything you like, my dear, but not *brave* Mummy."

Mummy's so strange and sarcastic sometimes, thought Elizabeth, anyone but me might think she was bitter, but I know her better. I know how brave and true and kind she is. I understand Daddy too, how much he needs my love. Richard never thinks about anything but his old books, so I have to help both of them. It's a kind of secret I have with myself—and God, she thought quickly. God loves and knows them all, even Grannie, though she laughs at

Him. It's true what Miss Anstruther says—life's ever so exciting
for anyone who's found Him; always something new and worth
while to do, not just silly messing around with boys like Penelope
Black and all those drips. That's what Sven wants, a lot of silly
girls swooning about over him, like soppy Sinatra. That's what
he would like from me, for all he keeps on saying I'm only a kid,
but there's no time for waste of time, Miss Anstruther says. I
wish Sven hadn't come here, it's all been beastly since he did.
It's ever since he came that Mummy's been snappy and Daddy
keeps on showing off, not that it's for Sven, he wouldn't want to
show off for a little pipsqueak like him. I oughtn't to talk like
that about him, I must learn to love him. Love everyone, pray for
them, and set a good example—that's all we can do. I can help
all of them, even Sven, if I show how Christ wants us to live. People don't say so, but they're watching us Christians all the time,
Miss Anstruther says. "Ye are the salt of the earth. . . . A city
that is set on a hill cannot be hid."

Monica's voice suddenly broke into her daughter's thoughts.
"Look, darling! On that larch tree there. See? A jay."

There, indeed very close at hand, sat a jay preening its rose
feathers, its pastel shades harmonizing delicately with the soft
green caterpillars of the larch. Suddenly it rose, with a flash of
blue-green wing feathers, and flew off, screaming harshly. Immediately all the birds in the wood seemed to break into chattering. A cold wind blew across the stream. Monica shivered and
drew her coat round her shoulders. "I think there's a storm coming up, darling," she said. "Let's go back to Grannie."

"I think there's a storm coming up, but I'm glad we came all
the same," said Edwin, as, somewhat out of breath, he reached the
crest of the hills. "We've gone much farther than I ever intended,
but the time's passed so quickly in talking. I'm afraid the others
may get rather anxious, but still I think one has a right to enjoy
oneself in one's own way sometimes, don't you?" Then, not waiting for answer, he continued, "The Saxon settlement must have
run right across the chain to the left here. Down below, you see,

is Milkford, the outskirts run right up to the foot of the hills. It's quite an important town still, a sort of watering place, but it was even more important in medieval times. Of course, there's nothing earlier, really, than thirteenth century," he said apologetically, "but the castle's quite interesting—fifteenth century, you know, when the fortress is turning into the country house. We might run down and look at it later, would you like that?" he asked.

"That would be most nice," said Sven, "but for some minutes I should like to rest here, please. The heat renders me most tired," and indeed beads of sweat were trickling down his brown chest where the line of his shirt lay open almost to his stomach.

Edwin turned away. "Yes, you lie there a bit while I explore round the place." But he did not move far off.

Suddenly Sven broke the silence. "That is so lovely, your signet ring. I should much like one of the same kind," he said.

"Would you?" said Edwin. "We must see what we can do about it."

Sven did not answer. It was nice to lie here in the sun and to feel that one was being watched, admired. It was boring staying with these Newmans. Richard, with his books, had been bad enough at home, but there it did not matter; if he did not choose to come out swimming or skiing with the girls, he could be left behind. But here there were no girls, no sports, only books and talking and talking. He had hoped to watch the English girls bathing and to go dancing with them; they were said to be prudish, but all the same he was usually very irresistible. They would have run their hands through his hair, like Karen, who looked so pretty when her own hair blew across her face and she smiled with those white teeth through the salt spray; or they would have stroked his fine brown legs, as Sigrid when she buried them in sand and he brought his face close to her firm white breasts showing through her costume; or perhaps even an English girl more bold than the others would lie naked and soft under him on the sand, like little Lili, who had licked the salt sweat from his chest when he had done his part with her—different girls, but all of them, all of them wanting him as he had a right to be wanted, so handsome, he felt that sometimes he almost wanted himself. But here there were no girls, only books and talking. He had hoped much of Richard's sister, but she was only a child of sixteen and even so she was taken up with some rubbish about religion. With Mrs. Newman too, he had thought he might have so much fun; after all, she was not so old as Mrs. Thomas, the American woman, who had taken him out to cabarets and dances and given him presents last year when he was only seventeen. It had been most pleasant, and he had learned from her so much that was useful. But this bitch treated him as though he were a child, it made him so glad that now he could hurt her. Even if Richard had made him his hero, like Ekki Blomquist, who followed him around with admiring eyes, little Ekki whom he liked to protect and pet and tease—but Richard thought only of his books. No, it was only Mr. Newman who had been kind to him and who admired him, who looked so gay and fine for forty-seven—he would be very pleased if he could look so at that age. But all the same it was very disturbing; it would not be pleasant if so kind a man should behave stupidly—it would be necessary to be very polite and very firm. For a little while still it would be nice to continue to be admired; also he would like to have the present of the ring; also he would like to make that bitch unhappy. Not that he liked to be naughty, but it was not pleasant when one was not admired. What strange little white shells there were on the ground, like little Lili's ears, or his own curls when they fell from the nape of his neck at the barber's shop.

The same little crustacea lay all around Edwin, pressed into the soft ground by the tightly winding mesh of moss-grass. Little balls of rabbit droppings were scattered here and there. The hillside was carpet smooth but for an occasional red-and-yellow vetch that rose above the even level. Edwin peered closely at the turf, but he noticed nothing for his thoughts were far away.

If only I could collect my ideas, thought Edwin, but the blood pounds so at my temples. If only I could piece together how it had all led up to this. I think I have been feeling shut in by them all for a long time now, at any rate all this year. Richard with his books and Elizabeth with this priggish religious talk, and lately even Monica has seemed to be so sure of her values, so determinedly living in a world of beauty. All the best that's written, only the actions God approves, only the most beautiful in nature and art—it almost sickens me at times. It all seems to come out in their lack of charity to Sven. I wanted so to be kind to him, to show him that he was wanted, to make up for their priggish lack of courtesy. I understood what they meant when they said he was materialistic, animal, superficial, vain—but in some degree I felt that I was too and I wanted them to realize that. The children will always be afraid of physical pleasure in sex, afraid of their own bodies' lusts, afraid of the lusts of others for them. It's worse, somehow, when Mrs. Rackham's here, because I can see the stunted, shy, self-satisfied life they're heading for. But Monica is different; all the years she has understood my feelings about it, and at times has shared in them gloriously, but recently she's changed, "trying to put sex in its perspective" she would call it, but that's only another name for avoiding it because it's distasteful. It's true she's given me this physical reason, but she said it so eagerly that it seemed like an excuse for doing what she's wanted to do for years. And now this has happened. What I thought to be kindness and sympathy for a rebel has reawakened the old feeling of twenty years ago, the old sensual pattern of Gilbert and Heinrich and Bernard and the others, only more violently as it seems, and the blood is pulsing in my head as it used to then, only more loudly.

Suddenly he heard himself saying in a clear, artificial voice, "I'm so glad that we should have become such good friends, Sven, and I hope you are too. I don't expect you realize what a very lonely man I am in some ways. Oh, I know how lucky I am in my family, but they're terribly narrow. I felt perhaps that you were feeling that too. Richard, for example"—by now Edwin was talking at break-neck speed—"he lives in books, takes no pleasure in the life around him. Now you must find that very strange, being so strong and lithe and well made. Yes, I'm afraid the truth of the matter is that my family are all what we call in England kill-joys, that is, they get no real fun out of life. That's what I've so admired about you—you obviously get so *much* fun out of life. I think it's probably because I've allowed my wife to dominate the family so. You'll think it funny of me to say so, but I'm not really very much of a woman's man. I think women are inclined rather to be kill-joys. Do *you* think so?"

"Do I?" said Sven. "Do I think that women kill joy? No, oh, no. Certainly not that," and he began to shake with laughter, but, seeing Edwin's face twisted with combined excitement and alarm, he controlled his amusement and added, "But I think I so well understand what you may mean, you must tell me about this. But not here, I think, for it is now getting so dark and a rain spot has fallen on my face so that I think there will be a storm. Shall you not tell me in the town down there?"

"Of course!" said Edwin eagerly, and he began to clamber down the hill. "We'll go into Milkford and I'll ring up from there to say we've been caught by the storm. If we can't get a car we may have to stay the night there. You won't mind that, will you? It'll give us a real chance to get to know each other, and they say the Bull's really a very decent old pub."

At first there had only been a few heavy drops of rain falling through the trees in the wood. Richard, who had reached the death of Stefan Trofimovich, positively refused to move, and even Mrs. Rackham, who was being once more horrified and entranced by the vulgarity of Mrs. Elton, preferred to take no notice. Then quite suddenly the storm had burst over their heads—the picnic things all shook under the blast of the thunderclap and the whole wood was lit up by a great fork of lightning, which seemed to strike obliquely at the nearby stream. Before a second and more deafening thunderclap had sounded, Mrs. Rackham had jumped to her feet.

"Come on, Richard, pack up the picnic basket. We mustn't stay under these trees with this lightning about. Make for the car and the clearing. Help me with the rugs, Elizabeth. Monica," she called, "don't stand there, my dear, we'll all get drenched soon if we don't move, apart from the danger of the lightning."

But Monica stood a little away from them, her face chalk-white and her eyes round with terror. As the next fork of lightning zig-zagged viciously in front of them she began to scream.

"Edwin, Edwin! My God, where are you? Oh, pray God nothing happens. We must find him, we must find him!" And she turned and ran down the little path. She had hardly gone a few paces when she tripped on a tree root and fell on her face, bruising her cheek and cutting the side of her chin.

Richard made as though to move towards her and then, blushing scarlet, turned in the direction of the car. But already Elizabeth had run to her mother and, throwing herself on her, she sobbed. "Mummy darling, Mummy darling, let's go away from this place."

"For heaven's sake, Monica," said Mrs. Rackham, "pull yourself together. You're scaring the child out of her wits." She took her daughter's arm and started to pull her to her feet, but Monica pulled her arm away roughly. "We must find him," she said and began to weep bitterly.

"Stop this at once," said Mrs. Rackham sternly. "Edwin's perfectly capable of looking after himself," and she led her sobbing daughter to the car.

By now the rain was pouring down. Monica's fashionable hair style was washed across onto her face and strands of hair got stuck to the cut on her chin, while the blood ran down onto the white dress beneath. As they came to the clearing there was a blinding flash of lightning, followed by a crash. In a few moments smoke was ascending from the other side of the stream—one of the larches had been struck.

"*You* must drive, Richard," said Mrs. Rackham. "Your mother's not at all well," and she helped her daughter into the back, and as she did so she heard her mumbling, "Oh, God! Don't let it happen! Oh, God! Don't let it happen!" That any daughter of mine should be superstitious over a storm, she thought.

"It's lucky, there's only the four of us this time," said Richard as he started the car.

Elizabeth kicked his leg. "You silly, thoughtless idiot, don't let Mummy hear you," she said.

I've failed again, thought Richard. When I was reading about Stefan Trofimovich's death, I wanted to be there so that I could make him happy, to tell him that for all his faults I knew he was a good man. But when my own mother is in trouble I can't say anything. It all sounds all right in books, but when I see people's faces—all that redness, wetness, and ugliness, and the noises they make—I feel ashamed for them, and then I'm speechless and that makes me angry and I say cruel things. It was just like that when Sven was unhappy over that girl; I wanted to be his friend, as Alyosha was to Kolya, to tell him that I knew he was often bad but that I didn't mind, but it was no good because I couldn't show my sympathy. I shall always live like this, cut off, although I think I understand more clearly than others. But how can I speak to Mother of her fears about Sven and that they are absurd? No, I must always be shut in like this.

Nevertheless when they arrived home he took his mother's arm. "Don't worry, darling, nothing could happen, I'm sure," he whispered. But Monica did not hear him, she was listening to the maid.

"Mr. Newman phoned, ma'am, to say that he and Mr. Sodeblom are stranded at Milkford and will be staying the night."

Monica walked straight into the drawing-room and sat, with set face, upon the sofa. "I am very tired, my dears, I'll have my dinner in my room. Mother, would you be very kind and see Agnes in the kitchen, I don't want to be worried."

Richard and Elizabeth began to speak at once as Mrs. Rackham went from the room.

"Can I get you some books, Mother?"

"Shall I help you to undress, Mummy?"

But such offers were premature, for at that moment a car sounded in the drive outside and a few minutes later Edwin rushed breathlessly into the room. "Oh, you're here before us!" he exclaimed. "So you got my message. As the storm cleared, I thought it wasn't necessary to stay the night."

Sven had come into the room very quietly behind Edwin and now his voice sounded, speaking very slowly. "Mr. Newman was so kind, he was so anxious that I should stay and see Milkford. But I thought you would be alarmed at our absence, Mrs. Newman. See, however, he has bought me this lovely ring, the stone has so strange a name—garnet. But he has not forgotten you, Mrs. Newman," and though Edwin motioned him to be silent he went on, "But, no, Mr. Newman, you must show your wife the gift or she will be upset that you gave me so lovely a ring and nothing for her. Look, it is a beautiful sapphire pendant. Is it not a lovely stone? I chose it for you myself, I have a great taste for jewels."

Monica got to her feet. "It is a pity," she said, "that you speak such ghastly English. You say unfortunate things that a boy of your age cannot understand," and she walked from the room.

A few moments later Mrs. Rackham returned. "Look," said Sven, "at the lovely pendant the kind Mr. Newman has bought for Mrs. Newman."

"Oh! But, Edwin, how sweet of you! It's charming-looking," said his mother-in-law.

"But Mrs. Newman does not at all seem to like it," said Sven.

"Oh, she will tomorrow," said Mrs. Rackham. "She's very over-tired tonight, the storm upset her a lot."

The rainfall ceased after dinner, and there was a calming silence as Monica sat before her dressing table, talking to her mother. Suddenly Edwin came into the room. He began to talk quickly as though he feared interruption.

"I've been talking to the children," he said, "and Sven thinks he ought to return home by the next boat—that is, in three days— I think he's right probably. He's got his exams coming on, and I don't know that it's been quite his sort of holiday or"—and he laughed—"that we're exactly his sort of family."

Monica said nothing, but Mrs. Rackham declared approvingly, "I'm sure it's a very wise decision."

"I'm glad you think so," he said, "because I was wondering if you'd mind looking after the three of them until he goes. I've suddenly remembered *Don Giovanni* comes off next week and it may not be done again for some time." He put his hand on his wife's shoulder. "Would you like to go up to the flat for two nights on our own?" he asked.

Monica nodded her head. "Yes, darling," she said. "I would."

"You'll have to wear that new pendant to celebrate," said Mrs. Rackham.

"No," said Monica, "I shan't do that. I don't think I shall ever wear that pendant. And now," she said, gathering her dressing-gown around her, "I must go and see that all Sven's clothes are properly mended. I can't have Mrs. Sodeblom thinking we didn't look after the child, she was so good to Richard," and she swept from the room.

Safe, thought Edwin, safe, thank God! But the room seemed without air, almost stifling. He threw open one of the windows and let in a refreshing breeze that blew across from the hills.

FROM

Such Darling Dodos

Such Darling Dodos

-»»×«««-

"I think it vastly disobliging in you, Cousin," said Tony, "to be at so much pains over me."

It was thirty years ago now since he had first adopted this imitation Jane Austen speech in addressing the academical branch of his family; it represented the furthest concession he felt prepared to make to the whimsical humour of North Oxford.

"I've brought you the *Times*," said Priscilla. "I hope that was right."

She was not expected to reply in the same jargon. She drew the curtains apart, letting the sunlight fall full upon her visitor as he sat up in bed. It was all that Tony could do not to scream. To be seen by anyone but Mrs. Fawcett before he had made his morning toilet was monstrous enough; to be revealed in every line and wrinkle was an outrage. Thus floodlit, he did indeed look far older than his fifty-five years, his long thin Greco features chalk-white against the crimson eiderdown, his nose, chin, and cheekbones all highlights where the sun shone upon the greasy cold cream, the artifice of the black waved hair too clearly revealed beneath the neat mesh of the slumber net. He looked with distaste at the bowl of Puffed Wheat and anticipated with dread the inevitable strong Indian tea.

"Is it all right?" said Priscilla anxiously. She stood with her

---

Written in 1948; first published in 1950; scene immediate post Second World War.

hands held awkwardly at her sides, rocking from one foot to another like a giant schoolgirl. Pathos always made her feel awkward and anxious, and at the moment she felt very deeply the
pathos of this lonely, ageing, snobbish old man whom she toler-
ated only through childhood ties. Pathos was Priscilla's dominat-
ing sensation. It had led her into Swaraj and Public Assistance
Committees, into Basque Relief and Child Psychiatry Clinics; at
the moment it kept her on a Rent Restriction Tribunal; it fixed her
emotionally as a child playing dolls' hospitals.

Tony smoothed his eyebrows with his fingers and looked at
the breakfast tray; he decided to take the remark as referring to
Priscilla's dress. "*All right,* my dear?" he said. "It's *quite* charming."

Priscilla was not surprised at the twist of the conversation; it
was so much a family tradition that Cousin Tony should know
about women's clothes and arranging flowers. Mother had always
referred to these accomplishments with a smile; it had been her
version of Father's "nincompoop." Later in the 1920s, after she
had married Robin, Priscilla herself had discussed the whole problem with him in more Freudian terms; but for the last twenty
years the family had been content to let the matter drop. The
thought that for Tony himself it must of course be still a living issue made her feel weary beyond measure. She looked down
for relief at her blue linen dress with its long, full skirt.

"Robin hates these long skirts," she said.

"My dear Priscilla," said Tony, "I should have hoped that, after
more than twenty years of matrimony, you would have ceased
to believe that men know anything whatsoever about their wives'
clothes. I should think a great deal less of dear Robin if he did
take kindly to changing fashion." Tony always put himself on
the feminine side of the fence in this way.

"You don't think the colour wrong?" asked Priscilla.

Tony closed his eyes in despair. "No, no, it's quite perfect,"
he said and reflected that, no matter how long or short, dresses on
Priscilla would always seem like hand-woven djibbahs.

With his long, bony, and blue-veined hands he spread out the

Times in front of him. It was more than he could endure to face the leaders nowadays; they were so dreadfully socialistic. Only last week he had said to his friend Mildred Brough-Owen, "I really believe that I should take the *Telegraph* if I wasn't so afraid of finding that I actually *knew* some of the curious people who announce their marriages in its columns. It would be too shaming."

"Let us see what fresh horror the government has in store for us," he said and then remembered that it was not the comforting, motherly tones of Mrs. Fawcett that would reply to him. Christian charity and good manners, he reminded himself, must be observed. After all, he was *in partibus infidelium*, the land of invincible ignorance, and he smiled to himself at his little Catholic joke.

"Ah," he went on quickly before Priscilla could protest, "this is surely the crowning horror of all. Violet Durrant's daughter is going to breed and they have the impudence to announce the fact in advance. Well, we can't say we haven't been warned. Anything more unpleasant than *that* young woman with a big belly I cannot imagine."

He often spoke in this way; it was a coarse directness that he felt to be a mark of the *grand seigneur*. It made Priscilla feel most uncomfortable, as though a curate had walked into the room naked but for his clerical collar, and yet, she reminded herself, she lived in a circle where frankness of speech was taken for granted. Tony was delighted at her embarrassment; it confirmed his cherished belief in the essentially middle-class narrowness of the university world, and, in particular, of his tiresome progressive relations.

He gazed with real distaste at Priscilla as she stood fingering the knob of the door. It was quite absurd that at over fifty she should not know what to say or when to go. With her enormous height and ample frame, her flaxen hair and bovine eyes, she was like a head prefect in the role of a Rhine maiden. Surely, he thought, there must be some delinquent child or unmarried mother to claim her attention even at this hour of the morning.

"You get more like Aunt Ethel every time I see you," he said acidly; remembering his aunt, he could think of no more satisfactory insult. But Priscilla smiled happily.

"Do you think so, Tony?" she asked. "I should be glad of that. Mother was such a very self-sufficient person. Some people thought her callous after Father died. She wasn't, of course, she felt it very deeply, but her life was too full to allow time for mourning and that sort of thing."

Too full of meddlesomeness, thought Tony, too little occupied with her duty as a mother. Maternity always wore a halo of sanctity for him.

"I doubt if we can any of us hope to be self-sufficient, Priscilla," he said. "I'm quite sure that we should be very unhappy if we were."

He had come here to help his cousin in her trouble and he was not going to be put off by sentimentality. Only his duty as a Catholic could have brought him to a house with such distasteful associations. It was something of this duty that he hoped to make clear to her.

"If Robin dies," Priscilla said, "I must be self-sufficient, you know, Tony. I'm not going to hang round Nick all the time. I've seen too many mothers like that."

"I should hope not indeed," said Tony, "though Nick, I am sure, will know his duty. No, my dear, if it's only human ties you're thinking of, I'm afraid you *will* be alone, very much alone."

Priscilla frowned. "Oh, I see what you mean," she said. "It's very kind of you, Tony dear, but don't you think God's rather a habit? I don't think I could acquire new habits at fifty. I don't mean to be shocking," she added.

Tony was delighted. Here was one of his favourite openings. He laughed gaily. "Oh, Priscilla darling, how little all these years of high thinking have done to break down your Protestant conscience. No, my dear, there's far too much real evil in the world to allow time for being shocked at human folly. I'm afraid being shocked is one of the indulgences we Catholics can't afford," and then he added less sharply, "*Fifty* years' habit, did you say? Surely, Priscilla, you can't be satisfied with a view of time which is, frankly, my dear, so provincial?"

"Provincial isn't the kind of word that affects me, Tony," said Priscilla. "It's all *my* life. There won't be so much more time, and I've been able to clear up so pitifully little of the muddle."

"Oh, my dear, if you're going to constitute yourself charwoman to the world!" His voice rose to coloratural heights and he smiled with Mona Lisa wisdom.

But Priscilla smiled too. "I'm afraid I took that job on a long time ago," she said and went out of the room.

What with the overharsh lighting and the dirty fly-blown glass of the dressing-table mirror, placed, of course, exactly where it should not have been, it took Tony quite a long time to give his skin that smooth stretched appearance, his cheeks that discreetly rosy shade with which he was accustomed to face the world, and even then he suddenly noticed a great white daub of shaving cream under the lobe of his left ear. He felt quite agitated and de-pressed as he combed the black waves into place—the side bits were no sooner tinted than they seemed to need re-doing. He sat by the window for a little, filing his nails—they were so brittle nowadays, he felt sure it was something to do with this horrible food. The front garden was as neglected and melancholy now as when he had first known it at the turn of the century. When all the other gardens of the Woodstock Road were ablaze with laburnum and lilac and red may, Courtwood always wore this lugubrious aspect—"*si triste, si morne*," he always said in de-scribing it. So often as a child he had sought relief from the op-pression of the house among the dusty golden privet and the spotted laurel bushes, the lower branches of which seemed al-ways hung with brown, dead leaves. He had sat so often on the mossy stones in the damp angles of the huge red-brick Italianate house, among broken stones and pieces of china covered by snail tracks and spiders' webs, companioned only by toads. No doubt at this very moment a few solitary Solomon's seal were in flower, to be followed later in the year by some pitiful straggling mont-bretia.

He turned from the window with a shudder. The Harkers had always been too busy to look after the house or the garden or the food; too busy, he reflected, covering reality over with reading and talking, too busy making things that were better not made and experimenting with things that should have been left alone, too busy urging rights and forgetting duties—a futile struggle to justify by works alone. And yet in their company it was *he* that always felt so very limited, so very uninteresting, so beside the point—absurdly, of course, because even before he came into the Church he had been infinitely more sensitive, more "alive to people," and afterwards—well, one must always beware of spiritual pride.

All the same, even now he had only to enter Courtwood's gates to feel dull and irrelevant. He could walk up the Woodstock Road with the sensitive approach of dear Mrs. Dalloway or the humorous eye of beloved Lizzie Bennet, and yet once past those gates his personality seemed to shrink; he would become aware of a curious, ridiculous sensation of having missed the essentials of life. He could only suppose that it was a hangover from childhood, when the great house and its occupants had loomed so large and solid above him, when his very protest against the lack of comfort and the ugliness had been made to seem petty and trivial. Safe in his bedroom, he used to pore over Richard Le Gallienne or, hidden among the laurels, bathe himself in the beauty of Beardsley's *Volpone* or Dowson's poems; but there had always been a return at last to the underboiled blue mutton, to Uncle Stephen with his telepathic communications in Ancient Greek and his White Knight electrical experiments, to Aunt Ethel protesting at the conditions of Chinese forced labour. With ears full of Stravinsky and eyes full of Bakst, he had later to suffer with a widowed Aunt Ethel as, tears in her eyes, she cast down forever the family Liberal gods and solemnly cursed Asquith and Grey for the outrage of Forcible Feeding.

Even when that dreadful guardianship was finally at an end, his visits, though more rare, more independent, had been, somehow, nonetheless humiliating. He had, for example, behaved so

well during that absurd little scene in the thirties, and yet the
memory of it was not exactly comfortable. He had entered that
awful sitting-room with its Heal's furniture, its depressingly sensible typewriter and long low bookcases, to be met by a phalanx
of grey-flannel-trousered young men and bespectacled young
women in cotton dresses busy with tea and leaflets and sandwiches for—of all enormities—these wretched, misguided Hunger
Marchers. Robin had been bustling about among them in a
butcher-blue shirt and a red tie quite unsuitable to a man of his
age with a mop of untidy white hair, and Priscilla presided like a
Roman matron in a terrible arty checked gingham dress and sandals; yet, caricatures though they looked, they had been familiar
and happy with the younger generation in a way that had made
him unaccountably envious. Of course that was the period of irresponsibility, not the gay irresponsibility of his own unregen-
erate days, but an awful, gloomy irresponsibility which was far
more dangerous, the period of that unfortunate "King and
Country" motion with its serious consequences abroad. He had
spoken most sharply to Robin—"with all your education and authority, to encourage these wretched men when the government's
doing everything it can." Robin had stared at him with his hard
blue eyes. "I think you should come and talk to them, Tony. Perhaps if you knew what was happening in Jarrow and South Wales
you would see why they needed encouragement." "I'm afraid,"
he'd answered, "that I should not feel justified in indulging my
sentimentality at the expense of the unfortunate." Then Priscilla had said abruptly, "There's no room for that sort of talk here,
Tony, at this time," and he had left. After that there had been the
Spanish War, and with the terrible outrages that he read of each
day, not only in the *Universe* but in non-Catholic papers like
the *Mail*, he had felt too angry to wish to see them.

Nevertheless, today as he made his way downstairs, almost a
slim young man in his well-cut tweeds, but for a strange stiffness in
the legs, a more kindly memory of the house came over him. The
war years had brought about a curious *rapprochement*. A
bomb exile from London, he had taken refuge in his wanderings

for a short while at the Mitre and had met his cousins by chance
one morning in The High. It had taken only a few minutes for the
memory of their disagreements to be glossed over, and then they
had found an underlying bond in their lack of enthusiasm for the
war. Tony was not, of course, unpatriotic, but he had been a great
Munichite and sometimes when he thought of the alliances we had
been led into he wondered if it was all quite wise; the Nazis were
only half the Devil, as dear Father Parrott said, and that not
the greater half. But it was more than that. He could not help
looking back with excitement to the old days of "the boys on
leave," the hectic fever of "The Bing Boys" and "Romance"
—what was it the girls had sung in that concert party? "Your arms
are our defence, our arms your recompense"—and now there
were hardly any boys on leave, only a few brave R.A.F. pilots,
and he didn't seem to know any of them. Priscilla and Robin on
their side were cast in an uncomfortably new role. They had almost literally "worked their insides out" with hastily snatched
cups of coffee and indigestible sandwiches to release Ossietsky
and imprison Mosley, for United Front and "Down the drain with
Chamberlain," but now, with Robin tied to Oxford, there was
little to do but combine with ex-colonels and Conservative ladies
in A.R.P. and W.V.S., or get hot round the collar listening to
Churchill, for it was still too early in the war to be building a
brave new world. So they really washed up together quite well for
a while, and built a little wall of family snaps and family jokes to
keep the tide of middle age from the door. Tony had almost succeeded in forgetting his fears of Courtwood in those days, almost,
but not quite.

Tony stopped cautiously at the foot of the stairs and peered
into the narrow hallway. Too often in the past he had been caught
among the mantraps that homely disorder assembled there, barking his shins upon croquet mallets or entangling himself in the
spokes of bicycle wheels. How often Uncle Stephen had mis-
quoted, "When bicycles stand in the halls"; it was one of those
little literary flippancies in which the household delighted. Everything seemed so securely smug still that Tony could hardly be-

lieve that his cousins were living in the shadow of death, and yet it was exactly that which had brought him to Courtwood on what might well be his last visit. He had been deeply and genuinely moved by Priscilla's letter, and, at the same time, had felt that faced by the reality of pain and death his relatives might surely at last take off their blinkers and stop trying to fit God's Universe to their own little home-made paper schemes. It provoked and depressed him to find so much unchanged.

Certainly Priscilla's letter had given every ground for belief that the foundations were crumbling. If pain and despair could shed forth rays of hope, then here indeed was the very sun of promise. "You will wonder, Tony, I expect, why I should write to you like this, but it seems so terrible to stand by and see him suffer and to know that I can do nothing." So she had written, and Tony reading the large sprawling handwriting had felt that his chance had come. "The doctors say the operation was a complete failure, and it is only a matter of a month or so. He is able to go on with his work for the moment, which is a great help. But there'll be a lot left over for me to finish, and I feel very proud that he is so confident of my powers. All the same I feel horribly afraid of the future loneliness—it is, I suppose, the inevitable price of our great happiness. Unfortunately I am not very good at thinking of life in terms of prices. I'm sure he would not like it if he knew I was writing all this to you, but we have agreed that there is no point in alarming Nick, as it would only be, I'm afraid, an emotional, messy sort of existence, and we're none of us very good at that"—that they should admit to "not being good" at so many things, thought Tony, was a salutary sign—"and so I'm telling you all this, Tony dear, perhaps because of the old days in the garden here and of the days on the river."

Tony could feel no warm glow of sentiment at these memories, but he reflected that there were so many roads by which a poor, weary soul could find its way to God.

"What worries me most, Tony, is that sometimes I think I've imposed my will too much upon him—you know how untidy and muddled he is, not in his thoughts, of course, but in his ways, and with his books and papers, and I—well, you know what I am. Perhaps he would have liked better just to have sat about and read and talked—been a kind of Coleridge. But I expect we all have regrets at these times; Mother used to worry about laughing at Father's old spirit-rapping. Anyhow, I take comfort from the long row of books sitting in front of me as I write—books that have influenced events too. A housing expert was down here last week and he said that Robin's work was the foundation of all they were doing, and without my system of files and indexes the work wouldn't have been done. . . ."

Tony shuddered as he read this passage; he could see the row of books so clearly—hard little bright-covered books full of facts, a dangerous array of so-called scientific knowledge that tried to treat man as a machine. How pitiful that she should still take comfort from the praise of some wretched civil servant! How pitiful that she could still believe in this illusory paradise of refrigerators for all! But still there was quite enough doubt and perplexity and contrition in the letter to give a hope of better things and so, despite Mrs. Fawcett's pleas "that he did more than enough for others" and "that Oxford never did him any good," Tony had appeared once more in the Woodstock Road.

The kindly memories of wartime hospitality were still with Tony as he entered the sitting-room, so that the aridity of taste betrayed in its furnishing did not jar upon him as much as usual. He certainly had no innate liking for oatmeal fabrics and unpolished oaks; he would have preferred *one* long low glass-fronted bookcase rather than four *walls* of them; while Marc's red horses in reproduction did not seem to him adequate pictorial decoration. But still it was an improvement on the smug, satisfied, late-Victorian ugliness of Aunt Ethel's day, a bit forbidding and austere, perhaps, but not impenetrably so—or was it that he felt some faint breath here of his own happy chromium-plated 1920s, now only permitted to be remembered as "those foolish, far-off days, my dear, when we were, I fear, as vulgar as we were misguided." Whatever the cause, he greeted Priscilla with a peculiarly gracious smile when she came in bearing a tray of cocoa and biscuits. How wise he had been to talk only of general matters during last night's depressingly inadequate meal, but now, with care and finesse, he might really succeed in saying something of what was in his mind.

"My dear, a dish of chocolate. I'm obleeged to you," he said, trying hard not to frown at the mauvish-grey liquid in his cup. "I quite forgot to tell you that I saw old Ada Lucas the other day in Knightsbridge."

"Did you?" Priscilla answered absently. She found it so difficult to concentrate on anything but Robin at the moment, and Tony's sudden appearance in the house was a particular perplexity for her.

"Yes, my dear, ten times as large as life and four hundred times as ugly. She seems to have eaten through all the alimony which she wrung out of that poor old major and is selling hats in Beauchamp Place. She bought the shop from a friend and, of *course*, there's some terrible law suit about the good will and the stock she took over. I longed to tell her that if the hat she was wearing was part of the stock, she had only to appear in court with it to prove *ill* will down to the hilt, but I couldn't get a word in edgeways. She went on and on about her frightful granddaughter— the one who was sick into Mabel Corbett's Sèvres bowl and said she thought it was a chamber—who it seems is ruling the Germans with a rod of iron. Has Nick mentioned meeting her by any chance?"

"He hasn't said anything," replied Priscilla vaguely. "I don't expect he'd be in her set at all."

"You'll send for him to come home, of course," said Tony suddenly and sharply.

"Oh, no, Tony, no," cried Priscilla, "Robin and I have talked it over. We've told him, of course, but Robin has asked him especially not to come in view of the importance of his work there. You see, he's just in the middle of reorganizing the whole teaching syllabus in the *Hochschule*."

"Priscilla darling," said Tony and he looked up at her gravely, "you'll forgive me if what I say seems impertinent, but this isn't a *game* that's happening. It's a very important, real thing."

Priscilla seemed like some huge Epstein figure seated with her legs apart, one elbow on her knee, her chin cupped in her hand.

"No, Tony, it's very far from a game," she said, "and its reality's with me every minute of the day, but it isn't *important*, at least Robin and I don't think so. It's all that Robin's done in his life that's important, not this. We've talked it over so often in the past; we're not children, you know, so we know where we stand. We've made mistakes, but on the whole we've been on the right lines; beside *that* fact, any feelings of fear or loneliness or doubt, even this beastly physical pain, are irrelevant—squalid and unnerving but irrelevant."

"You didn't feel that when you wrote to me, my dear," said Tony quietly.

"Oh, Tony, how can you?" cried his cousin. "Now that *does* shock me. To take advantage of a letter like that, the sort of wretched, hysterical outburst that one hopes so much will never happen, but which always does at these hateful, morbid times."

"So your grief was without reason then," said Tony.

"No, of course not. But that wasn't a letter of grief; it was an outburst of self-pity," answered Priscilla and then, as Tony was about to speak, she hit the arm of her chair and cried, "No, Tony, please. We shall only quarrel."

Tony got up slowly from the oatmeal sofa and stood for a moment, one hand on his corseted hip, the other fingering the rust-coloured window curtain. He gazed at the spotted laurels for some minutes and then turned suddenly towards his cousin.

"Priscilla," he said shrilly, "doesn't it mean anything to you that Robin is a Catholic?"

"A Catholic?" Priscilla asked. "I don't understand. Oh! You mean because those awful parents of his were Catholics for a time."

"No, Priscilla, there's no question of 'for a time.' Robin's parents were *Catholics*, bad Catholics, if you like, but Catholics; and Robin is a Catholic too. He was baptized into the Church."

"But, Tony, Robin didn't know anything about that, and in any case he's never given it a thought from that day to this," and as Tony's long white hands were waved in protest at her naïveté, she went on, "Oh, yes, I know what you're going to say. All about baptism and membership of the Church and Catholics having an especial grace. I'm not wholly ignorant. I've heard it all before and we've all said what strength it gave the R.C.s and how logical it was and so on and so on, and very often I've thought of you, because you're about the only Catholic I know well, and sometimes I've even envied you. But now I see what it's all about—Robin's parents passing through one of their crank phases and Robin happening to be born then and being baptized in the Catholic Church —and you apply all your same arguments by rule of thumb. That's your logic and it's just nonsense." Priscilla's heavy frame was shaking with anger. "It'll be Robin in mortal sin next, I suppose," she said.

"We're not a committee of film magnates, my dear, or whoever the people are who sit about making snap decisions," said Tony. "It's not for you nor me nor the greatest saint in the world to sit in judgment; God alone can do that. I should dispute every belief that Robin cherishes, and yours too for that matter, but if you *want* to make impertinent judgments I should say that you've escaped the contamination of your wrong-headed principles quite miraculously. You're certainly far better people than I am. But that isn't the point. Even if I thought you were the greatest sinners since Lucifer fell, it wouldn't be either here or there; no one can know the circumstances of a man's life, not even himself, perhaps. It would be easy, for example, to be led into criticism of Robin's parents in this matter, for undoubtedly they did him great wrong, but it would also be very foolish. We must recognize God's infinite wisdom and remember His infinite mercy and leave it at that. Certainly Robin himself has not lived in a world which could help him to see things clearly. After all"—and he laughed— "Courtwood is a very dark corner of pagan England. One could only pray and hope. At least so I thought, but your letter made me wonder a little."

"My letter?" echoed Priscilla.

"Yes, my dear, at the risk of annoying you I will repeat—your very human and wonderful letter. In an age in which shoddy thinking is only exceeded by shoddy living one doesn't see many marriages which come near to the meaning of Christian marriage." Tony's voice shook a little, as it did increasingly in old age when he spoke of motherhood or marriage. "Not even, I'm afraid, among those who have been privileged to know better. That's why I've always, despite our many differences, admired you and Robin. Without any guidance you've made a success of marriage that a Catholic couple might envy. You talk about your work and Robin's, but if it was all forgotten tomorrow, as I have no doubt it will be, you've created something far more enduring in the example you have given to Nick. When then, my dear, guided by a sound woman's instinct—a thing no amount of committees can entirely destroy—and by a great love, *you* express doubts about Robin's satisfaction with his life, then I *must* wonder whether perhaps that baptism, which as you say was so long ago, may not be nearer to Robin in his mind than I thought."

As Tony had been talking, Priscilla's bewilderment had grown; it seemed to her as though he was an embodiment of all that people thought of one without one's guessing. He was a nice old thing, and if it had not been so inopportune a time she would have been glad to see him, but he had nothing to do with her life or Robin's, and yet this strange story about them had been going on in his head, even impelling him to leave the comfort of his London flat for the discomfort of their home. She felt exhausted at all the endless projections of herself and Robin that she suddenly saw before her, living out their strange and separate existences in the minds of their friends. Mechanically she said, "I don't understand, Tony. What doubts? though she could guess wearily at what he would say in answer.

"The doubts, dearest Priscilla, that you so typically described as 'wishing he might have been a Coleridge,' though why you should have to drag Coleridge in, only your staunch North Oxford spirit can explain."

Priscilla got up from her chair and began to replace the cups on the tray. "I said Coleridge, you know, because I meant Coleridge, that and nothing more. You've done so many acrobatics inside your squirrel's cage that you've quite forgotten all the antics a monkey can get up to in a bigger one." She spoke as though reproving a precocious child. "The dreams and ambitions of what you call souls, Tony, are so many more than you seem to allow for. When I wrote to you that day, I had been watching Robin's imagination at work building patterns and shapes, some of them rather vague and overelaborate, but all of them rather interesting. It was one of his talkative days, and I thought of how he might have been a Coleridge instead of a good economist. But it wasn't very sensible of me really, because even if a Coleridge or a Wilde could expand today, I doubt if Robin would consider it either the time or the place in history."

"Certainly not for both of them at once." The directness of Priscilla's priggishness was always cloaked in Robin by a whimsicality, but his voice since his illness was less buoyant, more flat. Both Tony and his wife stared at him, and indeed to Tony his cadaverous appearance was a great shock, for he had always secretly admired his cousin's youthful grace. Now, however, the boyish head was like a skull surmounted by a plume of white feathers, and the emaciation of his body was emphasized by his student style of dress. The Adam's apple showed grotesquely above the open neck of his blue linen shirt; even his feet looked pitifully bony in their leather sandals.

"Tony says you're worried about being a Catholic and not having been one," said Priscilla defiantly. Tony moved his hand in protest, but she disregarded him. "*Do* you ever think about it, Robin? It's nonsense, isn't it?"

In personal matters, Robin was as pacific as his wife was pugnacious; only over social injustice did he ever lose control of his feelings.

"That was kind of you, Tony," he said.

"Kind? What do you mean?" asked Priscilla genuinely, for she was always ready to believe that her husband understood something of which she was ignorant.

"Well, perhaps not kind, but dutiful, and that's really more to the point," Robin replied.

"I know you'll understand my saying, Robin," Tony intervened, "that the whole matter is hardly one to be discussed in this way. Anyhow, it was foolish of me to intervene. If you wanted such help there are people far more qualified than I am. People to whom I should be glad to introduce you."

"Thank you," said Robin. "Yes, of course, it's a serious matter, but I should like to ask what gave you the idea?"

"A stupid letter I wrote," said Priscilla.

"Letter? What letter?" said Robin, and then regretted the question. In his present tired and painful condition he did not wish to touch any deep levels that affected his relations with Priscilla; he would prefer to let their marriage fade out on the same relatively successful plane on which it had always existed.

"A silly, hysterical, self-pitying letter. I wrote it in a state after Dr. Mainwaring left."

"It was a very moving letter," said Tony.

"It was good of you to be moved by it," answered Robin icily. It was the greatest anger he felt prepared to allow to his shattered body.

"I wrote it after you had been talking so brilliantly on Friday evening," his wife went on, "and I thought perhaps all my making you orderly and tidy had stopped you from being a great conversationalist like Coleridge and Wilde. It was silly of me, I know."

"I think it was rather sweet," said Robin, "but you need have no fears. I have never envied Coleridge; opium has never attracted me. As for Wilde"—he smiled across at Tony—"I've never had any inclination that way either. But I still don't really understand."

"Oh! Of course, as soon as Tony saw the letter, he thought you might be in doubt about what you'd done in life and then he imagined all this business about the Church."

"Well, darling," said Robin, "it was possibly a more constructive idea than Coleridge and Wilde. I'm afraid though, Tony, that I remain satisfied not with the amount I have done, God forbid, but with the kind."

"Satisfied with drains and baths and refrigerators?" Tony asked.

"Yes," said Robin, "only with more of them and better ones, and with sickness benefits and secure old age and works committees and"—here he smiled again—"the just wage. Strangely enough I did re-read William James the other day, but I'm sorry to say in all that welter of religious experience I could find nothing to accord with anything I had ever known. I'm sorry, Tony." He returned to Priscilla jovially. "You've forgotten, darling, that that young couple are coming for a drink before lunch."

"Oh, dear," Priscilla cried, "all these young people are so awful."

Tony welcomed the diversion as much as his hosts. "What's this heresy?" he asked. "You to speak ill of the young?"

"Well, they *are,*" said Priscilla, glad to take up a more social tone. "The undergraduates since the war have been absolutely bloody," and she rounded her eyes in childish defiance.

"Priscilla means that their opinions do not accord with ours," said Robin.

The social occasion proved most sticky. It would have taken more than Michael and Harriet Eccleston's rather prim presence to clear the emotional air. There were long silences in which glasses were twiddled and cigarettes refused. Neither Robin nor Priscilla could think of much to ask about Michael Eccleston's experiences in the desert or in Italy, and Tony racked his brain for another possible Wren officer colleague of Harriet's. The failure of his visit had brought all his old feelings of inadequacy back to him; Courtwood's triumph was complete. At least, however, on this occasion he could not be said to be out of things, for there was really nothing to be in. Robin and Priscilla were as ill at ease as he was, and they seemed determined to confine the conversation to the war—surely, he thought, with a new one in the offing, we could regard the last one as dead.

Gradually little undertones in the talk gave him the clue; they were deliberately avoiding general issues. Experience had taught them, as Robin had said, that undergraduate opinions did not accord with theirs. Poor Robin and Priscilla, how much they must hate that, and they were too tired to fight the younger generation. Only gradually did the converse dawn on him, however, that at last *he* was on youth's side. When Robin remarked that Michael must find chapel a bore, the young man stroked his moustache and murmured that he doubted if boredom was a possible reaction when something of the kind was so badly needed. Harriet too wondered if freedom was quite the issue when one looked at India; after all, responsibility was important. They *both* wondered about the death penalty—wasn't abolition rather an easy luxury in the face of social duty? Tony began to purr; he might have been back in Knightsbridge. In desperation Robin got out old snaps, in some of which Harriet's father, a former colleague of his, appeared.

"Oh, look, Michael," cried Harriet, "there's one of Daddy carrying an incredible banner. He wouldn't dare to show *that* at home."

There were photographs of Robin as a conscientious objector farm labourer in 1916, and pictures of Priscilla and himself relaxing at Fabian Summer Schools in Buxton and Brighton and Exeter. There was Robin with a Social-Democrat mayor being shown the Karl Marx Haus in Vienna—

"One of the few good things the Duke of Windsor did was to insist on seeing that, after Dollfuss came to power," said Robin.

"Rather irresponsible, wasn't it, sir?" asked Michael.

There were United Front groups—

"You don't look very united," said Harriet. "You look as though you were about to bite each other."

There were even pictures of the famous rally to feed the Hunger Marchers—

"I should have thought that sort of approach was rather theatrical in dealing with a national problem," remarked Michael.

"They were starving in Wales and in the north," said Priscilla savagely. "They wanted people down here to know about it."

Harriet said, "Oh, of course. No one would blame *them*. Only it seems so terrible that political capital should have been made out of their misery."

"Like the Tories did out of the General Strike," said Robin.

"Well, after all, two wrongs don't make a right. Anyhow, I think party politics are rather a dirty game." Michael was quite the gruff ex-officer.

"Yes," Priscilla answered, "so did Hitler."

They managed, however, to end the occasion on an easier note.

As Tony was to lunch at Balliol, he walked with the Ecclestons as far as St. Giles'. He felt completely at ease now; if the house still defeated him on the deeper levels, he had won a complete victory on more surface issues, and really, he reflected, to gain the support of young Oxford in his cousins' own home was the capture of an inner citadel. He had not even needed to voice his agreement with the Ecclestons; the atmosphere had been redolent with sympathies. But now he spoke.

"Of course," he said, "you realize that darling Priscilla and Robin were not representative of my generation. A good many of us thought quite differently."

"Oh, naturally, sir," said Michael. He loved old-world manners.

"I think it's rather pathetic," said Harriet, "and I suppose they *did* do very good work in a way."

"I am afraid," said Michael, "that so much of it was sentimentalism of a rather dangerous kind. You can't get past Munich, you know."

Even Tony realized there was some confusion here, but still it was on the right lines, so he did not contradict.

"I suppose it's always the same when people live in the past," said Harriet in a satisfied tone.

"Yes indeed," replied Tony. "Poor Robin and Priscilla are extinct, I'm afraid." He hadn't felt so modern since the first production of *L'Après Midi*.

"They're dodos really, but," he added more kindly, "such darling dodos."

A Little Companion

✦⇒⇒⟩⟨⟨⟨✦

They say in the village that Miss Arkwright has never been the same since the war broke out, but she knows that it all began a long time before that—on 24th July, 1936, to be exact, the day of her forty-seventh birthday.

She was in no way a remarkable person. Her appearance was not particularly distinguished and yet she was without any feature that could actively displease. She had enough personal eccentricities to fit into the pattern of English village life, but none so absurd or anti-social that they could embarrass or even arouse gossip beyond what was pleasant to her neighbours. She accepted her position as an old maid with that cheerful good humour and occasional irony which are essential to English spinsters since the deification of Jane Austen, or more sacredly Miss Austen, by the upper middle classes, and she attempted to counteract the inadequacy of the unmarried state by quiet, sensible, and tolerant social work in the local community. She was liked by nearly everyone, though she was not afraid of making enemies where she knew that her broad but deeply felt religious principles were being opposed. Any socially pretentious or undesirably extravagant conduct, too, was liable to call forth from her an unexpectedly caustic and well-aimed snub. She was invited everywhere and always accepted the invitations. You could see her at every tea or cocktail

---

Written in 1949; first published in 1950; scene laid in two years immediately before the outbreak of the Second World War.

party, occasionally drinking a third gin, but never more. Quietly but well dressed, with one or two very fine old pieces of jewellery that had come down to her from her grandmother, she would pass from one group to another, laughing or serious as the occasion demanded. She smoked continuously her own, rather expensive, brand of cigarettes—"My one vice," she used to say, "the only thing that stands between me and secret drinking." She listened with patience, but with a slight twinkle in the eye, to Mr. Hodgson's endless stories of life in Dar-es-Salaam or Myra Hope's breathless accounts of her latest system of diet. John Hobday in his somewhat ostentatiously gentleman-farmer attire would describe his next novel about East Anglian life to her before even his beloved daughter had heard of it. Richard Trelawney, just down from Oxford, found that she had read and really knew Donne's sermons, yet she could swap detective stories with Colonel Wright by the hour, and was his main source for quotations when the *Times* crossword was in question.

She it was who incorporated little Mrs. Grantham into village life, when that rather underbred, suburban woman came there as Colonel Grantham's second wife, checking her vulgar remarks about "the lower classes" with kindly humour but defending her against the formidable battery of Lady Vernon's antagonism. Yet she it was also who was first at Lady Vernon's when Sir Robert had his stroke, and her unobtrusive kindliness and real services gained her a singular position behind the grim reserve of the Vernon family. She could always banter the vicar away from his hobby horse of the Greek Rite when at parish meetings the agenda seemed to have been buried forever beneath a welter of Euchologia and Menaia. She checked Sir Robert's anti-Bolshevik phobia from victimizing the county librarian for her Fabianism, but was fierce in her attack on the local council when she thought that class prejudice had prevented Commander Osborne's widow from getting a council house. She led in fact an active and useful existence, yet when anyone praised her she would only laugh. "My dear," she would say, "hard work's the only excuse old maids like me have got for existing at all, and even then I don't know that they oughtn't to lethalize the lot of us." As the danger of war grew nearer in the thirties her favourite remark was, "Well, if they've got any sense this time they'll keep the young fellows at home and put us useless old maids in the trenches," and she said it with real conviction.

With her good carriage, ample figure, and large deep-blue eyes, she even began to acquire a certain beauty as middle age approached. People speculated as to why she had never married. She had in fact refused a number of quite personable suitors. The truth was that from girlhood she had always felt a certain repulsion from physical contact. Not that she was in any way prudish; she was remarkable for a rather eighteenth-century turn of coarse phrase. Indeed, verbal freedom was the easier for her in that sexual activity was the more remote. Nor would psychoanalysts have found anything of particular interest in her; she had no abnormal desires. As a child she had never felt any wish to change her sex or observed any peculiarly violent or crude incident that could have resulted in what is called a psychic trauma. She just wasn't interested, and was perhaps as a result a little overgiven to talking of "all this fuss and nonsense that's made over sex." She would, however, have liked to have had a child. She recognized this as a common phenomenon among childless women and accepted it, though she could never bring herself to admit it openly or laugh about it in the common-sensical way in which she treated her position as an old maid. As the middle years approached she found a sudden interest and even sometimes a sudden jealousy over other people's babies and children growing upon her, attacking her unexpectedly and with apparent irrelevancy to time or place. She was equally wide-awake to the dangers of the late forties and resolutely resisted such foolish fancies, though she became as a result a little snappish and overgruff with the very young. "Now, my dear," she told herself, "you *must* deal with this nonsense or you'll start getting odd." How very odd she could not guess.

The Granthams always gave a little party for her on her birthdays. "Awful nonsense at my age," she had been saying now for many years, "but I never say no to a drink." Her forty-seventh birthday party was a particular success. Mary Hatton was staying with the Granthams and, like Miss Arkwright, she was an ardent Janeite, so they'd been able to talk Mr. Collins and Mrs. Elton and the Elliots to their hearts' content; then Colonel Grantham had given her some tips about growing meconopsis, and finally Mrs. Osborne had been over to see the new rector at Longhurst, so they had a good-natured but thoroughly enjoyable "cat" about the state of the rectory there. She was just paying dutiful attention to her hostess's long complaint about the grocery deliveries, preparatory to saying good-bye, when suddenly a thin, whining, but remarkably clear child's voice said loudly in her ear, "Race you home, Mummy." She looked around her in surprise, then decided that her mind must have wandered from the boring details of Mrs. Grantham's saga, but almost immediately the voice sounded again. "Come on, Mummy, you are a slowcoach. I said, 'Race you home.'" This time Miss Arkwright was seriously disturbed. She wondered if Colonel Grantham's famous high spirits had got the better of him, but it could hardly have been so, she thought, as she saw his face earnest in conversation—"The point is, Vicar, not so much whether we want to intervene as whether we've got to." She began to feel most uncomfortable, and as soon as politeness allowed she made her way home.

The village street seemed particularly hot and dusty, the sunlight on the whitewashed cottages peculiarly glaring as she walked along. "One too many on a hot day, that's your trouble, my dear," she said to herself and felt comforted by so material an explanation. The familiar trimness of her own little house and the cool shade of the walnut tree on the front lawn further calmed her nerves. She stopped for a moment to pick up a basket of lettuce that old Pyecroft had left at the door and then walked in. After the sunlight outside, the hall seemed so dark that she could hardly discern even the shape of the grandfather clock. Out of this shadowy blackness came the child's voice loudly and clearly but, if anything, more nasal than before. "Beat you to it this time," it said. Miss Arkwright's heart stopped for a moment and her lungs seemed to contract, and then almost instantaneously she had seen it—a little white-faced boy, thin, with matchstick arms and legs growing out of shrunken clothes, with red-rimmed eyes and an adenoidal open-mouthed expression. Instantaneously, because the next moment he was not there, almost like a flickering image against the eye's retina. Miss Arkwright straightened her back, took a deep breath; then she went upstairs, took off her shoes, and lay down on her bed.

It was many weeks before anything fresh occurred, and she felt happily able to put the whole incident down to cocktails and the heat; indeed, she began to remember that she had woken next morning with a severe headache—"You're much too old to start suffering from hangovers," she told herself. But the next experience was really more alarming. She had been up to London to buy a wedding present at Harrods and, arriving somewhat late for the returning train, found herself sitting in a stuffy and overpacked carriage. She felt therefore particularly pleased to see the familiar slate quarries that heralded the approach of Brankston Station, when suddenly a sharp dig drove the bones of her stays into her ribs. She looked with annoyance at the woman next to her— a blowsy creature with feathers in her hat—when she saw to her surprise that the woman was quietly asleep, her arms folded in front of her. Then in her ears there sounded, "Chuff, chuff, chuff, chuff," followed by a little snort and a giggle, and then quite unmistakably the whining voice saying, "Rotten old train."

After that it seemed to her as though for a few moments pandemonium had broken loose in the carriage—shouts and cries and a monotonous thumping against the woodwork as though someone were beating an impatient rhythm with his foot—yet no other occupant seemed in the slightest degree disturbed. They were for Miss Arkwright moments of choking and agonizing fear. She dreaded that at any minute the noise would grow so loud that the others would notice, for she felt an inescapable responsibility for the incident. Yet had the whole carriage risen and flung her from the window as a witch it would in some degree have been a release from the terrible sense of personal obsession; it would have given objective reality to what now seemed an uncontrollable expansion of her own consciousness into space; it would at the least have shown that others were mad beside herself. But no slightest ripple broke the drowsy torpor of the hot carriage in the August sun. She was deeply relieved when the train at last drew into Brankston and the impatience of her invisible attendant was assuaged, but no sooner had she set foot on the platform than she heard once more the almost puling whine, the too familiar, "Race you home, Mummy." She knew then that whatever it was, it had come to stay, that her home-comings would no longer be to the familiar comfort of her house and servants, but that there would always be a childish voice, a childish face to greet her for one moment as she crossed the threshold.

And so it proved. Gradually at first, at more than weekly intervals, and then increasingly, so that even a short spell in the vegetable garden or with the rock plants would mean impatient whining, wanton scattering of precious flowers, overturning of baskets—and then that momentary vision, lengthened now sometimes to five minutes' duration, that sickly, cretinous face. The very squalor of the child's appearance was revolting to Miss Arkwright, for whom cheerful good health was the first of human qualities. Sometimes the sickliness of the features would be of the thick, flaccid, pasty appearance that suggested rich feeding and late hours, and then the creature would be dressed in a velvet suit and Fauntleroy collar that might have clothed an over-indulged French bourgeois child; at other times the appearance was more cretinous, adenoidal and emaciated, and then it would wear the shrunken uniform and thick black boots of an institution idiot. In either case it was a child quite out of keeping with the home it sought to possess—a home of quiet beauty, unostentatious comfort, and restrained good taste. Of course, Miss Arkwright argued, it was an emanation from the sick side of herself so that it was bound to be diseased, but this realization did not compensate for dribble marks on her best dresses or for sticky finger marks on her tweed skirts.

At first she tried to ignore the obsession with her deep reserve of stoic patience, but as it continued, she felt the need of the

Church. She became a daily communicant and delighted the more
"spikey" of her neighbours. She prayed ceaselessly for release or
resignation. A lurking sense of sin was roused in her, and she wondered if small frivolities and pleasures were the cause of her visitation; she remembered that after all it had first begun when she
was drinking gin. Her religion had always been of the "brisk" and
"sensible" variety, but now she began to fear that she had been
over-suspicious of "enthusiasm" or "pietism." She gave up all but
the most frugal meals, distributed a lot of her clothes to the poor,
slept on a board, and rose at one in the morning to say a special
Anglican office from a little book she had once been given by a
rather despised High Church cousin. The only result seemed to
be to cause scandal to her comfortable, old-fashioned parlour-
maid and cook. She mentioned her state of sin in general terms to
the vicar, and he lent her Neale's translations of the Coptic and
Nestorian rites, but they proved of little comfort. At Christmas
she rather shamefacedly and secretively placed a little bed with a
richly filled stocking in the corner of her bedroom, but the child
was not to be blackmailed. Throughout the day she could hear
faint but unsavory sounds of uncontrolled and slovenly guzzling,
like the distant sound of pigs feeding, and when evening came
she was pursued by ever louder retching and the disturbing smell
of vomit.

On Boxing Day she visited her old and sensible friend the bishop
and told him the whole story. He looked at her very steadily with
the large, dramatic brown eyes that were so telling in the pulpit,
and for a long time he remained silent. Miss Arkwright hoped
that he would advise her quickly, for she could feel a growing
tugging at her skirt. It was obvious that this quiet, spacious library
was no place for a child, and she could not have borne to see these
wonderful old books disturbed even if she was the sole observer
of the sacrilege.

At last the bishop spoke. "You say that the child appears ill and
depraved. Has this evil appearance been more marked in the last
weeks?" Miss Arkwright was forced to admit that it had. "My
dear old friend," said the bishop, and he put his hand on hers. "It

is your sick self that you are seeing, and all this foolish abstinence, this extravagant martyrdom are making you more sick." The bishop was a great Broad Churchman of the old school. "Go out into the world and take in its beauty and its colour. Enjoy what is yours and thank God for it." And without more ado, he persuaded Miss Arkwright to go to London for a few weeks.

Established at Berners', she set out to have a good time. She was always fond of expensive meals, but her first attempt to indulge at Claridge's proved an appalling failure, for with every course the voice grew louder and louder in her ears. "Coo! what rotten stuff," it kept on repeating, "I want an ice." Henceforth her meals were taken almost exclusively on Selfridge's roof or in ice-cream parlours, an unsatisfying and indigestible diet. Visits to the theatre were at first a greater success. She saw the new adaptation of *The Mill on the Floss*, and a version of *Lear* modelled on the original Kean production. The child had clearly never seen a play before and was held entranced by the mere spectacle. But soon it began to grow restless. A performance of *Hedda Gabler* was entirely ruined by rustlings, kicks, whispers, giggles, and a severe bout of hiccoughs. For a time it was kept quiet by musical comedies and farces, but in the end Miss Arkwright found herself attending only *Where the Rainbow Ends*, *Mother Goose*, and *Buckie's Bears*—it was not a sophisticated child. As the run of Christmas plays drew near their end she became desperate, and one afternoon she left a particularly dusty performance at the Circus and visited her old friend Madge Cleaver—once again to tell all. "Poor Bessie," said Madge Cleaver, and she smiled so spiritually, "how real Error can seem," for Madge was a Christian Scientist. "But it's so *un*real, dear, if we can only have the courage to see the Truth. Truth denies Animal Magnetism, Spiritualism, and all other false manifestations." She lent Miss Arkwright *Science and Health* and promised that she would give her "absent treatment."

At first Miss Arkwright felt most comforted. Mrs. Eddy's denial of the reality of most common phenomena and in particular of those that are evil seemed to offer a way out. Unfortunately, the child seemed quite unconvinced of its own non-existence. One

afternoon Miss Arkwright thought with horror that by adopting
a theology that denied the existence of Matter and gave reality
only to Spirit she might well be gradually removing herself from
the scene, while leaving the child in possession. After all, her
own considerable bulk was testimony enough to her material nature, while the child might well in some repulsive way be ac-
counted spirit. Terrified by the prospect before her, she speedily
renounced Christian Science.

She returned to her home and by reaction decided to treat the
whole phenomenon on the most material basis possible. She submitted her body to every old-fashioned purgative; she even indulged in a little amateur blood-letting, for might not the creature
be some ill humour or sickly emanation of the body itself? But
this antiquarian leechcraft only produced serious physical weakness and collapse. She was forced to call in Dr. Kent, who at once
terminated the purgatives and put her on to port wine and beef-
steak.

Failure of material remedies forced Miss Arkwright at last to a
conviction which she had feared from the start. The thing, she
decided, must be a genuine psychic phenomenon. It cost her much
to admit this, for she had always been very contemptuous of
spiritualism and regarded it as socially undesirable where it was
not consciously fraudulent. But she was by now very desperate
and willing to waive the deepest prejudices to free herself from
the vulgar and querulous apparition. For a month or more she attended seances in London, but though she received "happy" communications from enough small Indian or Red Indian children to
have started a nursery school, no medium or clairvoyant could
tell her anything that threw light on her little companion. At one
of the seances, however, she met a thin, red-haired, pre-Raphaelite
sort of lady in a long grey garment and sandals, who asked her to
attend the Circle of the Seventh Pentacle in the Earllands Road.
The people she found there did not attract Miss Arkwright; she
decided that the servants of the Devil were either common frauds
or of exceedingly doubtful morals, but the little group was enthusiastic when she told her story. How could she hope to fight

such Black Powers, they asked, unless she was prepared to invoke
the White Art? Although she resisted their arguments at first, she
finally found herself agreeing to a celebration of the Satanic Mass
in her own home. She sent cook and Annie away for a week and
prepared to receive the Circle. Their arrival in the village caused a
great stir, partly because of their retinue of goats and rabbits. It
had been decided that Miss Arkwright should celebrate the Mass
herself. An altar had been set up in the drawing room; she had
bought an immense white maternity gown from Debenham's and
had been busy all the week learning her words, but at the last
minute something within her rebelled. She could not bring herself to say the Lord's Prayer backwards and the Mass had to be
called off. In the morning the devotees of the Pentacle left with
many recriminations. The only result seemed to be that valuable
ornaments were missing from the bedrooms occupied by the less
reputable, while about those rooms in which the Devil's true servants had slept there hung an odour of goat that no fumigation
could remove.

Miss Arkwright had long since given up visiting her neighbours, though they had not ceased to speculate about her. A
chance remark that she had "two now to provide for" had led
them to think that she believed herself pregnant. After this last
visitation Lady Vernon decided that the time had come to act.
She visited Miss Arkwright early one morning and, seeing the
maternity gown which was still lying in the sitting-room, she was
confirmed in her suspicions. "Bessie dear," she said, "you've got
to realize that you're seriously ill, mentally ill," and she packed
Miss Arkwright off to a brain specialist in Welbeck Street. This
doctor, finding nothing physically wrong, sent her to a psychoanalyst. Poor Miss Arkwright! She was so convinced of her own insanity that she could think of no argument if they should wish to
shut her up. But the analyst, a smart, grey-haired Jew, laughed
when she murmured "madness." "We don't talk in those terms
any more, Miss Arkwright. You're a century out of date. It's true
there are certain disturbing psychotic features in what you tell
me, but nothing, I think, that won't yield to deep analysis," and

deep analysis she underwent for eight months or more, busily writing down dreams at night and lying on a couch "freely associating" by day.

At the end of that time the analyst began to form a few conclusions. "The child itself," he said, "is unimportant; the fact that you still see it even less so. What is important is that you now surround yourself with vulgarity and whining. You have clearly a need for these things which you have inhibited too long in an atmosphere of refinement." It was decided that Miss Arkwright should sublimate this need by learning the saxophone. Solemnly each day the poor lady sat in the drawing-room—that room which had resounded with Bach and Mozart—and practised the alto sax. At last one day when she had got so far as to be able to play the opening bars of "Alligator Stomp," her sense of the ridiculous rebelled and she would play no more, though her little companion showed great restlessness at the disappearance of noises which accorded all too closely with its vulgar taste.

I shall treat myself, she decided, and after long thought she came to the conclusion that the most salient feature of the business lay in the child's constant reiteration of the challenge "Race you home, Mummy"; with this it had started and with this it had continued. If, thought Miss Arkwright, I were to leave home completely, not only this house but also England, then perhaps it would withdraw its challenge and depart.

In January 1938, then, she set out on her travels. All across Europe, in museums and cafés and opera houses, it continued to throw down the gauntlet—"Race you home, Mummy"—and there it would be in her hotel bedroom. It seemed, however, anxious to take on local colour and would appear in a diversity of national costumes, often reviving for the purpose peasant dresses seen only at folk-dance festivals or when worn by beggars in order to attract tourists. For Miss Arkwright this rather vulgar and commercial World's Fair aspect of her life was particularly distressing. The child also attempted to alter its own colour, pale brown it achieved in India, in China a faint tinge of lemon, and in America, by some misunderstanding of the term Red Indian, it emerged bright scarlet. She was especially horrified by the purple swelling with which it attempted to emulate the black of the African natives. But whatever its colour, it was always there.

At last the menace of war in September found Miss Arkwright in Morocco, and along with thousands of other British travellers she hurried home, carrying, she felt, her greatest menace with her. It was only really after Munich that she became reconciled to its continued presence, learning gradually to incorporate its noises, its appearance, its whole personality into her daily life. She went out again among her neighbours and soon everyone had forgotten that she had ever been ill. It was true that she was forced to address her companion occasionally with a word of conciliation, or to administer a slap in its direction when it was particularly provoking, but she managed to disguise these peculiarities beneath her normal gestures.

One Saturday evening in September 1939 she was returning home from the rectory, worried by the threat of approaching war and wondering how she could best use her dual personality to serve her country, when she was suddenly disturbed to hear a clattering of hoofs and a thunderous bellow behind her. She turned to see, at some yards distance, a furious bull charging down the village street. She began immediately to run for her home, the little voice whining in her ear, "Race you home, Mummy." But the bull seemed to gain upon her, and in her terror she redoubled her speed, running as she had not run since she was a girl. She heard, it is true, a faint sighing in her ears as of dying breath, but she was too frightened to stop until she was safe at her own door. In she walked and, to her amazement, indeed to her horror, look where she would, the little child was *not* there. She had taken up his challenge to a race and she had won.

She lay in bed that night depressed and lonely. She realized only too clearly that difficult as it was to get rid of him—now that the child was gone she found herself thinking of "him" rather than "it"—it would be well-nigh impossible to get him back. The sirens that declared war next morning seemed only a confirmation of her personal loss. She went into mourning and rarely emerged from the house. For a short while, it is true, her spirits were re-vived when the evacuee children came from the East End; some of the more cretinous and adenoidal seemed curiously like her lost one. But country air and food soon gave them rosy cheeks and sturdy legs and she rapidly lost her interest. Before the year was out she was almost entirely dissociated from the external world, and those few friends who found time amid the cares of war to visit her in her bedroom decided that there was little that could be done for one who showed so little response. The vicar, who was busy translating St. Gregory Nazianzen's prayers for victory, spoke what was felt to be the easiest and kindest verdict when he described her as "just another war casualty."

Learning's Little Tribute

➤➤➤◄◄◄

As soon as the clergyman had murmured his last word over the coffin, Miss Wells was scuttling with almost unseemly haste down the yew-lined avenue towards the cemetery gates. It was one of her misfortunes that, though well equipped with the proper rules of conduct in life, she too often spoiled their effect in her anxiety to show her knowledge of them. It was right, of course, to leave the relatives to their private grief, but not perhaps at the double. Her haste was, however, dictated in part by the extreme cold, for though a glorious sunny day for January there was yet a bitter east wind and Miss Wells was above everything delicate. In part, also, she was genuinely moved to tears; she had not known Hugh Craddock well—just the ordinary requests for her services in typing and proof-reading—but the thought that he had died with his contribution to the great work still unfinished and the sight of the other encyclopædists gathered round the graveside, so noble, yet themselves no longer young and all too liable to be snatched away, were overmuch for her susceptible emotions. The little bows and ribbons with which she was decorated shook and trembled, the lucky charm bracelets and semi-precious necklaces jangled as she searched among the debris of memo notes, lipstick ends, and loose powder for her lace-bordered handkerchief. Who,

Written in 1948; first published in 1950; scene immediate post Second World War.

she wondered, could possibly take over "Art" now that Mr. Craddock was gone?

The same question was disturbing Dr. Earley, the assistant editor, as with solemn but springy steps he walked along the gravel pathway in conversation with the chief, attentive and deferential as befitted a subordinate, yet independent and forceful as was correct for an up-and-coming figure in the world of popular scholarship.

"It isn't easy, Brunton," he said, and his voice with its over-elocutionized vowels ill concealing their cockney origin sounded like some nineteenth-century roadside preacher, "to think of the world without Hugh Craddock. So modest and unobtrusive"—even at such a time he found it difficult to use these words without a slight note of contempt—"yet so painstaking and devoted a scholar. But however little we may wish to do so"—and here he felt himself free to resume a more jolly, ringing, confident tone, less denominational, more that of the popular radio lay preacher—"we have to think of the living, of those who are left behind, of his family, and of what—and perhaps only those of us who are scholars can understand this—was as dear to him as any wife or child, his work upon the encyclopædia. Poor Craddock! Thank God that a few of us at least were privileged to know something of what he proposed to do had he been spared."

Mr. Brunton's sharp little eyes glanced cynically for a moment from his heavy, blue-jowled face. "Yes, Earley," he said bitterly, "*I* shall have to think of the living. I have indeed already done so. But for the moment, if you please, I would like to allow my thoughts to remain with the dead."

The bitter east wind seemed to cut through all the warm pullovers with which his valet had provided him, through all the comfortable layers of fat which protected his body. Neither his wealth nor his everyday, jog-along common sense were sufficient guards against fears of mortality in such a setting. Never had he felt so cynical and contemptuous towards his subordinates, never so bitterly aware of the paltry nature of his "scholarly" hobby. He almost regretted that his autocratic character had prevented him from investing in some enterprise of real learning, even though he would have been forced to assume a less dominant role. At such a moment he felt painfully conscious of the truth of that title of the "Mæcenas of Hacks" which his enemies had given him. The quick intelligence which had brought him to the front rank of commerce had always prevented him from taking at their own valuation the imitation scholars with whom he had surrounded himself in launching *The People's History of the World*, the *Digest of Great Sayings*, and now *The Universal Encyclopædia of the Humanities*; but today at the grave of the only one of them for whom he had felt any respect and with the clay and worms of his own flesh threatening him so disturbingly, he was ready to bark and bluster at these self-deceiving, ambitious shams as he would at any secretary or clerk in his great City offices. At the sight of Miss Wells' tearful features, however, he softened. Her pathetic, disinterested belief in the great work for which she was proud to act as general dog's-body could only arouse an amused pity.

"Now don't you catch cold, Miss Wells. One corpse is enough for today, you know," he said and, moved by the shocked convention which she tried to conceal out of deference for his greatness, he added, "Poor Craddock. I should be content if I thought we could any of us know one-tenth of the happiness that *he* got from his work."

"Ah, yes, indeed. That at least must be a comfort to us."

Dr. Earley's unctuous cockney whine broke into his chief's words as the canting tones of some Puritan divine must often have broken into Cromwell's reflections and with much the same effect.

"I was thinking the same thing myself as I stood by the graveside of our dear friend and listened to those simple old words which were yet so poignant, perhaps *because* of their very simplicity, perhaps *because* we have heard them so often. We have suffered a great loss. But he? I wonder. He lived so much in the world of beauty, among his pictures and his cathedrals. No, I don't think he will suffer much from the loss of mere material things. Except, of course," he added hurriedly, "the separation from his dear ones. And them"—he took Miss Wells' hand and assured any possible doubts that might beset her by the steady gaze of his clear blue eyes—"and them he will see again."

It was typical of Dr. Earley that he should so soon cut across his chief's mood once more. The dramatic possibilities of the occasion were more than he could bear to forgo. Though he had forsaken the cruder aspects of Nonconformity for a wider, more all-embracing transcendentalism—he called it Christian humanism—as his devotion to the great heritage of English letters had advanced him in the social scale, there were still two Chadband marks upon him—his morbid curiosity and his histrionic moralizing.

"You will not, I know," he went on, "mistake the very deep nature of the grief that I feel, 'Thoughts that do often lie too deep for tears' "—and whatever might seem deficient in the quotation was amply compensated by the nobility of his handsome head with its mane of white hair as he uttered it—"when I say that it is with his dear ones, poor Mrs. Craddock, that boy and that girl, that my thoughts lie so closely today. The last days, I believe, were most harrowing. Great pain and an all too lively consciousness . . ." He spoke with relish. "Our poor friend, I fear, must have been oppressed by the thought of the circumstances in which he would be leaving those he loved. He had all that generous improvidence which we proverbially associate with the world of art which he so loved."

He allowed his listeners a slight twinkle of the eye at this mention of the childlike nature of artists, but there was bitterness in the tone of his voice as he recalled the disadvantageous light in which his late colleague's generosity had placed his own innate meanness. "I am not personally acquainted with the family, yet it would give me great pleasure to do all that I can to assist them" —and only by the twist of his smile did he allow his scepticism of such a possibility to appear.

"That's very good of you, Earley," said Mr. Brunton. "I may say now that I have certain schemes in mind and I shall not hesitate to call upon your generous promise."

Dr. Earley's Adam's apple wobbled slightly above the points

of the Gladstone collar with which, with morning coat and striped trousers, he habitually clothed the dignity of his old-world charm. "But of course, my dear friend," he said hurriedly, "I do beg also that you will not trouble yourself about the question of the Art Section of our little work." It was characteristic of him that where the others habitually spoke of their task as great he somehow magnified it by referring to it as little. "Poor Craddock naturally confided in me so many of his ideas; indeed, our paths so constantly crossed. The Sister Muses, you know, have an unfortunate habit of refusing to be divided so conveniently as we could wish, they are really quite Siamese twins, so that I feel no hesitation in saying that I can safely offer . . ."

But his offer was lost in the deep bellow of Mr. Cobbell's roar, as like a great Johnsonian lion he descended upon them, his huge chest covered by a double-breasted morning waistcoat across which his single eyeglass fluttered on its black silk ribbon like Beau Brummel's quiz. "The late duke, of course," he was saying, "resembled an ostler both in language and appearance, while there was, I remember, an ostler at Hutchings who was curiously like the late duke's father." It was a remark which had always drawn applause from the American audiences of his ten-minute lectures on "England's Great Families."

Dr. Noreen Maxwell gave him one of her Mona Lisa smiles. With her watery eyes, thin, wriggling body, and mysterious smiles she seemed like an enigmatic eel. "Mr. Brunton," she said, taking her chief's hand, "we feel a great loss, but then we expected to, yes, in these last months we expected to." No one asked her what she meant, for intuition and prophecy were her feminine contributions to the circle. Even in her historical work she was understood to feel and to apprehend rather than to know. "His work had gone as far as it could. Poor Mr. Craddock, he was beginning to look so puzzled. Men," she said, turning to Miss Wells, "are awful babies really. They go on fitting the bricks together and then when one of them doesn't go into place they just can't make it out. I suppose," she said with a laugh, "that's why God saw fit to make the illogical sex. We expect things to be a bit of a mystery and sometimes when one's dealing with the big things in life that's rather a help," and once again she smiled a little pityingly.

Now, at any rate, her listeners felt they knew the direction in which her thoughts were moving, and Mr. Cobbell hurried in with *his* claim to the vacant position.

"Poor Craddock," he roared, "I'm afraid his difficulty was a very *practical* one. He'd exhausted the public galleries and he simply couldn't get to see the private collections. Our great families, you know, have their funny little ways; they need humouring. Simborough, for example, apparently refused to let him see his Tintoretto. Of course, if I'd known I could have dealt with it straight-away. Dear old Simborough, all you've got to do is to praise his shorthorns."

The practical claims of the genealogist to take over the realm of art could not be set out more clearly. Any direct opposition that they might have met, however, was forgotten in the shock produced by the chief's next words.

"I had not intended to mention my ideas before our next weekly meeting," said Mr. Brunton. "I'd not really thought that the question of Craddock's successor would come up so soon," and he looked first at the white tombstones around them and then at his staff. "But I had forgotten your constant concern for the success of our enterprise. I am glad to say that I have thought of a scheme which, if we can put it into practice, will kill two birds with one stone. Craddock, who, by the way, seems to have been more generous with his confidences than I, at any rate, would ever have guessed, has talked to me a number of times in the last months about all the help his girl has been giving him. In fact I strongly suspect that a good number of the contributions that came in from him since last autumn were really her work, and if I'm right she not only knows what to say but also how to put it on paper. It's struck me that we could do ourselves and her a good turn by giving her the job. What do you think, Earley? Do you think you could use her?"

If Mr. Brunton had calculated that the suddenness of his proposal would carry the day he had reckoned without the evasive determination that lay beneath his assistant's buttery manner. Dr. Earley had no intention of committing himself.

"It's a lovely proposal," he said, "a lovely proposal," and he stood for a moment in reverence before the beauty of it, "and just what I would have expected from you. What a wonderful chance for an untried girl—to step straight into the shoes of a tried scholar, and, of course, a princely salary for someone of her age." He glanced quizzically at his chief.

"I naturally shouldn't pay the girl what Craddock got," said Mr. Brunton, meeting his thrust with a direct riposte.

"I see," said Dr. Earley, "I see," and by their looks the other scholars made it clear that they saw also. With such ammunition in their possession, and Mr. Brunton aware that they held it, they could afford to postpone the fight. Mr. Cobbell even felt able to venture upon Dr. Earley's preserve of trite quotations.

"'The air bites shrewdly,'" he bellowed. "'It is bitter cold.' Will Shakespeare always has the last word. I shall be getting what old Brakehampton always called the rheumatises—extraordinary how the dialects persist in some old families. The present duchess, you know, always speaks of lilocks for lilac."

"Yes, indeed," said Dr. Noreen, "*il fait un froid de loup.*"

"One moment before we break up," said Mr. Brunton, ready now with the next thrust. "The difference between the girl's salary and her father's I thought of paying to young Craddock. Of course he'd have to give us a hand with the work, but it'll keep him going until his call-up. I don't know what he's good for, but apparently he's interested in the theatre, so he might give you a hand with some of the literary articles, Earley. It might also prove possible to relieve Miss Wells of some of her burden by getting *Mrs.* Craddock in now and again."

Poor Miss Wells looked quite shrivelled and once again her necklaces jangled. It was not so much the inroad on her salary, meagre though it was, that she feared, but rather any interference in the work which she regarded as so sacred a trust.

As Mr. Brunton moved off to his waiting Daimler, the little group stood in bitter silence.

"Well," said Dr. Earley at last, "we have much food for thought from today's sad proceedings. Suppose we all assemble for tea before the meeting next week, at the A.B.C. shall we say?"

" 'The funeral baked meats,' " began Mr. Cobbell and then paused. Somehow the quotation seemed to be in poor taste, and to venture twice on the Tom Tiddler's ground of Dr. Earley's preserves would be courting disaster.

"Good-bye, Dr. Earley," said Dr. Noreen, taking his hand. "I have a most unwelcome guest awaiting me at home, one master Niccolò Machiavelli"—she was always on easy terms with the great. "He has such an unpleasant habit of putting poison in one's tea." She paused, then, smiling enigmatically, she threw her last bolt of woman's intuition. "I had such a strange feeling when Dr. Brunton was speaking that he meant something quite different to what his words implied," she said and was gone.

In a few seconds they had scattered to the four winds, to those sombre late-Victorian homes in which high tea or supper awaited them. If only some Georgian poet could have saluted them as they departed "for Highgate and Highbury, Barnet and Ealing, for Richmond and Roehampton, Purley and Cheam."

It was really quite a neat little scheme that they devised at the tea table, so much so that the ten minutes left to them before the meeting were passed in festive mood. Miss Wells, who was inclined to rich living, ordered a second Ovaltine; Dr. Earley sipped at his cold milk almost playfully; in a company of dyspeptics he alone had the distinction of a fully developed stomach ulcer. Mr. Cobbell became quite Horatian in mood as he discussed the Chablis at the last dinner of the "Friends of Old Books."

"When the secretary asked me what I thought of it," he boomed, "I replied that it was certainly water-stained but I doubted if it would leave me even *slightly* foxed."

Dr. Earley pinched Miss Wells' leg and made a joke about "half calf."

"My wicked Cæsar," said Dr. Noreen of her cat, "killed my favourite little sparrow last night, and he wasn't a bit ashamed even when I told him that I should call him Cæsar Borgia in future."

" 'Passer mortuus est meae puellae,' " bellowed Mr. Cobbell, and he looked almost lasciviously at Dr. Noreen as he added, "Passer, deliciae meae pullae.' "

"How lyrical, how musical they are!" cried Dr. Early. "Catullus and Tibullus. Only the Carolines, I think, ever caught the mood again exactly, and Austin Dobson," he added. "Austin Dobson, what a master of belles-lettres! Austin Dobson, Garnett, Gosse, no one reads them now, my girls tell me." He frequently made reference to his daughters in this way, sometimes even speaking of them as his girlies and always in so arch a manner that one might have fancied him master of a seraglio.

By the time they departed for the meeting the fun had reached a high pitch; everyone was talking at once. Through a maze of quotations given verbatim by Dr. Earley from his somewhat ambiguously titled reference book *Who Did What to Whom and Where*, Miss Wells could distinguish Dr. Noreen's report of an imaginary conversation held by her with "Kit" Marlowe in which she had whimsically indulged one evening the week before. Mr. Cobbell meanwhile was telling an amusing story of an American's encounter with the Earl of Crudeleigh, the realism of which must have been doubtful when he first heard it in 1921, and in which the American said to the Earl "Say, bo" and referred to York Cathedral as a "Godbox." It was, Miss Wells felt, a real intellectual treat.

They were somewhat late at the encyclopædia offices, where Mr. Brunton was already in impatient mood.

"We shall be able to have only the shortest possible discussion," he said, "because I've invited Mrs. Craddock here to talk over any plans we may have made for her and her children. I hope you've decided upon the best means of rearranging the work to fit the new circumstances, Earley."

"My dear friend"—and Dr. Earley's smile seemed to be all ill-fitting dentures—"if what we have to say should seem to hurt you, and I fear it will, for it hits at what you hold most dear—your charitable, your deeply charitable nature—remember that it is be-

cause we feel for once that your kindness, your too great sentiment, is in danger of sacrificing that standard of accuracy and
scholarship which must always be our *first* concern. In entrusting
the work of the encyclopædia to untried, I would almost say, unknown hands, you are allowing yourself an indulgence against
which it is our duty to warn you."

"I find it difficult, Earley, to understand quite what you mean.
If I remember rightly you were the *first* to urge our duty to the
living, as I think you called it."

"And that duty must not be tied by any conditions," said Dr.
Earley, "which may make the gift turn sour in the mouths of
giver and receiver alike. My dear old friend, indulge your
generous impulses, it is your right, your nature, but let this be
quite independent of our great work. A pension to the widow, for
example, would surely fit the case. We, on our side, have decided
to make a little collection among ourselves. It cannot of course be
given the importance of what may come from you as poor Craddock's employer, his patron and confidant, but a simple tribute to
the memory of a respected colleague." They had in fact computed
the Danegeld most carefully.

Mr. Brunton was, for the moment, checked. He was not a
wholly unkind man, but he was certainly not generous. He never
believed in giving something for nothing, particularly since he felt
certain that in securing Miss Craddock's services he would be getting a bargain. For a moment he sat silent. Then he said very de-
cisively, "I'm sorry I cannot agree. I think it only right in view
of Craddock's opinion of his girl that she should be given a trial.
As to the idea of a little monetary gift," he added, smiling, "I
think it excellent, so long as it is offered with due respect for Mrs.
Craddock's feelings. Nor can I think of your separating your-
selves from me in this way. In the work of the encyclopædia we
are all colleagues." He paused for a moment while he reached a
figure which would be an adequate embarrassment to them, then,
"Indeed I will start by putting myself down for fifty pounds," he
said.

Consternation was plain in every face, but any remonstrance was drowned by the loud grinding of a taxi's brakes as it drew up outside the windows. From this taxi, to their amazement, stepped Mrs. Craddock. It was a curious mode of transport for a suppliant woman.

Her appearance as she entered the room was even more amazing. They had none of them seen their colleague's wife except at the funeral, when their egocentric visions had painted in a conventional grief-stricken figure at the graveside, a stout, ageing female of no particular importance. Not that Mrs. Craddock would have claimed any importance for herself. She was the most modest of women, but she was decidedly not of the encyclopædists' world. Large she was, but of the stoutness of a Rubens Venus or of the Wife of Bath, with purple hair and plenty of make-up. If she had been shy they might have found it easier, but though she clearly felt unfamiliar, it was not in her nature to be other than "at home," and as soon as the introductions were complete she began to talk.

"It's very kind of you to let me come and see where Hugh worked, Mr. Brunton"—and what with her common accent and her flashy clothes, Miss Wells was hard put to it to know what to think. "Oh, yes, and thank you all for coming to the funeral," she added. "I'm afraid I didn't shake hands or anything as I should, but I always get upset when I'm meant to be dignified." She was so short of breath when she spoke that Dr. Noreen Maxwell decided that she drank.

"It was a sad occasion for all of us," said Mr. Brunton hesitatingly, for even he was rather put out. "I asked you here, Mrs. Craddock, because in association with your husband's colleagues I wanted to make you an offer of help. I know how suddenly poor Craddock's death came and I felt that perhaps with the two children to provide for, of whom, by the way, he always spoke to me so warmly, you might be somewhat difficultly placed."

"Nothing," said Mrs. Craddock, "except the house. Poor old Hugh, always meant to put aside, of course, but what with Vera always winning scholarships and Ronnie never winning them, we've spent a fortune on their education. But the house is mine,

I'm glad to say. Hugh saw to that." She smiled rather broadly, and Mr. Cobbell recognized, to his surprise, what in another sphere he had come to regard as the manner of a gracious lady. "Luckily I've got a bit in the post office that'll carry us through for a month or so, but it's very kind of you to think of it."

"As to money," said Mr. Brunton, "Craddock's colleagues and I will be deeply hurt if you will not accept a small sum we have collected to show our appreciation of all that he has done for the encyclopædia. I hope to be able to present you with a little cheque for a hundred pounds. Am I right, Earley?" he asked maliciously, and Dr. Earley said hurriedly, "About that, yes."

"Well, I'm certainly not going to refuse. Whatever I might do for myself, I couldn't possibly where the children are concerned. I'm glad you appreciated Hugh; he certainly took a lot of trouble over the work. And thank you very much."

"I didn't do that very well, I'm afraid," she said confidentially to Dr. Noreen, "but then I'm a bit nervous."

All Dr. Noreen's powers of enigmatic speech had vanished before Mrs. Craddock's buoyancy, so she twisted her face into what she felt to be a more than usually Mona Lisa smile—and succeeded somewhat unhappily in recalling to the widow the effects of Mr. Craddock's last paralytic stroke.

"What I chiefly had in mind, though," continued Mr. Brunton, "was the idea that your daughter, who I know from your husband's account, and from some of her writing that I've seen, is a most promising scholar, should take on her father's work on the encyclopædia. Part of it at first, perhaps, later possibly all."

"Well, that is good of you," said Mrs. Craddock, "but I don't somehow think that's what Vera's got in mind. It would mean refusing her scholarship and that wouldn't be right, would it? You see," she said in confident explanation to Dr. Earley, "really good qualifications are so important in scholarly work today. That was what held Hugh back really." She smiled happily at Mr. Brunton. "Thank you very much though," she said. "That was really a very kind thought and I can see it would be ever such fun for her working with you all"—here she looked particularly at

Miss Wells' emaciated features—"and I'll ask her, of course, but I think she'll say no."

"And how about your boy, Mrs. Craddock?" asked Dr. Earley. He could guess at the effect upon their chief of Mrs. Craddock's simple rejection of his well-laid schemes to secure a bargain, and he derived considerable pleasure in pursuing the matter. "After all, the men of the land still deserve some attention as I tell my girlies. It'll be a trying time for him, hanging about waiting to do his military service, to which no doubt he's looking forward like most of the young fellows."

"Well, as to that I'm surprised to hear it," said Mrs. Craddock. "But I expect you know best. Anyhow, Ronnie isn't, I'm afraid. Not of course that he doesn't want to do what he should, but he certainly isn't looking forward to it. He talks about getting some extra work at the studios while he's hanging about. He's stage mad, you know."

"Ah, yes," said Dr. Earley, "so I heard. Mr. Brunton was thinking he might like to give me a hand with the drama section."

"Oh, dear," said Mrs. Craddock, "I shouldn't think that would do at all. Ronnie's very frivolous, you know," she added, winking at Dr. Noreen Maxwell. "No, I'm afraid, you might as well ask me."

"And how," asked Mr. Cobbell—of all the party his social conceptions were most outraged—"and how do you propose to maintain these two young people?"

"Well," said Mrs. Craddock, "to be honest with you, I'm going to let the whole house out in lodgings. It's a large house and I'm used to students' ways and there's quite a lot of money to be made that way these days and still do a good part by them."

"I see," said Dr. Earley, "a good part," and he repeated the expression once or twice. It was not a concept with which he felt familiar.

Surprise and anger had prevented Mr. Brunton from speaking for some minutes. The more kindly genial side of his nature, which he reserved for his private life and particularly for his academic hobby, was not proof against the rush of more brutal sentiments which surged up in him as he saw his offer rejected in this offhand manner by a person of absolutely no importance. To lose his bargain through the obstinacy of a fool, to have his patronage overlooked by a subordinate, choked him with rage, and that this subordinate and fool should be a woman roused all the misogynistic fears that lay beneath his valeted bachelor existence.

"I only hope, Mrs. Craddock," he said with an icy fury, "that you will organize the rest of your children's future with the same frivolous obstinacy that you have shown here this afternoon. If so, you should have the pleasure of seeing them in the bread line before you have finished. Should that eventuality arise," he continued, "and I hardly see how it can be avoided, please remember that no assistance whatever will be forthcoming from me."

If the others had sensed the storm in the air, Mrs. Craddock was quite overwhelmed with astonishment when it broke upon her. For a moment her lips trembled, and then she spoke rather quietly. "I'm afraid I must have said the wrong thing. It's not easy to say what one means, is it?" she asked, turning to Dr. Noreen, but it was clear that this was not Dr. Noreen's experience, so Mrs. Craddock went on hurriedly, "I tried to say how grateful I was, and so I'm sure Ronnie and Vera will be. Maybe Vera will think differently; I'll certainly ask her."

"There will be no need," Mr. Brunton replied, for by now his fury had overruled his self-interest. "The offer is withdrawn. I should not wish anyone to work upon the encyclopædia who thought so poorly of it. You don't perhaps know that during these last months we were carrying your husband as a passenger; otherwise perhaps you would show us a little more gratitude."

But Mrs. Craddock's lips were no longer trembling; she was staring up at Mr. Brunton in disgust. "Well, of all the mean things," she said. "Now I know why Hugh looked so low sometimes." She was about to add something more sharp, when she cried out, "Oh, Lord, what's the good?" and gathering her handbag to her she went quickly out of the room, leaving behind her a trail of Californian Poppy.

Mr. Brunton sat hunched over the table for a moment. No one

dared to speak. Then he lifted his head; raising one eyebrow quizzically, he looked sharply at his staff with his little beady eyes.
"It'll take a good deal of hard work to get the taste of that out
of our mouths," he said and left them.

Though, in fact, they had won the day, though the encyclopædia remained uncontaminated and Mr. Craddock's job still
open to competition, they yet shared their chief's anger and disgust. That she should have taken the money and refused the advice, it was more than Miss Wells could have believed possible.
Dr. Noreen asked if they had not noticed something peculiar
about the woman's eyes? No? Well, if they hadn't, no matter; it
was probably one of those things that only a woman would see. Mr.
Cobbell remembered Lady Breconwood telling him of just such
a case of ingratitude from a housekeeper in the old viscount's day.
But Dr. Earley was at heart more realistic, or perhaps his belief
in himself was more securely grounded. He saw only that they
had secured their point. He preferred to take a more kindly view.

"She was not, I hasten to confirm it," he said, "one of our
world. That much is certain. But I think I detected some change,
some softening of her manner, suggesting that even on that stony
ground learning's little tribute had not fallen quite fruitlessly."

Necessity's Child

>>><<<

Four years ago I still could know the seashore, especially the summer seashore of purple sea anemones, of ribbon weed clear as coal-tar soap, of plimsoll rubber slipping upon seaweed slime, of crab bubbles from beneath the rock ledge, but now I have grown up—thirteen years old, too old to make my bucket the Sargasso Sea, too old to play at weddings in the cliff cave, too old to walk with handkerchief falling round my calf from a knee cut afresh each day on the rocks. Now there is only the great, far-stretching sea that frightens me. If I were like other boys, I should be getting to know the sea by swimming in it, treating it as my servant, somewhere to show off my strength, to dart in and out of the waves like a salmon, to lie basking on the surface like a seal. Mummy and Daddy and Uncle Reg can move like that. At one time they tried to teach me to join them, but now they have given me up as hopeless. I can watch their movements and wish to imitate them, but when I am in the water I am afraid. I am so alone there; its great strength is too great, it draws me under. I can lie on the beach and dream—I am Captain Scott watching the sea leopard catch the awkward penguins; I am the White Seal as he swam past the great, browsing sea cows; I am Salar the Salmon as he sported in the weir; I am Tarka the Otter as he learned to swim downstream; above all, nowadays I am lying in the sun on the deck of the

Written in 1946; first published in 1950; scene immediate post Second World War when petrol was still severely rationed.

Pequod with the Southern Cross above me. But there always comes the moment of fear—Captain Scott has dread in his heart as he reaches the Pole too late; the White Seal grows up to fear the hunter; Salar the Salmon must dart from the jaws of the conger eel; Tarka lies taut beneath the river bank as the hounds breathe overhead; on the *Pequod* is heard the ominous tapping of Ahab's ivory leg. Even in my dreams I must be afraid, must feel unprotected.

Mummy and Daddy are ashamed of my fears. They play games that are meant to be for my benefit, but they are their games really. I spoiled cricket on the beach as I used to spoil their sand castles. When we were playing last summer, Mummy called out that she did not want me on her side. "I'm not having Rodney on our side," she said. "I want to win. "We'll have to have you on *our* side, old man," Daddy said, "if your mother doesn't want you. I think we can carry a rabbit, don't you, Reggie?" And Uncle Reggie said, "Yes, you'll have to be the tail, Rodney. With luck it'll be lunchtime before the last man goes in." It was just the same building sand castles when I was little. Once I started to make a ruined tower. "What on earth is that, darling?" Mummy asked me, and when I told her, "Ruined is about right," she said. "Derek, my dear, what can make him suppose that we want a ruined tower when we're building the Clifton suspension bridge?" "Ye olde ruined and medieval suspension bridge, eh, Rodney?" said Uncle Reggie. But Daddy just took the sand to build one of his pediments. In the end I used to fetch and carry for them. "Get us some sea water in that bucket, there's a good little chap," or, "Darling, just dig all round here for me." Sometimes I used to forget about the game and stand dreaming; then it used to be, "Don't stand on the drawbridge, old chap, that'll never do," or "Darling, if Uncle Reggie takes the trouble to make this marvellous fort for you, I *do* think you might take some interest."

The truth is that I am in the way. I heard Mummy telling Auntie Eileen about it one afternoon in the garden. "Well, there it is," she said. "We can never have another and so we must face the situation. But you can say what you like, Eileen, I'm not having a mother's darling round the place. I suppose it's very awful of me to say so, but I realize now that the whole thing was the greatest mistake. Derek and I aren't the sort of people to make parents. We married because we were in love; we still are and we're going to stay that way. We like having fun and we like having it together. Derek doesn't want to come home to someone who's old and tired and scratchy at the end of the day, and I intend to see that he doesn't."

Auntie Eileen thinks she can make up for it. She's kind to me, and when I was little it was nice to play with her. But Mummy's right when she says that she's silly. She doesn't understand anything. She just likes to share silly secrets. "Well, Rodney, what little stories have you been making up today?" She likes to show off when people are there, too. She winks at me with her stupid, fat sheep's face. "Rodney and I have lots of little secrets, haven't we?" She made me ashamed when she came down to the Christmas play, talking to Mr. Rogers like that. "I'm not a bit surprised at Rodney's acting so well. You see, we've always been rather special friends and we've had our little plays since he was ever so small." But she didn't notice the look on Mr. Rogers' face.

I wish I was back at school. I wish this holiday was over. There'll be nets and missing catches, I know, and the bridge ladder and not knowing the answers in algebra and old Puffin banging his ruler down so that you can't think. "If you can't deal with X and Y, try and think what the answer would be if it was pears and apples, or the beloved pineapple chunks," as if *that* made it any easier. But then there'll be Tony and Gerald to talk to. Gerald said that he would read *Moby Dick* too, when Mr. Rogers told us about it, and even if Tony can't manage it, and lots of it *is* difficult to understand, we can tell him about all the important bits like Ahab's fight with the white whale, and the sea hawk, and Queequog praying to his idol. We'll all have read *The Wreckers* too, because Mr. Rogers set it as holiday reading. We'll be able to act lots of it and with any luck they'll let me act Pinkerton. Mr. Rogers said we should read *Barnaby Rudge* for English. It will be the last book I shall read in class at St. Bertram's, because in the autumn I shall be going on to Uppingham. To a public school! Mummy and Daddy like to talk about it, but I try not to listen because I'm so frightened. Oh, God, don't let me think about it! Oh, God, don't let me think about it! If I count one hundred and three before I get to the kiosk I shan't ever go to a public school. One, two, three, four, five, six, seven, eight . . .

"Talking to yourself? That's bad, that's very bad." The thick, unctuous voice sounded stern but jolly. Rodney, startled out of his thoughts, stared up at the flabby and rubicund face of Mr. Cartwright, the vicar of St. Barnabas'. "You know what they say about people who talk to themselves, don't you? Just a little bit cracked, getting ready for the looney bin," and Mr. Cartwright laughed with schoolboy glee.

"I'm afraid I didn't know I was doing it," mumbled Rodney.

"That's no excuse in the eyes of the law," boomed Mr. Cartwright, all mock magisterial severity. "And how have the holidays been? Pretty busy, eh? Gordon and Roger have got a craze" —and he dwelt lovingly on what he felt to be the juvenile *mot juste* —"on hockey at the moment. They tell me you don't play. You know, I'll let you into a secret if you won't tell the boys." He looked all conspiratorial. "I've no use for the game either. Fast enough, I know, but it always seems to me something of a girl's game. I tell you what though—Mr. Harker's lent the boys the gym at the high school. You must come up one evening for a rag."

Rodney murmured an assent; then, as Mr. Cartwright continued to talk of his sons and the April Fool they had played upon him, he suddenly became panic-stricken at the thought of the commitment. I can't go up there. I won't. "I'm afraid I shan't be able to come after all," he interrupted Mr. Cartwright breathlessly. "You see, Mummy's ill and she likes me to be about to help in the house."

"Oh! I'm sorry to hear that," said the vicar. "Not seriously, I hope. Mrs. Cartwright will want to call and help when she hears."

"Oh, please, no visitors or telephones at the moment," said Rodney.

"Dear, oh, dear. *You* must keep us posted then. It's a fine thing

for you that you can be such a help at this time. A great fellow
like you can do a lot to earn your living. You'll be leaving St. Bertram's soon for a wider world, I suppose. Uppingham, isn't it?
That's something to look forward to. Though mind you"—and
his voice took on a confirmation-class note—"it won't be all beer
and skittles at first. One gets to be rather a big pot at one's prep
school, and unfortunately when one goes on to a public school
they don't seem to quite see things that way. But you'll soon settle down. It's just a question," he added with ringing confidence,
"of not getting rattled."

He's speaking about it as though it was certain to happen, as
though it didn't matter, thought Rodney. How can I make myself not mind going there, if there are people like him about who
take all the bullying for granted, who seem to want it? If none
of it can happen to me, I won't even let *him* think it can. Aloud he
said, "I know heaps of other boys there already, so I expect I shall
be all right."

"Good show," said Mr. Cartwright. "Well, we shall expect to
hear great things of you," and with a pat on the boy's shoulder he
set off along the parade.

I've told him two lies, thought Rodney, and they're bound to
be found out. It's always happening like that. Why didn't I say
that I didn't want his rotten rag in the gym? Why did I have to
say I knew people at Uppingham when I didn't? Because you
were afraid of his knowing you were frightened. And now
Mummy and Daddy will find out that I lied and they'll despise me
for it. If I was dying like Thatcher when he had meningitis, they
wouldn't want me always to be with other boys; they would
want to have me with *them*. If Daddy was to die, I should be very
brave and Mummy would be very proud of me. *The Schoolroom
is filled for evening prayers when old Puffin calls out loudly,
"Brent, will you step outside, please. We have some rather serious
news about your father." White-faced and tense, but steady, I
walk out of the room. Mummy is sitting weeping in Puffin's study.
"I don't need an explanation, sir, I think I understand. My father
is dead!" and then with my arms round her, "Don't cry, darling, I*

will try to be all he would have wanted me to be," and then to
Puffin, *"I think, sir, if you could get my mother a little brandy."*
Making up horrible daydreams, that's all I ever do. I can't be any
good except in my imagination. It's not fair, really. There's nothing to be brave about, when all that is wanted of you is to keep
out of the way. I shall sit in the shelter here and read *The Wreckers* until long after suppertime and then perhaps they'll wonder
where I am and get worried about me.

The problem of the mysterious cargo of the wrecked ship was
so absorbing that it was some time before Rodney noticed that he
had been joined in the shelter by two other people. The stout old
lady in the heavy fur coat was the first to speak. "You *must* have
an interesting book to be carried away like that," she said. Rodney decided that with her long face, her tiny eyes, and the warts
on her cheek she looked like a huge furry hippopotamus. "A
really good yarn on a nice spring day—what could be jollier?"
said the old gentleman in slow, mournful tones, which seemed
somehow accentuated by the downward curve of his long white
moustaches and the watery blue of his protruding pug's eyes.

"It's Robert Louis Stevenson's *Wreckers*," said Rodney with
some pride.

"Ah," said the old gentleman, "the redoubtable Pinkerton.
Somebody you're not familiar with, my dear," he added to his
wife, "not unlike that American we met last year who'd patented
those revolting and peculiarly useless braces."

"I don't think I should have particularly wanted to read about
him," said his wife. "He had such very bad manners. But there I
expect it would be different if it was in a book."

"My wife's one of those unfortunate people who can't read,"
said the old gentleman with great seriousness. The old lady protested laughingly, and an expression of puzzled concern appeared
on Rodney's face. "Well, it's almost true," the old gentleman went
on. "She never learned the delight of books until she was too old.
Now when I was your age I lived half my time in the stories I
read, as I've no doubt you do. I remember being D'Artagnan for
weeks on end—a great, swaggering Gascon fellow. I'm not sure

it wasn't then that I grew these moustaches. One thing I am sure of though, I didn't keep to the book exactly. I remember I always saved milady from the block at the last minute. I know, of course, that she wasn't exactly a nice person, but still it's always the mark of a cad to refuse to help a beautiful woman when she's in trouble."

"I love the chapters where milady seduces Felton," said Rodney.

"Ah, yes, a nice juicy bit," said the old gentleman, looking sideways at his wife's shocked expression. "There's no need for alarm, my dear. The word seduce is used only in a very general sense, to imply dereliction of duty and that sort of thing, you know. But my wife does like *one* book"—he turned to Rodney—"our grandchildren read it to her last winter, and that's *Wind in the Willows*. Of course, she fell in love with Toad."

"I didn't," protested the old lady. "I thought he was odious."

"Oh, he wasn't really," said Rodney. "He was really a nice kind sort of person, only he boasted rather a lot."

"Yes, yes," said the old gentleman. "We're none of us free from weaknesses, not even you, my dear. And then he was a pioneer of motoring, though whether that's on the credit side I'm not so sure. However, he had a proper sense of his superiority to the teaching profession, which our friend here no doubt shares. 'The clever men at Oxford know all there is to be knowed,' " he recited, laughing heartily.

" 'But there's none of them knows half as much as intelligent Mr. Toad,' " finished Rodney, and he began to laugh too.

His enjoyment was suddenly halted, however, by the lady's next remark.

"I expect you read lots of books aloud to *your* mother," she said.

Rodney paused some moments before answering. "Yes," he said at last, "you see, Mummy's an invalid and she depends a lot on me."

"I'm sure you're a great help to her," said the old lady. "What does your father do?"

"Daddy's a solicitor," replied Rodney. "Poor Daddy," he added with a deep sigh.

"That's a very large sigh for so small a person," said the old lady.

"I was just thinking how difficult it is when people don't understand each other. Daddy's such a kind man really, only he gets so angry because Mummy's always snapping. It's only because she has dreadful pain to bear, but Daddy doesn't seem to understand. That's what makes him drink so. When he gets drunk he says dreadful things to Mummy and then she wishes she could die."

"Never mind, my dear," said the old lady. "If I understand how your Mummy feels, having you about will make life worth living."

"That's what Daddy says," Rodney went on in increasingly excited tones. "We have wonderful walks together in the country and along the seashore. He knows all about birds and fishes and makes everything so interesting. If only Mummy knew what he was like then—oh, I wish I could make them understand each other! I think I'm the only person who could."

The old gentleman left off drawing lines in the gravel with his walking stick. He looked quizzically for a moment at Rodney, then he said drily, "Making human beings understand one another can be quite a difficult task."

Rodney's look of bewilderment as he replied was appealing in its innocence. "Oh, I know how difficult it will be, and after all I am only a child."

The old gentleman's tone was more kindly as, rising from the seat, he patted Rodney's shoulder. "I shouldn't worry too much if I were you. Grown-up people are very strange creatures," he said. "They often seem to be in a bad way, but it's amazing how quickly they pull out of it. Well, we must be going, my dear," he added.

The old lady bent down and kissed Rodney's forehead, then she produced a visiting card from her handbag. "If you're ever in need of a friend, this is my name and address," she said. "I shall always think of you as a very brave boy."

It was well after teatime when Rodney returned home, but Mrs.

Brent did not appear to notice that he was late. For a moment as he saw her he remembered his lies to the vicar and wondered with dread whether Mrs. Cartwright had rung up. But his trained eye soon saw from his mother's face that no storm was brewing, and with long, acquired habit he pushed his fears aside. It hasn't led to trouble yet, he thought. Perhaps if I cross my fingers it never will. "Please, God, if it's all right this time I'll never tell any more stories," he murmured.

Mummy was wearing her black costume with the diamond shoulder clip, he noticed, and the black hat with the cockfeathers that curled over the ear. That meant that Daddy and she must be going out. They had only been in to dinner four times during the holidays and then there had been visitors, so that he had to have supper on his own. If only they would talk to him occasionally. Of course, Mummy *did* sometimes, but only if there was nobody there, and *usually*, if they were alone, she would say, "Thank goodness! an afternoon to ourselves. Now I can get on with something. I hope you've got things to do, Rodney, because I really must get this finished before Daddy comes home and I don't want to be constantly interrupted." Anyhow, Auntie Eileen was here for her to talk to this evening. Certainly no one could want a better listener, he thought as he watched his aunt's pale moon-face with its look of constant surprise, the eyebrows raised and the mouth eternally rounded and ready with exclamations of "Oh!" or "No!" to greet the speaker, her large earrings jangling with interest.

"Quite honestly, Eileen, I think she must have been canned," his mother was saying. "She's never a good player, but to go up five in a major suit, when she didn't even hold the top two honours, *and* they were vulnerable. Of course Derek was *furious*. I've promised him we'll never go there again. But it's a frightful bore, because she's been so useful over petrol coupons."

"Oh, Vera, how maddening for you!" said her sister-in-law.

"Yes, it is rather, isn't it? Actually, of course, Derek's bridge is so much too good for this town that it's rather a bore playing

anyway. You should see the look on the poor lamb's face sometimes when one of these old girls makes some terrible call. Anyhow, the summer's coming now so that with tennis and cricket
there won't be much time for bridge. You know, the new road-
house has opened on the London Road."

"No!" said Eileen. "Really? I didn't know."

It was amazing how few things his aunt *did* know, Rodney reflected.

"Yes, my dear, and it's really awfully gay. We're motoring out
there this evening after drinks at the Grahams'. Derek's crazy
to take up dancing in a big way again. He adores all this old-time
dancing. So the summer programme will be pretty full. There
really *does* look to be a chance of our getting abroad at the end
of August. Derek says all the money restrictions mean nothing
if you know the ropes."

"Rodney will like that," said Aunt Eileen.

"My dear," replied Mrs. Brent, "I honestly think it would be
madness to take him. Nothing could be less amusing for a
child than a Paris holiday, and it wouldn't be terribly fair on us.
No, thank goodness! The housemaster at Uppingham has been
amazingly kind about it. He's quite willing for him to arrive there
a few weeks early and be a sort of paying guest. There'll be other
boys there too, which will be very good for him."

"Oh, Mummy, please!" Rodney cried. "Don't make me go
there in the holidays. It'll be awful, I know it will."

"My dear child, there's no need to get excited. We're not pro-
posing to send you to prison or something. It'll be a marvellous
chance to get to know some of the boys before term begins.
You'll be one up on the other new boys."

"Rodney can come to me, Vera, if he likes," and Auntie Eileen
wrinkled her nose intimately at her nephew. "We'd have grand
times."

"There you are, Rodney. You can go to Auntie Eileen's,
though I'm not sure it wouldn't be better if you were to be with
other boys."

"I don't *want* to go to Auntie Eileen's"—Rodney was almost shouting—"I want to be with you and Daddy."

"Well, I'm afraid you'll have to want. Daddy and I are going abroad. And now apologize to your aunt for being so rude."

It was no good putting everybody against you, thought Rodney, so he said, "I'm sorry, Auntie Eileen." Then suddenly he kicked at the table. "But everything's so jolly dull. I get so bored and that makes me cross."

"What have you been doing this afternoon that bored your lordship so?" said his mother.

"Talking to an old lady and gentleman on the front."

"Well, really, Rodney! With hundreds of other children in the town you spend the afternoon talking to some old couple and then you say you're bored. I give up!"

"What about your book?" said Auntie Eileen. "You're not the person to be dull if there's a book about."

"Oh, it's all right," said Rodney, "but I'm tired of reading."

"Why not make up a story for yourself," said Auntie Eileen. "That ought to be great fun, and then you can tell it to me."

"Don't spoil the child," said his mother, and she began to tell her sister-in-law of their holiday plans.

Half an hour later Rodney's father returned. "Hullo, Eileen," he said to his sister. "What's the best news?" He leaned over his wife's chair and kissed her, running his hands down her breasts. "Had a good day, Tuppence?" he said.

His wife's somewhat hard, carefully made-up face softened as she answered, "This is the best moment."

"Same here," he replied, smiling boyishly. "How's the world treating you, old son?" he called to Rodney.

"He's been an absolute horror," said Mrs. Brent.

"Bad show," said her husband. "We must be moving, darling."

"You look tired, sweet," said Mrs. Brent.

"I am a bit," said her husband.

"Then *I* shall drive."

"I won't say no," and he gave her a smack on the bottom as

he pushed her out of the room. "Pass along the car there," he called.

"Will you be all right, Rodney, while I get your supper?" said Auntie Eileen. "Then we can have a nice long chat."

"I'm busy making up a story like you told me," said her nephew, and he smiled to himself.

A quarter of an hour later when Auntie Eileen returned, bringing a cup of Bovril and some jam tart on a tray, Rodney was sitting in the chair, his body tense and his face white and strained.

"Rodney, darling, what is the matter?" she cried.

"Oh, it's so horrible!" the boy said, his eyes rounded. "I couldn't tell Mummy. I can't tell anyone ever."

"You can tell *me*, darling."

"Oh, I do so want to. But if I do, you'll tell Mummy. Promise if I tell that you'll keep it a secret."

"Of course, of course I promise," said Auntie Eileen with relish.

"It happened this afternoon with that old gentleman," said Rodney, speaking in an excited, staccato voice. "He looked so nice, Auntie, and then he showed me pictures, horrible, beastly pictures."

"Oh, my darling," said Auntie Eileen, "how dreadful! What a wicked, wicked man!" Then she added, "But I thought you said there was an old lady with him. Had she gone away or what?"

There was a short silence and then, "No, Auntie," said Rodney bitterly. "No, she was there. She just laughed and said they had lots more like that at home and I'd better come back and see them, but I ran away. Promise, promise you'll never tell anyone. It was all so dreadful I don't want to think about it ever again."

"I wish I knew what was right," said Auntie Eileen, but at Rodney's look of alarm she added, "Very well, darling, it'll be our secret, a secret we'll just forget. But I shall always think of you as a very brave boy."

The sea swings away from me now, brown and sandy in patches, but without light, grey and cold. It heaves and tosses and lashes itself into white fury as it crashes and thunders against the breakwater. It flies into a mist that sprays against my cheeks. But always, however the waves may rush forward, tumbling over each other to smash upon the beach, the sea swings towards me and away from me. I am sitting upon a raft, and the calm, level water is swinging me so, back and forward. It is the Pacific Ocean everywhere, clear and green. Over the side of the raft I can see deep, deep down to strange, coloured fishes and seahorses and coral. I am all alone, "alone on a wide, wide sea." Mummy and Daddy have gone down with the ship, spinning round and round like the *Pequod*. See! She sinks in a whirlpool, and I am shot out, far out, alone on this raft. The heat will scorch and burn me, "the bloody sun at noon," and thirst and the following sharks. Don't let me be alone so, don't let me think of that! But now the sea is moving, violently, wildly, in high Atlantic waves. I am lashed to a raft. The sea is swinging me roughly, up on the crest, so that the wing of the albatross or the sea hawk brushes my cheek, raucous screams are in my ears, hooked beaks snap at my eyes, and now down, down into the trough where the white whale waits. Mummy and Daddy have gone down with the ship. It crashed and broke against the glass-green wall, the name *Titanic* staring forth in red letters as it reared into the air. Mummy's black evening dress floated on the surface of the water, and her shoulder showed white as she was sucked down. But I am left alone, tied to the raft, numbed, frozen, choking with the cold, or again, as it sails relentlessly on towards the next floating green giant, dashing me to pieces against the ice as I fight with the ropes too securely tied.

Christmas Day in the Workhouse

➤➤➤❮❮❮

Thea was showing one of the new girls how to mark the personnel cards when Major Prosser came in. She continued the demonstration without turning round, not because she thought the work of more importance than the Head of Section's visit, but because she guessed that his sense of his own position would be more flattered by assuming it so. After four years at the Bureau, actions tended to be guided by such purely personal considerations. Where all other values had been effaced by isolation and boredom, only sexual conquest or personal advantage remained as possible goals; most of the time Thea found only personal advantage within her range, but at a certain cost in hysteria she had made quite a success of it—she was, after all, the only woman head of a subsection under the age of thirty.

"Directed staff are marked green for sick leave, volunteers blue, established officers red," she explained, and as she looked at the new girl's pallid skin she wondered if green had been purposely chosen for the conscripts. She tried very hard to treat these bewildered and unattractive girls with kindness. Sometimes, however, a bitter despair would break through the deadness with which she had insulated herself from the place, and in her anger at the naïve enthusiasm with which *she* had first volunteered for the work, she would turn against those who had only come under

Written in 1948; first published in 1950; scene laid in the Second World War.

duress. At such times she would dwell with satisfaction upon these sickly, suburban ewe lambs—green-faced girls with pebble glasses, protruding teeth, and scurfy shoulders who had been hunted from the protecting parental arms to be sacrificed upon the pyre of communal existence. In fact, of course, as she fully realized, this monotony of ugliness was simply the ready response of the Ministry of Labour to the Bureau's call for "clever girls."

"For the dying, the dead, and those yet unborn, we use black," she went on. It was a joke she had inherited from her predecessor, who had thought it out way back in 1939, but as she made it she realized that it was not quite Tim Prosser's sort of remark. It reflected, if only faintly, a certain cynicism towards the Bureau, which he preferred to reserve only for expansive moods with his immediate subordinates. All the "old faithfuls" among the girls laughed obediently, and Joan Fowler even managed to impart a special note of devotion towards Thea into her little giggle.

Major Prosser's laugh was really more of an impatient cough. He was beginning to see this devotion to work as *lèse-majesté* rather than a compliment.

"Have you got Braddock's card there?" he said abruptly. He always used the girls' surnames when he wished to wound the remnants of humane feelings to which Thea clung as the last plank of her self-respect.

"Daphne's card?" she replied on a lingering note as she tried to puzzle out what he was after.

"Yes, yes." Major Prosser was impatient. "The girl with the migraines and the excess charm." He liked Thea's competence, but he genuinely despised her gentility and what he called her "blasted hard-boiled virginity."

Anxious to oblige, the new girl handed the card to him directly. He gave her a friendly, boyish smile that reminded her of her daddy.

"Away since September," he said sharply. "I say, Thea, you ought to have asked me for a replacement ages ago. Establishments is no sinecure at the best of times, but carrying pas-

sengers!" And he looked all admiraton for her silent self-sacri-
fice. "Let's see, who can we give you? I know—Turnbull. I'll see
Room 6 straight away."

My God, thought Thea, so that's it! As soon as he laid a new
wench—increasingly she found herself using the "tough" language affected by her superiors—there was always a shift round
of staff. He'd put his new little bit in charge of Room 6 and now
he'd got to weed out the duds for her. He would have his work
cut out in finding a home for Turnbull, whose black frizz with
its bleached streak made her absence from evening shift to have
a bit of fun with the messengers seem somehow more noticeable
than in "quieter" girls.

"Thank you, Tim," said Thea sweetly. The constant use of
Christian names among the heads and subheads was one of the
many external signs of the splendid, amateur, wartime spirit with
which they were making rings round the inflexible efficiency
of the enemy *and* having fun in doing it. Though Thea had no
doubts of the truth of this claim to improvised genius, she often
found its conscious expression embarrassing. She was, however,
rapidly learning the language by which modesty, reserve, and
reticence can be widely advertised.

"Thank you, Tim, I don't think there'll be any need," she went
on. "Joan Fowler had a letter from Daphne saying she would be
back within a fortnight. That's right, isn't it, Joan?"

Joan was so delighted that Thea should have turned to her
for support that she blushed wildly and her genteelly distorted
vowels tumbled over one another in an effort to please.

"Oh, yes, Thea, she's ever so much better, really almost all
right, and her doctor says that as long . . ."

Major Prosser laughed to disguise his disgust at Joan's lack of
sex appeal. "That's not perhaps quite the official report," he said.
"In any case"—and he looked round the room somewhat venom-
ously—"a drop of new blood might be a very good idea. We
all get a bit stale, anæmic . . ."

But Thea was ready for such a favourite generalization and
quoted another of his loved phrases back at him.

"Except, Tim, that in Establishments we have a highly integrated group of specially picked personnel." She knew the phrase from his last report to the chief. He took the joke against himself with a "good sport" smile, but she could see he was getting angry.

"Well, we'll talk about it later," he said.

Thea decided that the moment had come to push her victory home. "I don't suppose it matters," she said, "but in the report I did for the Duce"—it was their jolly name for the chief, originally bestowed in bitter contempt, but wisely accepted by him as a piece of family fun—"saying why the section needed more staff I did mention that we never cared to move people from one job to another."

Major Prosser was already somewhat alarmed by the difficulties of justifying his request for forty new personnel—a request made because other sections were increasing—so that the blow was a telling one. Nevertheless, Thea reflected, she would probably have to put up with Turnbull's bleached streak, for unless she was prepared to make a row about it, Tim could always override her wishes.

"No Christmas decorations yet?" he asked, dismissing the matter.

"We're putting them up tomorrow morning," said Thea. "We've got some wonderful caricatures this year."

"One of me, I hope," said Tim.

"Well, yes," laughed Thea. "Show him what you've done, Stephanie."

If Tim had been expecting giggles and shy refusal, he was sadly disappointed. Stephanie ignored him altogether, but taking the drawing from a folder on her table, she handed it to Thea.

"I've got to colour the uniform still," she remarked in her off-hand, dead voice. Tim looked at her long slender figure and her neatly rolled straight gold hair in fury and misery. He was always telling his cronies that these cold bitches with *Tatler* backgrounds weren't worth laying. "Their bed manners are so bloody awful," he used to say amid roars of laughter at the local, but lust and snobbery were too powerful to be resisted in her presence. Even his vanity could not fail to see the bank manager disguised in a uniform which her caricature of him underlined.

"Very good," he said, laughing. "I wonder about the moustache though. It's a shade too neat for mine."

Stephanie looked at him for a second. "No," she said, considering, "I don't think so. I took it from one of those hair-cream advertisements."

After Tim had gone, Joan Fowler came and fussed round Thea. "Oh, poor you," she said, "it's absolutely monstrous making you take that awful Turnbull on. I hate all these new people. I'm sure we got much more work done when there were only a few of us. Do you remember, Thea, when there was only you and me and Penelope, and then Stephanie came and poor Daphne? Of course, I think it's been *much* worse since Prosser came. A girl in Room 6 told me last night it was simply *frightful* since he'd pushed that creature of his in there. You don't think he'd ever try to do that here, do you? Oh, but he *couldn't*, not when you've made so much of Establishments. But then you simply can't tell *what* he might do. If he *did* try to push anyone new in here, I bet you anything nobody would work for them. Even these new girls are frightfully keen on working for you."

If Joan seized any occasion to surround Thea with a fog of vague perils and implied intrigues, it was not from hostility but from an ill-defined feeling that it united them more closely, made her own protective devotion more necessary—locked in each other's arms for safety, they could float forever upon a buoyant sea of treacly emotion. Unfortunately, however tonic such emotions might be to Joan, Thea only felt their stickiness sucking her down. Luckily, her experience as Guide leader in her father's parish had taught her to keep such silliness in hand.

"Don't forget you're chart-checker today, Joan," she said. "We keep a half-day chart for every section," she explained to the new girl. "Green and red for the two shifts, purple for those on half-days. That's if it's working properly. At the moment Joan's got more than half the section marked on leave." A little snub

worked wonders with these stupid girls, though, really, she had
to admit that Joan's devotion was less revolting than the so-called
normal attitude that Tim Prosser and the others professed so
loudly, a normality that apparently classed human beings with
pigs. The nostrils of her bony Roman nose dilated and her thin,
faintly coloured lips compressed as she thought of it. For a few
seconds she imagined the moment of release from it all, and how
Colin would be both disgusted and amused, and then the horrible realization of Colin's death surged through her head. It was
one of those appalling failures of memory that occurred, thank
God, increasingly less since his plane had crashed two years before.

Despite the freezing wind that blew across the dismal meadows,
where each month saw less trees and more concrete buildings,
the atmosphere in the canteen with its radiators and fluorescent
lighting was stifling. The white coats of the waitresses were
splashed with scraps of food and gravy stains; around their
thickly lipsticked mouths, their cheeks and chins shone greasy
and sweaty. The young technician who sat opposite to Thea spat
fragments of potato as he talked to his girl friend. She pushed
aside her plate and decided to leave before the roof of her mouth
was completely caked in suet. What a prelude to a Mozart concert! she thought. Nothing in her education had ever allowed her
to bridge the gap between the material and the cultural.

And yet in some curious way they did get entwined that night.
The concert hall was packed when she entered, and for a few
moments she thought with depression that she would have to
stand; of course, with the *Jupiter* to listen to, she was not likely to
mind, but she felt very exhausted. Then suddenly she saw Stephanie's delicate hand beckoning to a seat beside her. How cool
and restful her large grey eyes and sleek golden hair seemed above
the plain cable-stitch jumper and rope of pearls. Thea felt glad,
when she looked round the room at the vulgar evening frocks,
that she too had not "changed." She was not quite sure that her
angora jumper was exactly right, but at any rate her pearls—a

twenty-first birthday present from Daddy—were really good. Throughout the *Overture to Figaro* and the *Jupiter* she had no mind for anything but the music; for she had heard it often enough to be thinking all the time how important it was to know what was coming, otherwise one never really saw the relation of all the parts to each other. The piano concerto that followed was more difficult, and though she tried hard to listen for the themes she found her thoughts wandering.

It was amazing, she reflected, how one person of the right sort could help to make life tolerable. All the vulgarity, the intrigue, the anxiety that surrounded her life at the Bureau seemed to vanish in Stephanie's presence; but that, of course, was because she was so detached, so completely above them. Breeding did make a difference—there was no doubt of it. Not, Thea thought, that she had a reverence for titles in the vulgar, snobbish way that made so many of the girls excited when they saw Stephanie's picture in the *Tatler*. Half of the people in the *Tatler* were appalling, spending their time at night clubs and theatres when the country needed them; but the real aristocracy were quite different, living quietly in the country and doing so much good. The proof of it was, of course, that she'd never had one moment's trouble with Stephanie from the day she joined the section. She knew she had a job to do and she did it, which was exactly what one would have expected of course, and she did it so coolly and efficiently too, although she was only twenty, and had beauty that would have turned any other girl's head.

With the sound of the piano as an accompaniment, little pictures began to pass before Thea's eyes. She knew Stephanie's home, Garsett House, well from the outside; she used to pass the lodge gates in the bus from Aunt Evelyn's into Taunton, and she had seen the countess once at a meet of the staghounds near Minehead. Now she saw herself on a horse like Ropey only better, laughing and talking with Stephanie, who looked almost haughty in her habit and with her riding whip; or coming down a broad staircase in a plain black evening dress with her pearls, her arm round Stephanie's waist. Stephanie, of course, was in a simple

but lovely white frock. Black and white—she pulled herself together as she thought of the advertisement. The slow movement
was lovely but perhaps a little long. It was difficult to imagine
the inside of Garsett just from the lodge gates; and Thea felt more
safe as she saw Stephanie at the rectory, galloping on Ropey, for,
of course, she would not mind his being old and short-winded;
or, even better, laughing at the strange old hats and frocks in the
dressing-up box in the nursery. How pleased Mummy would be
with her new friend!

When they came out after the concert Thea almost gasped at
the beauty of the moonlight on the snow-covered lawn. After a
week's hard frost the wind was warmer, and already everywhere around them the snow was falling from the branches of
the trees with strange, sudden, little popping noises that relieved
the frozen tension. And then, "How beautiful it is," Stephanie
said, so that Thea almost jumped at the strange unity of their
thoughts. They sat waiting in their bus—for their billets were in
the same direction—while a crowd of noisy girls from the dance-
hall climbed into the back seats. Thea, turning round with horror
at the sacrilege, saw Turnbull in a dreadful gold lamé evening
dress, her bleached streak fallen across her eyes. "'When I say I
love you,'" she was crooning, "'I want you to know, it isn't because of moonlight, although moonlight becomes you so.'" Thea
had almost decided to demand silence when suddenly she saw
Stephanie's hair gleam pale golden-green in a haze of moon-
beams. Of course, these jazz tunes were very frightful, but in a
sense they were the folk music of the age, and she could not help
dwelling on the phrase "moonlight becomes you so." It was
strangely like something in a ballad.

"I don't think I can bear tomorrow's party," said Stephanie
suddenly. "Penelope Rogers has bought a special box of Christmas jokes." She looked at Thea quizzically, and they both burst
out laughing, almost hysterically. Stephanie was the first to re
cover. "You're tired, Thea," she said, "after the way that wretched
little man bothered you today. Do you have to come in tomorrow?" And she laid her long fingers on Thea's arm.

"Oh, I think I must," said Thea, "but I'm having a quiet Christmas dinner at the billet in the evening."

"You're lucky." Stephanie laughed. "My people have gone away. I shall cook myself an omelette and go to bed."

"You'll like that, I expect."

"Oh, I don't know. I'm rather fond of a Christmas celebration as long as it's not at the Bureau."

"You wouldn't care to come to us, would you?" asked Thea boldly. "It'll be very quiet, only me and my billetor. She's a dear." She was about to add that Mrs. Owens was a doctor's widow when she wondered if that was exactly the kind of thing that would be of interest to Stephanie, so she said rather pointlessly, "She's a widow. Do come."

"Thank you," said Stephanie, "I think I should like to," and then, almost abstractedly, she added, "You do know, don't you, Thea, what a compensation working for you has been? Compensation for the Bureau being so bloody, I mean."

It seemed to Thea as though she floated through the gates of the billet—with their brass plate, last remnant of the late Dr. Owens—and on up the drive, a cold, white river of moonshine. At any ordinary time she would have recoiled from the melting snow as it seeped through her stockings, for her fastidious feelings revolted from any unfamiliar physical touch, but tonight she was dancing on a lake of glass. No happiness, however, could allow her to forget the consideration due to others, so she removed her shoes most carefully as she closed the front door.

"Thea," Mrs. Owens called from her bedroom upstairs, "is that you?"

It was a nightly repeated ritual that usually formed the final torture of Thea's tiring and nerve-racked days, but tonight, "Yes, Mrs. Owens. Can I come in for a moment?"

She lay back in the armchair by the old lady's bed and ran her hand sensuously over the soft pink eiderdown, just as she did in the rare, happy, midnight "confabs" with Mummy when Daddy was visit-preaching.

"Does anybody in the world make such perfect Ovaltine?" she cried as she helped herself from the little spirit stove by the bedside. "Oh, isn't it nice that Christmas is here?" she asked.

"I wish I could do more to make it brighter for you," said Mrs. Owens. "I think it's a shame they don't send you all home. I've made the sausage rolls for you to take tomorrow. I'm afraid they won't go very far. I nearly let the pastry burn. I've been so excited all day. I've had a letter from Stephen, and he's getting leave in the New Year."

"Oh, darling!" cried Thea. "I'm so pleased." And she leaned over and kissed the old lady.

Mrs. Owens was quite surprised by the warmth of her embrace.

"We'll have a real celebration tomorrow evening," Thea said. "You must open a bottle of that champagne. Oh, and I've asked someone to come to dinner—Stephanie Reppington."

"That beautiful girl whose picture was in the *Tatler*? Oh, dear, I'm afraid we shan't be grand enough." It was one of Mrs. Owens' constant fears that she would not be able to live up to the social standards of her "wartime child."

"Oh, Stephanie's not like that," Thea protested. "She's tremendously simple and genuine. I know you'll like her."

"My dear," said Mrs. Owens, "you know that any friend of yours is welcome here," and she smiled so sweetly. It was the most wonderful Christmas Eve, just like a fairy story.

By Christmas afternoon the Establishments Room had been quite transformed, and everything was ready for the tea party. Each plywood table was covered with a lace-edged cloth, and right across the centre of the big middle table, where the adding machines usually stood, ran a row of little pots of holly made so cleverly from tinfoil and decorated with little cut-out black cats in bedsocks. A whole collection of "In" and "Out" trays had been lined with paper doilies and filled with every sort of delicious cake and sandwich—Thea's sausage rolls and Penelope's dainty bridge rolls filled with sandwich spread, Helen's raspberry fingers and little pyramids of chocolate powder and Post Toasties that Joan Fowler called "coconut kisses." The extra sugar ration of months had gone into the display. Caricatures of everybody were pinned on the walls, and some drawings of cuties modelled on "Jane" from the *Daily Mirror*, but less sexy and more whimsical. It had proved very difficult to fit the branches of holly and evergreen to the blue tubular lighting, but by a united effort it had been done; while from the central hanging light there swung an enormous and rather menacing bunch of mistletoe. Stephanie had brought six bottles of peaches in brandy from Fortnum's, and they stood in uncompromisingly lavish display on the table by the window until at the last minute Joan Fowler decided to decorate them with crackers and some silver "star-dust" that flew all over the room and stuck to everyone's clothes. At four sharp visitors from other rooms and sections began to arrive.

Never was the dissimilarity, the lack of basic compatibility of the staff of the Bureau, more apparent than on such customarily festive occasions as Christmas. Compelled by convention to put aside "shop" talk and the gossip of personalities which surrounded their working hours, the tightly welded machine parts soon collapsed into a motley collection of totally disparate individuals. The service officers found it impossible to continue to suggest that they were really intellectuals; the businessmen's service talk creaked badly; while the assumption of business toughness among the dons and schoolmasters was patently laughable. The women of all ages and classes, who so outnumbered the men at the Bureau, glimpsed with shame something of their failure to preserve the standards of glamour and charm normally offered to the other sex; they saw for a moment that in their fatigue and absorption with routine they had forgotten to turn the males out of the dressing-room before it was too late. Everywhere in the room the regulation masks of brightness and competence were slipping, and from behind them peeped forth pre-war faces, pale after so much confinement, and blinking a little at the strange light in which they were seeing the accustomed surroundings, but individual, shy, and faintly disgusted with their colleagues. Heaven knows to what anarchy the discipline of years might have slipped—for an hour or more must pass before the circulation of free beer would allow the tough, brassy, devil-take-the-hindmost gang to assume their wonted leadership—but luckily there was another stable, welding element for whom tea and buns was a familiar signal to take control. From Low Church and Chapel, from C.I.C.U. and O.I.C.U., from the hockey field and the football ground—"God who created me nimble and light of limb"—they were there when needed. All difference, all shyness, was dissolved in the rich strains of "Holy Night" from many baritones that were all but tenors, from contraltos in pious hootings, from the sweet sopranos of girls with nice home backgrounds. Unity was for a moment endangered when the girl who ran the Music Club got together with the polo-sweatered organist and tried to raise the artistic tone—it was, after all, the cultural end of England's war service. They just managed to steer through "All under the Leaves," but broke down badly on "Lullay My Liking," when once more the fine old strains with the good old words floated forth, and soon they had sunk from *Oxford Book of Carols* to plain A. and M.

Tim Prosser, like many of the heads, felt rather out of it. But he smiled patronizingly, as he always did when things took a religious turn, and even sang feebly once or twice when old favourites like "Once in Royal David's City" made their appearance. After a decent interval he turned to his favourite occupation of teasing flirtation. As a result of working with "highbrows" he had grafted a certain "clever" undergraduate diction onto his old bank technique with curious results.

"I'm surprised, Pamela," he said to his girl friend—it was part of the ritual always to repeat their Christian names—"that a fine, upstanding example of female emancipation like yourself should wear those outward and visible signs of servitude," and he gave her earrings a little tug that made her wince.

"Oh, stop it," she cried, "you're hurting!"

"Stop it!" he copied her in falsetto. "Does the slave bid her master to cease his attentions? Does Fatima cry to Bluebeard, 'Hold, enough'? Pamela"—and he looked stern—"I'm afraid that your visit to London has done you no good."

"You're the end," said Pamela.

"The end, Pamela, the end. You really must enlarge your vocabulary. Now the middle, Pamela, or the beginning, why not try them for a change?"

"Oh, stop talking nonsense," protested the girl.

"I know, Pamela, I know. 'Ow I do go on, as the tart said to the sailor. But it's nothing to how I *shall* go on, Pamela, if you wrinkle your nose up at me like that. Not that it is different by an inch from any other nose, a hair's-breadth shorter perhaps than Cleopatra's, but then, you see, Pamela, like Mark Antony, I'm funny that way," and with this he pinched her thigh.

Thea, who was standing nearby, tried not to give them the satisfaction of seeing her look the other way. Not that vulgarity could upset her this afternoon. Stephanie had brought her peach offering directly to her, and they had stood for a moment side by side. When the singing started, the girl had smiled. "It's easier really not to believe it's happening," she had said, and Thea, laughing, had agreed.

A few minutes later Stephanie had slipped away, and Thea stood by a window, gazing out onto the wet, shiny asphalt paths as though her dreams were reflected in their mirrored surface. She smiled gently at some of her girls from time to time and, after Stephanie had left, even joined in one of the carols. It was not the sort of singing that would have been favoured at the rectory—all too hearty and muscular for her father's almost Tractarian taste —so that, happy as she was, she could not feel quite "at home"; she was therefore dissociated enough to notice the strained, red face of one of the new conscripts. Clearly the simple emotion of the carols had brought "home" all too near. Thea's kindly impulses were liberated by her happiness, and, additionally urged by a personal horror of any public scene, she crossed the room, took the girl by the arm, and led her out before the pent-up sobbing had attracted much attention.

The empty workrooms, with their litter of papers and tin lids

full of cigarette stumps, were not ideal rest rooms, but at last
Thea found one with a battered cane armchair. Here she de-
posited the hysterical girl, provided her with a cigarette and a
copy of *Picture Post,* and left her comparatively restored. A
faint ray from the dying winter sun shining upon the wet leaves
of the laurels tempted Thea to take a turn through the shrubbery.

She had never been a light-hearted girl, had always walked a
tightrope across chasms of social anxiety and private phobia, and,
since Colin's death, she had been ceaselessly battling to keep
within her strict limits of propriety the violent anger and frustration into which it had plunged her. Now, therefore, that this sudden release from isolation had come, she was constrained by habit
to savour it in quietude rather than to laugh and sing out loud as
her excited senses urged. She sat on the garden seat under the
high cypress hedge that cut the shrubbery in two and gave herself up to hazy pictures of the future, as she had not dared to do
for over two years. She had just been dissuaded by Stephanie's
good sense from foolish investment of the proceeds of the little
hat shop they had both been so successfully running for some
years in Brook Street, when she heard voices approaching from
the other side of the cypress hedge. It was the sound of her own
name—how often had her self-consciousness imagined this over
the last years, but this time she was not mistaken—that recalled
her from her dreams.

"I simply don't understand all this Thea business," a man's voice
was saying. She recognized him as one of the boys from the Archives Section— "Noah's Ark Cubs" they were always called by
the others. "But do exactly what you like."

And then it was Stephanie's voice that replied, "But naturally,
Nigel, you know that I always do."

Thea stood up so that they should see her before more could
be said; it was one of the primary rules of conduct that her
mother had instilled into her. Stephanie's lips parted for a second
in surprise, then, "Oh, Thea," she said, "I was coming to look for

you. Nigel's asked us to go to their section dance. I said I had no idea what you'd arranged . . ."

"But of course you must go," cried Thea. She felt sure that her lips looked blue with the cold.

"But is it what *you* would like, darling?" asked Stephanie.

"Oh, *I* shouldn't be able to go, I'm afraid. You see I told Mrs. Owens . . ." Thea seemed to remember vaguely that this whole conversation had taken place many times before, could anticipate the disappointment and anger that burned her, as though it were a scene she had been rehearsing all her life.

"Oh, well, of course we can't come then, Nigel," Stephanie said hurriedly, and when the young man murmured something about promises she added sharply, "Don't be absurd, Nigel, you know I never make promises."

"Please, Stephanie," said Thea, "I'm sure you'd enjoy it much more. It'll only be a Christmas dinner at the billet. I'm afraid it'll be very boring."

Stephanie raised her eyebrows slightly and her voice was faintly disgusted as she answered, "My dear, as if everything here wasn't boring. See you tomorrow, Nigel," she added in dismissal. She was clearly anxious that he should not witness Thea's emotion further. They stood for a moment, silent, after Nigel had gone.

"You *would* have liked to have gone . . ." began Thea when Stephanie interrupted quite angrily. "Good heavens, I'm perfectly indifferent what I do," she cried. A moment later she laughed rather shrilly. "I'm sorry," she said, "I'm afraid I'm not very good at all this. You see, it never occurs to me to think of anything that happens here as being important," and she disappeared into the house.

After a little Thea crept back to the shadow of the building. She stood for a moment, leaning against the brick wall, deliberately feeling its harsh surface through her costume, controlling a violent impulse to run after Stephanie and beg her assurance that the whole conversation had been an illusion, had never taken place, had been a joke. . . . Then, carefully shaping her mouth with her lipstick, she returned to the party.

Already beer drinking had begun and the carol singers were giving way to Tim and the "gang." A gramophone was playing "Paper Doll." " 'I'd rather have a paper doll to call my own,' " the crooner sang, " 'than a fickle-minded real live girl.' " Thea accepted a strong gin, coughed at the first mouthful, and then with set expression joined the little group surrounding Tim and his girl friend.

"Cry-baby all right now?" the girl friend asked, and "Yes," answered Thea, "cry-baby's all right."

"My God! I don't know what they expect," said Tim.

"No," replied Thea, "you don't, Tim. You don't know what they expect."

"So that's for you, Tim," said one of the group.

"Oh, Thea and I understand each other, don't we, Thea?" said Tim, and "Oh, yes, we understand each other, Tim," Thea said. She felt sure this was the right manner—bitter, quick, hard. It brought back something she had read in Hemingway, and the loud noise of the gramophone seemed to clinch the scene. In reality she didn't feel at all bitter, only humiliated and unhappy.

"Well," said Tim, "here's to next Christmas, and the one after."

"Think we'll be here, Tim?" asked a young lieutenant.

"Shouldn't be surprised," said Tim. "Got 'em on the run, now, you know, and we've got to paste the bastards until they've forgotten *how* to squeal. Besides there's always the Nips." Two drinks always made him talk in this saloon-bar manner, unless one of his superiors was about, when he tried to preserve some of his hard-won gentlemanly behaviour.

"Two years from now you'll be deputy director, Tim, and won't that be nice," Thea said. She had taken another drink and was prepared to say anything if only they would like her.

"She's got you there, Tim," they cried, and Tim said, "*Touché.* But honestly, Thea, you know as well as I do we can't let up now." He looked serious.

Thea too looked grave. "I know, Tim," she said simply, though she wasn't quite sure to what he referred.

"Well, when you two have settled all our fates," said the girl friend, "we've got to move, darling."

Thea was amused to see that the girl was slightly jealous, so she smiled at Tim quizzically. Strangely enough he didn't respond but followed his girl friend. Thea was puzzled; her memory of scenes in the films had been different from this.

Suddenly everyone moved off, and Thea found herself isolated again. She felt so unhappy that she could hardly restrain her tears. She had worked up a special vulgar manner, and there she was left with it on her hands. Suddenly she saw Stephanie coming towards her, and desperately she made for where Joan Fowler stood.

"Oh, Joan, we ought to be going," she cried. "I told my billet eight o'clock sharp and I've ordered a special car."

Joan Fowler looked bemused but in a mist of happiness. "Oh, Thea, I didn't remember. I *did* say to Penelope . . . Oh, but it'll be quite all right. Shall I get my coat?" she cried.

Thea turned to Stephanie. "Oh, my dear," she said, drawling, "it's too awful of me. I quite forgot last night, when I asked you, that Joan was coming. I was half asleep, I think. I'm afraid I daren't spring an unexpected guest on poor Mrs. Owens; ours is such a *very* humble home. But you won't have missed anything. I'm sure you'd have found it an *awful* bore."

Mummy to the Rescue

→>><<<-

Nurse Ramsay was an incongruous figure in her friend Marjorie's dainty little room. Her muscular, almost masculine arms and legs seemed to emerge uneasily from the cosy chintz-covered chair, her broad, thick-fingered hands moved cumbrously among the Venetian-glass swans and crocheted silk table-mats. Tonight she seemed even more like an Amazon at rest. She was half asleep after a tiring and difficult day with her charge, yet the knowledge that she must get up from her hostess's cheerful fireside and make her way home along the deserted village street through torrents of rain and against a bitter gale forced her into painful, bad-tempered wakefulness. Her huge brow was puckered with lines of resentment, her lips set tight with envy of her friend's independence. It was easy enough to be dainty and sweet if you had a place of your own, but a nurse's position—neither servant nor companion—was a very different matter. She bit almost savagely into the chocolate biscuits, arranged so prettily by Marjorie in the little silver dish, and her glass of warm lemonade seemed only to add to the sourness of her mood.

"Of course, if they weren't so wealthy," she said, "they'd have to send her away, granddaughter or no granddaughter. She's got completely out of hand."

Written in 1948; first published in 1950; scene contemporary.

"I suppose the old people like to have her with them,'" said Marjorie in her jolly, refined voice. She licked the chocolate from her fingers, each in turn, holding them out in a babyish, captivating way, of which, however, Nurse Ramsay was too cross to take any notice. "But she *does* sound a holy terror. Poor old Joey,"—for so she called Nurse Ramsay—"you must have a time with her. They've spoiled her, that's the trouble."

Nurse Ramsay drew her legs apart, and the heavy woollen skirt hitched above her knees, displaying the thick grey of her winter knickers, allowing a suspender to glint in the firelight.

"Spoiled," she said in her deep voice with its Australian twang. "I should think *so* if you *can* spoil a cracked pot. I've had many tiresome ones, but our dear Celia takes the biscuit. The tempers, the sulking, you wouldn't believe, and violent too sometimes; of course, she doesn't know her own strength. So selfish with her toys—that's Mrs. Hartley's fault. 'Whatever she wants, Nurse,' she told me, 'we must give her. It's the least we can do.' Well! I ask you—of course, the old lady's getting a bit queer herself, that's the trouble, and the old gentleman's not much better. 'You're asking for trouble,' I told her, but you might as well talk to a stone wall. You should have heard the fuss the other day just because I couldn't find an old doll. 'If other little girls bit and scratched when they lost their dolls,' I said."

Marjorie gave a little scream of laughter. Nurse Ramsay scowled. She was always suspicious of ridicule.

"What's funny about that?" she asked.

"Oh, nothing, I s'pose," said Marjorie, "if you're used to it, but better you than me."

"I should think so," said Nurse Ramsay. "Why, Dr. Lardner said to me only the other day, 'Nobody but you would stand it, Nurse, you must have nerves of steel.' I suppose I am un-usually . . ."

But Marjorie had closed her ears to a familiar story. She was busy wiping a chocolate stain from her pretty blue crepe-de-Chine frock, liberally soaking her little lace-bordered hanky with

spittle to perform the task. Really Joey was always full of moans
nowadays.

It was so very dark in the little bed, and if you turned one
way you would fall out and if you turned the other it was wall
and you were shut in. Celia held her doll very tightly to her. She
was shaking all over with fright. Nanny had pushed and scratched
so because she wanted Mummy in bed with her. Nanny always
tried to stop her having Mummy, because she was jealous. But
you had to be careful, you had to watch your time, because however much you bit, squelching and driving the teeth into the arm-
flesh, cracking the bone, they could always tie you in, as they had
done before, and then even Granny didn't help you. So she had
pretended to Nanny that she was beaten, that she would do without Mummy. But Nanny did not know—Mummy was in bed.
Celia pushed back the clothes and looked at the familiar blue
wool by the light of the moonbeam from the window-shutter.
"It's all right when Mummy's with you, darling." So long ago
she had said that, before she went on the ship, leaving her with
Granny. "I shall be back with you before you can say Jack Rob-
inson," she had said as Celia sat on the edge of the cabin trunk
and wrapped her doll in the old blue cardigan. She did not come
and she did not come, and then she was there all the time in the
blue cardigan, and if she was with you it was all right. But you
had to be very careful not to let them part you from Mummy's
protection—they could do it by force, but only for a little because Granny wouldn't allow it; but the worst was when they
tricked you into losing. Nanny had done that once, and they had
searched and searched, at least all of them had except Nanny, and
she had pretended to, but all the time you could tell from her eyes
that she was wishing they would never find. The look in Nanny's
eyes had enraged Celia, and she had scratched until the blood ran.
That had meant a bad time following, with Granny angry and
Granddad's voice loud and stern, and being held into bed and little white pills. No, it was important never to be separated—so

Celia took Mummy and, very carefully passing the arms round her neck, she knotted them to the bedpost behind her. It was very difficult to do, but at last she was satisfied that Nanny could not separate them. Then she lay back and watched the yellow moonlight from the window. Yellow was the middle light, and as they drove behind Goddard in the car—Goddard who gave the barley-sugar—with Granny smelling of flowers, they would say yellow, that was the middle light, and green we move, and red we must stop, and green we move, and yellow was the middle light, and red we stop . . .

"It's simply a question of the money not being there," said old Mr. Hartley, and his voice was cracked and irritable. He didn't like the business any more than his wife, and yet her refusal to comprehend financial dealings—thirty-five years before he would have found it feminine, charming—was putting him into the role of advocate, of cruel realist. He had already succumbed to a glass of port in his agitation at the whole idea, and the thought of tomorrow's gout was a further irritant.

"Well, you know best, dear, of course," his wife answered in that calm, pacifying voice which had vexed him over so many years. "But you've often said we ought to change our lawyers, that Mr. Cartwright was a terrible old woman . . ."

"Yes, yes, I know," Mr. Hartley broke in. "Cartwright's an old fool, but he isn't responsible for taxation and this damned government. The truth is, my dear, we're living on very diminished capital and we just can't afford it."

"Well, I do my best to economize," said Mrs. Hartley, "but prices . . ."

"I know, I know," Mr. Hartley broke in again. "But it isn't a question of cheeseparing here and there. We've got to change our whole way of living. In the first place we've got to find somewhere cheaper and smaller to live."

"Well, I don't know how you think we're all going to fit into a smaller house," said his wife.

"That's just the point," he replied. "I don't." He pulled his up-per lip over the lower and stared into the fire, then he looked up at his wife as though he expected her to be waiting for him to say more. But she had no thought for his continuing, only a deep ab-horrence and refusal of the proposal he had implied. She folded her embroidery and, getting up, she moved the pot of cyclamens from the little table by the window. "You've been letting Nurse Ramsay get at you," she said.

"Letting Nurse Ramsay get at me," echoed the old man sav-agely. "What nonsense you do talk, dear. Anyone would think I was a child who couldn't think for myself."

"We're neither of us young, dear," Mrs. Hartley said drily. "Old people *are* a bit childish, you know."

Such flashes of realism in the even dullness of his wife's thought only irritated Mr. Hartley more.

"One thing is clear to me," he said sharply, "on this subject you'll never see sense. Celia gets worse and worse in her behaviour. Nurse Ramsay won't put up with it much longer and we'll never get another nurse nowadays."

Mrs. Hartley set out the patience cards on the little table. "Celia's always very sweet with me," she said. "I don't see what nurse has to grumble at."

"My dear," Mr. Hartley said, and his tone was tender and soothing, "be reasonable. It can't be very pleasant you know—all those rages and the difficulty with feeding, and really she's less able to be clean in her habits than two years ago."

The coarseness of the old man's allusion made Mrs. Hartley's hand tremble. She said nothing, however, but "Red on black." Her silence encouraged her husband.

"I want your help, Alice, over this, can't you see that? Don't force me to act alone. Come over with me and see this place at Dagmere. You're so much better at judging these things than I am."

Mrs. Hartley was silent for a few minutes, then, "Very well," she said, "we'll drive over tomorrow." But her daughter's voice was in her ears. "I'm leaving her with you, Mother. I know she'll be in good hands."

Celia was on the deck of the ship. The sun shone brightly, the gongs beat, the whistles blew, and her pink hair ribbons were flying in the wind. All the stair rails were painted bright red, pillar-box red, like blood, and that was Celia's favourite colour. Red meant we must stop, so Celia stopped. The gentleman in the postman's suit came up to her. "Go on," he said, "don't stand there gaping like a sawney." She wanted to tell him that it was red and that she couldn't go, but the whistles and the gongs made such a noise that he couldn't hear her. "Go on," he cried, and he clapped his hands over her head. Such a wind blew when he clapped his hands that her hair ribbons blew off. Celia began to cry. "A nice thing if every little girl cried when her ribbons blew away," said Nurse Ramsay. She hoped to make Celia run after them, although it was red and that meant we must stop. But there was Granny beckoning to her, and there were the hair ribbons dancing in the sunshine a little way ahead—they were two little pink dolls. So Celia ran, although it was red. And now the side of the ship had gone and great waves came up to pull her down, green and grey. "Mummy, Mummy," she cried, but the waves were folding over her. Mummy would not come, and suddenly there was Mummy holding out her arms to save her—Mummy all in blue. Celia ran into her mother's arms and she sobbed on her mother's bosom. She would not be lonely now, now she was safe. But Celia's Mummy's arms folded tight round her neck, tighter and tighter. "Don't, Mummy, don't. You're hurting me," Celia cried, and she looked up to see her Mummy's eyes cruel and hard like Nurse Ramsay's. Celia began to scream and to fight, but her Mummy's hands closed more and more tightly round her neck, crushing and pulping.

Nurse Ramsay heard the screams as she came up the dark drive. The battery in her torch had given out, and she was feeling her way beside the wet bushes. The screams penetrated slowly into her consciousness, for she was oppressed by the memory of that humiliating scene at the Flannel Hop when Ivy had made such a fool of her in front of Ronnie Armitage. Really, it's getting impossible, she thought at first; you can't leave her alone for half an hour now without trouble. Then suddenly something in the screams made her quicken her pace, and now she was running in panic, the branches of the rhododendron and laurel bushes catching at her like long spiky arms.

When she reached Celia's bedroom it was already too late. No efforts of poor old Mr. Hartley or even of Goddard could bring life back to those flushed, purple cheeks, that swollen black neck. Dr. Lardner, who came shortly after, said that death was due as much to failure of the heart as to strangulation. "She must have woken herself in struggling to free her neck from the woollen jacket," he said, "and the fright acted upon an already weakened heart." It was easy to believe as one surveyed the body: the wreck of a great Britannia blond, thirteen stone at least—she had put on weight ever since her twenty-fifth year; the round blue eyes might have fascinated had they not stared in childish idiocy, the masses of golden hair won praise had they not sprouted in tufts on the great pink cheeks, allying the poor lunatic to the animal world, marking her off from normal men and women.

Nurse Ramsay said the whole thing was a judgment. "If they hadn't been so obstinate and had agreed to send her to a proper home she'd have been alive today," she added. But Mrs. Hartley, who was a religious woman, offered thanks to God that night that Death had come in time to prevent her being taken away. It's almost as though her mother had come to help her when she was in trouble, she thought.

What Do Hippos Eat?

>><<

She seemed such a little bit of a thing as she peered through the railings at the huge, cumbrous bison, her neat boyish head of short-cut, tight red curls such a contrast to the matted chocolate wool that lay in patches around the beast's long, mournful features. "Ginger for pluck" Maurice always called her, and indeed her well-knit little figure and firm stance were redolent of determination and cheek, and cried out her virtues as a real good pal, her Dead-End-Kid appeal that went through to the heart.

"My, my," she said to the bison, "someone forgot to bring his comb." She was such a round-eyed urchin that one felt almost surprised when she did not put out her tongue.

Maurice smiled paternally and fingered his little grey First-World-War moustache. "How would you like to have a couple of rounds in the ring with that?" he asked, laughing.

"Oh, I'd take it on all right," she said and gave him one of her funny straight looks. She had only two roles with men—tomboy and good scout. Even they were very alike, except that the good scout was full of deep, silent understanding and could hold her drink.

Maurice guffawed. "My God, I believe you would! Size means nothing to you." His admiration was perfectly genuine, for under his ostentatious virility he was a physically timorous

Written in 1947; first published in *The Listener* in 1949; scene contemporary.

man with a taste for the brutal. As he looked appraisingly at her slender shoulders and tight little breasts he felt wonderfully protective and sentimental. All the same it irked him that he wasn't getting on faster with his scheme. It was true, he reflected, that he hadn't paid a sausage out in rent for the last two months and she'd cashed two stumers for him without batting an eyelid when they came back "R.D."; but now that he'd turned fifty-five he wanted a more secure berth than that. The truth was that Maurice had experienced some unpleasant bouts of giddiness in the mornings recently, and his heart—he called it "the old ticker" even to himself—often missed a beat when he climbed upstairs. Under such circumstances, a partnership in the boarding house—it was his name for legalized use of her capital—would just suit him, with a liberal supply of pocket money for the "dogs." Earls Court wasn't exactly the neighbourhood he would have chosen, indeed, when he remembered his brief residence in Clarges Street, now seen in retrospect as lasting for years. He felt ashamed that he should have sunk so low, but he had known too much of Camden Town and the York Road, Waterloo, in the interval not to count his blessings while they lasted. He was, in fact, worn out with schemes and lies and phony deals, he slept badly, and his nerves were giving way. Temporary setbacks made him act, as now, precipitately.

"It's grand to see you enjoying yourself, Greta," he said. "You ought to be having lots of fun while you're still young. It's a damned shame the way you have to work. You had a hard enough life as a kid, God knows, and now this blasted house hanging round your neck. It's too much even for your heavyweight shoulders," and he laughed.

Greta stuck out her chin. "I had my fun all right," she said. "You don't have to be rich to enjoy life as a kid."

"Oh, I know," Maurice replied with a smile, as though she had been referring to hopscotch in the back alley. "You can take it on the chin all right, I'll say that for you. But all the same," he continued with a sigh, "I'd give my right hand to have known you when I still had a bit of money. *I'd* have put an end to all these worries."

Greta had decided not to notice Maurice's remarks for a few moments, so she turned to watch a scarlet ibis wading in the pool behind them.

"Aren't you a lucky bird not to be a hat?" she asked. She had her special brand of humour—the gang at the local called it "Greta's dopey jokes." Then, "You're my only money worry, Maurice Legge," she said, her Manchester accent more emphasized than usual, "and what are you going to do about *that?*"

Self-pity and suppressed anger brought beads of sweat to his temples, and he mopped them with the silk handkerchief which he kept in his cuff—an old ex-officer habit, he was always careful to explain. Two pictures flashed before him in quick succession. First, the young ex-subaltern, a possible for the Harlequins: handsome, easygoing; a man to whom stockbrokers offered £2,000-a-year jobs on his social contacts alone. Then the other picture, still a handsome man, old and tired now, but unmistakably a gentleman for all the doubtful shifts into which life had forced him—he bent before the cheap snubs and insults of a common little creature, whom the ex-subaltern would not have noticed in a crowd. He could almost hear the commentator say, "Look upon this picture and on *this*," and his eyes filled with tears. This cinematographic representation of life had grown on him in middle age. It was not a surprising phenomenon, since his days were passed in a highly coloured histrionic blur. He would move from Prince's to the Cri, from the Cri to the Troc, from the Troc to Odennino's, trying with a closely knit web of circumstantial narrative to pull off complicated deals or, at the very least, to cadge a drink from some toughly sentimental, whisky-soaking colonial or American. In the intervals of this "work" he went to the "pictures" or sat before the gasfire of his bed-sitting-room working out large betting schemes, which he had not the capital to realize, or reading cheap thrillers. Past, present, and future, truth and lies, all moved before him in short, vivid, dramatic scenes that merged into a background mist of anxiety, imagined grandeur, and sticky sentiment. But behind it all was a certain hard core of determination to survive. It was this that made him swallow Greta's snub and turn to the buffaloes.

"Nice mild-looking fellows, you would say those were, wouldn't you?" he asked.

Greta looked at their large, brown calf's eyes and their shapely horns and nodded.

"How wrong you'd be," said Maurice. "I shall never forget once up country from Nairobi going through a village after buffalo had stampeded. Not a pleasant sight at all. Harry Brand was with me, and I've never seen a chap turn so green. 'So help me God, Maurice,' he said, 'I shall have to call it a day and turn back.' Funny thing, really, because he was a beefy sort of cove. But you remember him, anyhow."

Greta shook her head.

"Oh, yes, you do, darling," said Maurice. "Great red-faced fellow we met one evening outside the Plaza."

Greta looked puzzled but denied it.

"I'm sure you did," Maurice went on. Then he added thoughtfully, "But wait a minute though, perhaps you're right. Yes, you are. I was with Dolly." And, glad to have checked this point, he returned to Kenya with renewed ardour.

Greta listened to his stories with rapt attention. However her business acumen and natural hardness might protect her against his wilder financial schemes, her pride and delight in his recounted exploits were for once in her life quite unself-consciously childlike. His attraction as a gentleman was enhanced for her by the cosmopolitan background which every day of their intimacy revealed a little more. She felt, more justly than she realized, that it was an authentication of all that the films had hinted to her. The digressions, irrelevant ramifications, and long-winded checks of memory in which Maurice indulged might have been expected to bore his listeners, but, strangely enough, they were exactly the features which finally convinced the sceptical, banishing suspicions of glibness and lending realism to art. To Greta they

were the supreme pleasure, for they seemed somehow to involve
her own participation in these exciting adventures. After all,
she had, it seemed, only just missed meeting Harry Brand outside the Plaza. For Maurice himself they formed a reassurance
which his self-confidence badly needed. He had told so many
stories for so many years, truth and fiction were so inextricably
mixed, that to check a new falsehood by a poorly remembered
old one made him feel that in some way truth must be involved
somewhere.

As they walked into the Lion House, Maurice felt his confidence returning. He was ready for any audience. And there, gazing at the Siberian tiger, an audience awaited him—an elderly
solicitor and his wife, a working-class woman with two small
children. Maurice began to talk to Greta in a voice pitched
loudly enough for the others to hear.

"Siberian tiger, eh?" he said. "A present from our not such dear
friends the Russians. He's a beautiful creature though. Never had
any experience with them myself, but I should think they might
be very ugly customers. Don't you agree, sir?" he asked the solicitor, who replied embarrassedly, "Yes, yes, I should imagine
so."

"No," said Maurice loudly and self-depreciatingly. "I've only
run across this chap's Indian cousin, who's altogether smaller fry.
Most of this stuff about man-eaters, you know, is a lot of nonsense. No tiger turns to human flesh until he's too old to hold his
own in the jungle."

"Do you hear that, Billy?" said the woman to her son.

"Oh, yes," Maurice continued, "all these round-ups of tigers
for important people, makes you laugh if you know about it.
Half the poor blighters can hardly stand up with old age. So if
anyone asks you to a tiger shoot, laddy," he said to the boy, "you
can be sure of bringing your mother back a nice new rug."

"There you are, Billy," said the woman, "you hear what the
gentleman says," and everyone laughed.

Greta felt so proud of Maurice. He looked so handsome,
despite all his wrinkles and pouches, and the line of his arm ap-

peared so strong and manly as he gripped the rail in front of him, that she longed to take his hand in hers and to stroke it. He had told her so often, however, that physical caresses in public were "just not done," and she was able now to check herself in time. Greta was both anxious and quick to learn as she climbed up the economic ladder, and she felt it was one of the great advantages of her relations with Maurice that he could teach her so much. She no longer said "serviette" or dropped her shoes off under restaurant tables. She never went out now without gloves—Maurice's ideas of polite behaviour belonged rather to his early years —but she also no longer blew into them when she took them off. She could hardly guess that he had mixed little with respectable people of any class for over fifteen years, and thus she was able to retain many of her humorous phrases—"he's a smell on the landing to me" was a favourite—without qualms, for Maurice greeted them with a smile. She was jealous sometimes of his larking with waitresses, but he told her not to be suburban, and in any case she felt ready to forgive anything as she watched him finger the knot of his old school tie while he studied the menu, and heard him refer to her as "madam" when he finally gave the order.

As the keeper passed the tiger cage with a bucket of dung Maurice asked him which the biggest lion was now and how many pounds of meat the black leopard consumed in a day. He was one of the older keepers and received Maurice's officer-to-batman manner in a more friendly spirit than was often the case these days. Soon the whole party was being taken behind the scenes to watch a puma cross one of the little bridges to its outdoor cage. Greta felt quite queenly when she saw the respectful manner in which the keeper received Maurice's tip, and she attempted a new charming bow and smile as the party broke up. She even approved Maurice's giving sixpence to the two little children, though in general she did not care to spend her money too lavishly.

Maurice looked ten years younger as they walked away from

the Lion House. He had always been interested in wild animals, felt a mastery over them that he lacked with men, and these boyish sensations combined with a genuine æsthetic feeling for their shape and colour were now reawakened. It was so seldom that he experienced any pleasure divorced from his own schemes and anxieties these days, and his body expanded and revelled in the carefree mood. He stroked the soft nose of the caribou as it pushed through the bars in quest of food. It was not, therefore, surprising that he felt little pleasure in Greta's urchin impudence when she gave the animal the raspberry. But he was too happy to comment on her vulgarity. For her, wild animals were an alarming and remote tribe that, once secured behind bars or in travelling circuses, could be treated as comic turns.

But Greta's thoughts were not, in any case, on the beasts; they were very much upon Maurice. She had seldom felt him so desirable, and it worried her to see the creases of his suit—so overcleaned and repaired—shine in the sunlight. She knew the pitiable state of his few underclothes and threadbare second suit as they reposed in the chest of drawers in a litter of important-looking papers, solicitors' letters, unpaid bills, and pawn tickets—knew only too well, for in the first weeks of his failure to pay his rent she had searched in vain for any saleable articles. Though she could not allow him to handle her money since he was obviously so foolish about business, he *was* her man and she wanted him to look nice. She made up her mind to buy him a whole new outfit. She had done very well out of letting her rooms in the last few years and could afford to spend a little and still leave the good margin in the bank which represented respectability to her. Greta's realism had begun at sixteen as a waitress; Maurice's had never really got going. It was hardly an even match. In her greater sense of reality she was far clearer about what she did and did not want. She wanted a man, and the fact that he was twenty years older did not trouble her, for she liked experience. Nevertheless she did not want to tie herself to someone who might play fast and loose with her savings, nor even perhaps would she want that man at all when he had passed sixty. However, if he was not to have her money he should certainly have a suit.

Greta's friendly thoughts, her increased desire for him, communicated themselves to Maurice and, added to his own happy mood, made him walk on air. Tips passed lavishly as they fed the sea lions from the rocks—Greta screamed and jumped like a little girl as the shapely, blubbery creatures flopped about her; gave honey to the brown bear—Maurice smiled in his old way as she cried, "Who's got a bear behind?" How devil-may-care he was with a carefully selected snake coiled round his arm! The monkeys rather damped their ardour, for they were both united in their prudish disapproval of certain antics. But an incident in front of the spider monkeys' cage finally broke up their happy mood. They were laughing delightedly as the monkeys snatched the bread they offered and swung away with feet, hands, and tails alike, when a young couple approached the cage. In general Greta did not care for freaks, and there was certainly something a bit cranky about the young woman's long, shapeless grey frock and the young man's corduroys and knapsack. They were, in fact, R.A.D.A. students at play. But their studied seriousness and carefully beautiful voices impressed Greta.

"Their movements *are* rather heavenly," said the girl. "Almost a ghostlike flitting."

"It's immensely interesting that they should have developed prehensile tails," said the boy and, seeing Greta watching him, he smiled the new shy smile he was developing to play Oswald in *Ghosts*. Greta was completely conquered and smiled back. Maurice began to talk loudly, but Greta frowned impatiently, for the boy was speaking again.

"You see they're really gibbons, at least I think so"—and he smiled shyly again—"and yet they've developed prehensile tails as well as arms and legs for swinging. It's a complete vindication of Lamarck really."

"You do find the oddest things interesting, darling," said the girl.

Greta felt so angry with her. "You can always learn something if you keep your ears open," she said and smiled again at the boy.

"Come along," said Maurice impatiently. "We don't want to watch these damned monkeys all day."

But Greta waited a few minutes before following.

They stood surveying the hideous flat features of the lion-faced baboon in angry silence. "Why the hell you want to encourage that damned unwashed, long-haired young swine," said Maurice, "I can't imagine."

"Because," replied Greta—she snapped like a turtle when she was annoyed—"I'm willing to learn from others occasionally."

"And you've got a hell of a lot to learn."

"I fully appreciate the lessons," Greta cried, "and I hope you appreciate what I pay for them."

Maurice's eyes narrowed with rage. "What exactly do you mean by that?"

"Two months' rent—that's what I mean by that, Maurice Legge." He raised his fist as though to hit her, and she ran from him, calling, "You keep away from me."

An elderly woman turned to stare at them.

"I'll leave your bloody house tonight," he shouted. "You'll get your cheque tomorrow morning."

"Yes," said Greta, "and it'll come back R.D. by the end of the week."

"You little so-and-so," Maurice cried—it was one of his favourite phrases. He was trembling with rage, but behind his anger he could see all his hopes crumbling. He felt completely at the end of his tether; a night on the streets at his age might finish him off. With a tremendous effort he controlled his temper. "Don't let's be greater fools than God made us," he said.

Greta watched his collapse with genuine pity; she felt more than ever determined to look after him. But first, like all men, he must be taught a lesson, a lesson for spoiled children. From the pages of her favourite woman's journal she recalled the advice, "He will accept you at the price you put on yourself, so don't make yourself cheap"—it was not exactly the situation the editress had in mind, but it seemed to apply.

"No, thank you, Maurice. I've had enough. We're friends if you like, but friends apart." She felt very pleased with the phrase. Sturdy, jaunty, independent, she walked away from him, past the pelicans and the ravens, towards the tunnel.

Maurice stood sullenly for a few minutes, then he ran after her. He saw her at the far end of the tunnel and shouted "Greta! Greta!" until his ears were filled with the echoes. His heart was pounding heavily and his legs felt like lead. He noticed the flood-level mark and wished he were under the waters.

Greta stood and waited for him.

"I'm sorry, kiddie," he said. "I can't say more."

"That's all right," she replied, the perfect good scout. "We'll say no more about it."

They went slowly back through the tunnel to the tea-room.

The "set" tea with watercress *ad lib* was like a children's picnic as they laughed and teased away the memory of the angry outburst. Greta was determined to bring back Maurice's pleasure. She felt sure of her mastery now and was anxious to erase all trace of the events that had revealed it. She stuffed herself almost sick with bread and butter and buns because he so delighted to tease her about her "kid's appetite." "Greedy guts," he said, smiling, as she took a second helping of watercress. He was quite sentimental now as he thought of where he would be without her generosity; she might not be a lady but she certainly had a heart of gold. Ever sanguine and tenacious, he began to consider new ways of putting his little scheme to her.

"Shall we have a dekko at the elephants and then make for home?" he asked.

As they passed through the tunnel once more, Greta thought how alike all men are, just children really, and she purred as she thought how well she understood him. When they approached the pool where the orange-toothed coypus sat on the rocks, cleaning their whiskers, she began to sing, " 'He's my guy. Heaven knows why I love him, but he's my guy.' "

"There's your famous musquash coats," said Maurice, pointing at the huge rats with their wet, course bristles.

"I *should* believe you," Greta cried. They were both delighted when he convinced her—he because she was such a funny, ignorant little rascal, she because it really was surprising what he knew. "Well, I'll never have a musquash coat," she cried, "not from creatures with teeth like that."

They watched the otter as it swam in crazy circles round its pool, trying ceaselessly to dig a way through the concrete sides down to the open sea. "The way it keeps scrabbling," said Greta, "I should think it wanted to get out." They both had to laugh at its antics.

When they reached the Elephant House, Maurice asked the keeper if they could go to the back of the hippopotamus pool. He was quite a young cockney who didn't respond to Maurice's manner at all.

"It's not usual," he said. "There's nothing to see, you know, that you can't see from here."

"All the same," replied Maurice, "I'd like to take the lady round the back."

"Okay, colonel," the boy said, winking across at Greta, "but it's not the place I'd choose to take my girl friend."

It was, indeed, most unattractive on closer inspection. The hot steam from the muddy water smelled abominable, and the sides of the pool were slippery with slime. Every now and again the huge black forms would roll over, displacing ripples of brown foam-flecked water, and malevolent eyes on the ends of stalks would appear above the surface for a moment. Maurice offered the keeper a half crown.

"That's all right," he said. "You keep your money. I get paid, you know."

It was most difficult to walk on the slimy surface, and Maurice, who was exhausted from the afternoon's events, slipped and would have fallen had not the boy caught his arm. As he recovered his balance he noticed Greta returning the keeper's amused smile. A moment later a hippopotamus surfaced, blowing sprays of water from its great pink nostrils. Maurice's suit was flecked with mud.

"Sorry about that," said the keeper.

But Greta begged him not to worry. "It's a terrible old thing, anyway. I'm going to get him a new one tomorrow," she explained.

Maurice felt his throat fill with rage, anger that almost blinded him. He put his hands on her hips and in a moment he would have pushed her into the thick, vaporous water; then he suddenly realized that he had no idea what would happen. Hippos, he felt sure, were not carnivorous, but in their anger at the disturbance they might destroy her, and that would be the end of both of them, he reflected with bitter satisfaction. On the other hand, they might just turn away from the floating Greta in disgust, in which case he would simply have mucked up all his schemes. He withdrew his hands in despair. Once again he had to control his fury.

Greta was most surprised when she felt his hands on her waist. How funny men were, she reflected, just when you thought you understood them, they did something unexpected like that. Maurice, who was always lecturing her for showing her affection in public! She was really rather touched by the gesture. All the same, she decided, it would be wiser not to notice it then. So turning her wide-eyed gaze up at him, "What *do* hippos eat, darling?" she asked in her childlike way.

Totentanz

⬧⟫⟪⬧

The news of the Cappers' good fortune first became generally known at the Master's garden party. It was surprisingly well received, in view of the number of their enemies in the university, and for this the unusually fine weather was largely responsible. In their subarctic isolation, cut off from the main stream of Anglo-Saxon culture and its preferments, sodden with continual mists, pinched by perpetual northeast gales, kept always a little at bay by the natives with their self-satisfied homeliness and their smugly traditional hospitality, the dons and their wives formed a phalanx against spontaneous gaiety that would have satisfied John Knox himself. But rare though days of sunshine were, they transformed the town as completely as if it had been one of those scenes in a child's painting book on which you had only to sprinkle water for the brighter colours to emerge. The Master's lawns, surfeited with rain and mist, lay in flaunting spring green beneath the even deep blue of the July sky. The neat squares of the eighteenth-century burghers' houses and the twisted shapes of the massive grey lochside ruins recovered their designs from the blurring mists. The clumps of wallflowers, gold and copper, filling the crevices of the walls, seemed to mock the solemnity of the covenanting crows that croaked censoriously above them. The famous pale-blue silk of the scholars' gowns flashed like sil-

---

Written in 1948; first published in *Horizon* (London) in 1949; scene immediate post Second World War.

ver airships beneath the deeper sky. On such a day even the most mildewed and disappointed of the professors, the most blue and deadening of their wives, felt impulses of generosity, or at any rate a freedom from bitterness, that allowed them to rejoice at a fellow prisoner's release. Only the youngest and most naïve research students could be deceived by the sun into brushing the mould off their *own* hopes and ideals, but if others had found a way back to their aims, well, good luck to them!—in any case, the Cappers, especially Mrs. Capper, had only disturbed the general morass with their futile struggles, and most people would be glad to see them go.

The Master's wife, always so eccentric in her large fringed cape, said in her deep voice, "It's come just in time. Just in time, that is, for Isobel."

"Just in time," squeaked little Miss Thurkill, the assistant French lecturer. "I should have thought any time was right for a great legacy like that," and she giggled—really the old woman said such odd, personal things.

"Yes, just in time," repeated the Master's wife; she prided herself on understanding human beings and lost no opportunity of expounding them. "A few months more and she would have rotted away."

In the wide opening between the points of his old-fashioned high Gladstone collar, the Master's protrusive Adam's apple wobbled, gulped. In Oxford or Cambridge his wife's eccentricity would have been an assistance; up here, had he not known exactly how to isolate her, it might have been an embarrassment.

"How typical of women," he said in the unctuous but incisive voice that convinced so many businessmen and baillies that they were dealing with a scholar whose head was screwed on the right way. "How typical of women to consider only the legacy. Very nice of course, a great help in their new sphere." There was a trace of bitterness, for his own wife's fortune, so important when they had started, had vanished through his unfortunate investments. "But Capper's London Chair is the important thing. A new Chair too, Professor of the History of Technics and Art. Here, of course, we've come to accept so many of Capper's ideas into our everyday thoughts, as a result of his immense powers of persuasion and . . . and his great enthusiasm"—he paused, staring eaglelike beneath his bushy white eyebrows, the scholar who was judge of men—"that we forget how revolutionary some of them are." He had, indeed, the vaguest conception of anything that his subordinates thought, an administrator has to keep above detail. "No doubt there'll be fireworks, but I venture to suggest that Capper's youth and energy will win the day, don't you agree with me, Todhurst?"

Mr. Todhurst's white suet-pudding face tufted with sandy hair was unimpressed. He was a great deal younger than Capper and still determined to remember what a backwater he was stranded in. "Capper's not so young," he said, ostentatiously Yorkshire. "Maybe they'll have heard it all before, and happen they'll tell him so too."

But the Master was conveniently able to ignore Todhurst, for red-faced Sir George was approaching, the wealthiest, most influential businessman on the university board. A tough and rough diamond with his Glaswegian accent and his powerful, whiskied breath, Sir George was nevertheless impressed by the size of the legacy. "Five hundred thousand pounds." He gave a whistle. "That's no so bad a sum. Though, mind you, this government of robbers'll be taking a tidy part of it away in taxation. But still I'm glad for the sake of his missus." Perhaps, he thought, Mrs. Capper would help in getting Margaret presented at Court. How little he knew Isobel Capper—his wife would not have made the mistake.

"And this magnificent appointment coming along at the same time," said the Master.

"Aye," said Sir George—he did not understand that so well— "there's no doubt Capper's a smart young chap." Perhaps, he thought, the board has been a bit slow, the Master was getting on and they might need a level-headed, warm young fellow.

"Oh, there they are," squeaked Miss Thurkill excitedly. "I must say Isobel certainly looks . . ." But she could find no words to describe Isobel's appearance, it was really so very outré.

Nothing could have fitted Isobel Capper's combination of chic and Liberty artiness better than the ultra-smart dressing-gown effect of her New Look dress, the floating flimsiness of her little flowered hat. Her long stride was increased with excitement, even her thin white face had relaxed its tenseness and her amber eyes sparkled with triumph. Against the broad pink-and-black stripes of her elaborate bustled dress, her red hair clashed like fire. She was a little impatient with the tail end of an episode that she was glad to close, her mind was crowded with schemes, but still this victory parade, though petty and provincial, would be a pleasant start to a new life. Brian, too, looked nearer twenty than forty, most of his hard, boyish charm, his emphasized friendliness and sincerity, had returned with the prospect of his new appointment. He tossed his brown curly hair back from his forehead as, loose-limbed, athletic, he leaped a deck chair to speak to Sir George. "Hope so very much to see something of you and Lady Maclean if all those company meetings permit." Before the Master he stood erect, serious, a little abashed. "So impossible to speak adequately of what I shall carry away from here . . ."

There was no doubt that Brian was quite himself again. His even white teeth gleamed as he smiled at the Master's wife. To her he presented himself almost with a wink as the professional charmer, because after all she was not a woman you could fool. "The awful thing is that my first thought about it is for all the fun we're going to have." With Todhurst he shared their contempt for the backwater. "Not going to say I wish you'd got the appointment, because I don't. Besides, *Kunstgeschichte*, old man! —you and I know what a bloody fraud the whole thing is. Not that I don't intend to make something useful out of it all, and that's exactly why I've got to pick your brains before I go South." It was really amazing, Isobel thought, how the news had revived him—alive, so terribly keen and yet modest withal, and behind everything steady as a rock, a young chap of forty, in fact, who would go far.

Her own method was far more direct; she had never shared her husband's spontaneous sense of salesmanship, at times even found its nauseating. There was no need to bother about these people any more and she did not intend to do so. "Silly to say we shall meet again, Sir George," she told him before he could get round to asking. "It's only in the bonny North that the arts are conducted on purely business lines." Todhurst, along with all the other junior dons, she ignored. "You must be so happy," said Jessie Colquhoun, the poetess of the lochs. "I shan't be *quite* happy," Isobel replied, "until we've crossed the Border."

"Of *course* we shall lose touch," she said to the Master's wife, "but I'm not so pleased as you think I am." And really, she thought, if the old woman's eccentricity had not been quite so provincial and frowsty it might have been possible to invite her to London.

Her especial venom was reserved for the Master himself. "Dear Mrs. Capper," he intoned. "What a tremendous loss you will be to us, and Capper too, the ablest man on the faculty." "I wonder what you'll say to the board when they wake up to their loss, as I'm sure they will," replied Isobel. "It'll take a lot of explaining."

And yet the Master's wife was quite right, it was only just in time for both of them. Brian had begun to slip back badly in the last few years. His smile, the very centre of his charm, had grown too mechanical, gum recession was giving him an equine look. His self-satisfaction, which had once made him so friendly to all —useful and useless alike—had begun to appear as heavy indifference. When he had first come North he had danced like a shadow-boxer from one group to another, making the powerful heady with praise, giving to the embittered a cherished moment of flattery, yet never committing himself; engaging all hearts by his youthful belief in Utopia, so much more acceptable because he was obviously so fundamentally sound. But with the years his smiling sincerity had begun to change to dogmatism; he could

afford his own views and often they were not interesting, occasionally very dull. Younger colleagues annoyed him, he knew
that they thought him out of date. Though he still wanted always
to be liked, he had remained "a young man" too long to have
any technique for charming the *really* young. Faced by their contempt, he was often rude and sulky. The long apprenticeship in
pleasing—the endless years of scholarships and examinations, of
being the outstanding student of the year—was now too far behind to guard him from the warping atmosphere of the town.
Commonwealths and Harmsworths were becoming remote memories; the Dulwich trams of his schooldays, the laurel bushes of
his suburban childhood, were closer to him now than the dreams
and ambitions of Harvard, Oxford, and McGill. Had the Chair
come a year later he would probably have refused it. He had been
such a success at thirty-three, it would have been easy to forget
that at forty he was no longer an infant phenomenon.

If Brian had been rescued from the waters of Lethe in the nick
of time, Isobel had been torn from the flames of hell. Her hatred
of the university and the heat of her ambition had begun to burn
her from within, until the strained white face with cheekbones
almost bursting through the skin and the overintense eyes recalled some witch in death agonies. It did not take long for the
superiority of her wit and taste to cease to bother a world in
which they were unintelligible; depression and a lack of audience soon gave her irony a "governessy" flavour, until at last
the legend of Mrs. Capper's sharp tongue had begun to bore herself as much as others. The gold and white satin, the wooden
Negro page of her Regency room had begun to fret her nerves
with their shabbiness, yet it seemed pointless to furnish anew,
even if she could have afforded it, for a world she so much
despised. She made less and less pretence of reading or listening to music, and yet for months she would hardly stir outside.
Everything that might have been successful in a more sophisticated society was misunderstood here: her intellectual Angli-
canism was regarded as dowdy church-going, her beloved
Caravaggio was confused with Greuze, her Purcell enthusiasm

thought to be a hangover from the time when *The Beggar's Opera* was all the rage; she would have done far better, been thought more daring, with Medici, van Goghs, and some records of the "Bolero." She had come to watch all Brian's habits with horror, his little provincial don's sarcasms, his tobacco-jarred, golfy homeliness, his habit of pointing with his pipe and saying, "Now hold on a minute. I want to examine this average man or woman of yours more carefully"; or "Anarchism, now that's a very interesting word, but are we *quite* sure we know what it means?" She became steadily more afraid of "going to pieces," knew herself to be toppling on the edge of a neurotic apathy from which she would never recover.

It was not surprising, therefore, that as she said good-bye for the third time to old Professor Green, who was so absent-minded, she blessed the waves that had sucked Aunt Gladys down in a confusion of flannel petticoats and straggling grey hair, the real-istic sailor who had cut Uncle Joseph's bony fingers from the side of an overloaded lifeboat. She was rich, rich enough to realize her wildest ambitions; beside this, Brian's professorship seemed of little importance. And yet in Isobel's growing schemes it had its place, for she had determined to storm London, and she was quite shrewd enough to realize that she would never take that citadel by force of cash alone, far better to enter by the academic gate she knew so well.

By January six months of thick white mists and driving rain had finally dissipated the faint traces of July's charity, and with them all interest in the Cappers' fortunes. The Master's wife, dragged along by her two French bulldogs, was fighting her way through Aidan's arch against a battery of hail when she all but collided with Miss Thurkill returning from lunch at the British Restaurant. She would have passed on with a nod but Miss Thurkill's red fox-terrier nose was quivering with news.

"The Cappers' good fortune seems to have been quite a sell," she yelped. "They've got that great house of her uncle's on their hands."

"From all I hear about London conditions, Pentonville prison would be a prize these days," boomed the Master's wife.

"Oh, but that isn't all. It's quite grisly." Miss Thurkill giggled. "They've got to have the bodies in the house forever and ever. It's part of the conditions of the will."

Boredom had given the Master's wife a conviction of psychic as well as psychological powers, and she suddenly "felt aware of evil."

"I was wrong when I said that silly little woman was saved in time. Pathetic creature with her cheap ambitions and her dressing-up clothes, she's in for a very bad time."

Something of the old woman's prophetic mood was communicated to Miss Thurkill, and she found herself saying, "I know. Isn't it horrible?"

For a moment they stood outlined against the grey stormy sky, the Master's wife, her great black mackintosh cape billowing out behind like an evil bat, Miss Thurkill sharp and thin like a barking jackal. Then the younger woman laughed nervously. "Well, I must rush on or I'll be drenched to the skin."

She could not hear the other's reply for the howling of the wind, but it sounded curiously like "Why not?"

Miss Thurkill was, of course, exaggerating wildly when she spoke of "bodies" in the house, because the bones of Uncle Joseph and Aunt Gladys were long since irrevocably Atlantic coral or on the way to it. But there was a clause in the will that was troublesome enough to give Isobel great cause for anxiety in the midst of her triumphant campaign for power.

A very short time had been needed to prove that the Cappers were well on the way to a brilliant success. Todhurst had proved a false prophet—Brian had been received with acclamation in the London academic world, not only within the university but in the smart society of the museums and art galleries, and in the houses of rich connoisseurs, art dealers, smart sociologists and archæologists with chic that lay around its periphery. It has to be remembered that many of those with Brian's peculiar brand

of juvenile careerist charm were now getting a little passé and
tired, while the post-war generation were somehow too total in
outlook, too sure of their views, to achieve the necessary flexi-
bility, the required chameleon character. Brian might have passed
unnoticed in 1935; in 1949 he appeared as a refreshing draught
from the barbaric North. Already his name was current at the
high tables of All Souls and King's—a man to watch. He talked
on the Third Programme and on the Brains Trust—Isobel was a
bit doubtful about this—he reviewed for smart weeklies and
monthlies, he was commissioned to write a Pelican book.

Isobel was pleased with all this, but she aimed at something
more than an academical sphere however chic—she was incurably romantic, and over Brian's shoulder she saw a long line of
soldier-mystics back from Persia, introvert explorers, able
young Conservatives, important Dominicans, and Continental
novelists with international reputations snatched from the jaws
of O.G.P.U.—and at the centre, herself, the woman who counted.
Brian's success would be a help, their money more so. For the
moment her own role was a passive one; she was content if she
"went down," and for this her chic Anglo-Catholicism—almost
Dominican in theological flavour, almost Jesuit Counter-Refor-
mation in æsthetic taste—combined with her spiteful wit, power
of mimicry, and interesting appearance, sufficed. Meanwhile
she was watching and learning, entertaining lavishly, being pleasant to everyone and selecting carefully the important few who
were to carry them on to the next stage—the most influential
people within their present circle, but not, and here she was most
careful, people who were too many jumps ahead; they would
come later. By the time that this ridiculous, this insane clause in
the will had been definitely proved, she had already chosen the
four people who must be cultivated.

First and most obviously, Professor Cadaver, that long, gaunt
old man with his corseted figure, his military moustache, and his
almost too beautiful clothes; foremost of archæologists, author
of *Digging Up the Dead, The Tomb My Treasure House,* and
Where Grave Thy Victory? It was not only the tombs of the an-

cient world on which he was a final authority, for in the intervals between his expeditions to the Near East and North Africa
he had familiarized himself with all the principal cemeteries of
the British Isles and had formed a remarkable collection of photographs of unusual graves. His enthusiasm for the ornate ma-
sonry of the nineteenth century had given him *réclame* among
the devotees of Victorian art. He enthusiastically supported
Brian's views on the sociological importance of burial customs,
though he often irritated his younger colleague by the emphasis
he seemed to lay upon the state of preservation of the bodies
themselves. Over embalming in particular he would wax very
enthusiastic—"Every feature, every limb, preserved in their life-
time beauty," he would say, "and yet over all the odour of decay,
the sweet stillness of death." A strange old man! For Isobel too
he seemed to have a great admiration: he would watch her with
his old reptilian eyes for hours on end—"What wonderful bone
structure," he would say; "one can almost *see* the cheekbones."
"How few people one sees today, Mrs. Capper, with your perfect pallor, at times it seems almost livid."

Over Lady Maude she hesitated longer. There were so many
old women, well connected and rich, who were interested in art
history, and of these Lady Maude was physically the least pre-
possessing. With her little myopic pig's eyes, her wide-brimmed
hats insecurely pinned to falling coils of hennaed hair, and her
enormous body encased in musquash, she might have been
passed over by any eye less sharp than Isobel's. But Lady Maude
had been everywhere and seen everything. Treasures locked
from all other Western gaze by Soviet secrecy or Muslim piety
had been revealed to her. American millionaires had shown her
masterpieces of provenance so dubious that they could not be
publicly announced without international complications. She
had spent many hours watching the best modern fakers at
work. Her memory was detailed and exact, and though her eye-
sight was failing daily, her strong glasses still registered what she
saw as though it had been photographed by the camera. Outside
her knowledge of the arts she was intensely stupid and thought

only of her food. This passionate greed she tried to conceal, but Isobel soon discovered it and set out to win her with every delicacy that the black market could provide.

With Taste and Scholarship thus secured, Isobel began to cast about for a prop outside the smart academic world, a stake embedded deep in café society. The thorns that surrounded the legacy were beginning to prick. She still refused to believe that the fantastic, the wicked clause could really be valid and had set all London's lawyers to refute it. But even so there were snags. It was necessary, for example, that they should leave the large furnished flat which they had taken in Cadogan Street and occupy Uncle Joseph's rambling mansion in Portman Square, with its mass of miscellaneous middle-class junk assembled since 1890; so much the will made perfectly clear. The district, she felt, might do. But before the prospect of filling the house, and filling it correctly, with furniture, servants, and, above all, guests, she faltered. It was at this moment that she met Guy Rice. Since coming to London she had seen so many beautiful pansy young men, all with the same standard voices, jargon, bow-ties, and complicated hair-dos, that she tended now to ignore them. That some of them were important she felt no doubt, but it was difficult to distinguish amid such uniformity and she did not wish to make a mistake. Guy Rice, however, decided to know *her*. He sensed at once her insecurity, her hardness, and her determination. She was just the wealthy peg he needed on which to hang his great flair for pastiche, which he saw with alarm was in danger of becoming a drug on the market. Mutual robbery, after all, was fair exchange, he thought as he watched her talking to a little group before the fire.

"I can never understand," she was saying, "why people who've made a mess of things should excuse themselves by saying that they can't accept authority. But then *I* don't think insanity's a very good plea." It was one of her favourite themes.

Guy patted the couch beside him. "Come and sit here, dearie," he said in the flat cockney whine he had always refused to lose—it was, after all, a distinction.

"You *do* try hard, dear, don't you? But you know it won't do."
And then he proceeded to lecture and advise her on how to behave. Amazingly, Isobel did not find herself at all annoyed. As he
said, "You could be so cosy, dear, if you tried, and that would be
nice, wouldn't it? All this clever talk's very well, but what people
want is a good old-fashioned bit of fun. What they want is parties,
great big slap-up do's like we had in the old days," for Guy was a
rather old young man. "Lots of fun, childish, you know, elaborate
and a wee bit nasty; and you're just the girl to give it to them." He
looked closely at her emaciated white face. "The skeleton at the
feast, dear, that's you."

Their rather surprising friendship grew daily—shopping,
lunching, but mostly just sitting together over a cup of tea, for
they both dearly loved a good gossip. He put her wise about everyone, hard-boiled estimates with a dash of good-scout sentimentality—it was "I shouldn't see too much of them, dear,
they're on the out. Poor old dears! They say they were ever such
naughties once," or "Cling on for dear life. She's useful. Let her
talk, duckie, that's the thing. She likes it. Gets a bit lonely sometimes, I expect, like we all do." He reassured her too about her
husband.

"What do you think of Brian?" she had asked.

"Same as you do, dear. He bores me dizzy. But don't you
worry, there's thousands love that sort of thing. Takes all sorts
to make a world."

He put her clothes right for her, saying with a sigh, "Oh, Isobel, dear, you *do* look tatty," until she left behind that touch of
outré-artiness that the Master's wife had been so quick to see.
With his help she made a magnificent, if somewhat overperfect,
spectacle of the Portman Square mansion. His knowledge of interior decoration was very professional, and with enough money
and rooms he let his love of pastiche run wild. He was wise enough
to leave the show pieces—the Zurbarán, the Fragonard, the Samuel Palmers, and the Braques—to the Professor and Lady Maude,
but for the rest he just let rip. There were Regency bedrooms, a
Spanish Baroque dining-room, a Second Empire room, a Victo-

rian study, something amusing in Art Nouveau; but his greatest triumph of all was a large lavatory with tubular furniture, American cloth, and cacti in pots. "Let's have a dear old pre-war lav in the nice old-fashioned Munich style," he had said, and the Cappers, wondering, agreed.

On one point only did they differ: Isobel was adamant in favour of doing things as economically as possible; both she and Brian had an innate taste for saving. With this aspect of her life Guy refused to be concerned, but he introduced her to her fourth great prop, Tanya Mule.

"She's the biggest bitch unhung, duckie," he said, "but she'll touch propositions no one else will. She's had it all her own way ever since the war, when 'fiddling' began in a big way."

Mrs. Mule had been very beautiful in the style of Gladys Cooper, but now her face was ravaged into a million lines and wrinkles from which two large and deep-blue eyes stared in dead appeal; she wore her hair piled up very high and coloured very purple; she always dressed in the smartest black of Knightsbridge with a collar of pearls. She was of the greatest help to Isobel, for although she charged a high commission she knew every illegal avenue for getting servants and furniture and decorator's men and unrationed food; she could smell out bankruptcy over miles of territory and was always first at the sale; she knew every owner of objets d'art who was in distress and exactly how little they could be made to take. No wonder, then, that with four such allies Isobel felt sure of her campaign.

Suddenly, however, in the flush of victory the great blow struck her: the lawyers decided that the wicked, criminal, lunatic clause in Uncle Joseph's will must stand. Even Brian was forced up from beneath his life of lectures and talks and dinners to admit that the crisis was serious. Isobel was in despair. She looked at the still-unfurnished drawing-room—they had decided on Louis Treize—and thought of the horrors that must be perpetrated there. Certainly the issue was too big to be decided alone: they must call a council of their allies.

Isobel paced up and down in front of the great open fire as she

talked, pulling her cigarette out of her tautened mouth and blowing quick angry puffs of smoke. She looked now at the Zurbarán
friar with his ape and his owl, now at the blue and buff tapestried huntsmen who rode among the fleshy nymphs and satyrs;
occasionally she glanced at Guy as he lay sprawled on the floor,
twirling a Christmas rose, but never at Brian or Lady Maude, Mrs.
Mule or the Professor, as they sat upright on their high-backed
tapestried chairs. "I had hoped never to have to tell you," she said.
"Of course, it's absolutely clear that Uncle Joseph and Aunt
Gladys were completely insane at the time when the will was
made, but apparently the law doesn't care about that. Oh, it's so
typical of a country where sentimentalism reigns supreme without regard for God's authority or even for the natural law, for
that matter. A crazy, useless old couple, steeped in some Non-
conformist nonsense, decide on an act of tyrannous interference
with the future, and all the lawyers can talk about is the liberty of
an Englishman to dispose of his money as he wishes. Just because
of that, the whole of our lives—Brian's and mine—are to be ruined, we're to be made a laughingstock. Just listen to this:
    " 'If the great Harvester should see fit to gather my dear wife
and me to Him when we are on the high seas or in any other manner by which our mortal remains may not be recovered for proper
Christian burial and in places where our dear niece and nephew
or, under God, other heirs may not decently commune with us
and in other approved ways show us their respect and affection,
then I direct that two memorials, which I have already caused
to be made, shall be set in that room in our house in Portman
Square in which they entertain their friends, that we may in some
way share, assist, and participate in their happy pastimes. This is
absolutely to be carried out, so that if they shall not agree the
whole of our estate shall pass to the charities hereinafter named.'
    "And that," Isobel cried, "*that* is what the law says we shall
have to do." She paused, dramatically waving the document in
the air.
    "Well," said Guy, "I'm not partial to monuments myself, but
they can be very nice, Isobel dear."

"Nice," cried Isobel, "nice! Come and look," and she threw open the great double doors into the drawing-room. The little party followed her solemnly.

It was perfectly true that the monuments could not be called "nice." In the first place they were each seven feet high. Then they were made in white marble—not solid mid-Victorian, something could have been done with that; nor baroque, with angels and gold trumpets, which would have been better still. They were in the most exaggeratedly simple modern good taste by an amateur craftsman, a long way after Eric Gill.

"My dear," said Guy, "they're horrors"; and Lady Maude remarked that they were not the kind of thing one ever wanted to see.

The lettering too was bold, modern, and very artful; one read, "Joseph Briggs. Ready at the call," and the other, "Gladys Briggs. Steel true, blade straight, the Great Artificer made my mate." Professor Cadaver was most distressed by them. "Really, without *any*thing in them," he kept on saying. "Nothing, not even ashes. It all seems most unfortunate." He appeared to feel that a great opportunity had been missed.

No one had any suggestion to make. Mrs. Mule knew the names of many crooked lawyers and even a criminal undertaker, but this did not seem to be quite in their line. Lady Maude privately thought that as long as the dining-room and kitchen could function there was really very little reason for anxiety. They all were standing about in gloom when suddenly Guy cried, "What did you say the lawyers were called?"

"Robertson, Naismith and White," said Isobel, "but it's no good, we've gone over all that."

"Trust little Guy, dear," said her friend.

Soon his voice could be heard excitedly talking over the telephone. He was there for more than twenty minutes; they could hear little of what he said, though once he screamed rather angrily, "Never said I did say I did say I did," and at least twice he cried petulantly, "Aow, pooh!"

When he returned he put his hand on Isobel's shoulder. "It's all right, ducks," he said, "I've fixed it. Now we can all be cosy and that's nice, isn't it?" Sitting tailor-wise on the floor, he produced his solution with reasonable pride. "You see," he said, "it only says in the will 'set in that room in which they entertain their friends.' But it doesn't say you need entertain with those great horrors in the room more than once, and after a great deal of tiresome talk those lawyers have agreed that I'm right. For that one entertainment we'll build our setting round the horrors, Isobel dear, everything morbid and ghostly. Your first big reception, duckie, shall be a Totentanz. It's just the sort of special send-off you need. After that, pack the beastly things off, and presto, dear, back to normal."

The Totentanz was Isobel's greatest—alas! her last—triumph. The vast room was swathed in black and purple, against which the huge white monuments and other smaller tombstones specially designed for the occasion stood out in bold relief. The waiters and barmen were dressed as white skeletons or elaborate Victorian mutes with black ostrich plumes. The open fireplace was arranged as a crematorium fire, and the chairs and tables were coffins made in various woods. Musical archives had been ransacked for funeral music of every age and clime. A famous Jewish contralto wailed like the ghetto, an African beat the tomtom as it is played at human sacrifices, an Irish tenor made everyone weep with his wake songs. Supper was announced by "The Last Post" on a bugle, and hearses were provided to carry the guests home.

Some of the costumes were most original. Mrs. Mule came tritely but aptly enough as a vampire. Lady Maude, with her hair screwed up in a handkerchief and dressed in a shapeless gown, was strikingly successful as Marie Antoinette shaved for the guillotine. Professor Cadaver, dressed up as a Corpse Eater, was as good as Boris Karloff; he clearly enjoyed every minute of the party; indeed, his snakelike slit eyes darted in every direction at the many beautiful young women dressed as corpses, and his manner became so incoherent and excited before he left that Isobel felt quite afraid to let him go home alone. Guy had thought at first of coming as Millais' Ophelia, but he remembered the harm done to the original model's health and decided against it. With flowing hair and marbled features, however, he made a very handsome "Suicide of Chatterton." Isobel thought he seemed a little melancholy during the evening, but when she asked him if anything was wrong he replied quite absently, "No, dear, nothing really. 'Half in love with easeful Death,' I s'pose. I mean, all this fun *is* rather hell when it comes to the point, isn't it?" But when he saw her face cloud he said, "Don't you worry, ducks, you've arrived," and, in fact, Isobel was too happy to think of anyone but herself. For many hours after the last guests had departed she sat happily chipping away at the monuments with a hammer. She sang a little to herself: "I've beaten you, Uncle and Auntie dear, I hope it's the last time you'll bother us here."

Guy felt very old and weary as he let himself into his one-room luxury flat. He realized that Isobel would not be needing him much longer; soon she would be on the way to spheres beyond his ken. There were so many really young men who could do his stuff now and they didn't get bored or tired in the middle like he did. Suddenly he saw a letter in the familiar, uneducated handwriting lying on the mat. He turned giddy for a moment and leaned against the wall. It would be impossible to go on finding money like this forever. Perhaps this time he could get it from Isobel—after all, she owed most of her success to him—but it would hasten the inevitable break with her. And even if he had the courage to settle this, there were so many more demands in different uneducated hands, so much more past sentimentalism turned to fear. He lay for a long time in the deep green bath, then sat in front of his double mirror to perform a complicated routine with creams and powders. At last he put on a crimson-and-white silk dressing-gown and hung his Chatterton wig and costume in the wardrobe. He wished so much that Chatterton were there to talk to. Then, going to the white-painted medicine cupboard, he took out his bottle of luminal. "In times like these," he said aloud, "there's nothing like a good old overdose to pull one through."

Lady Maude enjoyed the party immensely. The funeral baked meats were delicious, and Isobel had seen that the old lady had all she wanted. She sat on the edge of her great double bed, with her grey hair straggling about her shoulders, and swung her thick white feet with their knobbly blue veins. The caviar and chicken mayonnaise and Omelette Surprise lay heavy upon her, but she found, as usual, that indigestion only made her the more hungry. Suddenly she remembered the game pie in the larder. She put on her ancient padded pink dressing-gown and tiptoed downstairs—it would not do for the Danbys to hear her, servants could make one look so foolish. But when she opened the larder she was horrified to find that someone had forestalled her, the delicious, rich game pie had been removed. The poor cheated lady was not long in finding the thief. She padded into the kitchen, and there, seated at the table, noisily guzzling the pie, was a very young man with long fair hair, a red-and-blue-checked shirt, and a white silk tie with girls in scarlet bathing costumes on it; he looked as though he suffered from adenoids. Lady Maude had read a good deal in her favourite newspapers about spivs and burglars so that she was not greatly surprised. Had he been in the act of removing the silver she would have fled in alarm, but as it was she felt nothing but anger. Her whole social foundation seemed to shake beneath the wanton looting of her favourite food. She immediately rushed towards him, shouting for help. The man—he was little more than a youth and very frightened—struck at her wildly with a heavy iron bar. Lady Maude fell backwards upon the table, almost unconscious and bleeding profusely. Then the boy completely lost his head and, seizing up the kitchen meat axe, with a few wild strokes he severed her head from her body. She died like a queen.

Only the moon lit the vast spaces of Brompton Cemetery, showing up here a tomb and there a yew tree. Professor Cadaver's eyes were wild and his hands shook as he glided down the central pathway. His head still whirled with the fumes of the party and a thousand beautiful corpses danced before his eyes. An early underground train rattled in the distance, and he hurried his steps. At last he reached his objective—a freshly dug grave on which wooden planks and dying wreaths were piled. The Professor began feverishly to tear these away, but he was getting old, and neither his sight nor his step was as sure as it had been; he caught his foot in a rope and fell nine or ten feet into the tomb. When they found him in the morning his neck was broken. The papers hushed up the affair, and a Sunday newspaper in an article entitled "Has Science the Right?" only confused the matter by describing him as a professor of anatomy and talking obscurely of Burke and Hare.

It was the end of Isobel's hopes. True, Mrs. Mule still remained to play the vampire, but without the others she was as nothing. Indeed, the position for Isobel was worse than when she arrived in London, for it would take a long time to live down her close association with the Professor and Guy. Brian was a little non-plussed at first, but there was so much to do at the university that he had little time to think of what might have been. He was now the centre of a circle of students and lecturers who listened to his every word. As Isobel's social schemes faded he began to fill the house with his friends. Sometimes she would find him standing full square before the Zurbarán, pointing the end of his pipe at a party of earnest young men sitting bolt upright on the tapestried chairs. "Ah," he would be saying jocosely, "but you haven't yet proved to me that your famous average man or woman is anything but a fiction," or "But look here, Wotherspoon, you can't just throw words like 'beauty' or 'formal design' about like that. We must define our terms." Once she discovered a tobacco pouch and a Dorothy Sayers' detective novel on a tubular chair in the "dear old lav."

But if Brian had turned the house into a W.E.A. lecture centre, Isobel would not have protested now. Her thoughts were too much with the dead. She sat all day in the vast, empty drawing-room, where the two great monuments threw their giant shadows over her. Here she would smoke an endless chain of cigarettes and drink tea off unopened packing cases. Occasionally she would glance up at the inscriptions with a look of mute appeal, but she never seemed to find an answer. She made less and less pretence of reading and listening to good music, and yet for months on end would hardly stir from the house.

A faint April sun shone down upon the wet pavements of the High Street, casting a faint and melancholy light upon the pools of rain that had gathered here and there among the cobblestones. It was a deceptive gleam, however, for the wind was piercingly cold. Miss Thurkill drew her B.A. gown tightly around her thin frame as she emerged from the lecture hall and hurried off to the Heather Café. Turning the corner by Strachan's bookshop, she saw the Master's wife advancing upon her. Despite the freezing weather, the old lady moved slowly, for the bitter winter's crop of influenza and bronchitis had weakened her heart; she seemed now as fat and waddling as her bulldogs.

"Did you get the London appointment?" she shouted. It was a cruel question, for she knew already the negative reply. "Back to the tomb, eh?" she went on. "Ah, well, at least we know we're dead here."

Miss Thurkill giggled nervously. "London didn't seem very alive," she said. "I went to see the Cappers, but I couldn't get any reply. The whole house seemed to be shut up."

"Got the plague, I expect," said the Master's wife; "took it from here," and as she laughed to herself she crouched forward like some huge, squat toad.

"Isobel certainly hasn't been the success she supposed," hissed Miss Thurkill, writhing like a malicious snake. "Well, I shall catch my death of cold if I stay here," she added and hurried on.

The old lady's voice came to her in the gale that blew down the street. "No one would notice the difference," it seemed to cry.

FROM
A Bit Off the Map

A Bit Off the Map

⸻❯❯❯❮❮❮⸻

See, some people go about like it doesn't matter why we're here or what it's all for, but I'm not like that. I want to get at the Truth. Of course, it's not easy because there's a lot that think they know, but even if they do, they're not telling anyone else. Same as it might be with the government. A lot's secret and we can't tell what they're doing. But about this other truth—the important one —like what the religions pretend to know, I think it's more of a question of keeping on worrying at it and making up your mind that you'll find out. At least that's how I see it. And now I've met Huggett and The Crowd, I'm likely to be lucky—because Huggett's a sort of philosopher and a mystic too. Only like me he's quite young.

They've sent me a parcel for my birthday. But I won't go back there. Not unless I was to go back and perhaps kill her, see; and I might do because I don't know my own strength. I'm not very tall, just average, but I'm well made all right. I could go for a model if I wanted. There's crowds of artists have asked me— sometimes it's just funny stuff, of course, but mostly it's genuine. They'd be glad to get me because I've got proportions; not just health and strength stuff—muscles and that just goes to fat. Well paid too, but you've got to be able to take it, because it's tiring work modelling, I could do it though if I wanted; I don't know

Written in 1956; first published in 1957; scene mid-1950s.

my own strength. I wouldn't take a job like that though, because maybe I'll be an artist and then it'd be bad if I'd been a model. At least that's how I see it. You never hear of models becoming artists. Models are usually just layabouts.

It could be I *might* be a painter too. I've got an eye for colours. But I haven't found myself yet. That's what I've got to do now—find what's really there, what really goes to make up the being they call Kennie Martin. (It's all right too, I can tell you—not just the physique like what I said already but the eyes and the mouth. If I use them most times I can get anything I want.) "Being they call Kennie Martin," that's like they put it in novels, see, it's more subtle. I notice things like that. That's why it might be I might be a writer. But I've got to find myself first. And that means going deep down. Of course, a lot of it's sex. I can get most what I want but I don't know what I want. See, it's like I read "the personality is a delicate balance between mind and body. In each personality the balance between male and female is delicate too," or something like that. That was in a book I bought second-hand—*The Balance of Being* by James T. Whiteway. Or it might have been Havelock Ellis, because I've read that too—cases and all. But I know all that anyway. Like you get a woman that fancies you but then she won't let you have it unless you're wearing a special sort of belt or socks or something. Or like it might be a queer that dresses up as a maid. I know it all, but I won't say whether I know it personally or not. I never admit. That's one thing you learn in the life I lead—never admit anything. Let the other man do the talking and if there's questions you don't like, just stare. Only you must put all the power you've got into it. It's a matter of Will Power—one or the other of you goes down. With me, the other man goes down. So I don't say what I know from experience—not in detail, that is.

Lots of times I don't work because the jobs they offer don't take you any place worth going or because like now I've got to be free until I find myself. Well, I've got to sleep somewhere, haven't I? That's all I'm saying. (If you answer like that and smile a bit sideways, it makes people interested—it's a mystery, see, and everyone's a sucker for a mystery.) But personal or not, I know all the prostitutes and the ponces and that. I shan't get stuck there, because I've something big in me that'll take me to the top when I find myself.

All the same it's a world that keeps you on your toes because you've got to think and talk quick in that world. I mean like a prostitute's got to think and act quick if she's to live. Anyhow I've read it too, how criminals and artists are all together; see, they've got to be because society's ranged against them. It was in *Picture Post* one week about it. Like Rimbaud. There was a bloke lived in Fulham who read some of Rimbaud's poems to me. "Souls of the Damned" or something, because art means you have to suffer. Huggett says Rimbaud found out about himself and then he quit. Went out for big money and made it. Slave trade or something. Lots of artists are sadists, see. But Huggett says he wasn't any good anyway. He says real genius means Will Power. All this art and suffering is just cock, Huggett says. (I don't like it when Huggett uses those words—cock and that. A lot of these intellectuals talk like that, "C—— this and f—— that"—but all as though the words would bite them. I just stare at them when they talk like that. They soon stop. But Huggett isn't like that. When he speaks he means it. All the same he uses the words—cock and all that. I don't know why.) Well, anyway Rimbaud once was sitting in a café—with the poets and all, queers a lot of them, the bloke who told me was queer himself. And he suddenly lashed out with a knife and cut the fingers of these others. On the table.

That's what I've done. I suddenly see red, especially if someone's done me a wrong thing. I don't forgive, I don't believe in that. I half killed another boy at school. That's what got me into trouble first. There's four or five people in the world that I'd like to cut the guts out of. I often think of that. It's like I said about my stepmother. If I went back there I'm liable to half kill her because I might see red and I don't know my own strength. So it's no good their sending me birthday presents. They're all earning good money there now but all they sent me's five pounds.

Not that I blame them. All the same a lot of that's going on what they wouldn't like. Haircut and that. And a bottle of good stuff—it doesn't dry the hair, see, because if you put spirit on it it's liable to crack; and it gives colour without any dye. "Pour les Hommes," it's called.

Well, as I say, they don't believe in me. They think I'm just a layabout or worse. But I don't worry. They'll see. I'm just finding myself, that's all. If my mother hadn't died she'd have understood. She saw to it that I speak well, because, see, I speak good English, but I can't write very easy. Of course, if I turned out to be a poet, that'd be different, because there it isn't writing, it's the words, like they have to have power. Poetry's like painting in words. That's how I see it. She took me to see the psychologist because I'd seen red and half killed that boy. But then she died and *he* didn't see any good to psychologists. And then he married this bitch. The psychologist said I'd got to find myself, at least I think he did. I don't remember very well. All the same I had a low I.Q. and that was the same in the army. I used to worry about that, but Huggett says all that's cock. And the same about that I didn't do very well at school.

Look, I'm trying to find out what it's all about. Because when you look at it, it doesn't seem very much good. But I've always known it did mean something—life and all, I mean. Not religion, mind you. I used to think that and I went to a lot of these churches. Because he and my stepmother didn't bother about that. A car and old-time dancing and the pictures. That's about all they think of—and sex, of course. I see red when I think of that. Chris, that's their son, has been given a Lambretta because he's got a grant to Teachers' Training College. I don't say I wish he'd kill himself on it, but pretty near. Well, anyway, with them not believing in religion and that, I used to think there must be something to it. My mother always went Christmas and Easter. (I wonder sometimes if there wasn't something funny about who my father was. I'd like to get at the truth of who I really am. I know my mother never wanted to have it with him. I wouldn't blame her even if it was someone else. I'd be glad although it'd mean

giving myself an ugly name. Also it would account for a lot, like
why I'm different.) So I went to all the churches—there's lots
nobody knows much about like the Church of the Latter-Day
Saints and that. And I listened at Marble Arch. But I didn't find
what I wanted. Like it's what Huggett says, they've only got a
part and they make out it's the whole. It stands to reason there
must be a whole Truth somewhere. Anyway what they said didn't
seem to go along the way I was looking. See, it's like I say when
I want to give someone the brush off—"I don't fancy anything
with you, thanks all the same." There was more in a book I bought
once—*A Triangle of Light. An Analysis of Mysticism*, by J. G.
Partridge, D.Litt. What I got through of it, that is. It gave, see,
the Inner Meaning. But Huggett says he's never heard of the
book and he doesn't go much for the idea of it, maybe it wasn't
much—see, I was only seventeen when I bought that book.

   Huggett's writing a book that's to go a long way for finding
out the Truth, but it'll take him years to write because it's not
only religion he's taking in but philosophy. So he works in
this shipping office, but he has poems published and he's got all
these followers—The Crowd they're called. Truth and Reality—
it's thousands of years men have been searching for it. What's
real?—Aristotle said it was what we see, and Plato said it was what
we couldn't see, like what's behind things. I read about that in a
digest. And Socrates said Know Thyself. But Huggett says that
it's more the Will. We've got to breed a new race with real Will
Power. It's Will Power that'll get you to the top too.

   Of course I could get jobs with prospects, but what's it mean?
There they go, like I see them on the tubes and buses and maybe
they'll have a house in the suburbs and a car and a wife and kids,
and mostly when they've got these they drop dead. Don't be an
anonymous man, Huggett says. That's what he calls them. We're
in a hurry, my generation. And anyway I've got to have time
to think and to find myself. So mostly I take short jobs like load-
ing things on vans (but I'm not very strong) and doorman and
working in the ice-cream factory and waiter. And mostly I
change rooms. We're restless, we're in a hurry. And sometimes I

just sleep around where I can find it, but, like, well it's not always to my taste, though it's company and I get lonely on my own. But still you've got to have the will to stand alone if you are going to get anywhere. Sometimes I've got a room of my own *and* I'm between jobs like now and that's the best.

Of course, maybe success might come sudden, like I saw a map the other day showing all the buried treasure that's been found in England (I don't know much of the country, except the approved school was in Yorkshire on the moors), or there's unclaimed moneys, you can get a list of them if you ask for it. I've got the figure and legs that could make a dancer and I could sing if only I could stop smoking. There's Elvis Presley's got all these cars and Tommy Steele started just in a skiffle group like in one of the coffee bars that I spend most time in. (You have to learn to make one coffee last.) Look at Carroll Levis's discoveries, those are all young, but that's not serious. Traditional's more serious. But in any case I don't go much for dreaming like that because, see, you've got to keep your wits about you if you're going to think about the Truth, and it's most only layabouts that dream of making millions on pools or like perhaps being England's Johnnie Ray overnight.

All the same it was chance that I met The Crowd. Susan's a school teacher. We got talking in the Italian coffee house and she was the girl friend then of Reg that's the next to Huggett. I think he'd like to be the principal himself, but Huggett's a genius and he's not. And Reg believes in Power and what he says is, Shit in the face of humanity—if millions have to be liquidated what's it matter? most people are never alive anyway—but Huggett believes in Power and Leadership for the Regeneration of the World. So they often quarrel. At first Reg didn't like for me to be there because it was obvious I appealed to Susan, but now he's with this other girl Rosa, see, who works as a typist. Reg doesn't work much himself. And then, see, they mostly (the men, that is) dress very badly—dirty old flannel trousers, I wouldn't think to wear, and coats (who wear coats?), and they don't have their hair cut anywhere good, if at all—partly it's they're too busy thinking and talking, partly it's they don't like anything that might look queer, mostly it's they don't like anything that looks bourgeois (only Huggett tells Susan not to be a fool when she calls a thing bourgeois). Well, me being dressed as I am—see, when I've got money I buy my jeans and sweaters at this place where they make specially for you(so you never see the same on anyone else) and my hair cut at Raymond, 15/- with Pour les Hommes, and my jeans very tight because I've got good legs. Well, see, The Crowd thought I might be on to some game (but what have they got to lose?) or a queer (The Crowd is strong against queers, but Susan could tell them different about me) or in with a Teddy boy lot (but I'm always alone). So they didn't act very friendly at first (except Susan—and the women in The Crowd, they don't count too much), but I thought, as it might well be I'd be an artist or a writer, this was my chance (because even Huggett says in England the world of artists and writers is very tough to make, you've got to smash your way through), and then what they talked about is what I want to hear—see, about Truth and Will Power and Genius—and especially Huggett; and I get very lonely. So when I was with Susan and we were with The Crowd, I didn't speak, I just listened. That's another trick, if you want something or somebody, don't say anything, it seems like a mystery, see, which as I say people like. Also The Crowd, even Huggett, like listeners. But mostly anyway I wanted to listen—it was what I must hear if I'm to find myself—and, see, I haven't had much education so I have to listen hard. At first I don't think Huggett noticed me. Then one day Reg started that there probably wasn't any Reason for it, any Truth about it, just being smarter than the next man. That made Huggett mad at him. So I said what Reg said couldn't be right because it stood to reason there was the Truth to find somewhere. And after that Huggett started to ask for me when I wasn't there and told Susan to bring me along. So now I go with them mostly. (And about being lonely—that's what I tell when someone's interested in me. I know how to do it all— about my mother being dead and that bitch my stepmother, and whether perhaps he's not my father at all. And mostly it gets them

—sometimes they say, "Look, take this couple of pounds and nothing asked in return." I tell it big-eyed and lost because I could be an actor; maybe I will when I find myself. But what's funny is it's true. I don't think too much about it because you have to be on your own and be tough. So it's like I'm shooting a line and it's true all the same, which is funny really.) But The Crowd's not the same as the Angry Young Men which you read about. Someone said it was and Huggett got very angry, because it's by Love and Leadership that the Will works. And all these Angry Young Men believe in democracy and freedom and a lot of stuff that Huggett says just gets in the way of real thinking.

All the same The Crowd *is* angry because what's being done and written now is all cock. Huggett says it's only time before their ideas come to the top, but all the same, like I said, our generation is in a hurry. And I get angry too, like I said, so that I could kill them all—the foremen and the headwaiters and the police and the girls that want to be kind and the queers that want to be kind and him writing from Southampton—"You know, Kennie, and I've told you often and again, there's a bed for you here and jobs too if you treat your stepmother right and don't mix with the rotten crowd off the ships that you did when you were here. For they are a rotten crowd, Kennie, you know. And you mustn't think we don't want you." I don't *think* about that, I *know*. The bitch worked to get me out and I'm not going back unless if I go back as something big that she'll have to listen to. But I mustn't think about it too much, for like I said I see red and then I am liable to do anything. I don't know my own strength. Like the man at the approved school wrote "psychopath" but I don't take much notice of that. But I must know what it's all about, what we're here for, what the Truth is. And sometimes I get so that I can't wait—I *must* know. Often I've thought I've found it, but it's been a bloody cheat. But I reckon I can learn a lot from Huggett because he's a genius. Well, anyway, that's where I'm going now, to the Italian coffee house to meet The Crowd and not to bloody Southampton and home. And Susan told Huggett it was my twenty-first birthday and The Crowd is giving me a party. And mostly I don't drink because I'm liable to get angry, but with The Crowd I feel good and maybe I shall get drunk at my party.

The Crowd sat at two long tables in the far corner of the window. If the polished yet wilting rubber plant which loomed above them had now the familiarity of the aspidistra—once, after all, also a modish exotic—the unself-conscious dowdiness of the members of The Crowd only seemed designed further to deny the tropical origin of the fleshy leaves, to insist on their complete acclimatization to the English lower middle-class world. Amid the uniformity of elaborate male hair styles and female horsehair tails, of jeans and fishermen's sweaters, the dilapidated grammar-school heartiness of The Crowd's male attire, the dead but fussy genteelness of their women might have suggested a sort of inverted exhibitionism. But the clothes of The Crowd—the tired suits, the stained flannels and grubby corduroys, the jumpers and skirts, the pathetically dim brooches and earrings—were no conscious protests, only the ends of inherited and accepted taste, the necessities of penurious earnings. Even Harold's blazer was just what he had always worn. They were as unconscious of the bejeaned world around them as they were of the rubber plant, the Chinese chequer players, or the guitar of the skiffle group. They always met at the Italian coffee house and they drank Cona. They were, as always, talking; or rather the men were talking and the women were seeming to listen. Clothes were the last thing that either sex would have noticed in the other. The young women, except for Susan, were plain, and, except for Rosa, without make-up; but Rosa alone had a bad skin. The young men had strong faces with weak chins, except for Harold Gattley, who was an older, simple-looking man with spectacles. He was probably over thirty. Huggett had a thin and freckled white face, unbrushed carroty hair, pale-grey eyes, and a rather feeble little reddish moustache. When, as now, the conversation had ceased to interest him, his face was quite without expression, his body absolutely still.

Reg was describing his present difficulties with his novel. "When Rawston gets back to London," he said, "he reads in the evening paper that there has been a big fire in Bristol and a woman has been burned, and he realizes that it is Beth." He paused.

Everyone knew the plot and the characters of Reg's novel well, but Susan, who had never shed an upper middle-class desire to say the right thing, asked, "Is that the whore?"

"Yes," said Reg. "What I'm worried about is Rawston's reaction. Beth had been the only living creature that he found when he returned home, the only being of force and will in Bristol, and by sleeping with her he'd renewed his energy. At the same time she represented the only claim the town and the past could make on him, now that his mother had married the school inspector, and, of course, he had to destroy her. I don't know whether to make him remember that he'd overturned the oil stove before he left her lodging house—a sort of subconscious half action that could be justifiable murder—or whether simply his will to be rid of her was enough to make her careless about the candle by her bed and so prepare her own destruction."

"If," observed Harold Gattley, "you give Rawston subconscious urges, you surely reduce his status as an expression of intellectually controlled will."

There was a general murmur of disapproval of the concept of the "subconscious" and one man even suggested that it sounded dangerously like Freudian rubbish.

Huggett flicked into life for moment. "I don't think Reg should be accused of infantilism," he said. "I imagine that by the subconscious he implies a reservoir of the Will that a man like Rawston, who is in training to realize himself, can call upon to strengthen his conscious powers. There are techniques for putting this reservoir more completely at command—prayer and contemplation and so on. I take it that Reg means Rawston to have some knowledge of these." There were disagreements between Huggett and Reg, but neither would have the other called a fool.

Reg nodded with a pleased smile. "Rawston," he said, "is not a homunculus, you know. He pitched old Daddy Freud with all the rest of the claptrap into the dung heap long before the book begins. As Huggett says, he knows the conventional exercises. Although, of course, he uses them for personal supremacy and not for all the old Christian rubbish. I have one chapter in which he reads Boehme and adapts his ideas for destructive ends."

Huggett closed his eyes wearily. "Oh, God," he cried, "all this dreary satanism, this nihilistic nonsense! You're just an old upside-down romantic, Reg," and, when Reg was about to answer, "No, no. We can't argue about all that again now," Huggett said firmly, "What *does* worry me is all this conventional concern with individual personalities. Rawston this and the harlot that. Of course, you've dug your own grave by using that rotting corpse, the novel. It's bound to be encumbered with humanistic dead wood."

"You need wood, Huggett, to make a fire," Reg answered in his special ruthless voice. "And, by God," he continued, "we'll light such a blaze that all their nice little civilized fire engines won't be able to put it out."

A frisson ran through the members of The Crowd present. The effect of Reg's and Huggett's talk on most of the girls and many of the men was always emotive rather than intellectual; it was always most powerful when the utterances were apocalyptic and mysteriously menacing to the old order.

Harold Gattley's new girl friend—a redhead—alone received no frisson; she was busily chasing with her tongue a seed that had lodged in her teeth. When she came to London to do a speech therapy course, she had determined to move in an artistic set, but this did not commit her to listening.

Susan, however, sought desperately for something nasty to say to Reg. She felt no sympathy with the ideas of The Crowd. She was held there solely by her strong physical desire for Reg and the hope that he would show interest in her again. Quiescence had proved no help, and she had determined on a course of opposition to arouse him. She could think, however, of no comment except, "Take care you don't burn your fingers." It sounded a bit child-

ish and, in any case, would only underline her schoolmarm manner, which Reg and Huggett both despised. Eventually she said,
"How boring all this intellectual pyromania is." But the words,
which had seemed so sophisticated, came too late, for Reg had begun to talk again.

"Rawston," he said, "as soon as he reads the news, goes to the
police and . . ." But the urges of Rawston's Heroic Will were to
remain unrevealed, for at that moment Kennie entered the bar
and made his way to their table.

Kennie's appearance, when as this evening he let his self-admi-
ration have rein, caused comment even in the most extravagant
world of jeans and hair-dos. Among The Crowd he seemed fla-
grant. His jeans were tighter than seemed altogether likely, and
they were striped. His belt was bigger and more decked with
brass studs. His sweater (the famous model) was unlikely ever to
be repeated in its zebralike weave. Beneath his swirling, sweep-
ing mass of black hair, luxuriant with the strong-scented Pour les
Hommes, his pale face was embarrassingly foolish and beautiful.
His huge eyes stared vacantly, his wide sensual lips fell apart in a
weak smile. Kennie always breathed through his mouth. He wore
one small brass earring. Above all, he was too short for so extravagant an attire. Reg frowned as Kennie took his seat by Susan,
and as soon as the first greetings had finished he continued, "You
see, Rawston has to impose his will, at some point, on authority . . ."

But Huggett would have none of it. He had adopted Kennie
as idiot mascot, and his mixed feelings of kindness and patronage
were not going to have his pocket Myshkin pushed to one side by
Reg. Huggett, he said to himself, was boss, not Reg.

"Shut up, Reg," he said. "Damn your Rawston and all the other
bloody little satanic nihilist heroes wreaking their puking little
vengeances on Society. What better are they than a lot of damned
Don Juans or Rastignacs or Sorels or the rest of the romantic rubbish? Keeping within the confines of their own clever little wills,
their own bloody little sanities, their all-too-human clever tricks.
Let them get the other side of sanity, that's where they'll find the

Vision and the true Will, in Bedlam with old Billie Blake." And when Reg seemed about to reply Huggett turned deliberately away from him. "Twenty-one-year-old Kennie," he said, "that's what we're celebrating today." It was final.

Susan took Kennie's hand. She had always aspired to teach the low I.Q.s, to reclaim the delinquents. Maternalism overwhelmed her, and she hoped against hope that Reg's jealousy might be lit by taking it for more. She had even hoped once that the maternalism would indeed turn to something more, but Kennie had lain so passive in their lovemaking, had rocked so cradle-content, that nothing had been woken in her. The Crowd had accepted it as proof that Kennie was not queer, and she had found in it her first doubts. Nevertheless she squeezed his hand and kissed him on the lips. "Many happy returns of the day, darling," she said. And all the others, save Reg and Rosa, echoed her cry.

Kennie felt suddenly shy with The Crowd. He had basked in their tolerance of him, feeling it as kindness that had no strings attached—he believed that he had known such things rarely in his life. But this sudden demonstration overwhelmed him. He wanted his party, of course, but, above all, he wanted to hear The Crowd talk. He had no liking for Reg, was indeed always glad to hear Huggett wham him down; but Reg was still someone very important, the next to Huggett, and that his birthday should be used to cut Reg's outpourings seemed to him almost sacrilegious. Kennie had learned over many years to please as well as to hate, and he sought a way now to please Reg. Nothing had surprised him more in his intercourse with The Crowd than the numbers of plays and novels and stories that the members were writing except, perhaps, the strange names of their heroes—not Christian names as in the books he had read, but strange-sounding surnames like Gorfitt, Sugden, Burlick, and Rawston. Knowing nothing of the D. H. Lawrence precedent, he had worked out for himself that leaders, men with will perhaps, dispensed with Christian names—after all, no one ever spoke of anything but Huggett. Perhaps all these strange characters in the books of The Crowd were a kind of homage to Huggett. He had carefully memorized all their names. So now he turned to Reg and said with all the appeal he could muster, "I should imagine Rawston's a good deal like Sugden in Harold's play. I mean, the way he does everything like for a purpose." Kennie's accent when he spoke was, unlike his grammar, very classy. Combined with his pretty looks, it was all that Reg detested most.

"Oh, for God's sake, Huggett," he cried, "if you want to believe all this Dostoevsky Myshkin balls, do you have to impose every little cretinous catamite on us? At least you can ask your protégé not to come the creeping jesus over me."

Susan and Huggett looked anxiously for a moment at Kennie; he had assured them so often of his "seeing red" and of his ignorance of his own strength. Fortunately there were words he had not found in Havelock Ellis; he was clearly bewildered at Reg's outburst.

"Look, Reg," said Huggett authoritatively, "D. H. Lawrence was a fool. Happily for the world, his corpse has long since mouldered. Don't bother to reincarnate it for us. You haven't got the right sort of beard." Then, turning to Susan, he announced, "Vitelloni's for the celebration dinner, I think, don't you, Susan?" And in a few minutes The Crowd had swept Kennie off for an orgy of pasta, risotto, and red chianti. It was all Reg could do to persuade Rosa to stay behind with him at the coffee house—as she said, "It's always silly to miss a party."

The idea, at first, was to go back to Huggett's room with plenty of bottles of Spanish red wine and play some records of unaccompanied Pennsylvania railroad songs. By the time, however, that they had reached the fruit salad and ice cream, Huggett's elation produced another scheme. "Let's go to Clara's," he cried, "she'll lionize Kennie. You'd like to be lionized, wouldn't you?" A very little drink affected Huggett; his manner became almost bullying.

The delights of Vitelloni's food had soon palled on Kennie; he had no great taste for food and drink, but he was used to being given more luxurious meals than The Crowd knew. With a few glasses of wine, his mind had returned to his urgent quest for the Truth. "I wanted like to hear what *you* had to say," he told Huggett, and he confided to Susan, whose protective arm round his waist he was now beginning also to feel an encumbrance to his quest, "See, I've not much time and I've got to find out such a lot about myself. I thought it might be that they'd be talking again about philosophy and truth and that."

"We shall," Huggett cried. "We shall talk of Truth and the true virtue of the Will until the small hours. But where better than at Clara's, Hetaira of Highgate, the Aspapia of the Archway. She holds the riddle of the Sphinx, Kennie, to say nothing of the secret of the Sibyls."

The Crowd goggled somewhat. One or two of the girls woke for a moment to hope and elation; Huggett seldom clowned, but when he did it meant only one thing—that he, who rigidly subordinated lust and, even more, emotion to the discipline of his great work, was in a sexy mood. The girls' hopes were soon dashed, however, for Huggett characteristically announced quite simply, "Besides, I think it's time that I took Clara to bed. She works too hard for the arts; she needs time off."

Huggett's laughter came rarely, but when it did it was always sufficient for eight men. Normally, however, it was reinforced by laughter from all The Crowd; tonight there was no reinforcement. There was silence. Then one of the girls, forgetting Huggett's admonitions to Susan, said, "She's such an *awful* bourgeois creature, Huggett." Another said, "She must be quite old." They meant the same thing. A young man in a grubby leather jacket said, "It's slumming, Huggett, that's what it is." Harold Gattley blinked owlishly through his spectacles. "I expect she sleeps in silk sheets," he said; "just because she got your poems published, Huggett, there's no need to be that friendly." Clara Turnbull-Henderson, in their view, was both untouchable and out of range. Harold's red-haired girl finished manoeuvring the last cherry in her fruit salad. She looked up and said primly, "I don't think I care to go all the way to Highgate, Harold."

Huggett was seldom faced with rebellion. On such occasions he always seemed younger even than his twenty-two years. He ran

his hand through his thick red hair in perplexity and stared at
them in distress. Nevertheless he was determined, and he said with
sudden boyish heartiness, "She's got heaps of drink there—
whisky, cherry brandy, crème de menthe." Then he got up from
the table and, edging through the narrow space between The
Crowd and the next table, he made his way up the stairs, behind
the cash desk, to the dark, unsanitary lavatory that Vitelloni's provided for clients. Huggett's rare evasions were of the simplest
kind.

Kennie, in whose life sex had been so frequent a burden, heard
Huggett's proposal with disappointment and perplexity. He had
felt so sure that tonight might be the crisis, the moment of revelation when he would learn what it was all about, what everything
was for. And now perhaps there would be no talk. He thought of
the unknown Clara with hatred.

Susan's grey eyes rested on him maternally. She guessed his disappointment. She had almost decided to take Kennie off on her
own when Reg and Rosa silently took their places with The
Crowd. Rosa's determination to be in on the party had won the
day, but her fat little made-up face still wore the sulky pout by
which she had gained her victory. Susan saw Reg and knew that
she had to stay, but she pressed Kennie's knee and said, "Don't
worry. There'll be lots of talking, Kennie."

The Crowd pooled their money to pay for the meal and, despite the prospect of Clara's drinks, bought bottles of red wine
to take with them. They would not let Kennie pay for anything.
They were eleven when they bundled into taxis for Highgate.
Kennie had to pay at the other end because The Crowd had now
hardly five shillings among them. Paying for the taxis gave Kennie
great pleasure, for he felt confident that he could come more
easily by money than The Crowd could.

The Crowd surged up the front steps of Miss Turnbull-Henderson's large late-Regency stuccoed house. A small elderly man
with flushed cheeks and greying black hair was already ringing the bell. He was soon swallowed up in the ocean of The
Crowd's talk, and when the door opened he was already being

gradually levered backwards down the steps by the unheeding young people. The Italian maid—Miss Turnbull's fourth change in as many months—was completely incapable either of comprehending or of restraining The Crowd. When Clara herself arrived on the scene The Crowd were already taking off the numerous scarves and gloves which both sexes wore at all times of the year. She was very disconcerted; her great dark eyes were round as a lemur's, her plump young face blushed crimson with shyness and alarm, her long earrings shook. Her shyness became her; and even Kennie, struck with surprise at her prettiness, felt the soundness of Huggett's desires.

"We've brought some drink," said Huggett, "we're celebrating a twenty-first birthday. I remembered that after that meeting you told me you'd like to meet the rest of The Crowd."

"Oh, my dear," Clara cried, and her silver dress shimmered and shook as she spoke, "I'm expecting Tristram Fleet." Then, with more alarm, she cried, "Mr. Fleet! Mr. Fleet! There you are." She smiled with gracious if excited welcome over the heads of The Crowd at the elderly stranger. Tristram Fleet smiled with equally gracious, old-world courtesy back at her. In between was an insurmountable barrier of sports coats and duffle coats, woollen scarves and raincoats.

For a moment it seemed as though Mr. Fleet and Clara were going to fight their way through to each other. But the situation was saved by Huggett. "I say," he said, "I had no idea you were Tristram Fleet. I'm Huggett, and this is Reg Bellwood."

"How do you do?" said Mr. Fleet. "May I say how satisfying I found your poem 'St. John of the Cross,' Mr. Huggett?"

" 'St. John *on* the Cross,' " Reg said angrily, but Huggett was genuinely delighted. "Thank you," he said, the pleased little boy; then, the angry small boy, he added, "We're against most of the stuff you write, of course."

"Ah . . ." Mr. Fleet sighed, and he made a coy little moue. "Ah, well."

It was beautifully done, Clara thought. Perhaps everything would be all right after all. To have brought Huggett and his group into contact with Tristram Fleet was quite something. What else was Mountside for? For what other purpose did all the money Mummy had left her serve, except to create an intellectual forum? She had been excited by the prospect of a tête-à-tête with Tristram Fleet, but her excitement had been tinged with alarm. Now she could simply assume the role of hostess to which she had dedicated her life.

"Mr. Huggett has already addressed the Club," she told Tristram Fleet, and to Huggett she said, "Mr. Fleet has come to talk over a discussion I'm hoping to get up." She left nothing for Huggett and Tristram Fleet to say. But there was no fear of silence for The Crowd were arguing loudly whether Fleet looked like his photographs, whether it mattered whether he did or not, whether it mattered *what* he looked like, whether, indeed, he mattered at all. Kennie was silent, for not reading either the Sunday or the weekly book reviews he had never heard of Tristram Fleet. Harold's red-haired girl friend was silent too; she read all the Sunday and weekly book reviews and she felt that at last she had *really* got into intellectual circles.

Only a few of her mother's Heal's chairs remained in the large drawing-room, which Clara was converting to Brighton Pavilion chinoiserie. Mr. Fleet, however, sat in one of the more comfortable of these and devoted himself to a few words of compliment to his hostess about the dragon panels she had put in. "They're charmingly monstrous," he said, "but," he added, for in taste he made no demurs, "don't hesitate to let the whole thing be a hundred times more monstrous. I should like to see twisted dragons entwining everywhere in monstrous embraces. Especially on the ceiling."

This was no sort of talk for The Crowd, and they set about consuming as much drink as they could in the shortest time. They persuaded Clara to let them make a "cup" in a large china bowl. The Crowd always mixed as many types of drink together as possible—it saved precious time that might be spent in the fuss of choosing.

Tristram Fleet was nervous of The Crowd and in particular of

Huggett. He would not otherwise have made his remark about the dragons, and he quickly realized its unsuitability. He had accepted Miss Turnbull-Henderson's invitation to address her Readers and Writers Get-Together Club with some apprehension, but she offered such a good fee that he felt justified in considering it his duty. To find that one of the leaders of the new generation had already found the same duty cheered him, but he was not happy that his first meeting with Huggett should take place on such unfamiliar ground. At such times he would normally have taken refuge—a very congenial refuge—in making advances to one of the young women. The girls of The Crowd, however, had naked faces and dirty hair; he was repelled by them. Clara's opulent if rather goofy prettiness he found charming—he regretted their lost tête-à-tête. But to commit himself to Clara, with all the absurd implications of her celebrity-hunting Club, before Huggett and The Crowd was a step he did not care to make. He was intensely relieved when Huggett squatted on the floor by his chair and began to make boyishly friendly conversation like any undergraduate fan. Soon they were discussing the economic possibilities in writing for a young man in modern England.

The Crowd relieved their nervousness of the chinoiserie by drinking continuously; Clara relieved her nervousness of The Crowd by filling their glasses as often as she could. A great deal was drunk very quickly.

Susan felt depressed because Reg and Rosa had begun smooching. She decided that it was abominable of Huggett so to neglect Kennie on his birthday treat. "This is Kennie Martin," she said to Clara, "it's *his* twenty-first birthday that we're celebrating."

If Clara found Kennie's clothes disconcerting, she thought his large-eyed face—a mixture of John Keats and cretinism—most disturbing. However, she thought someone so "interesting"-looking might well be a young genius. "I can't imagine anything more wonderful than to be twenty-one and have a whole creative future in front of you," she said.

Kennie did not answer. He was not, like The Crowd, particularly impressed by the chinoiserie; he had been taken back to far grander places in his time—rooms with concealed cocktail cabinets and fitted-in bars.

Clara tried again. "Are you a *dimanche* writer?" she asked.

Kennie turned and stared at her. "See," he said, "I've got to listen to what Huggett's saying to that bloke. It's important to me."

Clara blushed crimson once more, but, remembering the strange brusqueries so usual in young genius, she decided not to take offense and contented herself by filling up Kennie's glass even more often than those of the others.

It was not long before Huggett's conversation changed from the polite and the practical to the expounding of doctrine. He had great faith in his powers of conversion. Tristram Fleet, lulled by preliminary politenesses, felt only flattered by this friendly man-to-man challenge of the avant-garde. He was not among the established literary figures who made a profession of easy communication with youth; he only regretted now that more of his contemporaries were not present to witness his surprising success. He nodded attentively as Huggett gesticulated.

Kennie sat himself close to them and gazed as though into a fish tank at the aquarium. Around this little group the smoke gathered, and through it could be seen the increasingly drunk Crowd, petting and smooching and occasionally sitting bolt upright to listen with drunken pantomimic reverence to the talk. Even Susan, with her short straggly hair and red sunburnt face, began to look like a tipsy cricket Blue. Through the haze Clara glided and glinted like some graceful silvery fish. It was a success, she felt, but she did not dare to relax.

Kennie became increasingly sleepy. Huggett's dicta came to him in sudden wafts and then receded. What he heard, however, seemed to his drunken senses the revelation he was seeking.

"There is no other vision but a subjective one," Huggett was saying, "I make my own maps and mark my own paths on them. If people choose to follow me they'll find their own salvation."

"But your secret areas are so closely guarded. You keep your secrets too well. You've published no Defence of the Realm Act," Mr. Fleet said. It was all much easier than he had expected.

"It's my realm," Huggett shouted, "and I must protect it how I can."

Kennie saw how serious it all was from the look on Huggett's face. Later he heard Huggett protesting.

"Good God! Of course Rousseau was insane. What would be the possible point of taking any notice of him if he wasn't? If you sit on this side of sanity you'll fade away with the anonymous men, you'll be lost in the desert void of reason. Surely you can see that the only hope lies in the subtle and difficult patterns that lie beyond the reason. Why, even as an æsthete you must admit that. They're the only beautiful things left. Go to Blake, go to Maupassant in his last days, go to the Dukhobors and the followers of Jezreel. Why, even the next lunatic escaped from an asylum can tell you more of what the real truth is than fools like Hume or Bertrand Russell."

"Mm," said Mr. Fleet. " 'Great wits are sure to madness near allied.' I see." It was all far more banal than he had expected. He was beginning to find it quite tedious.

Then again, through a thicker haze and a room that was increasingly showing signs of revolving, Kennie heard Huggett say, "Oh, well, of course, if you don't recognize the humanist conspiracy to conceal the truth they've betrayed."

"Do you seriously mean," Mr. Fleet asked, "a conscious conspiracy?"

Huggett paused for a moment, then he replied gravely, "When I am talking to some people I am inclined to think that the only answer to that question is *yes*."

"Ah," said Mr. Fleet, "I see. Well, that takes me into fields with which I'm quite unfamiliar and quite unqualified to continue our argument." He got up and moved across the room.

Kennie could see that Huggett was very angry.

Distressed though he was at the course of his conversation with Huggett, Tristram Fleet felt on his mettle not to give up. He came over to Reg. "And what are you writing at the moment, Mr. Bellwood?" he asked.

Reg had been quite willing to be placated earlier, but he resented Tristram Fleet's sole attention to Huggett. He was annoyed with Rosa for making him come to the party and more deeply resentful than ever of Kennie as the cause of the occasion. He saw his chance. "Oh, nothing much. Thanks awfully," he said in an aggressive imitation of Mr. Fleet's voice. Then, taking Mr. Fleet by the arm, he said, "But you must meet the hero of this party. Our twenty-one-year-old Teddy boy. I expect you've read about the menace of the Teddy boys, but I bet you've never met one, Mr. Fleet."

He led the embarrassed critic over to where Kennie sat with his sensual mouth more than usually adenoidally open in a desperate attempt to sort out Huggett's vital words from a general drink-fumed haze.

"Kennie," Reg said, "here's the most distinguished guest of your party—Mr. Tristram Fleet. Mr. Fleet, meet our twenty-one-year-old guest of honour, Kennie Martin—as you can see by his attire, a genuine, guaranteed Teddy boy." He then moved away.

Kennie hated Reg for calling him a Teddy boy—everyone knew he was on his own. He remembered also that Tristram Fleet had made Huggett angry.

Mr. Fleet's first impulse on taking in Kennie's appearance was to turn his back and go away, but the boy's evident misery made him feel that he must soften Reg Bellwood's rudeness. "I'm afraid that in my secluded ignorance," he said, "I've had no acquaintance with any of the young people of today, Teddy boys or otherwise. I'm delighted to meet you though. Many happy returns of the day."

Something in the combined cultured tones and evident nervousness of Mr. Fleet gave Kennie a clue as to how he could avenge Huggett. He leaned forward in his chair and gave Mr. Fleet the slow, insolent smile with which he had often sent elderly gentlemen about their business. "Look," he said, "you've got the wrong

bloke. I shouldn't think you did know any Teddy boys, but if
you did, I know what they'd call you—a f——bent, see."

The slang was unfamiliar to Mr. Fleet but its intended meaning was painfully clear. He reddened with fury; his reputation
as a womanizer was known to everyone. He turned his back on
Kennie. For a moment he thought of leaving, but he somehow
felt that he must restore his reputation. He looked for Clara, but
to his disgust he saw that she had sunk at last onto the sofa
where she was holding Huggett's hand. His eyes swept the hideous nakedness of the young women's faces. Harold's red-haired
girl friend made a desperate effort to hold his glance, but he
pushed on hurriedly. At last he fixed upon Rosa. Her face, if a little spotty, was at least properly made up and not without a certain sophistication. Her clothes too made some offer of the
curves of her figure. Besides, it would be pleasant to annoy the
insufferable Mr. Bellwood. He lowered himself with a certain
difficulty to the floor by her chair and gave her his full attention.

Here he met with a greater triumph than perhaps he intended.
Rosa was already disgruntled with her victory over Reg. So far
it had given her no more than a little petting and, as this was from
Reg himself, she might have had it less grudgingly anywhere
else. Also, she alone of the women of The Crowd felt any envy
of Clara's looks, clothes, and money. Attention from Tristram
Fleet seemed at last to make sense of her triumph. She saw to it
that at least she left in his taxi. Susan too gained indirectly from
Rosa's triumph, for Reg could not bear to leave alone. Before
Reg took her off she bent over Kennie and asked, "Will you be all
right, Kennie?" but he was asleep. Two by two The Crowd
departed so that Huggett and Clara found themselves alone. When
he began to unhook her dress she pointed at Kennie. Turning out
the lights, she led Huggett upstairs.

It was quite dark in the room when Kennie woke. He felt very
sick. His first thought was to get outside, for, unless antago-
nized, he was naturally very polite and Clara had been the hostess of The Crowd. It would be awful if he vomited in her room,

but he managed to hold off until he got into the garden. Everything was very still when he bent down under a lilac bush. When he raised his head the sky seemed immense over him, the moonlight illumined remote distances. Far away the sound of a train whistle made his sense of loneliness almost unendurable. He was near to tears. He fought through the daze to hold on to the important things he had heard Huggett say. He set off to walk across the Heath and work out their meaning.

Colonel Lambourn looked at his watch and noted with annoyance that it was already half-past midnight. He liked to take his walk at half-past eleven exactly, but recently he had fallen asleep once or twice after his dinner and tonight he must have slept longer than usual. It was not altogether surprising after the unsatisfactory chat he'd had with that fellow at the Board of Trade—some subordinate without an ounce of gumption.

The Colonel locked the front door of his flat—always rather a business now that he'd had a third lock put on, but one couldn't be too careful with things as they stood—and set off briskly along Parliament Hill to the Heath. He carried his despatch case with him because, despite the three locks, there were things that he felt happier to have under his eye—in fairness to the community. He walked erectly and briskly for a man of seventy-four. He was still a handsome man with his rubicund cheeks and bright blue eyes, and he dressed smartly, although his black hat and overcoat were not new. He noticed with satisfaction how quickly a sleep had restored his energies after a very tiring day. Visits to the central offices of the Prudential, to the Royal Geographical Society, to the Treasury, to the Board of Trade, to Peter Jones, to the Bolivian Embassy, to the Wallace Collection, and to Church House— few men of his age could have carried programmes of this kind out day after day, wet or fine; but then few men of his age had his responsibilities, few men, indeed, of any age. He smiled grimly. His blue eyes had a watery glaze.

Reviewing the day's interviews—two events disturbed him: the incompetence of the subordinate at the Board of Trade, but, far more disturbing, the fellow at the Prudential. To begin with, he had no illusions that the fellow was really the high-up chap he represented himself to be and he'd told him so, but more disturbing than that, he had a shrewd idea that it was the same fellow who'd represented himself to be the curator of Kew Gardens a few days before, and, indeed, the same chap that had given himself out to be the Secretary of the Patent Office last month. In which case . . . However, discipline was the main essential. Every step in the campaign in its due order, and no panic.

He went over tomorrow's appointments: Willesden Borough Council, the Lord Chamberlain's Office, the Directors of Overseas Broadcasts, the Scottish Office, the Ranger of Richmond Park, the Arts Council, Friends' House, and the Secretary of the Junior Carlton. A tiring day. The colonel's eyelids shut, but a moment later he tensed the muscles of his face and marched on.

It was as he was passing a bench beneath a large oak tree that the colonel's attention was drawn to a bent figure seated there. Some young fellow in distress apparently. Well, there'd soon be a great deal of distress in the world unless the fellows in authority proved a great deal less idiotic than they had up to now. All the same, there was no more terrible sight in the world than a man in tears—most demoralizing thing that could happen.

The colonel was about to walk on when some sense of his own distress and loneliness made him decide to see if he could help at all. Used as he was to official business, however, he was not adept at establishing human contacts. He sat rather stiffly at the other end of the bench, and it was some minutes before he could bring himself to ask nervously, "Is there anything I can do to help?"

The boy turned enormous eyes upon him. "Look," he said, "I'm not interested."

Colonel Lambourn was familiar with these words. "I'm not surprised," he said, "few people are interested to find out the truth." To his amazement, however, the boy took him up on these words.

"Who says I'm not interested in the Truth. That's what I'm searching for, see."

"Ah!" said Colonel Lambourn. "In that case . . ." He felt in his breast pocket, took out a leather wallet, and presented the boy with his card. "Lieutenant-Colonel Lambourn (Rtd), 673, Parliament Hill, N.W."

The boy read the card, then he said, "I thought you looked like a colonel."

But Colonel Lambourn no longer seemed interested in the boy's remarks. He opened his despatch case and began to take out various maps. He spoke in a loud, rather colourless, official voice. "I'm perfectly aware, sir," he said, "that you are a very busy man." The boy looked surprised at this. "As I am myself," the colonel went on. "I shall not presume any further on your time than it takes to explain the essentials of the very serious situation which at present presents itself in this country. A situation which, however, I think you will see offers unlimited possibilities if comprehended properly and dealt with promptly. A situation which if, as I say, dealt with in this way offers to humanity a greater opportunity of grasping the essential truth of life than any that have previously existed. And now," he said, and his watery blue eyes glinted with a formal smile, "I shall cut out any further cackle and draw your attention to these three maps."

He seemed for a moment to search for a table in front of him, then, contenting himself with the ground, he spread out a map of England. "I do not have to remind you, sir," he said, "of the absolute secrecy which necessarily surrounds my statement. I don't wish"—he looked a little anxiously at the boy and his head shook a little—"to speak idly of a conspiracy. People are so often discouraged when I tell them of the continuous persecution to which I've been subjected." His voice sounded puzzled. "Fools find it so easy to avoid the truth by calling it madness."

The boy looked at the old man eagerly, then he asked with excitement, "Have you ever been in an asylum?"

Colonel Lambourn drew himself up stiffly. "My enemies," he said, "had me locked away at one time, but I'm glad to say justice prevailed." He folded up the map and showed signs of leaving.

"No, don't go," the boy cried, "I want to hear what you have to say. Like you'll be able to tell the truth of it all."

The old man spread out the map once more. "Thank you for your understanding, sir," he said, "you are a wise man." And now he began to explain the red lines and crosses on the map. "These, you see," he said, "are the old bridle paths of the eighteenth and nineteenth centuries. As far as I have been able to establish them," and he repeated somewhat vaguely, "As far as I have been able to establish them. Now"—and he spread out another map marked in blue—"here you have the government defence zones, atomic power stations, and gun sites laid down in the Defence of the Realm Act."

The boy's eyes grew rounder as Huggett's conversation with Fleet returned to him.

"You will notice that each of these bridle paths leads in fact to a defence zone. Hardly a coincidence, I suggest. Now look at this third map. A Map of Treasure Trove issued by the Office of Works. Notice the position of the bridle paths in relation to the buried treasures and in relation to the defence zones." The boy echoed, "Buried treasure," excitedly. "But," said the old man solemnly, "this map perhaps is the most conclusive. A diagram of the intersections of the three maps when superimposed. You see what they show?" he asked.

The boy stared, open-mouthed.

"No?" said the colonel. "Allow me to draw your attention. So, so, and so. You see. Three open pentacles." He sat back with a look of triumph, and the boy leaned forward excitedly.

"I think," Colonel Lambourn said, "that if the intersections of these pentacles themselves were to be fully explored, indeed I have no doubt, that humanity would be in possession of what I may call the putative treasure, and, if that were to happen, I have no doubt that our enemies would be, to put it mildly, seriously discomforted." He began to fold up the maps and replace them in the despatch case.

"What's it mean?" cried the boy. "What's it tell you?" And as the old man began to rise from the bench he seized his arm

roughly. "I want to know the Truth," he cried. "I want you to
tell me the Truth of it all. What's behind it?"

Colonel Lambourn turned and stared at the boy. His head
shook a little and for a moment a film came down over his blue
eyes; then he sat down, opened his despatch case, and took out
the first map. The boy's body trembled with excitement. "I'm
perfectly aware, sir," the colonel said, "that you are a very busy
man. As I am myself. So I shall not presume any further on your
time than it takes to explain the essentials of the very serious situation which at present presents itself in this country. . . ." The
boy stared, amazed. "A situation which, however," the colonel
went on, "I think you will see offers possibilities."

"It's a bloody cheat," Kennie cried.

The despair of his screams made the colonel turn towards him.
Kennie banged his fist down on the old man's face. Blood poured
from the colonel's nose and he fell backwards, hitting his head on
the bench corner. Kennie got up and ran away across the grass.

See, it's like I said when I see red I don't know my own
strength. And it's all, all of it, a bloody cheat and I don't know
what I shall do. But if there's questions, I'll be all right, see, be
cause what's an old bloke like that want talking to me on Hampstead Heath at one o'clock in the morning. That's what they'll
want to know.

A Flat Country Christmas

As usual Carola had to run back into the bungalow two or three times before they were ready to set off. First, she had forgotten her hanky, and then she thought she had put the hot plate on at "medium" instead of "low" for Mrs. Ramsden's stew; last, she was sure she had told the old lady wrong about the time for Deirdre's bottle. As a rule Ray used these delays to memorize for his exam, running over one of the set schemes for the General Paper that the Correspondence School had sent him, or reconstructing a chapter from the Hammonds—he expected to do rather well on the Industrial Revolution. Sometimes, when his headaches were bad, he tapped on the gate-post or called after Carola in the sharp, peremptory voice he had acquired as an officer. But this afternoon, although his head was splitting, his whole body seemed to resist any contact with the outside world. He merely stood, sucking at his empty pipe and staring at the houses around him.

Even on this unnaturally bright and sunny Christmas night of 1949, the rows of bungalows and council houses seemed silently disapproving, forbiddingly reserved. The Slaters' home stood on the very edge of the estate, commanding a panorama of flat, marshy fields, broken here and there by a muddy stream or a huge oak in the last decay of majesty—merging at last into the

Written in 1950; first published in the *New Statesman* in 1950; scene immediate post Second World War.

faint, shining vermilion of the roofs of the next "new town" some three miles away.

Carola's first reaction, as she saw the depression of Ray's stance, was to slip her arm through his and call his attention to "their view." With her new French-blue costume and red leather belt she felt very certain of herself; even her lipstick, she thought, was right for once, would give no hint of the chapel background of which she was always too aware when they visited Sheila.

In so unusual a mood of self-assurance, she was more than ever proud of the position of the bungalow, so almost in the country. But as she looked again at the shapeless waste land before her some faint breath of melancholy and despair seeped even into her busy, chattering world; she blew it aside with a gust of solicitude for her husband. "You haven't got a temperature, have you, darling?" she asked and put her cool little hand up to his brow. Ray only removed his pipe and said, "No." There was nothing Carola feared more than being a fusspot—not understanding, or nagging like the old Chapel cats; so she decided just to chatter on—Ray's funny little mouse. She was glad they were going to Eric and Sheila because they were such old friends, only she did hope there wouldn't be any politics. . . .

It was really just the neighbourhood to start life in, she thought as they made their way across the marshes. They didn't know anybody, of course, even after a year's residence, but at least there was none of the prying and gossip of her village home. Yes, an ideal place to start life in, so long as you didn't get stuck. But there wasn't much likelihood of that, she decided as she looked at Ray's tall, upright figure, his clear-cut features and steady, reliable blue eyes—a Technical Officer at the Ministry and about to take an Honours degree.

As if to echo her thoughts, Ray's voice cut across her chatter about Deirdre's attempts at speech. "I've applied for the Inspectorship," he said in his usual clear, confident voice, but a shade more loudly to cover his depression with words.

"With the degree behind me, I shall still be able to sit the Administrative in June. But it'll be the last Reconstruction entrance, and it's just as well to have a second string. Don't say anything to Eric. He's got some bee in his bonnet about sticking in the Technical Grade until the Association's taken the new claim to arbitration. He talks about it as a moral issue, as if *that* had any meaning. He's so unrealistic. We'll get from the Treasury exactly what they can give us, which at the moment is what we're already getting. I hope to God he doesn't start on it tonight. Rights to this and Rights to that: he's still with Tom Paine. He and the old man ought to get together. Did you see Dad's last letter? He's back to Keir Hardie now, and how we aren't a 'fighting party' any more. He'd do better fighting for Mother to have a bit of a rest."

Carola tucked her arm into his. "I know, darling," she said, and somewhere from her Baptist girlhood her mother's voice reached her. Pursing up her lips defiantly, she added, "As if we aren't all Labour, but we don't have to shout about it."

They had left the fields now and were passing through the overgrown shrubbery of some demolished nineteenth-century mansion. Through the rhododendrons and the laurels they could see the by-pass, its white concrete line of ships shining in the dying light—the snack bar, the Barclay's bank, the utility furniture store, Mme. Yvonne's beauty parlour.

At last they turned into the drive of a small Edwardian house. The lawn was planted with standard roses, but the conservatory stood glassless and derelict. The half-timbered upper storey of the house was a bold black and white; in the porch hung a wrought-iron lantern. Ray stopped dead in the middle of his loud discourse on his future, his thin lips and heroic eyes resumed their set of misery, then as suddenly grimaced into manly mateyness. "I could use a drink just about now," he said, and, giggling, Carola answered, "I hope Sheila doesn't make them as strong as last time."

Sheila, of course, had. If you have drinks, have them good, was only one of the many solid maxims of her rich Guildford business background that she had tried so hard but had failed to shed. She embodied three generations of business success—her own plain black dress and gay Jacqmar scarf speaking for bookish Roedean and Girton, something in her overcultured voice for her mother's feverish W.V.S. attempts to "make the county," and deep down a vulgar rumble that declared her grandmother's overjewelled, *nouveau riche* toughness.

"How are you, darling?" She kissed Carola. "And little Deirdre?"

"Terribly naughty, I'm afraid," said Carola, meaning really that as usual she was afraid of Sheila.

"That comes of feeding her on meat." Eric's cockney voice was at the top of his Max Miller form, his absurdly young face wore its most cheeky errand-boy look. He did not want a row with Ray, yet the news weighed on him so heavily that he doubted if he could avoid it. Only clowning, perhaps, could help; he would give them his every imitation, from "Eton and Oxford" to the flushing of the lavatory cistern, and so, perhaps, carry the evening through.

And now the party got under way. It was a curiously formal measure for close friends—rigid in its pattern like some saraband or pavane. They had broken down so many social barriers and prejudices to get there, and in the strange, flat isolation of the housing estate they depended so much on these bonds forged in the now-distant days in the Forces. They felt justly proud of the emancipation from class that they had achieved both in marriage and in friendship, but, though they had no wish to live on sentiment and memory, these were the only cement that riveted the fortress they had constructed against loneliness.

First, then, it must be ladies to the centre. Carola would admire the simplicity of Sheila's table-setting, though she wondered strangely at the lack of doilies, of little mats, and of colourfully arranged salads and fruit that she copied so carefully from women's magazines. Sheila must praise Carola's new blue dress and wish that she could speak about the dreadful little doggy brooch. She would first blame herself for snobbery and then decide that after all there was nothing morally right about bad taste and petty bourgeois gentility. They were happier when they got on to Ray's headaches, about which they could both be sensible, psychological, and practical. "What did the clinic say?" and "Oh, but that's the whole point. You can get decent psychiatric treatment now without being a millionaire." It was nice, they both thought, when common ground could be reached, because they did like each other, only they were rather thrown together.

Gentlemen to the side, meanwhile, were carefully avoiding politics. It was chaff and office personalities, and when these threatened to get too warm, questions from Eric about Robert Owen, and Ray trying to please by saying, "But the only really good analysis, of course, was Engel's *1844*." They could compromise and please each other as long as they stuck to the nineteenth century, giving full rein to the mutual admiration they had acquired in the army.

And now it was lady to gentleman. Sheila and Ray talked books. She, perhaps, found his approach a bit utilitarian. "I know," she said, "about comparing Fielding and Richardson, and Dickens and Thackeray, but I still don't think it's very helpful." After all, he decided, it was easy enough for her to say "damn Leavis, she still didn't think Conrad was any good"; she hadn't got to take the Reconstruction English paper. On the whole, however, they kept in step very well and were proud of their part of the measure. For Carola and Eric it was not easy. He thought her a nice little thing but as heavy as a suet pudding and far too like one in the face. She wished so much she didn't think him common. But they managed all right on praise of Ray and Sheila and glowed at each other in the process.

Finally it was all together to the centre with stories of the old war days and a good time had by all.

It wasn't Christmas every day, so they toasted "absent friends." Each now slid away in a *pas seul* of memory, back to the stifling family Christmas ritual from which they had escaped.

"Absent friends," Carola's mother had said as she raised her glass of ginger wine, "and I'm sorry so many of them should have been absent from Chapel this morning."

"If you mean Penelope," Carola had replied, red in the face above her gym tunic, "she was skating. After all, the river isn't frozen every Christmas. Is it so very serious for once?"

"It's pennies that make pounds, my dear. You can give a little here and a little there, and in the end there's nothing in the bank."

"Absent friends," Sheila's grandmother had said with a snort. "I suppose Sheila's thinking of her Mugginses or Fugginses or whatever they're called. A nice rumtcyfoo lot, not a penny to bless themselves with."

"Hush, darling," said Sheila's mother. "We don't use expressions like that now. All the same, Sheila, I do think they're rather a tatty crowd."

"I don't understand what you mean," said Sheila obstinately.

"I think you do, darling," replied her mother. "There are standards—gracious living, you know—that are surely worth something. It seems terrible to throw it all away unless you're very sure you've got something to put in its place."

"Absent friends!" Ray's father had said. "To the boys of the International Brigade, and damnation to Non-Intervention." Ray felt his collar stick to his neck. Of course he was against Franco, but what a moment to choose, and the sentimentality of it.

"Absent friends," Eric's spiv brother had said, "and from what I've seen of Eric's mob, the longer the bleeders are absent, the better."

Well, now it was these families who were absent; the friends had been kept through all the hazards of class. They felt warmer to one another, after their lonely childhood dances were over. There might be faults here and there, but their friendship was built on a common way of living—tolerant, forward-looking, never anti-social. Eric turned on the wireless to dispel the last clouds of melancholy. " 'Enjoy yourself, enjoy yourself, it's later than you think,' " sang the vocalist. It was then that Ray first lost control. Turning off the wireless abruptly—"I'm sorry. I don't think I can stand that," he said. The others searched about for a means of passing over the incident, and they fell back almost automatically upon a familiar dirge.

Carola spoke first; she felt she must excuse Ray's behaviour. "I don't think the air down here does Ray any good," she said.

"It's awfully depressing," Sheila agreed, "I think that's why there's so little going on in the place."

"Yes," said Carola, "you'd think there'd be a dramatic society or something," and she took Ray's hand, for they had met in a Forces show.

"Everyone seems half asleep," said Sheila.

"Asleep!" said Eric. "They call a man a live wire if he's only been dead three weeks."

They waited for Ray to speak; it was his buoyancy and confidence that usually carried them out of this mood. But his voice, when it came, was from the tomb. "It's such very flat country," he said.

Carola, once again, felt impelled to lead the party up to the heights. "Oh, well," she said brightly, "we're not likely to stick here long."

"God, no," said Sheila. "Eric's only waiting for the arbitration decision to apply for a move."

"That's right," said Eric. "And another thing, the Ministry won't be able to stand out long against the return to London. Devolution's had it . . ." But he stopped in the middle of the sentence. Illogically perhaps, he found that the name of London always brought the atom bomb to his mind. He'd been wanting to speak of it all the evening, but he'd promised Sheila to keep off it. They waited more than ever on Ray now, but he just stared into the distance.

"I've thought of the silliest thing," said Carola. She had to say something to cover Ray's silence. "Could we take one of the mirrors down, Sheila?"

"Of course, darling, but whatever for?"

"Well, I read about it in *Woman's Own* or somewhere. You decorate a mirror with mistletoe on Christmas Night and it acts as a sort of crystal to gaze in."

"Oh, do let's try," cried Sheila. Any port in a storm, she thought.

Even Eric seemed enthusiastic. " 'What the Stars Foretell.' Why not? I'm all for it."

But when Sheila looked into the mirror she could make nothing of it. "I'm afraid it's no good, darling," she said. "I never was psychic. Except that I do see how like Queen Elizabeth I am. My nose is fantastic."

Carola in her turn wasn't sure, but she really thought the mirror did get a bit cloudy, and she saw something awfully like a baby.

"Hundreds of darling little Deirdres, I expect," said Sheila rather sharply.

"Hallelujah," cried Eric as he bent over the glass, "fourteen Lana Turners doing the Veil Dance! And a kick in the pants for MacArthur, Deakin, and Ernie B. This is Heaven all right. 'Open up dem pearly gates, I'se a-coming, Lord.' "

They were all quite surprised when Ray agreed to sit down before the mirror, but he sat so long and so silently that they decided to disregard him.

"Well, I'll go and get me the wallop," said Eric. The sooner the evening was ended the better.

It was only the sound of Ray's sobbing that finally woke them to his condition.

"Ray!" cried Carola. "What's wrong, my darling?"

Ray's gaze was blank when he turned to them; only the tears running down his cheeks seemed alive. "Oh, my God!" he said. "Oh, my God! I've seen Nothing!"

"My poor poppet," said Sheila, all understanding. "Never mind. Come and sit over here." But Ray just continued to cry. "Darling, you must get him home," said Sheila.

Carola was so miserable and embarrassed. "If you won't think it awful . . ."

"My dear," said Sheila, practical, never alarmist, "there's nothing to worry about. He's just overworked. But you must put him to bed and get Dr. Rayesley. I'll ring Quiktax now."

Eric couldn't help it, he'd suppressed his apocalyptical thoughts so long, and now he said, "I know what. Ray's seen the future and we've all been atomized." It was a facetiousness he would never forgive himself.

But Ray only shook his head. "That's all to do with you. I'm not concerned with it. This is personal. I've felt it somewhere about for weeks, perhaps years, and now I've seen it. I've seen Nothing."

Carola's embarrassment was more than she could bear. "You old silly," she said, "we none of us saw anything. Sheila *said* so, and Eric was only joking. And as for me, you know I can imagine anything."

Ray turned on her savagely. "Why are you talking?" he shouted. "It doesn't matter to me what you do or say . . ." He broke off as suddenly. "I'm sorry," he said, "it's not of any importance," and he stared into the fire.

More Friend than Lodger

➤➤➤≪≪≪

As soon as Henry spoke of their new author, Rodney Galt, I knew that I should dislike him. "It's rather a feather in my cap to have got him for our list," he said. The publishing firm of which Henry is a junior partner is called Brodrick Layland, which as a name is surely a feather in no one's cap, but that's by the way. "I think Harkness were crazy to let him go," Henry said, "because although *Cuckoo* wasn't a great money-spinner, it was very well thought of indeed. But that's typical of Harkness, they think of nothing but sales."

I may say for those who don't know him that this speech was very typical of Henry: because, first, I should imagine most publishers think a lot about sales, and if Brodrick Layland don't, then I'm sorry to hear it; and, second, Henry would never naturally use expressions like "a great money-spinner," but since he's gone into publishing he thinks he ought to sound a bit like a businessman and doesn't really know how. The kind of thing that comes natural to Henry to say is that somebody or something is "very well thought of indeed," which doesn't sound like a businessman to anyone, I imagine. But what Henry is like ought to emerge from my story if I'm able to write it at all. And I must in fairness add that my comments about him probably tell quite a lot about me—for example, he isn't by any means mostly interested in the money in

Written in 1956; first published in *The New Yorker* in 1957; scene contemporary.

publishing but much more in "building up a good list," so that his comment on Harkness wasn't hypocritical. And, as his wife, I know this perfectly well, but I've got into the habit of talking like that about him.

Henry went on to tell me about *Cuckoo*. It was not either a novel, which one might have thought, or a book about birds or lunatics, which was less likely, although it's the kind of thing I might have pretended to think in order to annoy him. No, *Cuckoo* was an anthology and a history of famous cuckolds. Rodney Galt, it seemed, had a great reputation, not as a cuckold, for he was single, but as a seducer, although his victories were not only or even mainly among married women. He was particularly successful, as a matter of fact, at seducing younger daughters and debs. Henry told me all this in a special offhand sort of voice intended to suggest to me that at Brodrick Layland's they took that sort of thing for granted. Once again I'm being bitchy because, of course, if I had said "Come off it, Henry," or words to that effect, he would have changed his tone immediately. But I did not see why I should, because among our acquaintances we *do* number a few though not many seducers of virgins; and if I made Henry change his tone it would suggest that he was *quite* unfamiliar with such a phenomenon, which would be equally false. Fairness and truth are my greatest difficulties in life.

To return to Rodney Galt—the book he was going to write for Brodrick Layland was to be called *Honour and Civility*. Once again it was not to be a novel, however, like *Sense and Sensibility* or *The Naked and the Dead*. Rodney Galt used the words "honour" and "civility" in a special sense; some would say an archaic sense, but he did not see it that way because he preferred not to recognize the changes that had taken place in the English language in the last hundred years or so. "Honour" for him meant "the thing that is most precious to a man," but not in the sense that the Victorians meant that it was most precious to a woman. Rodney Galt, from what I could gather, would have liked to see men still killing each other in duels for their honour and offering civilities to one another in the shape of snuff and suchlike before they did so. He believed in "living dangerously" and in what is called "high courage," but exemplified preferably in sports and combats of long standing. He was, therefore, against motor-racing and even more against "track," but in favour of bull-fighting and perhaps pelota; he was also against dog-racing but in favour of baccarat for high stakes.

The book, however, was not to be just one of those books that used to be popular with my uncle Charles, called *Twelve Rakes* or *Twenty Famous Dandies*. It was to be more philosophical than that, involving all the author's view of society; for example, that we could not be civilized or great again unless we accepted cruelty as a part of living dangerously, and that without prejudice man could have no opinion, and, indeed, altogether what in Mr. Galt's view constituted the patrician life.

I told Henry that I did not care for the sound of him. Henry only smiled, however, and said, "I warn you that he's a snob, but on such a colossal scale and with such panache that one can't take exception to it." I told Henry firmly that I was not the kind of woman who could see things on such a large scale as that, and also, that if, as I suspected from his saying "I warn you," he intended to invite Rodney Galt to the house, only the strictest business necessity would reconcile me to it.

"There *is* the strictest business necessity," Henry said and added, "Don't be put off by his matinee-idol looks. He's indecently good-looking." He giggled when he said this, for he knew that he had turned the tables on me. Henry used to believe—his mother taught him the idea—that no woman liked men to be extremely good-looking. He knows different now, because I have told him again and again that I would not have married him if he had not been very handsome himself. His mother's code, however, dies hard with him, and even now, I suspect, he thinks that if his nose had not been broken at school I should have found him too perfect. He is quite wrong. I would willingly pay for him to have it straightened if I thought he would accept the offer.

Reading over what I have written, I see that it must appear as though Henry and I live on very whimsical terms—gilding the pill of our daily disagreements with a lot of private jokes and "sparring" and generally rather ghastly arch behaviour. Thinking over our life together, perhaps it is true. It is with no conscious intent, however—although I have read again and again in the women's papers to which I'm addicted that a sense of humour is the cement of marriage. Henry and I have a reasonable proportion of sense of humour, but no more. He gets his, which is dry, from his mother, who, as you will see in this story of Rodney Galt, is like a character from the novels of Miss Compton-Burnett, or, at least, when I read those novels I people them entirely with characters like Henry's mother. My parents had no vestige of humour; my father was too busy getting rich and my mother was too busy unsuccessfully trying to crash county society.

But it *is* true that Henry and I in our five years of marriage have built up a lot of private joking and whimsical talking, and I can offer what seem to be some good reasons for it, but who am I to say? First, there is what anyone would pick on—that our marriage is childless, which, I think, is really the least of the possible reasons. It certainly is with me, although it may count with Henry more than he can say. The second is that everything counts with Henry more than he can say. "Discerning" people who know Henry and his mother, and, indeed, all the Ravens, usually say that they are shy beneath their sharp manner. I don't quite believe this; I think it's just because they find it easier to be like this so that other people can't overstep the mark of intimacy and intrude too far on their personal lives. You can tell from the way Henry's mother shuts her eyes when she meets people that she has an interior life, and actually she is a devout Anglican. And Henry has an interior life which he has somehow or other put into his publishing. Well, anyhow, Henry's manner, shy or not, makes me shy, and I've got much more whimsical since I knew him.

But also there's my own attitude to our marriage. I can only sum it up by saying that it's like the attitude of almost everyone in England today to almost everything. I worked desperately hard to get out of the insecurity of my family—which in this case was not economic, because they were fairly rich and left me quite a little money of my own, but social—and when I married Henry I loved every minute of it because the Ravens are quite secure in their own way—which Henry's mother calls "good country middle class, June dear, and no more." And if that security is threatened for a moment I rush back to it for safety. But most of the time when it's not in danger, I keep longing for more adventure in life and a wider scope and more variety and even greater risks and perils. Well, all that you'll see in this story, I think. But, anyhow, this feeling about our marriage makes me uneasy with Henry and I keep him at a humorous distance. And he, knowing it, does so all the more too. All this, I hope, will explain our private jokes and so on, of which you will meet many. By the way, about security and risk, I don't really believe that one can't have one's cake and eat it—which also you'll see.

To return to Rodney Galt—Henry did, in fact, invite him to dinner a week later. He was not, of course, as bad as Henry made out; that is to say, as I have sketched above, because that description was part of Henry's ironical teasing of me. In fact, however, he was pretty bad. He said ghastly things in an Olympian way—not with humour like Henry and me, but with "wit," which is always rather awful. However, I must admit that even at that first dinner I didn't mind Rodney's wit as much as all that, partly because he had the most lovely speaking voice (I don't know why one says "speaking voice" as though most of one's friends used recitative), very deep and resonant, which always sends me; and partly because he introduced his ghastly views in a way that made them seem better than they were. For example:

Henry said, "I imagine that a good number of your best friends are Jews, Galt."

And Rodney raised his eyebrows and said, "Good heavens, why?"

And Henry answered, "Most anti-Semitic people make that claim."

And Rodney said, "I suppose that's why I'm not anti-Semitic. I can't imagine knowing any Jews. When would it arise? Oh, I suppose when one's buying pictures or objects, but then that's hardly knowing. It's simply one of the necessities. Or, of course, if one went to Palestine, but then that's hardly a necessity."

And I said, "What about Disraeli? He made the Tory Party of today." I said this with a side glance at Henry because he used then to describe himself as a Tory Democrat, although since Suez he has said that he had not realized how deeply Liberalism ran in his veins.

Rodney said, "What makes you speak of such unpleasant things?"

And I asked, "Aren't you a Tory then?"

And he answered, "I support the principles of Lord Eldon and respect the courage of Lord Sidmouth, if that's what you mean."

Henry said, "Oh, but what about the Suez Canal and the British Empire? Disraeli made those."

And Rodney looked distant and remarked, "The British Empire even at its height was never more than a convenient outlet for the middle-class high-mindedness of Winchester and Rugby. The plantations and the penal colonies, of course," he added, "were a different matter."

Henry, who makes more of his Charterhouse education than he admits, said, "Oh, come, Winchester and Rugby are hardly the same thing."

Rodney smiled and said in a special hearty voice, "No, I suppose not, old man." This was rude to Henry, of course, but slightly gratifying to me. Anyhow, he went straight on and said, "The thing that pleases me most about coming to Brodrick Layland is your book production, Raven. I do like to feel that what I have written, if it is worth publishing at all, deserves a comely presentation."

This, of course, was very gratifying to Henry. They talked about books, or rather the appearance of books, for some time, and I made little comment as I like the inside of books almost exclusively. It appeared, however, that Rodney was a great collector of books, as he was of so many other things: porcelain, enamels, Byzantine ivories, and Central American carvings. He was quick to tell us that, of course, with his modest income, he had to leave the big things alone and that, again with his modest income, it was increasingly difficult to pick up anything worth having, but that it could be done. He left us somehow with the impression that he would not really have cared for the big things anyway, and that his income could not be as modest as all that.

"Heaven defend me," he said, "from having the money to buy those tedious delights of the pedants—incunables. No, the little Elzevirs are my particular favourites, the decent classical authors charmingly produced. I have a delightful little Tully and the only erotica worth possessing, Ovid's *Amores*."

It was talking of Ovid that he said something which gave me a clue to my feelings about him.

"I know of no more moving thing in literature than Ovid's exiled lament for Rome. It's just how any civilized Englishman to-day must feel when, chained to his native land, he thinks of the Mediterranean, or almost anywhere else outside England for that matter. 'Breathes there a soul,' you know." He smiled as he said it. Of course, it was the most awful pretentious way of talking, but so often I do feel that I would rather be almost anywhere than in England that he made me feel guilty for not being as honest as he was.

It seemed, however, that after a great deal of travel in a great many places he *was* now for some time to be chained to his native land. He had, he said, a lot of family business to do. He was looking out for a house something like ours. He even hinted—it was the only hint of his commercially venturing side that he gave that evening—at the possibility of his buying a number of houses as an investment. Meanwhile he was staying with Lady Ann Denton. I ventured to suggest that this might be a little too much of a good thing, but he smiled and said that she was a very old friend, which, although it rather put me in my place, gave him a good mark for loyalty. (Henry scolded me afterwards and told me that Rodney was having an affair with Lady Ann. This surprised and disconcerted me. It didn't sound at all like "debs." Lady Ann is old —over forty—and very knocked about and ginny. She has an amusing malicious tongue and a heart of gold. Sometimes I accept her tongue because of her heart, and sometimes I put up with her heart because of her tongue. Sometimes I can't stand either. But, as you will have already seen, my attitude to people is rather ambiguous. However, Henry is very fond of her. She makes him feel broad-minded, which he likes very much.)

We had it out a little about snobbery that evening. "Heavens, I should hope so," Rodney said when I accused him of being a social snob, "it's one of the few furies worth having that are left to us—little opportunity though the modern world allows of finding anyone worth cultivating. There still do exist a few families, however, even in this country. It lends shape to my life as it did to Proust's." I said that though it had lent shape to Proust's work, I wasn't so sure about his life. "In any case," he said with a purposeful parody of a self-satisfied smile, "art and life are one." Then he burst out laughing and said, "Really, I've excelled myself this evening. It's your excellent food."

Looking back at what I have written, I see that I said that he wasn't as bad as Henry made out and then everything that I have reported him as saying is quite pretentious and awful. The truth is that it was his smile and his good looks that made it seem all right. Henry had said that he was like a matinee idol, but this is a ridiculous expression for nowadays (whatever it may have been in the days of Henry's mother and Owen Nares), because no one could go to a matinee with all those grey-haired old ladies up from the country rattling tea-trays and feel sexy about anything. But Rodney was like all the best film stars rolled into one and yet the kind of person it wasn't surprising to meet; and these, taken together, surely make a very sexy combination.

It was clear that evening that Henry liked him very much too. Not for that reason, of course—Henry hasn't ever even thought about having feelings of that kind, I'm glad to say. As a matter of fact, Henry doesn't have sexy feelings much anyway. No, that's quite unfair and bitchy of me again. Of course he has sexy feelings, but he has them at definite times, and the rest of the time such things don't come into his head. Whereas I don't ever have such strong sexy feelings as he has, but I have some of them all the time. This is a contrast that tends to make things difficult.

No, the reason Henry liked him I could see at once, and I said as soon as he had left, "Well, he's quite your cup of tea, isn't he? He's been everywhere and knows a lot about everything." I said the last sentence in inverted commas, because it's one of Henry's favourite expressions of admiration and I often tease him about it. It isn't very surprising because Henry went to Charterhouse and then in the last two years of the war he went with the F.S.P. to Italy, and then he went to the Queen's College, Oxford, and then he went into Brodrick Layland. So he hasn't been everywhere. In fact, however, he does know quite a lot about quite a number of things, but as soon as he knows something he doesn't think it can be very important.

We both agreed then that Rodney Galt was quite awful in most ways but that we rather liked him all the same. This is my usual experience with a great number of people that I meet, but Henry found it more surprising.

In the weeks that followed Henry seemed to see a good deal of Rodney Galt. He put him up for his club. I was rather surprised that Rodney should have wanted to be a member of Henry's club, which is rather dull and literary: I had imagined him belonging to a lot of clubs of a much grander kind already. Henry explained that Rodney did in fact belong to a lot of others but that he had been abroad so much that he had lost touch with those worlds. I thought that was very odd too, because I imagined that the point of clubs was that no matter how often you went round the world and no matter how long, when you came back the club was there. However, as I only knew about clubs from the novels of Evelyn Waugh, I was prepared to believe that I was mistaken. In any case it also seemed that Rodney wanted particularly to belong to this authors' sort of club, because he believed very strongly that one should do everything one did professionally, and as he was now going to write books he wanted to go to that sort of place.

"He's a strange fellow in many ways," Henry said, "a mass of contradictions." This didn't seem at all strange to me, because such people as I have met have all been a mass of contradictions. Nevertheless Rodney's particular contradiction in this case did seem odd to me. I had imagined that the whole point of his books would be that they should be thrown off in the midst of other activities—amateur productions that proved to be more brilliant than the professional. However, his new attitude, if less romantic, was more creditable and certainly more promising for Brodrick Layland. I decided, indeed, that he had probably only made this gesture to please Henry, which it did.

We dined once or twice with him and Lady Ann. She has rather a nice house in Chester Square and he seemed to be very comfortably installed—more permanently, indeed, than his earlier talk of buying houses suggested. However, this may well have been only the appearance that Lady Ann gave to things, for she made every effort short of absurdity to underline the nature of their relationship. I really could not blame her for this, for she had made a catch that someone a good deal less battered and ginny might have been proud of; and I had to admire the manner in which she avoided the absurdity, for, in fact, looking at him and at her, it *was* very absurd, apart from the large gap in their ages—fifteen years at least, I decided.

Lady Ann, as usual, talked most of the time. She has a special way of being funny: she speaks with a drawl and a very slight stutter and she ends her remarks suddenly with a word or expression that isn't what one expects she is going to lead up to. Well, of course one does expect it, because she always does it; and like a lot of things it gets less funny when you've heard it a few times. For example, she said she didn't agree with Rodney in not liking *Look Back in Anger*, she'd been three times, the music was so good. And again, she quite agreed with Henry, she wouldn't have missed the Braque exhibition for anything, but then she got a peculiar pleasure, almost a sensual one, from being jammed really tight in a crowd. And so on. Henry always laps up Lady Ann. She's a sort of tarty, substitute mother-figure for him, I think; and, indeed, if he wanted a tarty mother he had to find a substitute. I thought, perhaps, that Rodney would be a little bored with her carry-on, but if he was he didn't show it. This, of course, was very creditable of him but made me a little disappointed. Occasionally, it is true, he broke into the middle of her chatter; but then she interrupted him sometimes just as rudely. They might really have been a perfectly happy pair, which I found even more disappointing.

I can't help thinking that by this time you may have formed some rather unfavourable views about the kind of woman I am. Well, I've already said that often I have very bitchy moods; and it's true, but at least I know it. But if you ask me why I have bitchy moods it's more difficult to say. In the first place, life is frightfully boring nowadays, isn't it? And if you say I ought to try doing something with my time, well, I have. I did translation from French and German for Brodick Layland for a time, and I did prison visiting. They're quite different sorts of things to do, and it didn't take long for me to get very bored with each of them. Not that I should want wars and revolutions—whenever there's an international crisis I get a ghastly pain in my stomach like everybody else. But, as I said, like England, I want security and I don't.

However, what I was trying to explain about was my bitchy moods. Well, when I get very bored and depressed I hate everyone and it seems to me everyone hates me. (As a matter of fact, most people do like Henry better than me, although they think I'm more amusing.) But when the depressed moods lift I can't help feeling people are rather nice and they seem to like me too. I had these moods very badly when I was sixteen or so; and now in these last two years (since I was twenty-five) they've come back and they change much more quickly. When I talked to Henry about it once, he got so depressed and took such a "psychological" view that I've never mentioned it again. In any case it's so easy to take "psychological" views; but I'm by no means sure that it isn't just as true to say, like my old nurse, "Well, we all have our ups and downs," and certainly that's a more cosy view of the situation.

But enough about me, because all this is really about Rodney
Galt. Well, in those few times I saw him with Lady Ann (it
seems more comic always to call her that) I began to have a
theory about him, and when I get theories about people I get
very interested in them. Especially as, if my theory was right, then
Lady Ann and Henry and Mr. Brodrick and no doubt lots of
other people were liable to be sold all along the line or up the
river or whatever the expression is; but on the whole, if my
theory was right, it only made *me* feel that he was *more* fascinat-
ing. The best sort of theory to have. One thing I did want to
know more about was his family. In such cases I always believe
in asking directly, so I said, "Where are your family, Rodney?"

He smiled and said, "In the Midlothian, where they've been
for a sufficient number of recorded centuries to make them respectable. They're the best sort of people really," he added, "the
kind of people who've always been content to be trout in the local minnow pond. I'm the only one who's shown the cloven hoof
of fame-seeking. There must be a bounderish streak somewhere,
though not from mother's family, who were all perfectly good
dull country gentry. Of course, there was my great-great-great-
uncle the novelist. But his was a very respectable, middling sort
of local fame really."

Well, there wasn't much given away there, because after all
there are minnows and minnows and even "country gentry" is
rather a vague term. It was a bit disingenuous about Galt the
novelist, because even I have heard of him and I know nothing of
the Midlothian. And that was the chief annoyance—I knew absolutely no one with whom I could check up. But it didn't shake
my theory.

Now we come to the most important point in this story: when
Rodney Galt became our lodger. But first I shall have to explain
about "the lodger battle" which Henry and I had been then
waging for over a year, and this means explaining about our fi-
nances. Henry had some capital and he put that into Brodrick
Layland, and really, all things considered, he gets quite a good
income back. But the house which we live in is mine, and it was

left to me by my Aunt Agnes, and it's rather a big house, situated in that vague area known as behind Harrods. But it isn't, in fact, Pont Street Dutch. And in this big house there are only me and Henry and one or two foreign girls. They change usually every year, and at the time I'm speaking of, about six or seven months ago, there was only one girl, a Swiss called Henriette Vaudoyer. Henry had long been keen that we should have a lodger who could have a bedroom and sitting-room and bathroom of his own. He said it was because he didn't like my providing the house and getting nothing back from it. He thought that at least I ought to get pin money out of it. This was an absurd excuse because Daddy left me quite a little income—a great deal more than was required even if I were to set up a factory for sticking pins into wax images.

I think Henry had at least three real reasons for wanting this lodger: one, he thought it was wrong to have so much space when people couldn't find anywhere to live, and this, if I had thought of it first, I would have agreed with, because I have more social conscience really than Henry, when I remember it; two, the empty rooms (empty, that is, of human beings) reminded him of the tiny feet that might have pattered but did not; three, he had an idea that having a lodger would give me something to do and help with the moods I've already told you about. The last two of these reasons annoyed me very much and made me very unwilling to have a lodger.

So Henry was rather shy in suggesting that we should let the top floor to Rodney Galt. He only felt able to introduce the subject by way of the brilliant first chapter of Rodney's new book. Henry, it seemed, was bowled over by this chapter when Rodney had submitted it, and even Mr. Brodrick, who had his feet pretty firmly planted on the ground, rocked a little. If it had been a feather in Henry's cap getting Rodney Galt before, it became a whole plumage now. Nothing must get in the way of the book's completion. Well, it seemed that living at Lady Ann's did. Henry pointed out that, wonderful friend though Lady Ann was, she could be difficult to live with if you wanted to write because she talked so much. I said, yes, she did, and drank so much too. But I asked about the house that Rodney was going to buy. Henry said that Rodney hadn't seen the one he really wanted yet and he didn't want to do too much house-hunting while he was writing the book, which would require a lot of research. Above all, of course, he did not want to involve himself with what might turn out to be a white elephant. To this I thoroughly agreed. And, to Henry's surprise and pleasure, I said, yes, Rodney could come as a lodger.

I was a little puzzled about Lady Ann. I made some inquiries, and, as I suspected, Rodney had thrown her over and was said to have taken up with Susan Mullins, a very young girl but almost as rich as Lady Ann. However, Lady Ann was putting a good face on it before the world. I was glad to hear this because the face she usually put on before the world, although once good, was now rather a mess. But I didn't say anything to Henry about all this because he was so fond of Lady Ann, and I was feeling very friendly towards him for making such a sensible suggestion about a lodger.

Hardly had the lodger idea taken shape and Rodney was about to take up residence, when it almost lost its shape again. All because of Mr. Brodrick. I should tell you that Henry's senior partner was, again, one of the many people about whom my mood varied. He was a rather handsome, grey-templed, port-flushed old man of sixty-five or so—more like a barrister than a publisher, one would think. Anyway, what would one think a publisher looked like? He was a determinedly old-fashioned man—but not like Rodney, except that both of them talked a bit too much about wine and food. No, Mr. Brodrick was an old-world-mannered, "dear lady" sort of man—a widower who was gallant to the fair sex, is how he saw himself, I think. He had a single eyeglass on a black ribbon and ate mostly at his club. Sometimes I thought he was rather a sweet old thing and sometimes I thought he was a ghastly old bore and a bit common to boot.

At first, it seemed, he'd been delighted at Henry's capturing Rodney for their list, mainly because he was rather an old snob

and Rodney seemed to know well a lot of people whom he himself had only met once or twice but talked about a good deal. He
patted Henry on the back once or twice—literally, I imagine,
though not heartily—and saw him even more as "a son, my dear
boy, since I have not been blessed with any offspring myself."
(I often wondered whether Mr. Brodrick didn't say to Henry,
"When's the baby coming along?" He was so keen on heirs for
Brodrick Layland.)

But suddenly it seemed that one day Mr. Brodrick was talking
to Mr. Harkness of Harkness & Co., and Mr. Harkness said that
why they hadn't gone on with Rodney as an author was because
they'd had a lot of financial trouble with him—loans not repaid
and so on. Mr. Brodrick didn't care for the sound of that at all
and he thought that they should do what he called "Keeping a
very firm rein on Master Galt's activities." And as he saw Henry
as a son and perhaps me as a daughter-in-law (who knows?) he
was very much against our having Rodney as a lodger. The more
strictly commercial the relations with authors, the better, he said.

Henry was upset by all this and a good deal surprised at what
Mr. Harkness had said. I was not at all surprised but I did not say
so. I said that Harkness had no right to say such things and Mr.
Brodrick to listen to them. In any case, I said, how did we know
that Mr. Harkness had not just made them up out of sour grapes.
And as to commercial relations, I pointed out that Rodney's being
a lodger was commercial, and anyway the rent was being paid
to me. So Mr. Brodrick knew what he could do. But Henry still
seemed a little unhappy and then he told me that he had himself lent Rodney various sums. So then I saw there was nothing for
it but the brilliant first chapter—and I played that for all I was
worth.

Did Henry, I said, expect that anyone capable of that brilliant
first chapter was going to fit in with every bourgeois maxim of
life that people like Harkness and Mr. Brodrick laid down in their
narrow scheme of things? I was surprised, I said, that Henry, who
had a real flair for publishing because he cared about books, should
be led into this sort of "business is business" attitude that, if per-

severed in, would mean confining one's list to all the dullest books produced. Anyway, I made it clear I was determined that Rodney Galt should come if only as a matter of principle. When Henry saw that I was determined he decided to stand on principle too and on the great coup he had made for Brodrick Layland as forecast by that brilliant first chapter. So Rodney moved in.

What with all the research Rodney needed to do for his book and what with Susan Mullins, you may think that I was getting unduly excited about nothing. But if you have jumped to that conclusion, well then, I think you can't have a very interesting mind and you certainly don't understand me. When I say that I had become interested in Rodney that's exactly what I mean, and "being interested" with me comes to this—that I don't know really what I want or indeed if I want anything at all, but I know for certain that I don't want to let go. So for the first week or so Rodney went to the British Museum and read books about civility and honour, of which they have lots there—intended when they were published in the seventeenth and eighteenth centuries for people who were on the social make, I think. I rather used to like to think that after all this time they were being read again by Rodney. When he was not at the British Museum he was with Susan Mullins or on the telephone talking to her.

The British Museum fell out of Rodney's life before Susan Mullins. After only a fortnight it was replaced by books from the London Library which, as Rodney had a sitting-room, seemed only sensible. Then came a period when Susan did not telephone so often and once or twice Rodney telephoned to her and spoke instead to her mother (who was not called Mullins but Lady Newnham because she had been divorced and married again to a very rich Conservative industrialist peer) and then high words were exchanged. And finally one day when he rang he spoke to Lord Newnham and very high words were exchanged and that was the end of that. It became difficult then for Rodney to keep his mind even on the books from the London Library, let alone going to the British Museum. It seemed somehow that his mind was diverted more by financial schemes than by study. None of this surprised me much either, but I thought I would not worry Henry by telling him in case he began to be afraid that there would only be a brilliant first chapter and no more. In any case it might have only been temporary, though I was not inclined to think that.

So Rodney and I used to go out in his MG (and perhaps it would have been more in keeping if he had refused to use any kind of motorcar later than a De Dion but I was glad that he didn't.) We went here, there, and everywhere and all over the place. We saw a great number of lovely houses—a lot in London but gradually more and more outside London. Rodney came very near to taking some of them, he said. And then since he proposed to turn some of the houses when he bought them into furnished rooms or flats, we looked at a great number of antiques. The antiques we looked at were rather expensive for this purpose, but Rodney said that only good things interested him and what was the good of his expertise if he never used it. But it was quite true —that he had expertise, I mean. We also had a lot of very good luncheons. On my theory Rodney would pay for these during the first phase, but later I expected I would have to pay. But I was determined to make the first phase last as long as possible and I succeeded. We took to going suddenly, too, to places like Hampton Court and Cambridge and Hatfield House and Wilton. We did not go to see any friends though, partly because it wouldn't have done, but mostly because we really were very content to be alone together. However, often when we passed great parks or distant large houses, Rodney told me to which of his friends they belonged, and this was nice for him.

In fact we both had a wonderful time, although Rodney's time would have been more wonderful, he said, if I'd agreed to go to bed with him. Sometimes he cajoled; or at least he made himself as attractive and sweet as he could, which was a lot; and this, I imagine, is what "cajole" means. But often he took a very high-handed line, because in Rodney's theory of seducing there was a lot about women wanting to be mastered which fitted into his general social views. Then he would tell me that unless I let myself go and accepted his mastery, which was what I really wanted, I would soon become a tight little bitch. I had, he said, all the makings of one already at twenty-six. "You think," he cried, "that because you have attractive eyes and a good figure that you can go on having sex appeal just by cock-teasing every man you meet. But let me tell you it won't last, you'll quickly become a hard little bitch that no one will be interested in. It's happening already with your bitter humour and your whimsy and your melancholy moods. You're ceasing to be 'civilized.'" Civilization seemed to be his key to seduction, because he made light of my married position on the same grounds. "In any civilized century," he said, "the situation would be sensibly accepted," and then he talked of Congreve and Vanbrugh and Italian society. But I didn't care to decide too easily, because Vanbrugh and Congreve are no longer alive and this is not Italy of the *cicisbei* and affairs of this kind aren't easy to control and even if life was often boring it was secure. Also I quite enjoyed things as they were, even the violent things he said about my becoming a bitch, but I wasn't sure that I would like all that masterfulness on a physical plane.

So we went on as I wished and I enjoyed managing the double life, and if Rodney didn't exactly enjoy it he was very good at it. For example, one morning an absolutely ghastly thing happened; Henry's mother suddenly arrived as Rodney and I were about to set off for Brighton. I have already said about Henry's mother that you can feel two ways about her; I think that I would be prepared to feel the nicer way more often if she didn't seem to feel so consistently the nastier way about me. As it is, our relations are not very good, and as, like most people, we find it easier to fight battles on our home grounds we don't often meet.

Henry's mother doesn't bother much about dress, and that day being a rather cold summer day she was wearing an old squirrel-skin coat over her tweeds. As to her hats, you can never tell much about these, because her grey hair gets loose so much and festoons all over them. It is said in the Raven family that she should have been allowed by her father to go to the university and that she would then have been a very good scholar and happy to be so. As it is, she has lived most of her life in a large red-brick Queen Anne house in Hampshire, and the only way that you can tell that she is not happy like all the other ladies is that, as well as gardening and jam-making and local government, she does all the very difficult crossword puzzles very quickly, and as well as the travel books and biographies recommended in the Sunday papers she reads sometimes in French and even in German. She closed her eyes when she saw me, but this was no especial insult because, as I have said, she always does this when she speaks.

"You shouldn't live so close to Harrods, June dear, if you don't want morning callers," was how she greeted me.

As Rodney and I were both obviously about to go out there was not much to answer to this. But the Ravens have a habit of half-saying what is on their minds, and it immediately seemed certain to me that she had only come there because she'd heard about the lodger and wanted to pry. I said, "This is Rodney Galt, our lodger. This is Henry's mother."

Rodney must have formed the same conclusion for he immediately said, "How do you do? I'm afraid this is a very brief meeting because I'm just off to the London Library."

"Oh?" Henry's mother answered. "You must be one of those new members who have all the books out when one wants them. It's so difficult being a country member. Of course, when Mr. Cox was alive . . ." And she sighed, putting the blame onto Rodney but also making it quite clear to me that it was he whom she wanted to investigate. I thought it would be wise to deflect her so I said, "You'll stay and have a coffee or a drink or something, won't you?"

But she was not to be deflected. "What strange ideas you have about how I spend my mornings, June dear," she answered. "I haven't come up from Kingston, you know. I'm afraid you're one of those busy people who think everybody idle but yourself. I just thought it would be proper, since I was so close at Harrods, that we should show each other that we were both still alive. But I don't intend to waste your time, dear. Indeed, if Mr. Galt is going to the London Library I think I shall ask him if he will share a taxi with me. I'm getting a little old to be called 'duckie,' as these bus ladies seem to like to do now."

So Rodney was caught good and proper. However, I needn't have worried for him, because when Henry came home I learned that his mother had been round to Brodrick Layland and had spent her time singing Rodney's praises. It appeared that he'd been so helpful in finding her the best edition of Saint-Simon that she had offered him luncheon and he had suggested Wheeler's. His conversation must have been very pleasing to her for she made no grumble about the bill. She had only said to Henry, "I can't think why you described him as a beautiful-looking young man. He's most presentable and very well informed too." So we seemed to have got over that hurdle.

But Rodney was a success with all our friends; for example, with *les jeunes filles en fleur*. This is the name that Henry and I give to two ladies called Miss Jackie Reynolds and Miss Marcia Railton, and the point about the name is that although, like Andrée and Albertine, they are Lesbian ladies, they are by no means *jeunes filles* and certainly not *en fleur*. Henry is very fond of them because, like Lady Ann, they make him feel broad-minded. They are very generous, and this is particularly creditable because they do not make much money out of their business of interior decoration. They have lived together for a great many years—since they were young indeed, which must be a great, great many years ago—and Henry always says that this is very touching. Unfortunately they are often also very boring, and this seems to be all right for Henry because, when they have been particularly boring, he remembers how touching their constancy to each other is and this apparently compensates him. But it doesn't compensate me.

When the *jeunes filles* met Rodney, Jackie, who is short and stocky with an untidy black-dyed shingle, put her head on one side and said, "I say, isn't he a smasher!" And Marcia, who is petite rather than stocky and altogether dainty in her dress, said, "But of a Beauty!" This is the way they talk when they meet new people; Henry says it's because they are shy, and so it may be, but it usually makes everybody else rather shy too. I thought it would paralyse Rodney, but he took it in his stride and said, "Oh, come! I'm not as good-looking as all that." That was when I first realized that I preferred Rodney on his own, and this in itself is a difficulty because if one is going to be much with somebody you are bound to be with other people sometimes. However, the evening went swimmingly. Rodney decided that, although he would always have really good objects in his *own* house, the people to whom he let furnished flats would be much happier to be interior decorated and who better to do it than *les jeunes filles en fleur?* Well, that suited Marcia and Jackie all right. They got together, all three in a huddle, and a very funny huddle it was. Rodney already knew of some Americans, even apart from all the people who would be taking furnished flats from him when he had them to offer, and the rest of the evening was spent in deal discussions. Henry said afterwards he'd never felt so warm to Rodney as when he saw how decent he was to *les jeunes filles.* I wasn't quite sure what the decency meant but still . . .

The truth was that, much though I was enjoying Rodney's company, I was beginning to get a little depressed by the suit he was so ardently pressing and the decision that this ardour was forcing upon me. It would be so much nicer if there was no cause and effect in life, no one thing leading inevitably to another, but just everything being sufficient in itself. But I could see that Rodney was not the kind of person to take life in this way, and quite suddenly something forced this realization upon me rather strongly.

I have not said much about our Swiss, Henriette Vaudoyer, and I don't propose to say much now because nothing is more boring than talk about foreign domestics. I have to put up with it at three-quarters of the dinners we go to. Henriette was a very uninteresting girl but quite pretty. There were only four of us in the house: Henry and me in one bedroom and Rodney and Henriette in two bedrooms. Well, no one can be surprised that Rodney and Henriette began to be in one bedroom sometimes too. I wasn't surprised but I was upset; it gave me a pain in my stomach. Clearly there were only two things I could do about that pain:

get rid of Rodney or get rid of Henriette. The brave thing would have been to get rid of Rodney before I got worse pains; but already the pain was so bad that I was not brave enough. I gave Henriette notice. She said some very unpleasant, smug, Swiss sort of things to me and she began to say them to Henry, which was more worrying. Luckily one of Henry's great virtues is that he never listens to tale-bearing and he did what is called "cut her short." However, he was a bit worried that I should decide to be without a foreign girl because we'd always had one and sometimes two. But I explained that we had Mrs. Golfin coming in, and she was only too pleased to come in even more, and for the rest, having more to do would be wonderful for my moods about which I was getting worried. So Henry saw the necessity and Henriette went. But I saw clearly too that I would have to decide either to accept Rodney's importuning or not, because soon he would take no answer as the same as "answer—no."

I think maybe I might have answered no, only at the time Henry annoyed me very much over the holiday question. This is a very old and annoying question with us. Every year since we've been married Henry says, "Well, I don't know why we shouldn't manage Venice (or Madrid, or Rome) this year. I think we've deserved it." And first, I want to say that people don't deserve holidays, they just take them; and second, I want to point out that we're really quite rich and there's no question of our not being able to "manage" Venice or Rome. I long, in fact, for the day when he will say, "Well, I don't know why we shouldn't manage Lima this year, taking in Honolulu and Madagascar on the way home." But if he can't say that—and he can't—then I would prefer him to ask, "Shall we go to Italy or Spain or North Africa this year, June? The choice is yours." However, just about the time that Henriette left he came out with it. "Well, I don't see why we shouldn't manage Florence this year." So I said, "Well, I do, Henry, because I don't bloody well want to go there." And then he was very upset, and as I was feeling rather guilty anyway I apologized and said how silly my moods were and Florence would be rather enchanting.

Henry cheered up a good deal at this. "If that is so," he said, "I'm very glad, because it makes it much easier for me to tell you something. It's been decided on the spur of the moment that I'm to go to New York on business. It's only for a fortnight but I must leave next week."

Now I wouldn't really have wanted to go to New York for Brodrick Layland on a rush visit, but somehow everything conspired together to make me furious and I decided then and there that what I wanted was what Rodney wanted, physical mastery or no. And actually, when the time came, the physical mastery wasn't such a trial. I mean there was nothing "extra" or worrying about it. And for the rest I was very pleased.

So that when Henry set off for New York I was committed on a new course of life, as they say. But the weekend before Henry left he insisted on running me down to a country hotel in Sussex and making a fuss of me. I suppose I should have felt very bad about it because really he did his best to make the fuss as good as possible. But all I could think of was that I did hope cause and effect and one thing following another weren't going to make life worse instead of better. After all, I had made this committal to a new course in order to make life *less* boring, but if it meant that there were going to be more decisions and choices in front of me, it would be much *more* boring. One thing, however, I *did* decide was that I would try not to talk about Rodney to Henry even if I did have to think of him. After all, talking about Rodney would not have been a very kind return for the fussing.

In the end, however, it was Henry who raised the subject of Rodney. It seemed that Lady Ann had not been able to put a good face on all the time. One day at a cocktail party when even she had found the gin stronger than usual she had dropped her face in front of Henry. She said that the money she had spent on Rodney nobody knew—this I thought was hypocritical because she was just telling Henry how much it was—and the return he'd made had been beneath anything she'd ever experienced. I must say she couldn't have said worse, considering the sort of life she's led. Henry was very upset because, although he liked

Rodney, Lady Ann was such a very old friend. But I said that age in friendship was not the proper basis for judgment (after all, just because Lady Ann was so old!), and I also reminded him that hell had no fury. I succeeded in pacifying him because he didn't want his fussing of me to be spoiled, but I could see that things would never be the same between Rodney and Henry, as now, indeed, they were not between any of the three of us.

Well, there we were—Rodney and I alone for ten days. And Rodney did exactly the right thing—he suggested that we spend most of the time in Paris. How right this was! First, there was the note of absurdity of adultery in Paris. "That," said Rodney, "should satisfy your lack of self-assurance. Your passion to put all your actions in inverted commas." It must be said that Rodney, for someone only my age, understands me very well, because I do feel less troubled about doing anything when I can see it as faintly absurd. Of course the reasons he gives don't satisfy me very well; when I asked him why I was like that he said, "Because you're incurably middle class, June darling." On the whole though, by this time Rodney gave me less of his "patrician line." However, things had not yet reached the pass that I could tell Rodney my theory about him.

This theory, you will already have guessed, was that he was little better or little worse or whatever than an adventurer, not to say a potential crook. I did indeed know that his affairs had reached a serious state because of some of the telephone conversations that I overheard and because of the bills that kept arriving. The nicest thing was that Rodney paid the whole of the Paris trip. It is true that he hadn't paid for his rent for some weeks; it is also true that his trip to Paris was intended as an investment; nevertheless I think it was very lovely of him to have paid the Paris trip when he was up to his eyes in debts. Let me say that until the last day or so the Paris trip was everything I could ask or that money could buy. Also, though I don't think Rodney realized this, it was a great relief to me not to be committing adultery in Henry's house (for in a sense it *was* Henry's although it belonged to me).

It was only the last day but one of our trip, when we were sitting at a café looking at the Fontainebleau twiddly staircase and drinking Pernod, that Rodney began to press his further suit. I had been expecting it of course; indeed, it was the choice that lay ahead, the inevitable decision, and all the other things that I had so hoped would not happen but that I knew would. He asked me, in fact, to leave Henry for him. At first he just said it was what we both wanted. Then he said he loved me too much to see me go on living with Henry in such a dead, pretence life, getting more bitterly whimsical and harder every year. Then he said I was made like him to use life up and enjoy people and things and then pass on to others. It was all very unreal; but if he had only known, it was exactly this confidence trick part of him that attracted me. I could quite clearly see the life of travel and hotels we should have on my money and the bump there would be when we got through my money, which I think Rodney would have done rather quickly. But it was the bogusness, the insecurity, and even perhaps the *boue* beneath for which I had such a *nostalgie*.

Somehow, however, he didn't grasp this, or perhaps he was too anxious to secure his aims. For he suddenly changed his tone and became a pathetic, dishonest little boy pleading for a chance. He was desperate, he said, and it must look as though he was after my money, for he was sure I had put two and two together. This I had to admit. "Well," he said, "then you know the worst." But he begged me to believe, if he could have me with him, it would be different. He had real talent and he only needed some support to use it. Did I understand, he asked me, exactly what his life had been? And then he told me of his background—his father was a narrow, not very successful builder in a small Scots town—he described to me most movingly his hatred of it all, his hard if dishonest fight to get into a different world, the odds against him. It was I, he begged, who could get him onto the tram-lines again.

I don't think I'm very maternal really, because I didn't find myself moved; I only felt cheated. If I hadn't been sure that in fact, whatever he said, life with Rodney would have been much more like what I imagined than what he was now promising, I should have turned him down on the spot. As it was, I said I must think about it. He must leave me alone in London for at least a fortnight and then I would give him an answer. He accepted this because anyway he had business in France, so I returned to London alone.

Henry was glad on his return to find Rodney absent, I think. And in a short while he was even more glad still. Or, at any rate, I was, because if Rodney had been in our house I think that Henry would have hit him. This, of course, might have fitted into Rodney's ideas of the violence of life, even if not into his view of civilization; and probably Rodney, being much younger, would have won the fight, which would have made me very angry because of Henry. But it is just possible that Henry would have won, and this would have made me very sad because of my ideal picture of Rodney.

What put the lid on it (as they used to say at some period which I'm not sure of the date of) for Henry was a visit he made to his mother shortly after his return, when he discovered that Rodney had borrowed money from her. I could only think that if Rodney could get money from Henry's mother he had little to fear about the future (and maybe if my future was joined to his, though precarious, it would not founder). But Henry, of course, saw it differently and so did I, when I heard of the sum involved, which was only £50, a sum of money insufficient to prevent foundering.

Hardly had Henry's mother dealt Henry's new-found friendship a blow from the right, when up came *les jeunes filles* and dealt it a knockout from the left. It seemed that they had busily decorated and furnished two flats for American friends of Rodney's—one for Mrs. Milton Brothers and one for Robert J. Masterson and family—and as these American people were visiting the Continent before settling in England, the bills had been given to Rodney to send to them. The bills were quite large because Rodney had told *les jeunes filles* not to cheesepare. Now Mrs. Brothers and Mr. Masterson and family had arrived in London and it seemed that they had already given the money for *les jeunes filles* to Rodney plus his commission. Jackie said, "You can imagine what it makes us look like," and Marcia said, "Yes, really it *is*

pretty grim." Then Jackie said, "We look such awful chumps"—
and that, I think, was what I agreed with most. Henry said he
felt sure that when Rodney returned he would have some explanation to offer. I didn't think this likely and I didn't think Henry
did. "Well," said Jackie, "that's just it. I'm not sure that Rodney
ought to return because if Mrs. Brothers goes on as she is now I
think there'll be a warrant out for him soon."

I felt miserable when they had gone and so did Henry, but for
different reasons. All I could find to do was to pray that Mrs.
Brothers should die in her bath before she could start issuing warrants. Henry said, "I only hope he doesn't come near this house
again because I'm not sure what my duty would be."

Then, the very next morning, at about eleven o'clock the telephone rang and it *was* Rodney. I told him what Henry had said,
and we agreed that it was most important that he should come to
the house when Henry was out. He came, in fact, just before
lunch.

I had expected him to look a little haunted, like Humphrey
Bogart sometimes used to in fugitive films; he did look a little
haunted but it wasn't quite like the films. Less to my taste. As I
looked at him I suddenly thought of something. So I made an
excuse and ran upstairs and hid my jewel box. I would have hated
to have been issuing warrants for Rodney. Then we had a long
chat and something more. About that I will only say I have
rather a "time and a place" view, and so it ended things as far as
I was concerned with a whimper rather than a bang. As to the
chat, I said that I had thought things over and the answer was no,
very reluctantly. And when people say, "You don't know what
it cost me," I think it's rather stupid because they could always
tell you. So I will tell what this cost me—it cost me the whole of
a possible, different life with someone very attractive. I shall always regret it when the life I am leading is particularly boring,
which it often is. But that, after all, is the nature of decisions. The
answer had to be no. And I do not despair of other chances. But
life is indeed a cheat.

What Rodney said after my negative answer was a pity. He

went on again about how soon I would become a hard little bitch and rather depressing with all my "amusing" talk. He even said, "I should think you might go off your head. People who get the idea that they can make a game of other people's lives often do."

I must say that I thought, everything considered about Rodney's own life, this was a bit too much. And in any case all this toughness and bullying was all right when Rodney was pressing his suit, but now that the suit had been pressed and sent back, I thought it all rather boring. And so I changed the conversation to the warrant that might be out at any moment. Rodney was well aware of this, he said, and he had almost enough but not quite to get abroad that night. I said I would see what I could find in ready cash because obviously cheques would be no good. He didn't seem sure about this, but I stuck to my point, emphasizing how little he understood money matters as evidenced in his life.

While I was looking for what cash I had he went upstairs to the lavatory and I heard him walking about in my bedroom, so I was glad for his sake that I had hidden my jewel box. And I did find enough to help him overseas because I had put some aside in case he turned up, although I did not tell him this. Away, looking rather hunted but still very handsome, he went out of my life.

It was all rather an anticlimax without Rodney, although his name was kept alive, what with Henry's mother, and *les jeunes filles*, and the Americans, and Mr. Brodrick furious at only having a first chapter, however brilliant, after paying so much in advances. But all this was not the same for me as Rodney's physical presence, not at all the same.

It was only a month later that it got into the papers in quite a small column that he'd been arrested for stealing some money at the house of the Marchesa Ghirlaindini in Rome, where he was a guest. It mentioned also about Mrs. Brothers' warrant.

Well, I did miss the excitement of life with him and the decision that I hated so much when I had to make it; so I got talking to an old friend of mine—Mary Mudie, who writes a long, gossipy column in a Sunday newspaper. And sure enough there was a featured bit about him the very next Sunday. All about the well-known people he'd dined with and about Lady Ann Denton, how he was one of the "many fortunate young men of talent and charm who had profited by her friendship," and how valuable she was as a bridge between her generation and the young. Then there was a bit about Rodney's great brilliance as a writer and how few who knew him in this capacity realized his double life. It told us with what expectancy connoisseurs of the fresh and original in modern writing had awaited his new book and how ironic its title *Honour and Civility* now seemed. So brilliant was the first chapter of this, it said, that an old established publishing firm, famed for its cautious policy, had gone to unusual lengths to assist its young author. Realizing the supreme importance to a writer of congenial surroundings in which to work, the enterprising junior partner, Mr. Henry Raven, even installed their brilliant protégé as a tenant in his own house. Then came a block heading, "More Friend than Lodger," and it was followed by a bit about me. " 'I can hardly believe that Rodney was leading this double life,' said almond-eyed, brunette June Raven, well-known young London hostess and wife of publisher Raven, 'he was more of a friend than a lodger as far as I was concerned. He was not only clever and witty, but he had the rare gift of easy intimacy.' "

Dear Mary followed this up immediately with a mention of Rodney's first book, *Cuckoo*—"a study of married infidelity in history's pages as witty as it was scholarly." The paragraphs went on with a little interview with Rodney's parents. " 'Rodney never took to the building trade,' his father told me in the front parlour of his typical unpretentious little Scots 'hame'; 'he always wanted big things out of life.' " And then Mary ended on a moral note. "Rodney Galt got his big things—bigger, perhaps, than he imagined—when an Italian court on Monday last sentenced him . . ." It was a sad little article, but I did think it was clever of Mary to have made so much of what I told her.

I'm afraid Rodney will be very upset by the piece about his parents, but he did say very nasty things to me. And Henry, too, won't like the "more friend than lodger" part, but Henry ought to pay for my being faithful to him too, 1 think. At least that's how I feel, after life has presented me with such awful choices.

Sure enough Henry read Mary's article and got into a terrible rage. "I'm pretty sure it's actionable," he said. So I looked very nonchalant and said, "I don't think so, darling, because I supplied Mary with all the information." Then he looked at me and said, "I think you should be very careful, June, this sort of mischievous behaviour is frequently a danger signal. It may seem a strange thing to say to you, but you'd only have yourself to blame if you went off your head." He was trembling when he went out of the room, so I think it likely that he'd known about me and Rodney for some time.

Well, there you are—both Henry and Rodney take a "psychological" view of me. But as I said before, I often think that common-sense views are wiser. I spoke before of my old nurse and what she used to say of me was, "Miss June wants to have her cake and eat it." Well, so do most people one meets nowadays. But I think perhaps I want it more than the rest, which makes me think that in the end I'll get it.

Once a Lady

﹥﹥≪≪

Eileen Carter tightened the cord of her sandy Jaeger dressing-gown around her full waist, for the routine of preparing for bed was a lengthy one, and her pink-and-white-striped boy's flannel pyjamas were loose and inclined, when not controlled, to impede her actions. Habitual though all the preparation was, she went at it doggedly, her heavy face—a rosy-cheeked bulldog's—set in childish concentration. First she heated the milk in the little saucepan on the spirit stove in the corner of her bedroom; then she poured three dessert-spoons of whisky into the milk. She placed the milk with two Marie biscuits on her bedside table with her reading glasses, her sleeping pills, and *The Cloud of Unknowing* (Mrs. Underhill's translation). Then she knelt beside her bed and said the Lord's Prayer. Once in bed, she kicked the hot bottle to rest at her feet, slowly drank the milk and ate both biscuits while she read from the book. "All men will they reprove of their defaults, right as they had cure of their souls; and yet they think that they do not else for God, unless they tell him their defaults that they see. And they say that they be stirred thereto by the fire of charity, and of God's love in their hearts: and truly they lie, for it is with the fire of hell welling in their brains and in their imagination." But the passage seemed inapposite to her this night. She had of course been guilty of moral righteousness and cen-

Written in 1956; first published in *The New Yorker* in 1957; scene contemporary.

soriousness in the past—often and often—lonely people, she reflected, are prone to this sin, but at this moment she only wished
to dwell on one person's virtues, to give praise to the one she
loved. And this, too, was sin also to which lonely people were
prone. She tried to deflect her mind by reading other passages,
but the obtrusive thoughts kept breaking in. She was not unaware
that the Devil sometimes increased his power by forcing his vic-
tims to fight him, but rather in withdrawal lay victory; she therefore put by her book, put off her dressing-gown, and, taking a
small green pill with the last drains of the milk, prepared for sleep.
It came quickly, but just before she slept she saw Esther's dear
face smiling at her and she smiled lovingly in return.

Far across the village, over the pond and the pub and the crescent of new council houses, in the big bedroom above the shop,
Esther Barrington lay awake beside her husband Jim. Esther
was used now to waking suddenly in the night, sometimes from
alarming dreams, sometimes just from nothing, but always appal-
lingly and hopelessly awake. Tonight she tried, as so often, to at-
tribute her wakefulness to the screech owl that settled on the
telegraph wire above the outside lavatory and watched the chick-
ens in their sleep. She blamed it upon the sudden stirrings of
young jackdaws in the roof eaves. She was tempted to wake Jim
from his heavy sleep and tell him it was all his fault—for despite
his deep sleeping he constantly turned and muttered. When the
despair at being awake became urgent she thought of getting up
and running into Mother's room and telling her it was her fault
for having become senile and for moaning senselessly in the night.
You're not my mother, she thought to shout at her. Just because
you stood by Jim and me "at the time" doesn't mean that we
have to support you forever. You must leave. But how could a
semi-paralysed old woman of seventy leave? In any case this hysterical attempt to put the blame on others did not last long, for
her very wakefulness seemed to come from so deep within her
that it pushed out everything except consciousness of herself. She

could think of nothing, see nothing, feel nothing, but herself awake.

She tried desperately to force some issue—some thoughts or at the least some memory—out of this blank selfness. In the years before, when she had not been drained by work and futility, she had been able to imagine and think with willed concentration—curiously able for one with only a genteel girl's education. Now memory came only in flashed pictures that jolted shakily before her eyes as from a badly operated magic lantern, trembled there for a moment and then flicked out as though the electricity had failed. As for thoughts, they led nowhere.

She heard Mother moaning in the next room and told herself that it was just child's crying, with no more meaning than that; and then she set herself to reflect whether indeed a child's crying meant so little, whether its terrors were indeed so transitory. Her mind, however, would make nothing of it. Scenes of her own childhood misery, of the cupboard in the vicarage nursery where she had taken her sorrows, or of the dank, rotting-leaved ground behind the hibiscus where she had fled grown-up solicitude, came before her sharply and were as sharply gone. And then, as though flashed on the local cinema screen, the old tedious generalities. *You* have no children. It's worked out badly. Perhaps I'm to blame, I'm to blame. I'm tired of it all. She heard in recollection Lottie Washington's dismal droning next door, " 'Oh, I never felt more like crying all night, for everything's wrong and nothing ain't right.' " Then, defeated by the fact that all her attempts at thinking had ended only in recollection of a vulgar popular song, she turned to doing sums in her head.

After all, her true anxieties were practical. She went over the biscuit orders they had placed, did the confectionery accounts, and measured the dwindling returns from egg sales against the possible returns from home-made jam; but everything always depended on bills and figures that lay downstairs in the sawdusty, soapy-smelling dark of the shop. Past accounts now came into her head, and the large sums that had once spelled the failure of their farming venture became inextricably involved with the little bills of the shop that now kept their heads just above water. She saw herself and Jim swimming in the water-filled shop, their heads bobbing up and down like ducks, she thought indignantly—an *absurd* position for a woman who had once given scandal to her family, a woman who had married beneath her for love, a woman who had stolen another woman's husband. She checked a sudden loud laugh as she realized to what novelettish terms she had reduced the central action of her life. The laughter turned to bitter sobbing, which in turn she checked. She had no right to add to Jim's already cruelly heavy day by disturbing his sleep.

The church clock sounded four. "I'm not a bit tired," she said to herself, "sleeplessness is only harmful if you allow yourself to think it so." She knew, however, how tired she would be when the alarm sounded at half-past five. And now to calm her came the reflection which increasingly supported her resolution to hold on. It took great courage for someone brought up as I was to do what I did. She hated the snobbish implication of the thought; nevertheless she moved away from Jim in the bed and pride at her reflection gave her calm.

Polly Washington had climbed over the fence and was talking to the hens. Since Miss Cleaver had taken her up in Sunday school, teaching her little poems to recite and encouraging her to make up little dances for herself, she had become so ladylike and hardly played with the other village children any more.

She was forever picking little bunches of flowers and holding little conversations with the animals. At first Lottie and Reg Washington had encouraged her and made her show off her dance in a little peach silk party frock every Sunday afternoon to visitors. After a while they had lost patience with her little whimsies; Lottie was too busy to have a child hanging round all day; and even old Granny Washington had slapped her and called her "a little madam." She spent more and more of her time now at the Barringtons', following Esther round with stories or giving "pretence

presents" to old Mrs. Barrington, who was too senile to grasp that
they were not real and said, "Thank you, my dear," so that the
little girl broke into giggles.

"Good morning, Mrs. Speckly Hen," Polly said to the Plym-
outh Rock fowl in the special, puking, ladylike little voice that
Miss Cleaver had taught her to use for pretending games.

Esther had already given Jim his breakfast and had sent him
out on the milk round for Clarkson's before she came out into
the dust-blowing October gale to feed the hens. It was one of
Jim's jobbing gardening days, and she had sandwiches to cut for
him as well as the usual chores—beds to make, Mother to put on
the commode—before she opened the shop. Gusts of cold wind
blew up her sleeves, licked round her legs, reminding her of the
approaching winter she so dreaded. How long would Jim's obstinacy refuse to accept that the fowls—last sentimental relic of
their farm's high hopes—added nothing but trouble to their lives?

"Good morning, Mrs. Barrington," Polly said in a special sweet
voice. Miss Cleaver had told her that she must always be a very
kind, polite little girl to poor pretty little Mrs. Barrington.

Esther started into recognition of the child's presence with irritation. Polly round her feet at seven o'clock in the morning! There
seemed to be no hour at which those wretched people cared for
their offspring. Did the child get no breakfast? They trade on
the weakness of my barrenness, she thought bitterly.

"Good morning, Polly," she said, "and a very busy morning
for everybody." The hard lines that now lay beneath the soft surface of her pretty little birdlike face snapped into place as she
spoke.

"*My* mummy isn't busy," Polly answered, "she's listening to
the wireless."

Esther made no reply as she forced open the rickety fowl-house
door and fought her way through the acrid-smelling, clucking
birds. Polly ran excitedly behind her, increasing the hens' alarms,
getting in the way of the scattering corn. "Mrs. Speckly Hen had
a dream last night, Mrs. Barrington," she cried, and she paused,
her face red and bursting with imaginative effort, for, despite all

Miss Cleaver's encouragement, she was a girl of very limited fancy. "She dreamed she laid a big, big, big chocolate egg," she said triumphantly. "Oh, look, look, Mrs. Barrington, there's the greedy one with the little yellow patch on her foot. What shall we call her? Mrs. Yellow Patch?"

"I haven't time to give hens names this morning, Polly."

From over the hedge Esther could hear Lottie Washington's droning, " 'I never felt so like singing the blues.' " Out of the corners of her eyes she saw the cigarette dangling from Lottie's fresh full mouth, her lazy, easy, sensual movements as she reached up to fix the clothes pegs on the line. "You *must* not come over here so early, Polly," Esther said loudly and sternly.

Lottie immediately called raucously, "Polly, Polly, come back here at once."

"I'm sorry, Mrs. Washington," Esther said. "I cannot have Polly here at all hours of the day."

Lottie did not answer, but as the little girl scrambled red-faced over the hedge she caught her by the arm, twisted it, and slapped her face. "Don't you go where you're not wanted," she said and pushed the crying child towards the back door.

Esther scattered the last of the corn, shut the hen-house door, and returned indoors, feeling a little sick.

She was already behind the counter serving, or rather listening to old Mrs. Sumper when Jim returned from his milk round. "She were like a little sleeping child as she lay there. Doctor said 'e'd never seen one go so peaceful, not as 'ad gone with the cancer."

Through the old woman's words Esther saw her husband for a moment as a stranger entering the shop. Swarthily handsome, strong but gentle, a strong, steady face set in heavy lines of patience. People said that she too had kept her prettiness. And as to the lines, they only gave more interest to the face, people said. Well, let them say; that was all right if every line didn't speak of past worries and of back-breaking labours. As to the gentleness and patience, if only she didn't resent them. He ought to be more angry, more resentful, she thought; I've cheated him and he ought to hate me for it. What does love mean if it breeds only gentleness? She indicated his sandwiches to him, but he only smiled and went upstairs.

When he came down again Mrs. Sumper had finished her story. "Well, there it is," she said, "you haven't got 'em so I'll have to get 'em at Rayner's when I go into Lichfield Saturday." She sniffed resentfully and waddled out of the shop.

"Mother's waiting for her breakfast," Jim said.

"Oh, Jim," Esther cried, "she's *had* her breakfast, I gave it to her half an hour ago."

"Ah, the poor old thing's forgotten then."

"Well, she really shouldn't have done. I gave her two sardines and she insisted on dipping them into her tea." For some reason Esther heard herself laugh loudly.

Jim's dark, calf's eyes looked sadly hurt for a moment, then, "You've got enough to do without extra burdens," he said, "we'll have to send her away."

It annoyed her that after fifteen years of married life with her, peasant fears and ignorance showed through his good sense and independence in phrases like "send her away." She admired him still so much that it enraged her to think of his humility before authorities like hospitals or doctors. He had been so meek and uncomplaining three years ago when the failure of the farm had ended in two bouts of pneumonia.

"Don't be silly, Jim, we've discussed all that," she said, and she began bustling about behind the counter, rearranging tins on the shelves. The Maxwell children—a huddle of cheeping, underfed sparrows—came in for their daily supply of liquorice allsorts. When they had gone she said, "You'll be late at Major Driver's, Jim. See that they give you some tea with your lunch. It's a bit windy."

She felt ashamed of her solicitude for his health, remembering how hostile scandal had said that she only married him for his physical strength; and now it was her "wiry" strength which never failed. But this time he countered her sympathy. "I don't like you not sleeping," he said, "you must speak to the doctor about it. They can give you something for that nowadays."

"What do you know about my sleeping," she cried with mocking indignation, "snoring your head off." She was overcome with tenderness for him and resented it. What could the underlying tenderness do to mend the broken surface of their daily life together? "Besides, it's early closing, thank heaven," she said brightly. "I'm going to tea with Eileen Carter."

"Ah, that'll do you good," he said, smiling, showing the perfect, even white teeth she still delighted to see. She knew, however, how little he liked her friendship with Eileen—that ladylike companion of books and gardening and religion in which he had no part.

Miss Meadows came in for some elastic, but Jim disregarded her presence. He went up to Esther and whispered, "It'd be far better to let the old woman go, as the doctor wants."

Esther only shook her head in reply. She had brought him no children to care for, she was not going to let his mother be taken away. She turned away from him towards Miss Meadows, but as she passed him he pressed the back of his hand against hers and whispered, "Thank you, my old Esther." It was a gesture and words he had not used for so long, a gesture which recalled intensely the days of their clandestine lovemaking, their occasional secret pressures and touches when they met in shop or market square, wherever there were people who made open recognition impossible in the days before the scandal broke. The tenderness that filled her this time was so little touched by irritation that Miss Meadows, receiving her card of elastic, said, "The cold weather agrees with you all right, Mrs. Barrington, but there, you're always on the move."

Perhaps the reawakened and unalloyed tenderness for Jim would have died beneath the anæsthetic of the day's tedious chores had not a chance customer revived the past in Esther's feelings. For all those years in the remoteness of their Yorkshire farm, she had dreaded an utterly improbable chance contact with neighbours from Sussex who would revive the years of scandal, who even at worst might break down the wall which she had built around Jim's wounded self-esteem. But in these last years, with her father dead and her mother gone to join Rosamund in Kenya, the Sussex faces had faded out in dimness, the thought of their intrusion had ceased to fret her. Yet here, of course, in the shop, remote though their Midland village was from the South, the chance was far greater and on that very morning it turned to certainty.

The face of the man who entered the shop was familiar, the voice that asked for cigarettes made her sure. It was Charles Stanton, still bearing traces of the fourteen-year-old boy who, round-eyed, had once stared at her so fascinatedly as the subject of mysterious adult whispering. Childhood visual memory was apparently less enduring, for he left the shop without recognizing her. She peered through the stacked boxes of Puffed Wheat and tins of cocoa in the window. There, indeed, in the Ford Consul sat Mrs. Stanton, motherly, vulgar, overdressed, hardly changed, indeed, from the woman who, with more titillated curiosity than her small son's, had befriended her in those isolated days after the scandal broke. For a moment memory of the woman's kindness made Esther start for the door to hail the passing tourists; then a sharp recollection of how difficult even kindness had been to endure forced her back into the shop's safety. With relief she heard the car drive off; but that momentary impulse of Charles Stanton to stop for cigarettes, Mrs. Stanton's love for touring with her son, had broken through the blanketing mist that weariness had interposed between Esther and the "worst fortnight of her life."

If she had had her way, indeed if her mother's will had prevailed, she would not have stayed one day at the vicarage after Jim's wife had made her scene. But her father had been so determined. "If you care for me at all, Esther, you will stay and fight it out. I will try to help you, even to forgive you, as long as you do not run away. I can forgive anything—indeed I should hardly be a minister of Christ if I could not—but cowards I will not forgive." It had been nothing to do with her of course; it was part of his relentless fight against his parishioners. "I will teach these people Christ's charity even if I can do so only with the rod of shame." Of course he could not, and at the end of a fortnight he had been relieved when she ended his fight for him by running away.

Why, indeed, should the parish have forgiven her? She had betrayed her class, her Church, and her sex. They had not shared the passion which had sustained and driven her. If she had been outside that passion she would have been on their side. Only Mrs. Stanton—"My dear, you're always welcome here I'm sure. Not that that'll help you with the county, I'm afraid. You know what they think of Henry and me. Rich trade, that's us. But who cares what they say? They think the days of carriage folk are still with us, stupid creatures." And then her sentimental curiosity—"Well, love certainly suits her, doesn't it, Henry? I never seen you in such good features, my dear." Mr. Stanton too, just a little more familiar than he should have been. Esther had hated herself for needing their support and hated herself too for disliking it; but she could not bear their coating her passion with their sticky sentimentalism—"You must always follow your heart in life, my dear." She had longed to reject Mrs. Stanton as Marianne had rejected Mrs. Jennings, but then Marianne had not committed adultery with her Willoughby.

Little by little the memories faded from her mind at the chivvying and poking, the day's demands—the accounts, the customers' gossip, the orders, the telephone. She was left, as she closed the shop at one o'clock, only with an overwhelming tenderness for Jim.

As teatime approached, Eileen Carter became as excited as a schoolgirl. Although a strict guardian of her conscience, she was not inclined to be conscious of her own moods—to have been so would have seemed to her dangerously near to emotional fudge. Her present elation, however, was too violent to escape her notice, and she told herself sharply not to be swoony. Esther Bar-

rington was a good, brave little woman; it was lucky for both of
them that they had broken through the barriers of shyness, for
loneliness helped nobody in this world; she was only so pleased
that her comfortable sufficiency in life allowed her to brighten a
little the drudgelike existence of someone so decent; that was all
there was to it. All the rest *was* fudge.

As she passed through the kitchen to the garden old Madge
glowed warmth at her. "I'm making some of those griddle cakes
Mrs. Barrington loves. It does one good to see her enjoying herself, doesn't it, Miss Eileen?"

Eileen's usual gruff notes were almost a bark as she answered,
"All right, Madge, but don't worry me with it. I'm up to my eyes
in work." And so she was, she thought, with twenty herbaceous
plants to move; the work ought to have been done a week ago.

It was, therefore, a vast prospect of buttocks stretching tight a
chocolate-and-white-striped cloth skirt that confronted Esther
as she turned into the garden at a quarter to four that afternoon.

"Heavens above! Eileen," she cried, "surely you're not putting
more plants into that border."

Eileen's pink cheeks were scarlet almost to apoplexy point as
she swung her broad shoulders round to face her visitor. "I'm
only moving these damned phloxes," she said, grunting. "Every
one's got a hell of a great root. God knows whether they're worth
moving, they're probably riddled with bloody eelworm." It was
a mark of her shyness that she used to Eileen the "bad language"
that she normally only employed in her voluntary social work
to show that she was not an old frump.

"But surely you can tell."

"No, I *can't*," Eileen said emphatically. "The damned leaves
are all floppy, but that may be due to this summer's drought."

"You should let Jim come and advise you," Esther said. In her
present mood she rushed to get in her husband's name as soon as
possible.

Eileen Carter ran her hand through her untidy, greying black
bob with impatience. "I have some pretensions to being a gardener myself, Esther," she said.

"A very good one," her friend replied, "but Jim, poor dear, has to know these things professionally."

"Professional gardeners in my experiences," Eileen said, "always make a balls-up."

Esther's pretty blue eyes flashed angrily for a moment in her thinned, lined face, then she decided that the poor old thing was in one of her moods. "Most of them do, of course," she said. "Double begonias and calceolarias, they couldn't have more ghastly taste." Her voice, as she spoke, took on the upper middle-class drawl she had only found again recently in her friendship with Eileen.

They talked for a while about gardening, and as they talked Eileen lost her shy coarseness and Esther slipped more completely into drawling assurance.

"Well," Eileen asked as they sat over China tea, griddle cakes, and home-made quince cheese, "and how is the mum, dotty as ever?" She habitually referred to the mothers she visited in her family welfare work as "the mums"; it was a mark of her attitude to Jim that she called old Mrs. Barrington by this name.

"Oh, dear!" Esther said. "Poor old thing, her memory gets worse every day. She was such a good, kind person, Eileen, even if she was always a very simple soul. I can't bear to see her in this childish state. I gave her sardines for breakfast and nothing would stop her dipping them in her tea."

Eileen threw back her bulldog head and wheezed with laughter. For a moment Esther was on the point of joining in when she remembered Jim. "It isn't a laughing matter, Eileen," she said. Her handkerchief was rolled into a ball in the palm of her hand; she dug her nails into it with anger at betraying Jim—she should never have spoken of Mother's pathetic childishness.

Eileen looked at her, unperturbed. "Oh, yes it is, my dear," she said. "Sickness, death, even sin—all have their absurdities. And God intended that we should laugh at them. As long as it's not cruel laughter." She lit one of her small cheroots—her only capitulation to eccentricity. "Jane understood it well enough, as you know. She could laugh at Mrs. Musgrove's fat tears over her scapegoat son, but Emma's cruel jibe at Miss Bates could not be forgiven. It's as simple as that or rather, like everything else in life, as difficult." When she spoke her ethical convictions her gruff voice became almost absurdly offhand and flat.

Esther took a last piece of currant bread to finish her quince cheese. "Jane Austen was awfully clever," she said, "but even when I'm enjoying her books most, I sometimes wonder whether she ever knew what it was like to be laughed at."

"What?" Eileen questioned. "A surplus old maid?" Then, embarrassed by this degree of self-revelation, she added, "The trouble with you, my dear, is that you're a Jane Bennet and not an Eliza. You take too good a view of the world. You let it trample on you."

"Oh," cried Esther, "I have had enough of revolt to last me for my life! I don't ever want to fight people again. I just want to be left alone to get on with my work, and, God knows, there's enough of it." Then she looked across at Eileen's glowing fire, the samplers, the bellows, the etchings of Lichfield Cathedral. "What I'd most like in all the world," she said, stretching her thin body with an easiness unusual for her neat, trim manner, "would be some comfort, some ease of living like this. Or rather," she added earnestly, "I should like it for Jim."

Eileen's heavy face seemed to lose all life, to become a smooth, fleshy mass. "I can't quite see dear old Jim at Throckings," she said with a chuckle that was not somehow warm.

Esther still stretched, relaxed. "Can't you?" She spoke from far away. "You don't know Jim at all, do you, Eileen?"

"He's not very easy to know," Eileen answered stiffly.

"Isn't that the best kind?" Esther asked; then, as though she had returned to the room again suddenly, she said in a light, gay voice, "Oh, Eileen, you can't think how much it means to be able to come and relax here. You *are* a dear person, you know."

Eileen's heavy head bent down for a moment in girlish shyness. "I wish you would come far more often," she said.

"Oh, my dear, if I could . . ." Esther laughed. "But how could I? Who's to give Jim his tea?"

Eileen got up and stood for a moment by her chair, her thick legs ungainly set apart. " 'Thou shalt not make unto thyself any graven image,' " she said. She moved across the room and fingered the dried hydrangeas on the window table. "It's awful here on rainy days," she said absently. Then, coming behind Esther, she placed a square hand on her shoulder and pressed it. The gesture of intimacy was familiar to her friend. "You're worth such a lot more than you think," Eileen said, then she stroked Esther's greying fair hair.

It was a gesture entirely unfamiliar to her friend, and she got up hurriedly, pushing Eileen's hand to one side. She went over to the mirror above the fireplace and patted her hair into place. Eileen sat down on the sofa, legs apart, heavy bosom forward, squat and lowering.

Esther stared into the mirror and spoke without turning round. "I suppose I've lost the art of friendship," she said. "You've no idea what's it like to be a lawbreaker in decent society. And that's what Jim and I were. We broke every rule in the book. I pray for forgiveness and God, I trust, will forgive me. But the world—especially the village world—isn't God."

Eileen laughed. "Oh, you make it sound like one of those novels I used to read as a girl. By Sheila Kaye-Smith or someone like that. Fifteen years ago in Sussex! My dear, times have changed."

"Oh, I know"—Esther still did not look at her friend—"but the county haven't. About adultery perhaps, but they don't forgive anyone who oversteps their precious class barrier."

"You live in the past," Eileen declared. A gleam appeared in her usually dulled eyes, "Besides, even if you're right, it isn't as noticeable as all that. You've acquired a good deal of protective colouring through the years, you know."

Esther swung round; for a moment her soft blue eyes showed horror.

"Oh, my dear," Eileen boomed, "I've said the wrong thing. If that's what worries you, put your mind at rest. 'Once a lady,' as our mums used to say. For what it's worth."

Higher Standards

➤➤➤❰❰❰

"Come along then, both," said Mrs. Corfe. It had been the form of her call to tea at half-past six every evening for more than fifteen years. Perhaps it had lost some of its accuracy since Mr. Corfe's stroke some four years before, but home would not have been the same without it; and if Mrs. Corfe's conception of "home" was a trifle ill defined, her determination that it should never be other than "the same" was the central thread of all her actions and words.

There was nothing to upset her mother's love of sameness in her daughter's slow response to her call. It merely meant that Elsie had come home in one of her moods. There was a time, of course, before the war when Elsie had not had "moods." Indeed, there was a sort of tacit agreement between mother and daughter that the blackness of these moods should be indicated by the length of time that Elsie remained in her bedroom after the summons to meals. If, as on that evening, Mrs. Corfe had time to hoist her husband from his chair and support him, doll-like, on his dangling legs to the loaded table, before her daughter appeared at the foot of the stairs, peering myopically with refined distaste at the jelly and the jam puffs, then it was clearly one of Elsie's bad evenings. Not that this particularly distressed Mrs. Corfe, for it allowed her to say brightly, "Waiting for late folk never made an egg fresher or the tea hotter."

Written in 1953; first published in *The Listener* in 1953; scene contemporary.

Elsie's rejoinder to the implied moral rebuke was æsthetic. She carefully removed one by one from the overcrowded table the many half-empty pots of jam and bottles of sauce without which her mother felt the evening meal to be incomplete. Then, going to the mirror, she set the little lemon crepe-de-Chine scarf she wore in the evenings into pretty artistic folds; she further asserted her more refined canons of taste by loosening the beech leaves in the vase on the mantlepiece. Such autumn decoration was the sole incursion on the more traditional furnishing of the parlour that her rebellion had ever achieved. Her mother's revenge came each morning when she crammed the branches back into the vase.

Boiled eggs in egg-cups shaped like kittens and roosters were followed by a "grunter," a traditional local dish to which, under the stress of rationing, Mrs. Corfe had become increasingly attached. Originally designed as a baked suet roll to contain strips of pork or bacon, it had become a convenient receptacle for all unattractive scraps. Mrs. Corfe, however, retained the humour of the tradition by inserting two burned currants for the pig's eyes and a sprig of parsley for its tail.

Elsie, like her mother in so many things, shared her love of quaint local customs, but the grunter was a whimsy against which her stomach had long revolted at the end of a tiring day's teaching. She selected three Brussels sprouts and, cutting them very exactly into four parts each, chewed them very carefully with her front teeth. Mrs. Corfe ate heartily, continually spearing fresh pieces of the grunter with her knife. The noise of her mother's feeding brought to Elsie's pale features a fixed expression of attention to higher things.

Neither her daughter's aura of self-pity nor her own preoccupation with feeding in any way inhibited Mrs. Corfe's continuous flow of talk. After a day of housework and sick nursing, she looked forward to her daughter's return with a greed that was almost physical. To scatter the weariness and frustration of life's daily round in an evening's censorious gossip, to indulge herself in little disapproving jokes about less thrifty, less respectable neighbours, seemed the least that so many years of godly living and duty and deadening physical labour might be expected to give to a tired old woman. It was perhaps her only real grudge against Elsie that the girl refused to apply to her jaded nerves the sharp restorative of a little vinegary talk about her neighbours. How soon these black moods would pass from her daughter, she reflected, if only she would allow herself the soothing easement of village scandal or discharge the heavy, burdened soul in a righteous jibe or two.

"Carters' have refused to serve The Laurels again," she said. "The woman's half distracted. It's nice enough to have grand folk from London coming for the weekend; it's another thing to feed them from an empty larder. Oh!" She drew in her breath with disapproving relish. "The woman's been on the telephone all day to the other shops. She'll make use of *that* at any rate until it's cut off. But for any effect it's had, she might have saved her breath. On *one* tradesman's black books, on *all*. There might be a pint of milk and a plate of porridge for the city folks *if* they're lucky . . ." She paused for a second and then added, "And there might not. But still she's got her fur coat to keep her warm outside, if there's no soup to cheer the inner man."

Elsie tried hard not to envy Mrs. Hardy her musquash. She pictured as vividly as she could the vulgarity, the terrible, clashing bright colours of the drawing-room at The Laurels when she attended the Red Cross committee meetings there. But it was no good, she wanted the fur coat.

Mrs. Corfe tried another tack. If the punishment of the godless brought no comfort, then the distresses of the back-sliding would surely answer.

"It's been a day of wonders at the Fitchetts'," she announced with mock solemnity. "At eight o'clock our Bess had won ten thousand on the Pools. It was *pounds* then, but when the morning post brought nothing, it was down to shillings. All the same the old man quite bit Miss Rennett's head off when she mentioned principles. Nothing against Pools in The Book, it seems. But when the afternoon post went by, there was quite a change around.

Nasty, ungodly things, the Pools. Mrs. Fitchett's given our Bess a talking to, so we'll have *her* yellow bonnet back in Chapel next Sunday. Ah, well, it takes more than the Fitchetts and such turn-abouts to change the ways of old Nick."

Elsie remembered the lecture she had given to Standard Four only that morning against gambling. Television and Pools and space robots, that was all the children of today thought about. But somewhere at the back of her vision a tall, dark stranger leaned over to loosen her sable wrap for her as she settled herself in the gondola.

"How heavenly St. Mark's looks tonight," she said with ex-quisite taste, and "*Our* St. Mark's," he replied.

Of course, the Pools were a terrible drain on the nation's de-cency, but . . .

Mrs. Corfe was playing her last card now in the macabre vein. She had almost finished the jelly, and soon it would be time to put Father to bed, so there was not a moment to lose if the eve-ning was to bring any cosy exchange.

"They doubt," she said, "if old Mary will last the night. The poor old soul's been wandering terribly and bringing up every scrap she's taken . . ."

But Elsie had endured enough of the sordid aspects of life. She leaned across the table, speaking very distinctly. "And what did *you* do today, Father?" she asked.

A twitch of anger shot through Mrs. Corfe's wrinkled cheek. Now that *was* selfish of Elsie, selfish and thoughtless. Her father who had been such a fine man, so hard-working and thrifty, and such a splendid lay preacher too, for all that he'd had no education —what had he *done* today, indeed? What *could* he do since this wicked thing had struck him? And what, indeed, could *she* do but keep him neat and clean before their neighbors as he would have wished.

"Well, gel," Mr. Corfe replied, "I sat up at back window and watched the fowls. It's a wonder the way that crookity-backed one gets the scraps. Why should *she* have had the crooked back? I asked myself. Oh, the ways of Providence are strange: all they fowls and only one crookity-backed, and yet she gets her share. There's a thing to think upon, and to talk upon . . ."

"Yes, yes, indeed," said Mrs. Corfe, "but not now." It shamed her that her husband, who had always been so clear in his thoughts, so upstanding, should at last wander so unsuitably in his words. Elsie too felt the need to protect her father from what his failing body had made him; and so, when her mother began to question her on the events at school that day, she forced herself to answer.

"It's been a Standard Four day for you—I know, my girl, by your tired looks," said Mrs. Corfe. And when Elsie began to recount the exploits of that famous undisciplined class her mother listened avidly. Such sad happenings, such examples of human frailty in the nearby town, were second only to village misdemeanours in her catalogue of pleasures.

"Ah, the Mardykes, I thought they'd be somewhere in it. There's a couple of old Nick's own that'll come to sorry ends," she said with fervour when Elsie mentioned the notorious bad boys of the form. "And the woman had sent them out with nothing but a rumble in their stomachs for breakfast, I'll be bound." It was the fecklessness of city workers that so fascinated Mrs. Corfe. And then, as though her bitterness had sated itself, she added, "You must take them some apples tomorrow, Elsie. They're a couple of comics if ever there were any."

"Miss Teasdale's away with the flu," said Elsie, "so I've got *her* handful to deal with too."

"And why can't they get a Supply in?" asked her mother impatiently.

"Supply teachers need notification. Why do you use words you don't understand?" Elsie asked angrily.

It was lucky that noises in the village street came so suddenly to prevent a family quarrel. Shrill whistles could be heard, loud shouting, the sharp swerve of bicycle wheels followed by guffaws of coarse laughter.

"Hm," said Mrs. Corfe. "Well, there's *our* Standard Four anyway." It was their favourite name for the youths who nightly rode the length of the village street to call after girls.

Half an hour later when Elsie went to the pillar-box with a letter to an old friend of her Teachers' Training College days, a group of these young men were leaning on the nearby fence. Well, she thought, Bill Daly and Jim Soker among them, they ought to be ashamed wasting their time like that! At their age too. Why, Jim was a year older than herself, quite twenty-six. She was about to pass by with her usual self-conscious, majestic disregard when her loneliness was shot through with an aching for those childhood days before awakening prudery and her scholarship to the "County" had cut her off from the village Standard Four. She paused for a moment at the pillar-box and looked back at them.

One of the younger boys let out a wolf whistle, but Bill Daly stopped him short. "Hullo, Elsie," he said in the usual imitation American, "how about a little walk?"

The retort came easily to Elsie's lips. "Does teacher know you're out of school, Bill Daly?" she said, but the words came strangely—not in her customary schoolmarm tone but with a long-buried, common, cheeky giggle. She even smiled and waved, and her walk as she left them was almost tarty in its jauntiness. She was tempted to look back, but another wolf whistle recalled her to her superior taste, her isolated social position in the village.

Mrs. Corfe had her old black outdoor coat on when Elsie returned. "Who was that you were talking to?" she asked.

"Oh, Standard Four," Elsie answered. "Bill Daly was there. He ought to be ashamed, fooling about like that at his age."

"Well, it's lucky there are folks with *higher* standards," said her mother. "Father's not too good," she added. "The grunter's turned on him. I'm just off down to old Mary's. I've promised to sit with the poor creature. It may help to keep the bogies away."

Elsie's outing seemed to have softened her mood. She touched her mother's arm. "You do too much for them all," she said.

"Oh, well," Mrs. Corfe replied gruffly, "if the poor won't help the poor, I'd like to know who will. I don't like leaving your father though."

Through the flat acceptance of their life implied in her mother's tone came once more the wolf whistles and guffaws, and mingled with them now the high giggle of the village girls. Elsie's laugh was hard and hysterical. "Oh, don't fuss so, Mother!" she cried. "I'll sit up with Father. You haven't got a monopoly of higher standards, you know."

A Sad Fall

Mrs. Tanner stood in the porch watching the hired car disappear down the drive, taking her son to the London train—first short lap of his long journey overseas. She waved once or twice, but it was not Jeremy's face that turned to smile at her, only Naomi's, so she bent her heavy body ostentatiously to examine the loose paving in the front steps. Her sudden attention to the cracked paving would make clear her deliberate rejection of the smile, for her daughter-in-law knew well enough that the dilapidation of the house was one of the things that least concerned her. It was surely enough that she shared this wartime rural isolation with Naomi, had allowed her to go alone with Jeremy for his embarkation; she had earned a right to a single act of rudeness to this stranger brought in by marriage. In any case Naomi was well aware of the mutual indifference upon which their friendly relationship rested.

From the drawing room came the sound of a piano duet. Mozart or Beethoven—Mrs. Tanner made no attempt to guess. Music was not one of the cultural horizons which her isolation and ill health had extended. Even her uninclined ear, however, noted Roger's stumbling treble in contrast to John Appleby's practised bass. She felt a now rare sense of pleasure in anticipating John's continued stay in her house. The weakening of once agonizing maternal love was not all that old age brought in compensation for its other

---

Writtten in 1956; first published in 1957; scene laid in England after the end of the war with Germany but before the defeat of Japan.

more depressing physical weaknesses; for the first time for many years she had found real delight in the company of a stranger. He had become one of those few whom she could put trust in if she had a sudden seizure; in her new diabetic scheme of life such people were the elect. Of course, an attentive audience of any sort was relief to the imprisonment of solitude. Then, too, John Appleby was not truly a stranger but a wanderer returned from the happy lost days of Jeremy's youth. Nevertheless she knew that it was not just "company" nor the past that had attracted her to the young man during his week's visit.

Going into the hall lobby to leave the light tweed overcoat which the cold September afternoon had demanded, Mrs. Tanner gave an unwonted glance to the dusty mirror and patted her white, shingled hair into place on each side of her plump, wrinkled cheeks. A look of almost coy merriment tempered the usual self-mourning gaze of her spaniel-brown eyes as she went upstairs to take her insulin dose before joining the others in the drawing-room.

In that room Roger crashed his square-topped fingers down onto the keys. "It's no good," he cried, "I can't keep it up. You see, I haven't kept my practising going this holiday," and he broke into a long, giggling laugh that seemed oddly hysterically edged in so stolid and square-framed a boy.

"Yes," said John Appleby, "I do see." His smile took from his deliberate tones their touch of rebuke. He got up from the piano stool and, crumpling his long, thin body into an armchair, he began to fill his pipe.

The boy swung round on the other stool—a revolving one which he had brought to the piano from the desk in the dining-room. Legs apart, he drummed with his fingers on the stool's edge. He looked towards John, his lower lip pouting a little as though he feared his refusal to continue the duet had brought the conversation to an end. But John, as he sucked at his pipe, looked up at him over the bowl and between his suckings asked, "Do you give up with most of your prep like that?"

His note was schoolmasterly, but this must have been long accepted between them, for Roger said, "Yes, professor," and laughed. "I get bored when things are difficult," he added.

"Or you think you do," John observed.

"I do," Roger repeated; the touch of petulance underlined the cockney strain in his speech.

"So Tompkins is top of the form and not you. But you manage to get moved up each term, so why worry?" John's smile was quizzical. Roger's cheeks flushed, their high colour spreading up to the edge of his smoothly brilliantined fair hair. John's quizzical smile spread across his thin, monkeylike face. He shook his head. "No, no, I mean it," he said, "it's the perfect recipe for sensible moderate success."

If there was an undertone to the gay, friendly note of his voice, it was beyond the range of the boy's thirteen years. He swung round again on the stool, his plump bare knees catching the light as he moved. He began to play "Chopsticks," then changed to "The March of the Wooden Soldiers." " 'I had a hen and she laid such eggs that I gave her trousers for her legs,' " he sang. He bawled the words at the top of his voice.

Mrs. Tanner, coming into the room, took in the boy's high spirits and smiled across at John. "Heavens, what a noise!" she cried.

The boy stopped singing but continued to play the tune. "He's been lecturing me," he called over his shoulder.

"I made an observation," John said. "Roger took it as a rebuke."

"It wasn't an *observationem*," the boy threw back, "it was a jawing."

"No doubt deserved," Mrs. Tanner concluded, "however little you liked it."

Roger refused the conclusion. "Oh, but I did like it," he said and swung round again, facing them rather primly. "I don't mind a bit with him."

"And I thought you were busy with your Mozart," Mrs. Tanner said.

"Beethoven," John pretended to mutter but cast a teasing look at her.

"Don't you make any of your observations to me, Mr. Appleby," she cried; then, deflecting the conversation from herself, "You mustn't take up all Mr. Appleby's time, Roger, he's got his paper to write."

"Oh, my poor paper," John said. "You bring it in like a penance, Mrs. Tanner. A hundred Hail Marys."

"Well, I don't like the idea of an old woman and a schoolboy coming between you and a certain vague number." She brought out the technical phrase with a certain coquetry.

"Good heavens, you've remembered it. I beg you not to clutter your head with such awful stuff."

"It might displace some of the useless lumber," Mrs. Tanner said. "There's precious little else there."

"Oh, no, just the whole of Gibbon and *The Ring and the Book* and *Clarissa*."

"I wish I'd never told you about my wartime reading," Mrs. Tanner replied. "It was simply a solitary old woman's chance of repairing a bit of her abysmal ignorance. In any case," she went on, "I thought scientists and mathematicians weren't interested in human beings of any sort, let alone old women and schoolboys."

"We live among them"—John smiled—"we must learn to deal with them. Otherwise we should leave it all to humanists like Hitler."

"Hitler was vilely inhuman."

"It's the same thing upside down. Too much attachment."

Mrs. Tanner could make nothing of it, but if she intended to voice her perplexity she was prevented by Roger. "I bet Hitler isn't dead really," he cried, "is he? You know about it, don't you, Mr. Appleby? That's your job, spying."

"Now, Roger, I've told you you're not to question Mr. Appleby about his job."

"But I'm not questioning him, Mrs. Tanner, I'm just telling him he's a spy. Anyway, what's clever about spying? I'll spy on you today, Mr. Appleby, and you won't know I'm doing it."

John spoke in a heavy German accent. "Good morning, General Hannay," he said, "I did not recognize you at first in those grey flannel knickers." Roger gave way once more to his giggling laughter.

"General Hannay," Mrs. Tanner said firmly, "must set the table for luncheon. You and I will have to share the chores, Roger, while Mrs. Jeremy's in London. We usually have a roster of three," she explained to John.

"Oh, there's plenty of time," Roger said.

"No, there is not. I've taken my insulin. I shall want my food sharp at one."

The boy's face assumed a look of reverence. Mrs. Tanner's diabetes involved holy rituals. "I'll go straight-away," he said. "It it fish?"

"Yes"—Mrs. Tanner laughed—"I'm afraid it *is* fish, Roger."

As the boy opened the door to leave he turned to John. If he seemed for a moment coy, it was no more than the coquetry their visitor inspired in Mrs. Tanner. "If I promise to practise, will you take me to the cinema tomorrow, Mr. Appleby?" he asked.

"I'll take you to the cinema, but without any promises. We don't appease any more, you know, in our brave new world," John said, and then, as though in fear that his moralizing had offended the boy, he added, "Who knows, we might see a Gumble-duck."

Whatever the intimacy offered, Roger did not receive it well. "How could we?" he asked and went out of the room.

Mrs. Tanner let herself down into a deep armchair, slowly filling its every crevice with her bulging flesh. She took up some sewing from the side table. "I hope you realize what you're letting yourself in for," she said. "There'll be only Roger and me to talk to in the whole place." She waved her hand, incongruously small for her fat body, around the sitting-room to indicate the vast spaces in which he was to be bored.

It was in fact, John Appleby reflected, only a moderate-sized room in a smallish house with a smallish garden, less than half the size of the house the Tanners had occupied when he had visited them in his adolescence, yet she habitually spoke as though she were the unwilling mistress of a large estate. With his usual methodical approach to human behaviour, he sought an answer to the paradox and guessed that a house without servants seemed vast to her in the work it imposed.

He smiled with the teasing gallantry he had come to use with her. "I like talking to *Roger* very much," he said. "He's both sensible and ordinary. An extremely pleasant combination in a small boy."

Mrs. Tanner, playing her part, pretended not to notice the teasing omission. "I'm so glad you like him," she said. "You're certainly very good with him. Not that he's at all difficult. I can't tell you how pleased Naomi and I were that out of all the evacuees he should be the only one who hasn't drifted back to London. I oughtn't to say it, of course, because, poor child, it's dreadful that his mother shouldn't want him. But from the very start he gave me no trouble. I suppose, as you say, he is a very ordinary boy. He'll never set the world on fire, but then the others only set the *house* on fire or lied or wet their beds. Not a very pleasing sort of extraordinariness, and certainly not the sort that an old woman of seventy wants to cope with. All the same, Roger or no Roger, I warn you that the house will be no place for an intelligent man to spend his leave in. You've only seen it when Jeremy and Naomi were here, you don't know how dead it can be."

"I can't remember," he answered, "that Jeremy showed any sign this week of wanting to talk to anyone but Naomi, or Naomi, for that matter, of noticing anyone but him. She put up the better show of pretending, of course, but then I'm not *her* old school friend. But they were neither of them aching to be sociable. All the same, as far as I remember, I've had a great deal of very pleasant conversation and it hasn't all been with Roger."

Mrs. Tanner laughed, but once again she disregarded the compliment. "They're terribly in love," she cried, "you must forgive them. *I* try to, even though he is my son. As a matter of fact," she said, "old age and infirmity free one from a lot of encumbrances, and one of them is an excessive mother love." She had bent over her sewing so that John speculated whether she was hiding a face that could belie her assured tone. "I can honestly say that I was glad to let Naomi go alone to see him off in London," she said emphatically. "I've ached for him at times during these war years, of course; after all, he is my only one, and I worry too when he's been in London during air raids. But I live much more with a past Jeremy now than with the real one. That's one of the reasons I've been so pleased to get to know you. You're a link with his past. Of course, it's only *one* of the reasons," she added with a smile.

It was John's turn gracefully to ignore the compliment. "I hope you're not worried about his going to Calcutta," he said. "He'll be in less danger there, you know, than he was in London."

"Oh, heavens," she cried, "I'm not so blindly selfish that I'm unaware of the enormous luck we have had that he should be doing this Intelligence work, whatever it is." She threw him an amused glance; it was one of the customary jokes of their friendship that she should be a little arch about the secret work that he and Jeremy were engaged in. "Oh, no, he's safe enough. I feel quite guilty about it at times. One of the few compensations of my isolation down here is not having to face the other poor women whose wretched men are *not* safely in Intelligence. Naomi feels it at the hospital. So many of the nurses are married or engaged to pilots. Perhaps Jeremy's going to Calcutta will at least give her the peace of conformity with the others."

John raised his eyebrows slightly.

Mrs. Tanner put down her sewing and, removing her amber-rimmed spectacles, she turned her large, anxious, yellow-flecked brown eyes upon him. "No, I don't mean it like that. Not even unconsciously, I'm sure of it. I really *don't* grudge her Jeremy's love." She stroked the pale-lemon silk of the cushion cover she was sewing as for a moment she pondered. "Of course, I can't help remembering that *she* will have Jeremy again in a world of peace and decency. While as for me, a fat, diabetic old woman—who can say how long this awful Japanese war will last? But it's not really him I'm thinking of. I've honestly and truly let him go. No, it's of myself. Oh, I know it's only a vegetable life I live down here and it'll never be much more. But to have got through this awful time, to have seen the horror fade away in Europe. For I'm sure it will. And then to face years more of it. I'm sorry I can't believe in this Far Eastern war or the necessity for it. I want so much to see a world of gentleness again. That's why"— she smiled—"I've loved your courtesy in bothering with me and Roger. You're so gentle in a violent, hurrying world."

"Oh," John exclaimed, "I'm civil enough, I suppose." He ran his hand through his long black hair, pulling his head down to the chairback so that his high-cheekboned white face stared out at her against the dark red fabric. "I shouldn't," he added, "put much trust in a world of gentleness again though. It'll take an age to teach manners again—if they *ever* come back."

This time Mrs. Tanner's brown eyes showed no gleam, they were all hurt spaniel, Charles I, reproach. "Oh, it's more than manners that we need. It's love."

John, pipe between his teeth, ventured no more than, "Ah?"

"Oh, yes," Mrs. Tanner appealed, "surely. I know something about it. You see"—now her eyes seemed old pools of wisdom— "I used to love possessively, holding tight—husband, son, a London house I was proud of. Well, I lost them all. Or at least I lost Oliver, and then my health went, and the meaning of my life in London went from me. I think I learned then that holding tight could only hurt me and others. That was why I was able to let Jeremy go. And as to personal possessions—well, you see the state of this house and the garden! I allow them to be no more than somewhere I live in, someplace where I can take the air. Of course"—she laughed—"I can't do much else anyway, with only a charwoman and no gardener. But all the same"—she changed to the serious with a degree of ostentation—"I have learned a little at last of how to love, I think, to love without holding."

Again John gave only the slightest interrogative, "Ah?"

"It's allowed me, for example, to be good friends with Naomi simply because she's the woman my son loves." Provided with no comment, Mrs. Tanner drew to her conclusion quickly. "Well, anyway that's the way the world has got to learn to love if we're ever to be done with all these horrors. And I think it will."

The fitful yet strong September sunshine had lit upon John's chalk-white, furrowed forehead. Mrs. Tanner took it as a way out of her one-sided conversation. "Shall we seize the sunshine while it lasts?" she asked. "If, that is, you don't mind walking at a fat old woman's slow pace."

"We've talked so much about me and so little about you," Mrs. Tanner remarked as they walked at indeed a very slow pace across the ill-kept lawn. "Women and especially old inquisitive women can be such a nuisance that I have purposely not asked questions. But that doesn't mean I'm not curious, of course I am."

"A lecturer in mathematics at Oxford," John replied, "educated at Shrewsbury with Jeremy Tanner. The best of educations surely?"

"Oh, indeed." Mrs. Tanner laughed. "My father was headmaster of the school, you know. I always felt it had gone down by the time Jeremy went there. But then I was bound to."

"Well," he went on, "what else is there? Born in Brighton thirty-two years ago, father a stockbroker. Oh, and, of course, engaged twice but never married."

If he supposed that the romantic note was what Mrs. Tanner was waiting for, he seemed to be wrong, for she exclaimed impatiently, "Oh, I know all that. But were you happy as a child? I'm sure you must have been, and yet no woman can quite believe it about other people's children. And sometimes you seem so silent."

"I'm sorry." John laughed. "I'm usually listening."

"Oh, you're a wonderful listener—who else would have allowed me to go on about my wretched diabetes as you have? Oh, it's absurd of me, of course; you're bound to be abstracted with your brain, but you're so kind and put up such a show of interest that when for a moment you're not absolutely with one it seems strange."

John reached over and began to free a tall head of Michaelmas daisy from the bindweed that entangled it.

"Oh, if you once begin," Mrs. Tanner said, "there'll be no end to it. Look at it—what a wilderness!" And indeed the herbaceous border seemed a mass of weed—docks, polygonum, thistles, and, over all, bindweed; only the Michaelmas daisies still fought a losing battle. "I warned you," she cried, "I've just let it all go. I can manage a few roses but for the rest I've let it go. And it's released me. Old age must beware of property."

John too released the daisy, and it swayed back to its weedy height.

"And they loved you, your parents?" Mrs. Tanner asked.

"They were ideal," John replied. "We respected each other. They helped me to grow up and then, just when I had, they died."

For a moment Mrs. Tanner could make nothing of it, then she cried, "There! I knew it. I'm never wrong. You *were* loved. Good, gentle, friendly people always have been. It's the one thing I'm proud to have given Jeremy—a loved childhood and . . ." But once again her thoughts led on to silence. Then, as the grass path passed between the rhododendrons of the shrubbery out onto a meadow, she said, "Well, there it is. Our famous view. You said you liked it yesterday when it was clouded in mist, but now you can see what the mist hid. The vague red and grey to the left is Ludlow. And there you have Wenlock Edge. And beyond you're supposed to see The Long Mynd and on to the Welsh hills. And so you could, I suppose, if Wenlock Edge was not so high." She had a number of such little jokes to express her love-hatred of her home of exile.

"As a matter of fact, I think I can," John said.

"Oh, I don't believe it. And if you can, what do you see but a faint, dark shape. And they call that *seeing* the Welsh hills." Nevertheless she was pleased. She turned back to the shrubbery, striking at the struggling arms of rhododendrons with her ash-plant. "Is this seat too wet?" she asked, but before he could answer she had sat down. "Don't ever get fat," she said, "or rather, don't get too fat, for you could do with some extra weight."

Before John sat down next to her he carefully folded the mackintosh he was carrying and made a cushion for himself. "I was really interested about the diabetes, you know," he said.

"Oh, my dear boy!" Mrs. Tanner exclaimed. "All the same I'm sure you're right, it began with the shock of Oliver's death."

"It's only a hypothesis."

Mrs. Tanner, however, would have no modifications. "And none of those wretched doctors have seen it."

"It wouldn't have helped really, if they had, would it? It couldn't have brought your husband back."

"It always helps to know that our wretched bodies are under the control of our minds," Mrs. Tanner declared. "It's a great comfort."

John smiled. "The modern world should hold great comfort for you then," he said.

"No," she went on, "your understanding of that has given me even more confidence in you. You see, every illness brings its fears and, although, of course, it's quite irrational, the only thing I fear is having one of those dreadful seizures when people are around whom I don't trust. It's quite absurd, as I say, because it's only a question of regular meals, and if I go out I carry some sugar with me just in case. All the same, there's some people I have confidence in. Roger, for instance, although he's only a small boy, and now you, but not, I'm afraid, Naomi."

John took out his pipe and knocked it on the wooden bench. "You say these things about Naomi, and yet what I so admire is your friendly relationship with her. It can't be easy for two women together for all these years—and anxious years."

"Oh, it's not so bad. Of course she's difficult at times, but then so am I. She comes back from the hospital tired and then she tells me everything she's going to do. 'I'm just going to put on a kettle for the hot-water bottles, Mother,' or 'I'm only going upstairs for some wool, Mother.' As if I wanted to know. But there, as you say, two women living together."

"That's interesting," John observed; then he said by way of solution, "She probably needs to protect her tiredness from comment, so she covers it up with trivialities."

"There you are," Mrs. Tanner cried. "You see, you understand us all, Naomi and me and little Roger."

"Oh, Roger," John said, "he's not difficult surely."

"No, but you've won his confidence so quickly. What was all that about Gumbleducks?"

"Oh, it's an imaginary race of little men with whiskers and top hats that his father made up for him."

"Ah," Mrs. Tanner put in, "he doesn't tell us things like that. I thought he'd forgotten his home, poor boy."

"I was interested," John remarked, "because he's really such a sensible boy. He lives in the present. No ties or fears. I thought I'd found a chink. But I was wrong. He was resentful when I brought it up. He knows that his life is here and now. The Gumbleducks are over."

Mrs. Tanner sighed. "I'm afraid so," she said, "with those dreadful parents." She hoisted herself to her feet. "Time for my meal," she declared. "All the same," she said, "I'm right about love. We all need it but not too much. I was so interested when I read about Dr. Johnson. He needed love so much—too much, of course —that's why he behaved so badly when poor Mrs. Thrale married her Piozzi."

"You know your Johnson too?" John asked.

"Why shouldn't I?" Mrs. Tanner asked, laughing.

"No reason, I just haven't known many mothers. And those I have didn't read much. My mother never read."

"She was probably far too busy. I used to be until all this ill-ness and exile happened. But don't think I understand half of what I read. Only about people. Yes," she declared, "I can really judge people. After all, you know, I kept house for my father after my mother died, and headmasters of public schools entertain a wide range of people. And then Oliver was a very successful barrister. Oh, yes, I know the world. But not books. Do you know many lawyers?" she asked.

John took a moment to answer. "I'm so sorry," he said, "I thought I saw something creeping by the corner of the roof."

"The cat," Mrs. Tanner said, a little nettled.

"No," John cried, "it's Roger. Heavens, his idea of spying!"

Mrs. Tanner looked towards the square, two-storeyed Victorian house, and there, spread flat against the purplish tiled roof, was Roger, shuffling his feet sideways along the guttering. He was dressed in an old coat of Jeremy's, its belt flying loose, and an old felt hat of Mrs. Tanner's.

"Oh, he mustn't!" she said. "Those tiles are so loose."

"Well, don't call to him," John said, but he spoke too late.

"Roger!" she cried. "Roger! Come down!"

The small head turned, displaying a large pair of dark glasses. "I don't know what you mean," he called. "I'm mending Mrs. Tanner's roof. I've come in from Ludlow special to do it."

But Mrs. Tanner was not playing. "Come down, Roger," she called sternly.

"Oh, all right! But I spied on you all the way to the meadow and you didn't see me."

"No," said John, "you're a first-rate spy. But you'd better come down now. Mrs. Tanner wants her lunch."

The boy began hastily to edge his way back to the corner of the roof above a derelict conservatory—too hastily, for his foot wedged in the guttering, and as he pulled at it to release himself he threw his whole weight onto the rotting lead. It was the cracking of the guttering rather than Roger's scream that made Mrs. Tanner retch. For a moment she saw him clinging batlike in the flapping black coat against the shining tiles, then something loosened and he fell down through the sunshine pool of glass beneath.

For a second John stood trying in vain to distinguish the boy's screams from the crash of breaking glass, then he sprinted across the lawn.

When Mrs. Tanner arrived, panting, John seemed to be letting the small, stolid body roll back face down to the ground where it had fallen. "He's alive," he said and, not looking up, he turned the boy's face towards him and began to wipe the blood away. "He's unconscious. Concussion probably. He must have caught his head in falling. I daren't move him. I think a rib may be broken." He looked up at her. "Telephone for a doctor and an ambulance at once," he said. He seemed angry.

Mrs. Tanner cursed her size as she tried to hurry to the house, but she welcomed relief from the nausea which the spattered blood in the greenhouse had brought upon her. When she returned from the house John had slid his mackintosh and his coat under the boy; he had also torn a sleeve from his shirt and had tied it in a bandage below the boy's elbow.

"The ambulance is coming from Ludlow, but it may not be here for twenty minutes," Mrs. Tanner said. She produced a small bottle of brandy.

"No, no, no stimulants," John said impatiently.

She lowered herself to the ground with difficulty. "I've asked the hospital people to phone to his mother," she said wearily.

"Look," John said, disregarding the information, "you sit by him while I get a basin of water. Call me *if* he comes to."

She could see nothing to do but hold Roger's hand, but every now and then she stroked the fair hair from his forehead. In a minute John was back with a bowl of warm water and a napkin. He began methodically to wipe the wounds on the boy's legs and arms.

"I daren't touch the bits of glass. In any case these cuts are not serious. There was a hæmorrhage of the arm but I've stopped that for the time being."

Mrs. Tanner said, "Thank God you were here." She stroked Roger's hand and gazed at his square little face, whiter now than John's. It was this whiteness that gradually made her panic. "Why doesn't the ambulance come?" she said, and then again, "They'll be too late, I know they will. Oh, they can't let him die, poor little Roger," she cried, "I shall never forgive myself if he dies."

John got up and stood over her. "Look," he said, "he is feeling no pain, that's the important thing. It doesn't matter if he does die."

For a moment she could find no words, then she said, "How can you say that? He's a good, fine boy." Anger added to her growing hysteria and she began to weep.

"Yes," he said, "a very good, decent, ordinary boy. And with luck he'll grow up into the same sort of man. But there are millions of good, decent, ordinary men. It just *doesn't* matter."

Mrs. Tanner fought to hold back her tears. A moment later she said appealingly, "You said that, didn't you, to help me? You thought it would help me."

John turned round from his kneeling position beside the boy's legs. "Good heavens," he cried, "do you think this is a time to bother about helping *you?*" A minute later he turned round again. "I'm sorry," he said, "if the remark upset you. Please think I said it to help or anything else you like."

It came to Mrs. Tanner that she was alone with John Appleby. She got up slowly from the ground. "I'm going into the house to pack a small bag," she said urgently. "I shall go with the ambulance. I must be at the hospital tonight."

"Of course," John said and turned back to his task.

She hurried along the gravel path to the house and almost ran to the kitchen. Her panic died as she swallowed her dose of sugar. Such fears, of course, were entirely irrational.

After the Show

-->><<--

All the way home in the taxi and in the lift up to her flat on the
seventh floor Mrs. Liebig kept on talking. Sometimes she spoke
of the play, making comments to Maurice in the form of questions to which she did not await the answer. The lights of Regent
Street and Oxford Street flashed momentarily through the taxi
window, caught in the saxe-blue spangles of the ornament that
crowned her almost saxe-blue, neatly waved hair, reflected in
the mirror of her powder compact, which seemed always to
occupy her attention in taxis. "Was the father of the girl a fraud
then?" she asked, and "Why didn't the mother make him work?"
"I suppose," she said, "that the old man had used him to get rid
of his mistress." Then, "What a play," she exclaimed, "for a boy of
your age to take his grandmother to! But it's clever, of course,
too clever, I think. There weren't any real animals, you know,
in the cage. That was clever."

More often she commented on family affairs. "Your father
needs a real rest," she said. "Let's hope your mother sees that he
gets it. It's not the way to take holidays—mixing business up with
pleasure. Of course, your mother will want to spend a lot of
time with her own people, that's only natural. They have a very
nice house, you know, the Engelmanns in Cologne. Or they

Written in 1956; first published in 1957; scene contemporary.

used to have. Anything might have happened to it now. But she *must* think of your father all the same. That won't be much of a holiday for Norman, talking German all the time. Though he's a wonderful linguist, your father, you know."

Once she said, "Well, we must try to imagine what they are doing now," but the effort was apparently too great for her because she went straight on. "Lending her house to those Parkinsons. What a thing for your mother to do! But then they don't have to think about money, so there'd be no sense in all the trouble of letting." Her tone was at once reverent and sarcastic.

Maurice said nothing, indeed he hardly stirred, except once or twice to light Mrs. Liebig's cigarette with the lighter she handed him from her bag. She shared his parents' constant concern that he should have perfect manners with women. After the theatre, his slim body, usually so loosely and naturally elegant, remained tense—a tailor's-dummy woodenness perhaps more in keeping with the slightly overcareful elegance of his clothes than his usual poise. A tension too came into the expression of his large dark eyes, ordinarily a trifle cowlike in their placid, liquid sensuality. It was not so much that he remained hypnotically bewitched by the play's deception, but rather that he dreaded returning from its dramatic reality to the fraudulent flatness of his own life. He seemed to strain every nerve to keep the play in action, to spin out at least its mood from the theatre into the commonplace texture of his own life. His apprehension announced his experience that the task was vain, his nervous elation a certain fear that he might on this occasion succeed. It was the same, too, with every theatrical performance, from Shakespeare to musical comedy. In addition to this adolescent histrionic restlessness, however, there was a somewhat plodding seriousness which demanded a peculiarly strong response to "good" plays.

Tonight, after *The Wild Duck* then, his earnest good taste reinforced his emotions in their struggle against the invasion of his grandmother's voice. The underlying Jewish-cockney note of her cracked contralto jarred more than usual, and he could not condemn his unfeeling snobbery without also condemning his mother, for Mrs. Norman Liebig was forever saying that "Grandmother's voice was such a pity."

As they entered the hall of the flat, old Mrs. Liebig's well-corsetted plump body collided as usual against one of the giant-size Japanese pots as she searched for the light switch, but she still continued to talk. "Well, there it is," she said, "so the poor little girl committed suicide. No wonder, with a father who was a liar and did nothing all day. All the same," she said, and the electric light shone brightly upon heavily rouged high cheekbones, "I don't think a little girl like that would shoot herself. More likely the mother—tied to such a man."

Maurice took her black moiré silk evening coat off her shoulders and folded it carefully, smoothing the squirrel-skin collar; then he said, "Gregers Werle was a fanatic. In his false determination to expose the truth he destroyed the poetry in Hedvig's life and drove her to her death." His voice was a shade higher than usual, and its normal slight sibilance had a hissing edge.

Even Mrs. Liebig was struck by the fierceness of his tone. She looked up for a moment from the telephone pad on which the maid had noted a message. "Oh, it's a dreadful thing all right," she said, "to destroy young people's dreams." But there was a limit to her sentiment, or perhaps she remembered her own comfortable, prosaic childhood, for she added, "What a way to bring a child up! With all those fancies. No," she said emphatically, "it's not the sort of thing I'd have gone to if you hadn't taken me. But I'm glad I've seen it. The acting was fine."

In the sitting-room the brown velvet sofa and easy chairs looked hot and uninviting on this warm spring evening. Mrs. Liebig automatically moved one or two of the daffodils in the thick, shell-shaped white earthenware vase. She crossed the room and drew the long, heavy velvet curtains, shutting out the night breeze. "Go on, Maurice," she said, "help yourself, tuck in." And she slapped the handle of the silver-shaded, green metal cocktail wagon. "Your father said you could have two beers or one whisky."

Maurice gave himself a lager and turned to his grandmother, but she answered his gesture before he spoke. "No, I'll have my nightcap after my bath," she said, but she helped herself to a large canapé of prawns in aspic from a white-and-gold-painted metal table. "Go on," she said again, "tuck in."

Maurice surveyed the array of gelatinous hors d'œuvres. The Norman Liebigs also always had a mass of foodstuff awaiting their return from the theatre, but true to her German origin, Mrs. Norman saw that everything was cooked at home. Maurice could hear his mother's disapproving tones—"Poor Grandmother lives from Selfridge's cooked provision counter"—so he contented himself with a cheese straw.

Mrs. Liebig trotted out of the room and came back with the rubber ice container from the refrigerator. She dropped a square of ice with the tongs into Maurice's beer and kissed his forehead. She was happy to have for a while a man to wait on. "So there you are, my dear," she said. "That was your Uncle Victor phoned while we were out. Ah, well, some trouble again. Money for the dogs or for that Sylvia. It comes to the same thing, my dear. In any case it can wait for tomorrow."

At the mention of his Uncle Victor's name, Maurice's curved nostrils dilated for a moment, adding to the camel-like arrogance of his thin, sensitive face. Mrs. Liebig flushed above her rouged cheekbones to her temples.

"Oh, there's no good putting your head in the air at your uncle's name, my dear. He hasn't had your father's luck nor his brain. But business brains aren't everything. I know. I've got them. I've made money, but that's not all in life." Her grandson's complete stillness seemed to anger her, for she added loudly, "Who built your father's business up, eh? And they can't do anything now, you know, my dear, unless *I* agree. I'm still a director. What does your mother say to that?"

To this attack on his mother Maurice answered quietly, "We see Aunt Paula regularly."

It had all the effect he desired. Mrs. Liebig's large dark eyes narrowed with fury. "All right, you see your Aunt Paula. So do I.

And she's a clever buyer and she knows it. But that's not flesh and blood. What if your Uncle Victor did leave her? How did she treat him? I can't understand your father. He knows the world. He knows well enough that Paula only married Victor because she thought he would be a success. And when he wasn't, she turned to and made success for herself. All right, she's a clever girl. But all the time she let him know it. That's not love."

"Father helped Uncle Victor for years," Maurice said coldly. He took out an orange-wood stick and began to clean his nails.

"And you've got clean nails and he hasn't," Mrs. Liebig cried. "Very good. Yes, your father helped Victor. So did I. So should we all, his family. Rose sends him money from New York. It's flesh and blood, my dear. I could hardly *tell* Rose that your father doesn't see Victor any more. She asked me how the hell can they be like that when they're brothers. And now *you're* not to see Victor. Your mother told me, 'We don't wish Maurice to meet Victor.' She wants to have it every way. The Liebigs are no good because they have no culture. 'Norman doesn't care for music. I want Maurice to care for things besides money.' Very well. Your Uncle Victor cares for things besides money and he's a Liebig. He's a good artist. His cartoons made money and then those film people changed their minds and so he didn't make any more money. Oh, yes, your mother likes artists, but she doesn't like them to be out of work. I know."

Maurice rose and picked up a book from the table. "I can't listen to you if you talk about Mother like this," he said.

"What do you mean, you can't listen? A boy of your age," Mrs. Liebig cried. "You'll listen to what I choose to tell you, my dear. You're going to Cambridge and you're going to be a lawyer. Nothing to do with the rag business for Gertrude Liebig's son. Well, designing dresses and selling them has more art in it than arguing in law courts. You listen to sense for once instead of to your 'wild ducks.' Mustn't meet your own uncle. You're old enough to decide for yourself."

She was breathless by now with anger and sweating through her heavy make-up. She put her hand to her breast. "That's the sort of fool I am, upsetting myself for a foolish boy. All this has nothing to do with you," she shouted, "discussing your uncle at your age. Why, you're only just seventeen." She drew her compact, plump little body to its full five-feet-four. "I'm going to have my bath," she said and walked trimly out of the room, teetering a little as always in her very high heels.

Maurice arranged himself negligently on the striped, period Regency couch in order to control his rising hysteria. Because these people, his father, his mother, his grandmother, had conditioned him to love them, they had no scruple in tearing him apart. "Very well," as his grandmother said, they had him emotionally, but his mind remained entirely indifferent, even contemptuous—no, not contemptuous, for that involved some engagement—to them. He chose carefully the words in which he set his thoughts—"emotionally," "involved," "engagement"— for words shaped one's thinking. He could forgive them working off their loneliness, their ambitions, their nervous exhaustion on him; what he could not forgive—or rather accept, for forgiveness suggested some demand on his part and he asked nothing of them—what he could not *accept* was this inclusion in their empty, flat lives. Yes, even his mother, with her cultural aspirations; it was almost easier for someone with ideas to accept a woman like his grandmother with her tough, vulgar, pushing ways.

Carefully adjusting the sharp creases of his chocolate-brown trousers as he crossed his legs, he applied himself to Burke's speeches. Through the clever passion and the stirring elegance of the oratory he tried to control his impatience, his furious wish to have the years pass more quickly so that he could live a proper life of high responsibility, of tempered adult courage. For this age of mediocrity, of grubbing merchants and sordid artisans—this age of Liebigs would pass; he and his generation would see to that. But meanwhile, if only something would happen—something real and not just on the stage.

When Mrs. Liebig emerged from the bathroom she poked her head round the sitting-room door. Between the folds of her gold-thread dressing-gown her breasts showed sagging; her face was

flat, dead with vanishing cream; her blued hair frizzed out from a
silver hairnet. "How's your book, Maurice?" she asked with a
smile. Anger was soon gone with her. "We must get the man to
the T.V., my dear. It's not right for it to go wrong like this. I
paid a lot of money for that machine. Get me my nightcap,"
she said, "I'll be back in a minute. On the rocks," she added. She
had brought the phrase back from her visit to her daughter Rose
in New York and she loved to use it.

When she returned to her strong whisky she settled down to
her favourite half an hour's chat before bed. She had the impression that the daily routine of her life left no time for real conversation, although she had never been silent even at the height of
her active career as Madame Clara, Modiste.

She tried this evening to keep her talk off family matters. "I
don't know what I shall do next winter," she said. "The Palace is
closing down. There's not another hotel like it in Madeira.
They've known me since before your grandfather died. The head
porter always asks after you—the young gentleman with the
books."

As Maurice made no answer she tried hard to connect with
him. "The boys still dive, you know," she said. "Crabs and
sponges." The words in her mouth brought Maurice no evocation
of subtropical romance. "I wonder if Senhora Paloes will be at
Biarritz this year. She plays very high stakes. These Brazilians are
so rich, you know, my dear." But her annual holidays—Madeira
in February, Biarritz in June—were so much a routine even to
her that she could find little to say of them.

"Well," she asked, "who are you meeting tomorrow? The
Clarkson girl or Betty Lewis?"

"I'm going out with some friends from school," Maurice said
firmly to avoid his grandmother's roguish innuendo, but to no
avail.

"You prefer the little blondes, don't you, Maurice? She was
very pretty, that girl in the stalls."

Despite his annoyance at her noticing his glances in the theatre,
he did not wish to appear priggish, so he said, "Yes, wasn't she?"

"That's what I tell your mother," Mrs. Liebig said. "Let Maurice find his girls for himself. Always arranging theatre parties for the Clarksons or dinner dances with Adela Siegl's girl. He'll go out with his old grandmother when he's with *me,* I said. Let him find his girls for himself."

Maurice did not wish to side too openly with her against his mother, so he merely smiled.

"And tomorrow evening a nice show for *me,*" Mrs. Liebig continued, "a nice musical show, *The Pajama Game.* Rose saw it in New York. She said it was tops. Not a show for *you* this time. A show for the children. For the old girl." She laughed in delight at her little joke—a harsh, braying jay sound that seemed almost to call forth an answering note from the telephone.

"Oh, my dear, so late," Mrs. Liebig exclaimed. "You answer, Maurice. Is it Victor? What does he want? I can't speak now. It's too late." She chattered on, so that Maurice had to stop one ear with a finger to hear his correspondent.

"You're wanted at once," he said. "Sylvia is very ill. Uncle Victor's not there. They can't find him."

"Well, I can't go like this." Mrs. Liebig was indignant. "What's she got? A pain or something?"

"It's very urgent," Maurice said, speaking gravely as though the person at the other side might hear Mrs. Liebig's levity. "She's had an accident."

"Oh, my God!" Mrs. Liebig cried. "The damned fool girl. Poor Victor! Well, what can I do?"

"Mrs. Liebig will come as soon as possible. I shall come immediately," Maurice said into the telephone. "I'm Mrs. Victor Liebig's nephew."

Mrs. Liebig got up from her chair, drawing the gold-and-green dressing-gown round her, slopping a little in her mules. "You can't go *there,*" she said. "What do you mean, 'Mrs. Victor Liebig's nephew'? You've never seen the girl."

Maurice said, "Someone must go. The woman on the phone wouldn't say exactly, but she implied that it wasn't an accident. I think she wanted to say that Sylvia had tried to kill herself." His eyes were no longer flat and dead. "She couldn't find anyone else," he said as though that clinched the matter.

But for his grandmother it did not. "Oh, my God!" she cried. "What does Victor want to mix up with such little fools for? I should never have agreed to meet the girl," she added—as though her recognition of her son's mistress had given the girl aspirations above her station, encouraged her to ideas of suicide.

Maurice seemed not to hear her. "You'd better get dressed as soon as you can and follow me over there," he said and moved to the door.

Mrs. Liebig ran after him; holding her dressing-gown round her with one hand, she put the other on his arm. "I don't know what . . ." she said. "Norman will never forgive me. You'll have to answer to your mother, you know. You're not to meet Victor and now you rush off to see his girl. I don't know . . ." Maurice went out of the room. She followed him, shouting into the darkness of the hall, "They're not married, you know." She knew perfectly well that he knew—she shouted it as though it were a threat. Only the click of the front door latch answered her.

At first, in the taxi, sailing down an empty Baker Street, Maurice was only aware that monotony had been broken; held up by lights at the Edgware Road junction, however, he became nervous of what he would find at the end of his journey. The urgent and mysterious voice on the telephone had enveloped him at once in drama; he couldn't at that moment have handed over his part to his grandmother, however little he knew his lines. Now, however, apprehension made him search for evasions: if the Liebigs were in the cast, he thought, even courtesy Liebigs like Sylvia, it was bound to turn out to be some sordid melodrama. With the taxi in progress again, he felt the elation of duty; if the cause he was serving had neither quite the glory nor the high intent that he would have liked, at least there was a cause to serve—and this, as all his little group knew well, was what their generation had been cheated of. Besides, how few of his friends were likely to be involved with mistresses who tried to commit suicide, he reflected with a glow of pride.

Pride, however, has its fall, and as the taxi-driver braked
sharply to avoid a drunk at Westbourne Grove, Maurice was
jolted into disgust at his childishness. He blushed with shame, as
though one of his friends—Gervase or Selwyn Adcock—had heard
his thoughts. They were all agreed, of course, the whole group,
that sin today was as drab and inglorious as virtue. "Simply the
blowsy Brittania on the reverse of the fake coin," Gervase had
said last term. By the time the taxi drew up at 42, Branksombe
Terrace, Maurice had found many reasons to support his anxious
dislike of his self-imposed chivalry.

As he looked out at the dirty mid-Victorian house with its peel-
ing stucco and straggles of grimy Virginia creeper, he saw a
world whose unfamiliarity daunted him. He longed for the central heating, the books, the modern reading lamp, the iced
drink, of his bedroom in his grandmother's flat. There were theatres too cheap and squalid to play in. Maurice was about to tear up
his contract and tell the taxi-driver to take him home when the
front door opened and a thin, dark-haired young woman in blue
jeans came out on to the steps. "Mr. Liebig," she called, in an
overrefined, slightly petulant voice. "Mr. Liebig? This is the
house." Maurice got out and paid the fare.

"I'm Freda Cherrill," the young woman said, "the person who
phoned to you." Her thin, yellowish face looked so drawn and
tired and her voice was so languid that Maurice felt that he dared
not question her. She drew him into a little ill-lit hall and bent
her long neck—yellow and grubby above her blue-and-white-
striped shirt—down towards him. Her large dark eyes were vacant rather than sad. Her breath came scented but a little sour as
she whispered into his face. "I'd better give you all the gen before you go in," she said, pointing towards the door at their side.
"She's in there."

Maurice felt able to assert himself. "Is the doctor with her?"
he asked.

"I'm afraid not," Miss Cherrill replied a little petulantly. "He
was dining in Putney but he's on his way."

"But surely," Maurice cried, "there was some doctor nearer."

"I only know Dr. Waters," Miss Cherrill replied. "She doesn't seem to have a doctor of her own." Her languid voice became quite sharp with disapproval. "So naturally I had to send for mine. He's always been very good with my anæmia and he's a very understanding man."

"I don't know what has happened," Maurice said, cutting through her petulance with a certain hauteur.

"Well, I couldn't very well say everything on the phone, could I?" Miss Cherrill was quite annoyed. "She doesn't want Mr. Morello and everybody else involved."

"Where is my uncle?" Maurice asked.

"Oh," Miss Cherrill said scornfully, "if we knew that! She's comfortable enough now. I kept walking her up and down the room at first. I thought I had to keep her awake, she was so dozy, but Dr. Waters said she hadn't taken enough to make it serious and in any case with aspirins . . ."

"So she *has* tried to commit suicide."

"I told you so," Miss Cherrill said angrily.

"I didn't quite understand."

"Well, you can see the telephone's in the hall. She asked me not to bring everybody into it. Morello's room's only down there." She pointed along the hall. "I don't know them." She spoke quite loudly in her annoyance. "I heard her crying. My room's next door. It went on for ages so I went in."

"You've been very good," Maurice said. "Thank you."

"It was lucky I was washing my hair," Miss Cherrill replied. "I nearly always go out of a Wednesday. Besides, it's not often anything happens in life, is it?"

Maurice felt disgusted by his own emotions expressed from another mouth, so he said, "I think I'd better go in and see her."

"Of course," Miss Cherrill said, "someone ought to be very stern with her. I told her myself that it could have meant a police case, and would do now if I hadn't had a word with Dr. Waters. Not that he probably won't be pretty sharp with her himself, I expect. She's *got* to be frightened." All Miss Cherrill's sympathy, even her pleasure at events out of the ordinary, was dissipating now that someone else was taking over: she was very tired, she was going out the next evening, and her hair was still filthy. "Well," she said in final tones, "I'm glad there's somebody else here she knows at last. She's still very weepy and a bit dazed. She's been awfully sick, you know."

"I'm afraid," said Maurice, "that she doesn't know me at all. We've never met."

Miss Cherrill stared at him in disgust. "Well," she said, "I suppose it's all right. You're very young, aren't you? But it's only someone to sit with her. And, anyway, she doesn't seem to have any real people." She opened Sylvia's door and peered in. "She's all right for you to come in," she said and then, her refined petulance leaving her for a moment, "The smell of sick isn't too bad, is it? I've drenched the room in eau de Cologne." She whispered loudly and with relish.

Maurice said nothing; even the faintest smell of vomit made his stomach heave in protest.

Apart from the double bed in the corner and one broken-down, hair-oil-stained armchair, the room seemed as bare as it was large. The only dressing table was made from something that looked like an inverted packing-case. On it were crowded lotions, creams, and powders; above it hung some home-made contraption that had brought the electricity by means of a profusion of wires from its lonely eminence in the centre of the high ceiling. The walls were cream-distempered and dirty; someone had started to cover one of them with a cheap "modernistic" wallpaper. Over an old towel-horse hung a black skirt, a white muslin blouse, stockings and underwear. There were books and magazines in scattered heaps on the matting-covered floor; an uncovered typewriter crowded, with a portable gramophone and records, the small top of a rickety, varnished bedside-table. On the walls were pinned, in profuse disorder, Victor's drawings, giving the room the appearance of a school art exhibition. In the bed Sylvia lay. Against the blue whiteness of her face the bed linen showed grey, and the pillowcase shone greasy under her thick but dirty fair hair.

Despite all the pallor and the grubbiness, however, she looked so young and delicious to Maurice—especially so much younger than he had expected, no older, perhaps, than he was—that he was unable to speak, and he felt the giddiness and trembling of the legs which lust always brought to his repressed body. Her eyes seemed to him extraordinarily sensual under their drowsing, half-closed red lids; her white cheeks were nevertheless plump about their high pommets and her heavy lips were half opened in a Greuze-like pout. She looked altogether like some eighteenth-century print of a young dying harlot—ostensibly a morality, in fact a bait for prurient eyes.

Maurice felt embarrassed that Miss Cherrill's eyes were upon him, putting his manhood to the test. He summoned all his wits to find something to say, something that would mark his authority. Before he could find words, however, Sylvia's sobbing swelled to convulsive breathing and then burst into a loud, hysterical weeping—the hideous, uncontrolled crying of a frightened, spoiled child. With children Maurice knew himself to be powerless.

Miss Cherrill looked at him for a moment, then she walked over and shook Sylvia roughly. "Stop that noise at once," she said. "You'll look a fool if the doctor finds you like this."

Her action had no effect except that Sylvia hit out at her flat bosom. "Go away," she cried. "Go away, all of you. I won't see you or your bloody doctor."

It seemed to Maurice that if he could do nothing with Sylvia he could at least order Miss Cherrill about. "I think you'd better leave us," he said.

"I'm sure I've no wish to stay," Miss Cherrill replied. "This has been a lesson to me, I can tell you."

Maurice opened the door for her. "Thank you very much for all you have done," he said, but she went out without looking at him.

He stood for a moment staring at Sylvia. He was embarrassed at the pleasure her crying brought to him. It was not, however, his first intimation of the quirks of sexual desire. He hastened to efface the disturbing emotion with redoubled kindness. "I should like very much to help you if I can." The words when they came seemed very inadequate and stiffly formal; their effect on Sylvia, however, was immediate.

"Get out of here, get out of here!" she screamed. "I want to be left alone."

The request seemed to Maurice so reasonable that he was about to walk out, when Sylvia leaned over the side of the bed and, picking up a slipper from the floor, threw it at his head. Her half-doped aim was feebly wide of the mark. Nevertheless it produced a strange effect on Maurice; he walked very deliberately over to the bed and smacked Sylvia's face. Then he kissed her clumsily and excitedly on the mouth. Her breath, sour through the eau-de-Cologne fumes, checked his excitement. The whole chain of his behaviour was so surprising to him that he just sat on the bed and stared, not at Sylvia, but slightly over her head.

"You look like a fish," she said. She was not crying now, but he realized that her ordinary speaking voice was strangely husky.

"I'm sorry," he said, "I came here to help you."

"You do," she said.

To Maurice her strangely direct but slightly goofy manner recalled so much that he had heard in the theatre. If he had met neither the tragedy nor even the melodrama for which he had been prepared, here surely at least was English comedy at its best. He tried to forget the appearance of the room. Décor was after all an overrated aspect of the stage. He too must be laconic, offhand, bohemian, modern.

"Why did you do it?" he asked.

The question, alas, only brought on crying so violent that he could hardly hear himself speak. "You'll only bring Miss Cherrill back," he shouted.

"She's an interfering cow," Sylvia said, sobbing. "I hate her."

"She's been very kind, I should have thought."

"She wasn't, she just wanted to gloat."

"Oh, please," Maurice cried, "don't let's discuss that. Can't you tell me what's wrong?"

"Why should I?" Sylvia asked. "I don't know you."

This, however, seemed unreasonable, so Maurice said, "Why did you get Miss Cherrill to ring up my grandmother if you didn't want our help?"

This again set Sylvia crying. "You think I didn't mean to do it. You think I got frightened. That's what you'll tell Victor, isn't it? It's easy to say someone is just a hysteric." And when he made no answer—"Go on, that's what you think, isn't it?" she cried.

It was, in fact, what Maurice was thinking, as far as he could in her presence; but as he had had no experience of hysterics he did not feel fully justified in making the judgment; and in any case, if she was, it was surely most important to calm her, since both shaking and slapping, which he had always supposed to be the sovereign remedies, had failed. "I think you must be very unhappy," he said, "and if I can help you I should like to do so." It was not, perhaps, the high purpose in life which his generation was seeking, but it was a sincere wish.

It did, indeed, also succeed in calming Sylvia a little. "I'm in such a mess," she said, "such a terrible mess. I've let myself love a man who's a liar, a real hopeless liar. And that's a terrible thing to do!" She announced this gravely as one of the profound, the ultimate truths of life. "He says there isn't someone else," she said, "but I know better. I know her name. It's Hilda. Isn't it awful?" She began once more to sob.

Maurice could not feel this so deeply, but he said, "It's not a very nice name certainly."

Sylvia immediately began to pound on his leg with her small clenched fists. "Oh, you silly little fool!" she shouted. "Victor's left me. Can't you understand? He's left me. All Thursday I guessed he was going and I said to him, 'Victor, if you don't love me any more, well, then tell me. I can take it,' I said. But he just smiled, smiled to madden me. 'You want me to get mad at you,' I said, 'so that you can have your excuse. Well, I'm not going to do it. I can take the truth,' I told him. Well," she cried, turning suddenly on Maurice, "if I am hard and tough before I should be,

what made me that way? What's life done for little Sylvia
Wright?"

If she had intended an answer to this vital question Maurice was
not to hear it, for at that moment there was a noise of braking outside the house, of voices raised, of bells rung. Among the voices
Maurice could hear his grandmother's. He moved to the door,
wishing that he could kiss Sylvia again before Mrs. Liebig came
on the scene.

"You can't even bother to listen to me and yet you ask me how
it happened. I think you are despicable," Sylvia said.

It was true that he had ceased listening to her as soon as a rival
noise came to attract his attention, but then her torrent of words
had been so sudden and so uncontrolled.

"You think because I've been in prison . . ."

"I knew nothing about that," Maurice interrupted. "But in any
case I can't let my grandmother stand out there forever."

When he came into the hall a little old woman in a dressing-
gown was making her way crabwise and very slowly down the
stairs. "Everyone's in such a hurry nowadays," she said. "I'm coming as quickly as I can."

"I think they're ringing for me," Maurice said.

"Well, I didn't suppose they were ringing for *me*," the old
woman replied, but she began slowly and with heavy dragging
of her feet to go back up the stairs.

Before Maurice could get to the front door, however, another
door at the end of the passage opened and a plump, dark young
man, also in a dressing-gown, stuck his head out. "If that ringing's
for you," he said, "I should be obliged if you'd answer it quickly."
Before Maurice could answer he added, "If you're connected
with Mrs. Liebig I may as well tell you now that I have the whole
matter under review." The door closed again and he was gone.

When Maurice opened the front door he found a clean-shaven,
middle-aged man in evening dress standing on the step. He was
smoking a pipe and looked, Maurice thought, like a naval officer.
There was no sign of Mrs. Liebig.

"Liebig?" asked the man shortly. It was clear that he found the name unpleasant to pronounce.

"Are you Dr. Waters?" Maurice asked; he had already resented the delay in the doctor's arrival sufficiently to pronounce his name with equal distaste.

"Yes, yes," said Dr. Waters impatiently. "I'd better see this young woman as soon as possible."

"I'm her nephew," Maurice announced himself. "I think she's all right now."

"That's really for me to decide, old chap. It's far from what Miss Cherrill said. I suppose she's with the girl."

"No," Maurice said, "she's gone to her room."

Dr. Waters turned and grinned boyishly. "Well, I daresay we can get over that little loss," he said. "Lead the way, old chap, will you?"

Maurice indicated Sylvia's door. "If you don't mind, I think I ought to look for my grandmother. I heard her voice outside."

"There's an old girl knocking daylight out of a taxi-driver," Dr. Waters said, and he knocked on Sylvia's door. Maurice, wondering if the doctor was drunk, went out into the darkness.

There, indeed, was Mrs. Liebig arguing with a taxi-driver. She had reacted to the emergency by putting on a pair of royal blue slacks, a short fur coat, and a cyclamen silk scarf wound turban-wise round her head. It was the costume in which she had braved the air raids, but as Maurice's memory did not go back to this time he felt only acute embarrassment at her appearance.

When she saw her grandson she called raucously, "Well, it's all right, my dear, he's going to wait." She came up the steps, puffing and grumbling. "What do they think we are?" she asked. "Paupers? 'You'll get good money,' I told him. Ring for another taxi—what does he mean? I'll pay him to wait. I've got the money. 'Ring up and perhaps there aren't any more taxis.' I told him. 'I'm an old woman,' I told him. 'Do you think I want to wait about all night in a place like this?' "

Maurice said sharply, "Sylvia's been very ill. The doctor's with her now. She tried to kill herself but she only made herself sick."

"Well, there you are," Mrs. Liebig said. "Victor should never have picked up with her."

"You've no need to worry about *him*," Maurice said bitterly. "He's left her for some other woman." And when he saw that his grandmother was about to defend her son he interrupted violently, "He's lucky not to have a murder on his hands."

"Murder?" Mrs. Liebig said. "Don't talk nonsense. You don't know what you are talking about. A boy of your age mixed up in all this. Where's her own people, anyway? What's her mother doing? My God, what a rotten world we live in."

At his grandmother's words, all Maurice's heroic mood shrivelled inside of him. He felt that he had simply muddled the whole affair; he had never inquired about Sylvia's parents. "She's very young," he said hesitatingly; he could think of nothing else to express what he felt for Sylvia.

"Young," Mrs. Liebig echoed scornfully. "That's the trouble. A lot of children's nonsense, the lot of you. Well, where is the girl?" And when Maurice moved towards Sylvia's door she pushed past him and brusquely forced her way in.

Sylvia was lying back on the pillows—a ghostlike little waif. To Maurice's eyes she seemed to have faded surprisingly far out of life in the short while he had been gone.

"Well," said Dr. Waters, "she's going to be all right. Aren't you, young woman? If she'd taken anything but aspirins she'd be dead. As it is, I've given her an injection just to help nature along."

Maurice, who was sceptical of the knowledge of general practitioners, assumed the air of an educated mission schoolboy before the tribal witchdoctor, but Mrs. Liebig exclaimed knowingly, "Ah, there you are."

Dr. Waters now assumed a stern look. "I need to know a bit more about all this though. I'll have to examine the patient a bit further. I must ask you to wait outside," he announced

"Yes, yes," Mrs. Liebig cried, "you can't be here when the doctor's examining her, Maurice. That wouldn't do at all." Maurice moved towards the door. "I'll call you when the doctor's done," Mrs. Liebig said.

Dr. Waters swung on her angrily. "Will you kindly follow him. I want to talk to the young woman alone."

Mrs. Liebig's face was crimson. "Don't you order me about," she cried. "I've no intention of leaving this girl in here with you."

It was Dr. Waters' turn to approach apoplexy. "I would remind you, madam," he said, "that it may well be my duty to turn this matter over to the police, with unpleasant consequences for those responsible for this girl's welfare."

Mrs. Liebig was too astonished to reply. Maurice looked for some contradiction of the doctor's innuendo from Sylvia, but she had only faded further away into the ghost world.

"Now then," Dr. Waters cried sharply. "Out with the lot of you."

In the passage Mrs. Liebig gave it to Maurice good and proper. "Can't you behave like a gentleman?" she asked. "Good God! What would your father say? So I've had to wait for my old age to watch my grandson stand by and see me insulted. How do you know he's a doctor?" she asked. "What's he doing in there with that girl? They're pretty filthy, some of these doctors; I could tell you stories. What does Victor think I am? To be at the beck and call of every little tart he picks up off the street—his own mother!" And so on.

Maurice said nothing; indeed he heard very little—his thoughts were entirely upon Sylvia, a little puzzled at her sudden languishing, but in the main just dwelling on her.

It was over ten minutes before Dr. Waters emerged from the room. Mrs. Liebig was already urging that they should leave. "Let her stew in her own dirty juice," she said. "She got what she was after with her tricks. Good God, I should think Victor *has* left her, and if he never takes up with her again, good riddance to bad rubbish."

Dr. Waters cut into all this abruptly. "I think she'll be all right now," he said. "I apologize if I seemed rude but one must have a free hand in these affairs. I should like," he added, "someone to stay with her. She's still a little hysterical, and I can't say that I'm surprised. Besides, when that husband of hers comes back, heaven knows what may happen. Can I rely on one of you to stop with her?"

Mrs. Liebig's expression was so unpromising that Dr. Waters seemed finally to decide on Maurice as his assistant, despite his youth. He took him by the arm and drew him aside. "If that brute comes back and pesters her," he said, "you may tell him that I shall be over in the morning and that I shall have one or two very unpleasant words to say to him. You can say"—he chuckled sardonically—"that if he's so anxious for a thrashing he may well get it from an unexpected quarter. Filthy brute! Keep her quiet," he added. "Poor little creature!"

Before he left the house he bowed to Mrs. Liebig. "Good night to you, madam," he said. But she did not acknowledge his salute.

Back in the bedroom, Maurice had scarcely time to register the charm of Sylvia's wan smile before the old, crab-sidling woman came hobbling in. Like Dr. Waters, she disregarded Mrs. Liebig, so that Maurice began to wonder whether his grandmother's trousers, so unsuitable to her age, had robbed her of all claim on public respect.

"Mr. Morello wants to see you right away," the old woman mumbled to him.

"I shan't be a few minutes," he said to Mrs. Liebig and, determined on his new authority, he was gone from the room before she could protest.

Mr. Morello seemed also to accept Maurice's authority; indeed, he appeared anxious to counter with a demonstration of his own powers of command. He had changed his dressing-gown for a dark, rather too carefully "City suit" and had seated himself at a large roll-topped desk, which loomed incongruously in the obvious bed-sitting-room. His stature as landlord was asserted only in the neat divan bed and the unvarnished "modernistic" wardrobe and chest of drawers—a setting two whole "bed-sitter" social grades above the furnishings he provided for his tenants. Even to Maurice's eye Mr. Morello seemed ill at ease in his authority. His plump young face was smooth with massage, the bluish stubble of his heavy jowl was carefully powdered; but on his neck was an angry boil and his fingers seemed unable to leave it alone.

"I'm afraid this can't go on, you know," he said. His voice was surprisingly light for so heavy a man; his accent was Birmingham.

Maurice looked round the room and sat down on the divan.

"Of course, of course," Mr. Morello said. He was clearly embarrassed at his failure as host. "You'll excuse this spot," he said; and when Maurice did not answer, he added in extenuation, "It's a boil, you know. There's nothing to do but wait for them to come to a head." Feeling that he had gone too far, perhaps, in excuses, he sat back in his swivel chair and folded his hands over his stomach. "I know things are difficult," he said with paternal pomposity. "It's a very bad time indeed for artists." He spoke with the authority of a gamekeeper pronouncing on the partridge season. "We all get to the end of our tether at times. Some quite small trouble or other comes along and we break. I've felt like that with this boil." He laughed deprecatingly, but it was clear that he did not feel the irritation to be a small one.

To Maurice he seemed so like a vulgar parody of his form master that he expected him to add, "But do *I* break down and try to commit suicide?"

Instead Mr. Morello pushed out his thick underlip, looking like a sea elephant. "This house is a good part of my living," he announced, "and I can't have it getting a bad name. This sort of thing might easily lose me tenants. Good tenants. Paying tenants," he added ominously. "With all due allowance and having every sympathy, I hope—if it happens again they'll have to go. Will you please tell Mrs. Liebig that, when she's recovered enough to face the facts of the situation." He paused and then, as though resolving the situation from superior wisdom, he said, "It may well be a good thing to frighten her a bit."

Maurice was annoyed at the man's patronizing tone; he felt

dissatisfied too with his own lack of command over the situation. He searched for some means of asserting himself; then, "I think it was quite unnecessary of Miss Cherrill to have shouted my aunt's private affairs about the house."

Only his dislike of Mr. Morello had made him speak, and he immediately expected a sharp rebuff, but the landlord only pouted like a fat, cross baby. "I don't want any trouble with Miss Cherrill, please," he said pleadingly. "She's a good, paying tenant. I'm sure I'm glad to have made contact with one of Mrs. Liebig's family." He smiled. "It's a thousand pities she's had such bad luck. There's money to be made in dancing today. Really good dancing." He was clearly a man who prided himself on knowing how things stood in the world of today. "But there you are, accidents may happen to anyone."

Maurice could make nothing of this so he did not reply.

"Well," Mr. Morello cried cheerily, "she'll be all right with you there, I can see." He got up and opened the door for Maurice; he was clearly anxious to efface his previous insufficient manners. "I feel a lot happier for our little chat," he said. "You really must excuse me receiving you in this state." Once more his fingers went up to the boil on his neck. "If there's hot water or anything needed, I'm sure Martha will be glad to oblige."

Mrs. Liebig was standing in the hall when Maurice came out. "Ah, good God, there you are," she cried. "Do you think I'm made of money—keeping that taxi there all night?"

As though to underline her anxiety the door-bell buzzed loudly; and when Maurice opened it, there was, indeed, the taxi-driver.

"All right, all right," Mrs. Liebig cried, "I'm coming. Do you think you're going to lose your money?"

The little, grey-faced old taxi-driver seemed so cowed by her that he only said, "Well, it's a long time, lady."

"A long time?" Mrs. Liebig cried. "There's illness here, of course it's a long time. Well, Maurice, are you ready?"

"I must stay here. The doctor asked me to." Maurice tried to sound as casual as he could manage, but he felt, though he could not explain why, that his whole future happiness depended upon his getting his way about this.

"Stay here? Good God! The girl's all right now. Stay here? Of course you can't stay here with that girl alone in her bedroom, a young man of your age. What good would you be anyway, a boy like you?"

"The doctor . . ." Maurice began, but she broke in furiously.

"What do we know about the doctor anyway? You and your doctors—you wait until you know a bit more about life," she added darkly.

Maurice's thin face was tensed. "Either you or I must stay," he said, "unless we're to risk a death on our hands."

Perhaps it was the sibilance of his voice betraying to her his emotional state, or perhaps it was the fear that she might indeed have to stay—whatever the cause, Mrs. Liebig gave a hard little laugh. "All right," she cried, "I wash my hands. You and your morbid ideas. But *you* must explain to your mother. I hope you enjoy upsetting everybody like this, for that's what you're doing."

To Maurice's surprise she then went into Sylvia's room and, crossing to the bed, kissed the girl warmly on both cheeks. "Maurice is staying to see you're a good girl," she said. "Now don't you worry. You're a good girl, even if you are a little fool. Victor'll find his luck again. You don't have to blame yourself. That Paula must give him a divorce. You'll see, it'll turn out all right. Oh, yes," she cried, turning to Maurice, "I know. Happy endings aren't good enough for your clever ways. It's all got to be deaths and suicides and wild ducks. But Sylvia isn't such a little fool as that. She'll be all right." She kissed the girl again.

Once more Maurice felt surprise, for Sylvia looked at Mrs. Liebig with little girl's rounded eyes. "Thank you," she whispered gently, "you've been so very kind. You've helped me to believe again a little."

Mrs. Liebig only said, "Now you sleep, my dear, and you let her sleep, Maurice."

Now that he was alone with Sylvia, Maurice was completely

bewildered. He had asserted his right to remain on the stage, but of what the play was about he was entirely ignorant. For two years now, since his sixteenth birthday, he had been schooling himself to the sense of authority, the power of command, the heroic role which he and his friends in the Upper Sixth were determined to assume. They had discussed it so often, schooled themselves for the task of leadership which would fall to their generation—leadership out of the desert of the television world, out of the even more degrading swamps of espresso-bar rebellion. They had fed themselves on high purposes and self-discipline, on gallantry and panache, on Carlyle and Burke. Now for the first time he was called upon to control a situation, however paltry the occasion, and yet the situation seemed to drift by while he stood like a night stroller on the towing-path, scarcely able to distinguish water from land. He was emerging not as the hero leader but as that feeble figure, the *homme moyen sensuel* —the "hero" type of all the literature that he and his friends most despised. And he saw no way out of it.

Sylvia accepted his silence at first, lying back on her pillows. With the eyes closed, her face seemed strangely smooth and empty of life; she looked both older and lost. Gradually her underlip protruded in a sulky pout and her forehead wrinkled in a frown. To Maurice she now appeared like a sullen, bored child; but as he could make no sense of all that he had seen and heard of her, he tried to ignore this new ugly impression that she made on him. Suddenly the frown and the pout disappeared; opening her eyes, she looked at him tragically. "Why do you think God hates me so?" she asked.

A question based on so many doubtful premises shocked Maurice deeply; such melodramatic speech from such attractive lips disturbed him even more.

Sylvia sensed his disquiet; she let her hand fall on the eiderdown in front of her in a gesture of hopelessness. "Oh, God, always trying to find a way out, always trying to find someone else to put the blame on, even poor old God! Do you ever hate yourself like hell?" she asked.

This question was somewhat easier for Maurice to answer, although he found its formulation hardly more to his taste. "Quite often," he said. "I should think most people of any intelligence or feeling do at some time or other."

Sylvia seemed to ponder for a moment. "You understand things so well and yet you're so young," she said simply.

It was so exactly what Maurice had hoped to think of himself, and yet so exactly what he now doubted, that he looked at her covertly to see if she was speaking sarcastically; but her expression was one of childlike wonderment.

"How old are you?" she asked.

"Almost eighteen."

"Almost," she said, and she smiled. "That makes me terribly old. I'm twenty-three," she said.

"That's not old really." Maurice tried not to sound a little disappointed.

"Almost eighteen and you know so much. I wish you could teach me some of it." Sylvia's wondering, far-away voice would not have disgraced a performance of Marie Rose.

His age was not exactly what Maurice wished to harp upon, and her praise, though pleasing, was an indulgence high purpose did not allow him. "I'm afraid there isn't much point in our discussing these things unless you tell me why you wanted"—he paused a moment and then, determinedly realistic, ended—"to kill yourself. Something Miss Cherrill said made me think . . ." he went on and then stopped again—to speak about pregnancy was embarrassing, but then Dr. Waters' suggestion about Uncle Victor's depraved sexual tastes was an even less possible topic of conversation.

Sylvia's pupils contracted to two minute forget-me-nots. "What did Miss Cherrill say?" she asked, her husky voice now edgy.

"That you were going to have a baby . . ."

Maurice wished now that he had set about assuming control in a different way, but he was left little time to regret, for Sylvia burst out in fury. "That lying cow," she said. "Anyway, I've got a bloody sight better chance than her. No man would give her one. How dare she open her filthy mouth about my affairs? I'll have it out with her now." She began to lift herself with difficulty from the bed.

Maurice put his hand on her arm. "No," he said, "you must stay where you are. Perhaps I misunderstood her."

For whatever reason, Sylvia seemed willing to accept his restraint. "And if I *were* going to, as if I shouldn't know where to go to get rid of it. Better than that silly bitch would," she said and lay back on the pillows once more, smiling to herself.

Maurice's silence weighed down upon her satisfaction, however, and broke it. She turned to him angrily again. "You think I'm pretty sordid, don't you?" she asked.

"I wasn't making any judgment. I was just trying to understand, that's all," he replied. The words came out automatically, and he blushed not only for their priggishness but for their untruth—he *had* been thinking the whole episode sordid.

"Well, you *should* think it sordid—sordid and disgusting. For that's what it is. You've no idea of the foul things . . ."

"I think I have," Maurice said. "Dr. Waters told me something."

Sylvia began to giggle. "What did *he* say?"

Maurice found this quite difficult; to begin with, he wasn't quite sure if he had interpreted Dr. Waters aright, and then he was also very uncertain if his interpretation might not be nonsense. He knew there were such sexual deviations, but applied to Sylvia and Victor it seemed absurd. He did not want to make a fool of himself.

"Come on," said Sylvia sharply. "What did he say?"

So urged, Maurice blurted it out crudely. "He said Victor made you beat him and that was why you'd . . ."

Sylvia, to his consternation, roared with laughter. "Dr. Waters is a fool," she said. "Dr. Waters made a pass, and that was naughty of Dr. Waters, so Sylvia told him where he could put his pass."

It was, perhaps, the theatricality of her manner that suddenly decided Maurice. All his bewilderment suddenly vanished as a pattern formed before him. "That's not true. None of what you've been saying is true—to Dr. Waters or to Morello or to Grandmother or to me. You just make up stories about yourself."

Sylvia leaned quickly out of the bed and smacked his face. "You get out of here," she said, "go on, get out."

Maurice rose. There seemed nothing else to do but go. He had not moved, however, before she burst into tears.

"It's true," she cried. "Oh, God, it's true! But what else is there to do when I'm so unhappy? That or get out of it, out of all this useless, meaningless squalor. I'm so unhappy," she said again, "and so bored. What's the point of life? Oh, it's different for you . . ."

"No," said Maurice, "it isn't." And he told her of his own despair and boredom.

She listened for a while like an attentive child, then she seemed to grow restless with her own silence. Once or twice she tried to break in, but Maurice was intent on confiding his troubles. At last she cried, "Well then, if you feel like that, what's the hope for someone like me? You don't know what real dull respectability is like, or, worse still, this sort of sordid, disreputable life."

Then in her turn she told her story—a more vivid recitation than Maurice's. The large family, the dead drudgery of the Luton newspaper shop her parents owned, running away to London, film-extra work, Woolworth's soap counter, hostess at a little club, Victor.

It was at once a story so familiar to Maurice from what he had read in the newspapers, and so personal from her vivid narration, that he was spellbound. He only interrupted her once. "And prison?" he asked.

"Oh, the whole thing's a prison," she cried.

"Is all this true that you're telling me?" he demanded. "No, I shouldn't have said that. Only it's all so difficult."

"Oh, yes, you should," she replied. "How can you believe me when I've told you so many lies? But it *is* true. Not what I've said before. That about prison was just to make myself interesting. It wasn't even true about Victor. He hasn't been unfaithful.

He just didn't come back tonight because it's all so hopeless. He feels he can't help me and he's right, nobody can. I'm no use."

It was now, Maurice knew, that he ought to convince her of what life could be, *was* going to be when his generation got their chance, but he found himself taking advantage of a quite different chance. He got up and kissed her. When he found that she lay so passive in his embrace, his shyness left him and he kissed her excitedly, if a little clumsily, on mouth and cheeks, ears and neck. She lay purring like a white cat that has found warmth.

"It's nice," she said in her husky voice, "we're both young, and that's right, isn't it?"

He had hardly started to stroke her arms again a little clumsily before she seemed to become drowsy. Then she pushed him away—but gently.

"No," she said, "it's no good. Victor and I belong to each other. It may be hell but that's the way it is." Maurice noticed for the first time that her voice had assumed a faint American note. "Victor and I are down-hillers," she said. "You're not. Look," she went on, "I like you. You understand so much and you've helped. I need a friend who I can talk to. Will you be my friend?"

Maurice could not remember feeling so depressed, but he summoned all his courage to assent.

"I want to sleep now," she said. "And you must go, because if Victor comes back he'll be worried if you're here, and I'm too tired to face any more trouble."

"The doctor said . . ." Maurice began.

"Please, don't make it worse."

"All right," Maurice said. "But you won't be silly again?"

"Cross my heart," she said. "Come and see me again. I like to hear you talk."

Maurice moved to the door. "Of course. I shall come tomorrow to see how you are."

Sylvia seemed to hesitate, then she smiled lazily. "Okay," she said, "but don't come before five. I'm going to have a lovely long sleep," and she curled down among the grubby sheets and blankets.

Maurice could find no taxi until he reached Marble Arch, and by that time he was so absorbed in trying to sort out his emotions that he preferred to walk home.

He too slept long and heavily. Mrs. Liebig was already lunching when he woke. She seemed anxious at first that he should have been involved in last night's trouble. "I don't know what to say to Norman," she said. "He ought to be pleased that you did so much for his brother's girl. But heaven knows what your mother may say. I can't tell their ideas. Better say nothing. Yes, that's it," she cried, "tell them nothing. Do you hear?—you're to tell them nothing. All the same you behaved well, Maurice."

When she found that he ate a good lunch she seemed less worried. "Victor's got in a fine mess," she said. "All the same it's his life. That Paula must give him a divorce. I shall tell her. She's got a good job; what's she want to hang on to him for?" but when Maurice asked her if she had arranged to see Aunt Paula she answered vaguely. "Time enough," she said. "Besides, it's all nonsense. You're not to think any more of it, do you hear? At your age. There's quite enough with your wild ducks. All that Sylvia and Victor. It's a lot of nonsense. It's just the way they live." And with that she dismissed the subject. She was more intent that he should meet her on time for *The Pajama Game*.

Maurice found himself near Westbourne Grove long before five o'clock, but he passed the time impatiently in a tea-room. When at last five o'clock sounded from a nearby church he ran all the way to Sylvia's house for fear that she might be annoyed at his lack of punctuality. When Sylvia opened the door his fears seemed to be realized, for she scowled at him. Her appearance in daylight surprised him; she was shorter than he had expected, and as a result her plumpness seemed a little gross. Her breasts reared at him aggressively through her tight white sweater and her hips seemed almost tyrelike beneath her tighter black skirt. Heavy, bright lipstick made her cheeks seem waxen. Her fair hair fell loosely across her forehead. All in all, however, she sharpened his desire.

"Oh, hullo," she said a little crossly. "I'm nearly ready. You'd better come in while I finish my face. Victor's expecting us at the club."

In the bedroom she put an Elvis Presley record on the gramophone and sat before the mirror, doing her eyebrows. Maurice tried to make conversation, but her inattention and the deafening volume of "Blue Suede Shoes" made it impossible. He sat on the bed and stared disconsolately into the distance. When at last she had finished he met her turning glance with a smile. She smiled in return and stopped the record. "Elvis the pelvis," she said, but there seemed to be no possible reply.

"It's only a little drinking club," she announced, "but we always go there." Before they left the house she added, "It was sweet of you to come round."

The club was up three flights of bare wooden stairs and very dark when you entered. The radiogram here was playing "Dickie Valentine." There were only three people sitting at the bar and none of them was Victor.

"Hullo, Sylvia," the barman said, and a thin, dark girl cried, "Sylvia, darling!"

"Hullo," said Sylvia. "I expected Victor."

"He's gone to the little boys' room," said the girl. "He'll be back in a jiffy."

"This is Maurice," Sylvia said. "Maurice, meet Joy and Davy. King of his own frontier," she added and laughed depressedly.

"What's it to he?" Davy asked.

"Gin," said Sylvia. "Gin and what, Maurice?"

But Maurice was seized with panic. He must be gone before Victor returned. "I really think I'll have to go," he said. "I've got to be at the theatre."

"Oh, God!" cried Sylvia. "Do you really go to the theatre? It's ghastly."

"I haven't been to the theatre for years," Joy announced. "We always go to the pictures."

"I'm afraid I must go though," Maurice said.

"Well, yours was a quick one all right," Davy said.

Just as Maurice was stumbling out onto the top step in the

darkness he found Sylvia beside him. "I'm being bloody, I know," she said, "but that's how it has to be." Once more her accent was American. "I do need your friendship though. More than you know. I can't go on with it all much longer, even for Vic's sake. Can I call on you to help if things get too bad?"

Maurice was afraid of falling down the stairs, so it was with difficulty that he said, "Yes, of course."

"It may be sooner than you think. It may be tonight," Sylvia answered and kissed him on the mouth. Then she went back into the club-room.

Maurice stumbled down the stairs.

All the way back in the taxi from *The Pajama Game*, Mrs. Liebig hummed "Hernando's Hideaway." "That was a good show," she said. "Something to take away with you." She was tired, however, and had her nightcap in bed.

Maurice sat up and read Burke's chivalrous challenge to arms in defence of the fair, unhappy Queen of France. He found it difficult, however, to feel sufficiently for Marie Antoinette's wrongs, and once or twice he half rose from his chair, thinking that he had heard the ring of the telephone.